RESISTANCE

KIM BISHOP

THE REVELATIONS

RESISTANCE

TATE PUBLISHING
AND ENTERPRISES, LLC

Published by Tate Publishing & Enterprises, LLC
127 E. Trade Center Terrace | Mustang, Oklahoma 73064 USA
1.888.361.9473 | www.tatepublishing.com

Tate Publishing is committed to excellence in the publishing industry. The company reflects the philosophy established by the founders, based on Psalm 68:11,
"The Lord gave the word and great was the company of those who published it."

Book design copyright © 2015 by Tate Publishing, LLC. All rights reserved.
Cover design by Jim Villaflores
Interior design by Gram Telen

Published in the United States of America

ISBN: 978-1-68142-210-7
1. Fiction / Christian / Futuristic
2. Fiction / Christian / General
15.05.28

To everyone who dares to believe
in something greater than themselves

Put on the full armor of God, that you may be able to stand firm against the schemes of the devil.

For our struggle is not against flesh and blood, but against the rulers, against the powers, against the world forces of this darkness, against the spiritual forces of wickedness in the heavenly places.

—Ephesians 6:11–12

As government expands, liberty contracts.

—Ronald Reagan

Cast of Characters

Archeology Crew

Jason Fox—Archaeologist

Richard Wolfe—Archaeologist and Jason Fox's best friend

William Tempess—In charge of Techne-Corp, Jason Fox's nemesis

Resurrection Church Members

Donald Stewart—Missing pastor

Andrew Stone—Pastor

Burke Smith—Elder

Bob Johnson—Elder

Miriam Matiska—Secretary

Kevin Davies—Treasurer

Prayer warriors—Thomas Amos, Doris White, James Rickman, Debbie Cardinale, Yvonne Davies (Kevin Davies's wife)

Scott Abrams—Youth Leader

Youth—Kara, Peter, Kat, Josh, Eryn, Zac

New Life Foundation

Michael Damious—CEO

Isabelle Zenn—Spiritual leader

Jerry Holmes—Worker, student

Angels

Amicus—Messenger to Jerry

Veritas—Messenger to Isabelle

United Global States of the Earth (UGSE)

Justin Wright—Head administrator of the United Global Society Administration (UGSA)

Catherine Sunsteen—Head administrator of the United Global Health Administration (UGHA)

Amanda Wright—Global News Network (GNN) reporter

Rachel Vecler—United Global Society Administration (UGSA) social anthropologist, and coauthor of the Sustainable Societal Development plan

Demons

Angelous—Michael Damious's master

Adder—Isabelle's spirit guide

Trycon—Sent to the Abyss for failure

Jezeel—Justin Wright's master

Lucius—Jerry Holmes's guide

Morpheus—Torturer

Resistance

Marcus Daedalus—Head of the African and Los Angeles Resistance

Chef Daniel—Spy who infiltrated New Life Foundation

Jenna Wallace—Covert airfield maintenance

Jared Miller—Spy garage owner

Rick—Handyman

Chapter 1

A villain may disguise himself, but he will not deceive
the wise.

—Aesop's Fables

For nothing is hidden that shall not become evident, nor
anything secret that shall not be known
and come to light.

—Luke 8:17

In the one-hundred-plus-degree heat of the desert area in
southeastern California, archaeologist Jason Fox tied a red-
white-and-blue bandanna over his sandy-blond hair in hopes of
preventing another attack of heat sickness. He silently cursed the
ungodly, hot temperature of the desert to no avail as he placed
sunglasses over his light blue eyes. Looking from the top of what
the natives called Devil's Mesa, he felt discouraged at his lack of
success in this, his latest adventure.

It had been two weeks, and still he had not discovered the secret
underground laboratory for which he had been commissioned.
Standing near the edge of the small mesa, he slathered sunblock
over his tanned skin. As he looked down, he noticed a small point
in the otherwise flat barren floor of the mesa. Taking one of the
many tools from his knapsack, he began to dig and brush away
dirt from the strange object. As he dug, he began to unearth what
appeared to be the tip of a large structure. Buried beneath the
baked surface of the desert lay a find almost impossible to believe.

Fox excitedly called into his radio, "Base. This is Fox. Come in, base."

"Roger, Fox. What've you got?" replied his partner, Richard Wolfe, a friendly brawny guy with a green-white-and-orange bandanna tied pirate-style over his reddish-blond hair.

"Wolfe, man, you are not gonna believe this. I don't know how to describe it. It looks like the top of a pyramid or temple or something. Definitely man-made, not natural. You gotta send an extra team out here with fresh supplies!"

"Are you sure, Fox? I don't want to go to the big guy for nothing."

"Listen to me! I've found something big! I don't know what it is, but I know Tempess will definitely be interested in it!"

"All right, hold on. I'll get him."

William Tempess, a balding, stocky, hardheaded businessman in charge of Techne-Corp, had funded a dig in Death Valley to examine the possibility of a secret underground base developed by Uni-Tech in the early 1970s. Rumor had it that Uni-Tech, funded by the US government, began building the laboratory for the creation of secret weapons and technology. Two months into the venture, something went wrong. The project was scrapped after many of their employees began mysteriously disappearing. The natives in the area claimed the land had been cursed. William Tempess, however, did not believe in curses and was determined to find and plunder what Uni-Tech left behind.

Taking the headset from Wolfe, Tempess spoke into the receiver, "Tempess here. What's going on out there, Fox?"

"Tempess, this is huge! I don't think it's the laboratory...I don't know what it is or how it got here, but if you want it, you better get me some more people and supplies."

"Hold on, Fox. We'll get out there ASAP. Base out." Turning to Wolfe, he said, "That guy had better have something extraordinary. He may be the best, but he's a complete pain in the neck. Wolfe, call out the helicopter and get some supplies set up. You and I are going for a ride."

* * *

After serving as the pastor of Resurrection Church for twenty years, Donald Stewart mysteriously disappeared. A tall handsome man with unruly red hair, Donald had always been a mystery to his congregation. When first arriving at Resurrection, his demeanor puzzled many of the parishioners. His priestly duties of serving at the altar and preaching the word were of the highest caliber, but despite his warm smile, he held people at bay as his hazel eyes probed deep into their souls. It seemed as though he was always looking over his shoulder, as if waiting for someone to attack him. However, as the years rolled by and gray peppered his hair, he grew into the role of a father figure—stern but loving. He was always willing to listen, pray, or lend a helping hand. The paranoia had been replaced by a trusting and peaceful spirit, which was why his disappearance came as such a shock.

After much discussion and debate, the congregation decided that until his return, if he returned, they would call another pastor. Pastor Andrew Stone received the call and decided to accept. He was tall and handsome, slightly muscular, with medium-length brown hair and emerald eyes. His smile, always warm and sincere, could put anyone at ease. Enthusiastic and filled with purpose, he had opened his door for members to come get to know him and vice versa. Since speaking with a majority of members, his smile felt forced, and his heart had been troubled. The vast difference between the members amazed him, and he contemplated the reasons why in his journal.

June 3, 2020

> I'm perplexed at the difference between members in this church. After only three weeks, I'm feeling a loss to know what to do. On one hand, there are the followers, those members who are only looking for guidance and place to fit in—perfectly normal. Then there are the members who are extraordinarily zealous about the faith and worried

about where the church is heading—also a very normal part of the church. But I've never not seen any middle liners. There seems to be no one striving to bring the two sides together.

I'm sensing real spiritual fighting. This is wearing on me. I have yet to have anyone tell me exactly what's been going on. I'm hoping when the church's secretary comes back from vacation, she will be able to shed some light on the subject. From what I've seen, though, I'm tending to side with the more zealous members. I can't put my finger on it, but something just doesn't seem right. The complacency of the majority is questionable. They seem almost too willing to do anything I say. It's almost like they're brainwashed. Sheesh! Just reading that statement sounds so foreign to me, and yet I can't think of any better way to put it.

The head elder and other leaders in the church seem unhappy about me being here. For now I plan to keep my observations to myself, but I will definitely keep an eye on their doings. I am also concerned about their open views on certain moral and ethical behaviors. Soon I will have to say something about the policies of Pastor Stewart. I'm just not certain of the timing. Being so new to this congregation, I just don't know quite how to handle the situation. I guess all I can do is to take it to the Lord in prayer. Unfortunately, the Lord seems to be slow to answer me on this one. Wait on the Lord, Andrew—I have to constantly remind myself of that! It's me signing off for now!

* * *

After moving base camp closer to the mesa, Fox, Wolfe, and their team had begun the painstaking work of unearthing the treasure that lay beneath. Tempess could barely contain his excitement over the dig. Never in his wildest dreams did he think he would find something of this magnitude. The secret laboratory had all but been forgotten.

After weeks of digging and blasting, no one could believe what they were seeing. Within the small mesa, an ancient cave buried centuries earlier was being brought back to life under the cruel heat of the desert.

The tip that Jason Fox found was actually the peak of what appeared to be a crude portico carved into the mesa declaring the entrance to something truly amazing. Two pillars roughly etched into the stone stood beneath the portico, one to the right and one to the left, far enough apart to allow large vehicles to enter. Fox thought that someone sure went to a lot of trouble to hide whatever lay inside. The entrance had been covered from top to bottom with small boulders. Over the past centuries, the elements had fused the rocks together, making detection nearly impossible. How an ancient people or person had placed the boulders as high as to cover the entire entrance was baffling, but that was a thought for another time.

After clearing away the debris, the small band of adventurers prepared to enter the cave. With flashlights blazing, the men walked slowly and carefully into the strange opening. After about ten feet, it opened up to reveal a large cavern perfectly round and as large as a football stadium. Everyone stood in silent awe, for what was around and before them was truly amazing. Thirteen enormous stone pillars surrounded the perimeter of the cavern. Each displayed strange pictographs that had been carved into them and intricately painted. The scenes displayed horrible winged creatures with scaly skin and shark-like teeth, with fangs protruding through grotesque smiles. The creatures plunged long dagger-like claws into the heads of their human victims. Strangely, though, the people did not appear to be dying or dead. Rather, the creatures seemed to become one with whomever they grasped.

In the center of the pillars, a rectangular stone rested, covering a seven-by-five-foot area of the cavern's floor. The three-foot-high stone held the same pictographs as the pillars, with the exception of an even larger creature. It was grotesquely handsome and seated on a large black throne above the carnage created by the other winged creatures. The larger creature, exquisitely carved, appeared almost to be alive, and if Fox didn't know any better, he would swear it called to him.

* * *

Resurrection's secretary, Miriam Matiska, a lovely young woman with long dark hair and sapphire eyes, returned from a month-long vacation visiting her family in Israel to find a pile of junk in her office. It looked like Pastor Stewart hadn't done a thing in her absence. She stormed into his office for an explanation and was startled to see an unfamiliar man seated at his desk.

"Excuse me, sir, but who on earth are you, and what are you doing in Pastor Stewart's office?"

Looking up, Pastor Stone answered in a friendly voice, "Oh. Hello. You must be Miriam. My name is Andrew Stone."

"Well, Mr. Stone, it's nice to meet you, but that still doesn't explain what you're doing in Pastor Stewart's office without him present."

"I'm sorry. You haven't heard?"

"Heard what?"

"Pastor Stewart disappeared about a month ago."

"What do you mean disappeared?"

"I mean disappeared, vanished. All I know is that I got a call from the congregation to fill in for Pastor Stewart. When I arrived, the police came and questioned me about his disappearance, although I don't know why since I've never even met the man. Come to think of it, they wanted to talk to you too."

"Talk to me?" she replied, alarmed. "I can't talk to the police."

"What do you mean? Do you know something? If you do, you've got to tell the police."

"I promised him that I wouldn't tell the authorities. He said my life could be in jeopardy if I did, not by him but by…"

"By who, Miriam?"

"Oh, call me Mir. Everyone does," she said, looking up at him. "I'm afraid, Pastor…uh…oh yeah, Pastor Stone. How do I know I can trust you? How do I know you're not behind all of this?"

"Behind all of what?" He looked her in the eye. "I can see you're upset, but all I can do is promise you that I am who I say." He smiled warmly, and immediately she felt at ease. "I promise to help in any way that I can. Why don't you sit down and tell me about it?"

"Okay. Pastor Stewart told me that about forty-five years ago, he worked for a company called Uni-Tech. They dealt in weapons and weapons systems. He said that they were going to build some kind of bunker or underground laboratory in the desert for research. He never really went into what kind of research, and I never really cared to ask. He also told me that the place they were building around was cursed and that a lot of people began to change and disappear."

"Change how?"

"He claimed demons and ghosts haunted the camp and were taking over people's minds. Afraid for their lives, the workers began sabotaging all of the company's plans, causing them to have to desert the site. He said the company went belly-up after that. He also told me that there was another organization involved. I forget who, but he said that they still kept track of everyone who was there, which I found to be kind of strange. I mean, who does that? Anyway, earlier this year, he began getting phone calls from people I didn't know. I mean, they weren't church officials or members. I thought it was kind of strange because he always asked me to leave the office while he was talking with them.

"About a month and a half ago, I got a letter from my family saying that my grandma was ill and that I should come and see her. He suggested that I go on vacation for a month to visit them. I was a little hesitant at first because I had a lot to do here, and I just had a feeling, ya know? But he insisted and said it would be silly for me to not go. I figured since I hadn't seen my family in so long that I would go, seeing as how things in the Middle East have been improving."

"You went to the Middle East?"

"Oh, yes. My parents are Israelis. After getting permission to emigrate from Europe, my mom's family settled in Jerusalem. That's where my mom and dad met. When I was seventeen, some Christian missionaries came through and shared the gospel with us. I accepted Jesus as my savior and decided to follow them to America—Florida, to be exact. My parents, needless to say, were not happy, but they didn't stand in my way. The missionaries I came here with went back to the Middle East, and I decided to stay. That's about all there is."

"That's pretty interesting," he replied, lacing his fingers behind his head. "What brought you here?"

"Well, I visited Colorado with some friends five years ago before the war started and fell in love with it. I visited Resurrection three years ago and shared my story with Pastor Stewart. He said that he thought I would be a great asset to the church due to my Jewish background and then gave me the secretary job. I've been here ever since."

"Three years, huh? I guess you would know quite a bit about the church then?"

"Yeah, I guess. Why? What do you want to know?"

"Well, I've been talking with some of the parishioners, trying to get to know them. Some seem very pleased with the church, but others are quite disgruntled. Has something changed recently?"

Unconsciously lowering her voice, she replied in an unsettled voice, "Yeah. Pastor Stewart changed a lot in the last year."

"Changed how?"

"Well, he—how do I put it? He lost his spark. When I first came here, he was full of fire! He preached on living the Christian life through hearing the Word and receiving the sacraments rightly, not just talking the talk but walking the talk. Then just this year, he changed. He began to preach tolerance for sin. He began to remove the strong Christian leaders in the church and replaced them with brand-new members who were openly sinning and unrepentant. It wasn't so much that he allowed sinners in the church—I mean, after all, we're all sinners—but he began to *accept* sin. He started saying stuff like, 'Only God knows the heart, so keep your judgments to yourself,' even though we weren't judging. We were following scripture by trying to remove sin from the church body. We couldn't even admonish sinful behavior without being taken to task ourselves. A year ago, he would've been the one rebuking them.

"However, the strangest things began happening when he changed the service. He removed the confession and absolution, the Lord's Prayer, and the creeds. He replaced them with some feel-good mumbo-jumbo liturgy that one of the new ministry leaders came up with. He said it would make the service more real for everyone and not so boring and traditional. Then the new treasurer allowed the new music minister to take out a loan and buy an entirely new sound system even though there was nothing wrong with our old one. He said it would improve the clarity of the music, and that with the new mixing equipment, we could tape our services and share them with others. Worst of all, though, Pastor Stewart started letting random speakers come in and pitch their agendas during the sermon time. I simply couldn't believe it.

"After a few months of the new services, some of the members quit living for God and started living for the church. Again, a year ago, Pastor Stewart never would've allowed the congregation to switch their focus off God. I can't understand why so many members accepted what was happening when a small group of us couldn't accept any of it. We have been praying and trying to fight the changes, but like I said, Pastor Stewart replaced nearly half of the elders and other leaders in the church with the new so-called laissez-faire Christians. I wonder if the changes had something to do with those phone calls, although I don't know how. I don't really think he wanted to do the things he was doing. It seemed that he wasn't in control. Sounds pretty weird, aye?"

Confident, Pastor Stone replied, "Not at all. As a matter of fact, it sounds a lot like you've got massive spiritual warfare going on here. Mir, did all this begin when Stewart began getting those phone calls?"

"Come to think of it, yes. You know, he only told me his story the day before I left for Israel. Thinking back on it now, he actually seemed like his old self. I remember that he said he was going to fight them. I didn't know what he was talking about and, sad to say, kind of just drowned him out. Like I said, he changed recently. I never knew what to expect from him next. But you know, something's always struck me as kind of strange about the changes he made within the leadership. He knew I didn't agree with the changes, and yet *I* was the only dissenting person not replaced by a new member. Pastor Stone, I'm honestly a little bit afraid. I mean, what if these people come after me?" Starting to cry, she said, "I never thought anything like this could…"

"Don't worry, Miriam. We'll work this out together." *I have a few secrets of my own,* he thought. "If God is in control, and I believe He is, it will be His doing that changes things, not ours. Why don't we pray together?"

The two of them prayed for a long time for help, comfort, guidance, and mostly protection. When they had finished, Pastor Stone helped Miriam get her office back on track. It took most of the day. When they had finished, they continued their conversation over dinner.

* * *

"Hey, Fox!" called Richard Wolfe, concerned after his friend passed out. "Hey! Wake up!" he said while slapping Fox's face.

"How did someone so averse to heat become an archeologist?" Tempess mocked. "I swear, every time we get ready to do something, the man gets sick or passes out. I'm about to fire the prat."

"Come on, Will, chill out. If it weren't for Fox, you would've never even found this thing."

"Don't ever address me common again! You will call me Mr. Tempess. And as for Fox, I don't care how good he is and whether or not he found the site. It's my money and my equipment, and I'm fed up. If he isn't up in ten minutes, I will fire him and, while I'm at it, you too." Continuing his tirade against Fox, Tempess stomped away like a spoiled child.

"Just great, Fox," Wolfe muttered under his breath. Looking around the tent that served as an infirmary, Wolfe spied some smelling salts on a shelf. While crossing the tent to retrieve them, he looked out the rear flap and noticed Tempess preparing to move the stone. Hastily, he grabbed the smelling salts and dashed back to where Fox lay. Opening the vial and placing it under Fox's nose, Wolfe impatiently waited for the vapors to wake his closest friend. It didn't take but a second or two for him to react and come to.

As Fox, half unconscious, stirred, Wolfe thought back on their longtime friendship. As long as Richard Wolfe could remember, there had always been Jason Fox. They met in fourth grade after beating each other senseless over a girl they both wanted. As usual, Fox won the girl even though Wolfe won the fight. Since shaking hands and complimenting each other on their fighting skills, the two had become inseparable. Unlike most boys, the two had no interest in baseball or football, only ancient cultures and artifacts. Both wanted to be Indiana Jones, discovering cool artifacts and, of course, getting all the girls. After graduating high school, the young men joined an archaeological dig going on in Mexico and soon learned that the excitement of the movies was in fact not true in reality. Still, the promise of finding that one life-changing piece of history called them like a siren calling sailors to their death. Now here they were on the brink of finding a possible treasure trove hiding under the baked sand of the desert, and good ol' Fox has one of his spells.

"Wake up, man!" Wolfe said while shaking his friend. "Tempess is really ticked and just about to move the stone."

"What?" Fox responded groggily. "What!" he exclaimed while sitting up a little too quickly. "That dirtbag! This is my find. How dare he open it without me!" Fox's legs buckled under him as he abruptly tried to get to his feet.

"Hold on. Let me get you some water. You stroked out again." Wolfe gave him a bottle of water. "Tempess is steaming. We've got"—Wolfe checked his watch—"jeez, we've only got four minutes left."

"Left in what?"

"Left before Tempess goes ahead without us. He threatened to fire us if we weren't there in ten minutes, and that was six—no, make that seven minutes ago."

"Well, then let's get out there," Fox said sarcastically, regaining his strength.

Quickly, they exited the tent and ran to the dig.

* * *

Early Sunday morning as he sat on the porch in the cool morning air, Pastor Stone's prayers were full of apprehension and concern. "Dear Lord, I pray that You will be with me today. Send Your Holy Spirit to guide my words and fill the congregation with Your truth. You know the worry I have, Lord, and I pray You will help me to be strong, fight the good fight, and hold fast to the task ahead. Give me and the members the understanding and guidance we so desperately need to bring this body of believers back into the full, flourishing, glorious grace You've given to Your church. In Jesus's name, I pray. Amen." Contemplating the task ahead, he stood up, went into the parsonage, and began to prepare for the service, one that would change Resurrection forever.

The morning was glorious. The sun, rising in a cloudless sky, shone through the stained glass windows of the church, causing them to come alive with the stories that they told. Suspended on the wall above the altar hung a plain wooden cross. The altar was draped with a purple cloth to show the royalty of Christ. Two white candles in brass holders adorned either side of the altar. Between the candles lay the Holy Bible, propped up on a brass pedestal and opened to the eighteenth chapter of the Gospel according to Matthew. The pews had been recently oiled, and the sanctuary held the pleasant odor of lemon polish. Stone's favorite sight to see was the eternal flame, a candle that was never extinguished mounted on the wall. It symbolized God's eternal love for all and the promise fulfilled in Christ's death and resurrection—eternal life.

The congregation began to file into the sanctuary just before eleven o'clock. The service began with a favorite hymn, "Holy, Holy, Holy," followed by the praise song "How Majestic Is Thy Name." The congregation seemed in high spirits today and held nothing back in their praise to God. After speaking with Miriam, Pastor Stone decided to change the service by returning to the more traditional liturgy. Not surprisingly, the elders, along with the newer, more progressive members of the church, openly disliked the more structured service; however, the rest of the laity seemed to enjoy it immensely. After the group confession and absolution, everyone was seated. Pastor Stone had decided to invite one member a week to read the lessons for the day. Today, Bob Johnson, one of the more zealous members, a large middle-aged man with a good heart and love of scripture, began by saying, "Please open to the twenty-seventh Psalm, verses one and thirteen to fourteen. 'The Lord is my light and my salvation; Whom shall I fear? The Lord is the defense of my life; Whom shall I dread? I would have despaired unless I had believed that I would see the goodness of the Lord in the land of the living. Wait for the Lord; Be strong, and let you heart take courage; Yes, wait for the Lord.'

"Now turn to Ephesians chapter four, verses seven and fourteen to sixteen. 'But to each one of us grace was given according to the measure of Christ's gift...As a result, we are no longer to be children, tossed here and there by waves, and carried about by every wind of doctrine, by the trickery of men, by craftiness in deceitful scheming; but speaking the truth in love, we are to grow up in all aspects into Him, who is the head, even Christ, from whom the whole body, being fitted and held together by that which every joint supplies, according to the proper working of each individual part, causes the growth of the body for the building up of itself in love.' Please stand for the reading of the gospel."

"Thank you, Bob," said Pastor Stone. "Please rise and open your Bible to Matthew the eighteenth chapter, verses fifteen to twenty. 'And if your brother sins, go and reprove him in private; if he listens to you, you have won your brother. But if he does not listen to you, take one or two more with you, so that by the mouth of two or three witnesses every fact may be confirmed. And if he refuses to listen to them, tell it to the church; and if he refuses to listen even to the church, let him be to you as a Gentile and a tax gatherer. Truly I say to you, whatever you shall bind on earth shall be bound in heaven; and whatever you loose on earth shall be loosed in heaven. Again I say to you that if two of you agree on earth about anything that they may ask, it shall be done for them by My Father who is in heaven. For where two or three have gathered together in My name, there I am in their midst.' This is the gospel lesson."

Another favorite hymn, "The Old Rugged Cross," was sung. When the song was finished, Pastor Stone took a deep breath and approached the pulpit. "Please be seated. Good morning."

"Good morning," the congregation answered back.

In a confident voice, he began his sermon. "Today's sermon will be shorter than usual because there will be a congregational meeting directly after service. I have decided to preach on the necessity of a unified church under Christ. The lessons for today are basically the sermon. I just want to hit the main points that have to do with some of the problems that I have observed since my arrival.

"To begin, we hear the psalmist telling us that God is our strength and our defense, and with Him, we need not fear anyone. He also tells us that even though we see so much negativity in our world, with His help, we can see goodness, even in the bad, if we allow Him to lead our sight. He reminds us to wait for the Lord, to be strong and let our hearts take courage.

"How do we be strong and courageous? We do it through the grace given us through Christ. We do it through the strength we get from Him because we accept the promise that there is more for us than this life. What we do in this life reflects what we believe.

"Paul tells us that we are not to be as children, believing everything we are told by the world. The church needs to be aware of the schemes of Satan brought to us through the doctrine of man so that we do not blindly follow that which only makes us feel good. Now does that mean that Christians aren't supposed to feel good? Heck no. It means that the ways of this world which make us feel good in our worldly selves will make us feel uncomfortable if we are in Christ. We should be happy where we are, and we should be happy with what God gives us, those things being our spouses, our jobs, our children, our lives.

"We should not be going after things of the flesh. We should not be having affairs or premarital sex. We should not be living homosexual lifestyles. We should not be having abortions. We should not be lazy in our jobs. We should not be living on government welfare. We should not be stealing. We should not be lying. We should not be coveting, *and* we should not be supporting these things.

"'What!' I hear you saying. No one can live up to that, right? Wrong. Obviously, no one can keep all God's commandments through their *own* strength, but through the power of the Holy Spirit, knowing that we are forgiven when we make mistakes, we can. We need to be repentant when we fall. We need to be embarrassed and not proud of our faults. Christ's church, being the whole *and* the individual, should be taking a stand against worldly lusts and desires. The church should speak out in love against the schemes of Satan.

"What does it mean to speak out in love? Does that mean that we say, 'Oh, that's okay. It's not right, but God forgives, so be who He made you to be and do what you feel is right because God knows your heart'? I say no, no, no! The time for tolerance of sin within the church is gone! We need to take a stand and say, 'No more!'"

"Amen!" shouted some parishioners.

"The church needs to show the world that we stand for the truth of the gospel and set ourselves apart as Christ has done. We need to speak the gospel with truth and strength. We need to look Satan in the eye and say, 'No more!'"

"Amen! Praise God! Yeah!" responded some parishioners.

"To speak out in love is to be strong and take a stand. We need to ask ourselves if being nice is love, or is love saying, 'I want to see you in heaven, and what you're doing could lead you down the wrong path, down a path that could lead you to choose a sinful lifestyle over the life God wants you to have'? I say, the latter is *true love*. I have been honest with all of you ever since I came here, and honestly, I will tell you that I would rather have you hate me on earth for showing you what the Bible sees as sin and you repenting and going to heaven than having you love me on earth for looking the other way and knowing you went to hell.

"Our church needs to work together to build it into a place open to all sinners, but also to take a stand and let all of us sinners know that open unrepentant sin will not be accepted. Any person or persons proudly living or accepting such open sin may come to hear the truth, but they must know that their beliefs are not welcome here. That is love—not feel-good love, but practical love. When we allow open sin in the church and accept it, we begin to follow the path to destruction and lead others with us. Our gospel lesson today, spoken by Christ, says not to tolerate open sin in the church. He gave us steps to follow, and as a church, that is where I want Resurrection to go.

"In conclusion, at the end of Matthew 18, we see hope, as always with Jesus, that 'where two or more are gathered in My name, there I am in their midst.' God gives us every chance to repent, and He is always there to forgive. Take notice that while we are gathered together today, Christ is with us, next to you and next to me. We are not citizens of this world but citizens of heaven, and I hope we all eagerly wait for His coming. Let us pray."

Chapter 2

War is Peace. Freedom is slavery. Ignorance is strength.

—George Orwell, *1984*

Now when the unclean spirit goes out of a man, it passes
through waterless places, seeking rest,
and does not find it.

—Matthew 12:43

Isabelle Zenn, granddaughter of the founder of the New Life
Foundation, had felt great excitement from her spiritual master,
Adder. For the past few months, it came to her, often without her
channeling it. Adder encouraged her to bring more converts to
the foundation for the great spiritual awakening that would be
coming soon.

Isabelle, a beautiful, voluptuous woman, resembled what many
would call a gypsy. Her long thick black hair was usually tied
with a colorful scarf. It cascaded over her olive skin, ending at
her waist. Dressed in her usual colorful peasant blouse and long
flowing skirt, she looked in the mirror and was pleased with what
she saw. Her violet eyes held a mystical quality. They sparkled like
crystal and needed no enhancement from makeup. Isabelle never
wore makeup. She felt it interrupted the flow of Mother Earth's
life force into the soul and insisted that no one at the foundation
use it either.

The foundation was run by Michael Damious, a man obsessed
with the occult, especially the use of black magic. Tall, dark, and
handsome, Damious claimed that the archangel Michael guided

him to help bring in the peaceful age of enlightenment. Not that he believed it, but it was a means to an end and aided greatly in his control of the mind-numbed believers that flocked to the foundation.

The New Life Foundation helped searching souls find peace, love, and a place to be in the world. Most followers were young adults, usually in their twenties. They desired to perform some significant purpose in the universe and were helped by Damious and Isabelle. Dreams of world harmony filled their idealistic heads and hearts, seeds planted into their frail minds from preschool through high school, and especially in college. The foundation had been printing school curricula for both public and private schools since the early 1970s, when progressive educators gained control of most of the education system. Their philosophy of self-love, cleverly disguised by the word *self-esteem*, and nonjudgementalism had finally taken root even in the most conservative bastions of society. Self-love had replaced all other thoughts of right and wrong. The notion of "I'm okay, you're okay" had convinced most of society to worry about their own morality and leave others to choose their own paths. Unless, of course, their path included a definite sense of right and wrong, in which case they were considered mean-spirited, politically incorrect, and more recently, possibly mentally ill.

At the foundation, everything was community property. It was the perfect utopian hideaway. Isabelle believed the way to oneness would be found only when no one worried about personal possessions. Damious, on the other hand, found the lack of want by his followers to be a wonderful way for him to become rich and powerful with minimal effort.

Most of the New Life family dwelled happily working and living communally within the vast campus. For others, though, their purpose lay far beyond the walls of the estate. The foundation had found its way into every area of global life. Doctors, teachers, governors, senators, clergy, even presidents and kings belonged to

New Life. The beginning of world conquest or, as the foundation would say, world harmony would be brought to life through these mindless puppets. To Damious, they were nothing more than feeble imbeciles, free labor, and slaves he controlled. For Isabelle, however, they were wonderful and open to the thoughts and ideas brought forth by each of their spiritual guides. Her belief in the forces of nature and her innocent belief in the goodness of people blinded her to the true nature of Damious, who would ultimately be the undoing of her peaceful life.

* * *

Fox and Wolfe made it to the site with no time to spare. Gasping for air and sipping water from his canteen, Fox snidely remarked, "Sorry to disappoint ya, Willie. Gee, I guess we made it in time, you backstabbing—"

"Watch your mouth, Fox, or you might not like the consequences," Tempess said condescendingly. "Maybe I should ask how such a wimp as yourself ever made it in this field. You're pathetic! Oh, what's wrong Fox? You look like you're about to pass out again, you little sissy."

"You're about to get a fist in your mouth, Tempess. Let your little yes-men kiss your butt. You'll never get the satisfaction from me, and as for your job, you can shove it!"

Preparing to break up the ensuing fight, Wolfe interrupted. "Hey! Why don't the two of you grow up? The heat is getting to all of us. Let's get the stone moved and find out what's down there, if anything. Now shake hands and get over it!"

"He can shake his own hand!" spit Fox.

"Shut up, you prat!" Tempess replied, trying to regain his composure. "I'll deal with you later. For now, Wolfe is right. We need to focus on that stone. Fox, have you found anything on those markings yet? About what they mean?"

Still seething but not willing to give Tempess the satisfaction of thinking he'd won, Fox replied, "No, nothing yet. I've connected with everyone I can think of, but no one has seen these pictographs before."

Trying to lighten the mood a little, Wolfe chimed in, "Since those things look like devils, maybe you should give up on asking archaeologists and scholars and call in a priest."

"Oh yeah! Great idea, Rich," quipped Fox. "Yeah, a priest. Hey, maybe he'll do an exorcism, and the stone will just fly up all by itself. I swear, sometimes you just don't think."

Tempess snickered as he walked away from the two friends.

"Hey man," replied Wolfe dejectedly, "I was just trying to lighten things up here. Don't take your problems with Tempess out on me!"

"Yeah, you're right. Sorry, man. I'm just over anxious and too hot. This stupid desert is as hot as hell itself." Turning toward the direction Tempess had strolled, Fox yelled, "Hey Tempess, I thought you wanted to move this stone? Let's do it before we fry!"

"You don't give the orders here, Fox. The crane is coming now. You'd know that if you'd open your eyes and shut your mouth. Call in the rest of the crew—if you can manage without passing out!" Tempess walked off, laughing loudly.

"I swear, Wolfe, man, someday that guy is gonna get what's coming to him. I just hope I'm there to rub it in his face!"

After the crane moved into position, the crew began securing heavy chains tightly to the large steel anchors that they had fastened to the stone. As the crane lifted the slab, the air became heavy, almost unbreathable. A large hole was revealed in the cavern's floor. The whole crew fell silent as the thought of riches and fame filled everyone's mind.

"History is being made today, gentlemen!" crooned Tempess. "Get your oxygen masks and supplies, men. We enter the abyss in a half an hour."

The fetid smell of hot stale air was too much for Jason Fox. He felt himself begin to slip away. He staggered backward toward the cave entrance and out into the desert. Before unconsciousness took him again, he glimpsed the most frightening sight of his life; hundreds of what looked like the largest bats he had ever seen shot out of the dark hole, and he fell into oblivion.

* * *

After worship, Pastor Stone released the children to play outside and gave visitors the opportunity to leave. Apologetically, Pastor Stone began, "I'm sorry about springing this surprise meeting at the last minute, but several members have shown concern about the direction Resurrection is heading. In the sermon, I made my opinions quite clear. Now I would like your feedback on my thoughts."

The head elder, Burke Smith, a short rotund man with dull gray eyes and half a head of hair, chimed in, "Well, Pastor, your sermon was quite…thought-provoking, but I think it was very intolerant. We just can't tell people that they aren't welcome. What kind of church would that be?"

"I didn't say that we shouldn't welcome everyone. What I said was that we shouldn't accept open unrepentant sin within the church."

"Ah, come on now, Andrew, even though you're the pastor, you have sin. I would hate to see you removed from your position because of any impropriety. After all, how will people ever come to *your* repentance if they aren't even allowed into the church? Oh, and by the way, who will decide what sins are punishable, and what will those punishments be?"

"Burke, if you listened to my sermon, you would understand that *being* a sinner and *openly living* in sin are two different things. I never claimed to be sinless, but I do claim to be repentant of all my known and unknown sins. And no one comes to *my* repentance. They come to God's repentance. If the church doesn't state what it stands against, as well as what it stands for, no one will come to repentance. We must confront all sin head-on, or else we cannot be called Christ's church."

The two men held each other's stare with icy coldness as an uncomfortable silence fell over the church. Breaking the silence, Scott Abrams, the good-looking twenty-eight-year old youth leader with curly blond hair and fiery blue eyes, interjected, "I have to agree with Pastor Stone. I don't understand what has happened to this church in the past year, but we've steered way off course. I for one think we should move it back to the straight and narrow path. Pastor Stewart, for some reason, put us on this open path. I don't know why. He used to be the first one to speak out at sin, but he's gone now, and I think we should allow Pastor Stone to try it another way."

The congregation began mumbling to each other, discussing their thoughts. Many who were confused and unfocused looked toward Pastor Stone, Burke, and Scott.

Bob Johnson cut short the congregational chatter, saying, "I know we've only just begun the meeting, but I think most of you have your minds set. I think we should take a show of hands for who wants Pastor Stewart's way and who wants Pastor Stone's way."

Burke perked up at the suggestion. "I agree. All in favor of Pastor Stewart's way, raise your hands." About one-third of the congregation raised their hands. Disappointed, he said, "All right. All in favor of trying Pastor Stone's way, raise your hands." About one-half of the congregation raised their hands. "Well, I guess Pastor Stone's way wins, and those of you who didn't raise your hands are undecided. Since the church has decided to go the route of intolerance, I have no other course but to resign my eldership. Good day."

The members who voted for the more progressive service followed him as he walked out the doors. As Burke passed Stone, he whispered, "You've messed with something bigger than you can imagine. I look forward to seeing you squashed."

"Get thee behind me, Satan. Burke, you'd be surprised at how wrong you are."

"We shall see, man of God. We shall see."

*　*　*

Lying and meditating in one of the fragrant flower gardens of the foundation, Isabelle Zenn found herself transported to a different world, a world she invented for herself a long time ago. Even though she grew up on the beautiful campus of New Life, she had always longed for more. Her ability to channel spirits had pleased her father immensely. Sadly, her mother died in childbirth, and although she tried, she could never call her spirit back from the other side. Her father told her the reason was that her mother had reached her highest self and had become a goddess. It took Isabelle a long time to understand, but now she felt her own potential might bring them together in the end; she knew it.

From the time of her birth, her father had given her over to the spirit realm. As long as she could remember, whenever she felt lonely or afraid, she relaxed herself to this world where her oldest friend lived. It didn't matter to her that it was a spirit. The fact that it existed for her and no one else made her feel special. Its name was Adder.

In the beginning, it manifested itself as a cute little wood sprite, something she had read about in a fairy book. When she became older, it showed her its true self, a beautiful spirit of light. It claimed to be an ancient master, her own spirit guide. It promised to help her fulfill her potential and find her higher self. When her father died, Adder replaced him, leading her farther down the path of enlightenment. If only she could see its true reflection: a drooling scaly creature with long claws and fangs, which it had long ago plunged into her soul, taking her forever. For now, though, she spoke with it, loving it as a father.

"Adder, why is now so important for the foundation?"

It answered soothingly, "The time for the great awakening is near. Soon all of our trapped brothers and sisters will be released and the world will be brought together in unity, in oneness. In the desert, one of our associates is preparing to free many of us from centuries of imprisonment. He will bring in the beginning. You, my special one, have helped greatly and will continue to help. We need more converts. You must increase our numbers."

"I will tell Michael. He will let the others know. Have you heard from the others? Have they brought back the one who left us? Um…Stewart, I think?"

"Don't you worry about that! He has eluded us for now, but we will have him back. You just worry about the foundation."

"I'm sorry. I was only curious—"

"Never mind! Go back now!"

For the first time, instead of floating back to the foundation, she jerked awake. With tears streaming down her lovely face, she thought to herself, *What did I do?* Before she could think about it, she remembered how Adder had angrily ordered her around. For the first time, she feared it and quickly set out to find Michael Damious.

* * *

As Jason Fox regained consciousness and began to examine his surroundings, an imposing feeling of fear washed over him like a tidal wave. It took every ounce of restraint he could muster to keep from screaming out like a child awakening from a nightmare. He looked up at the night sky. The stars seemed to help calm his agitated state of mind. As he attempted to sit up, his head began to swim, and he decided to lay down a while longer. He wondered why he was lying on the desert floor.

"Hey, Fox, man!" exclaimed Richard Wolfe. "Welcome back to the land of the living! I saw ya try and sit up. Man, you look rough."

"Well, how do you think you would look after baking in the sun all day? Why on earth did you leave me out here? Jeez, you could've at least dragged me back to the tent."

"Quit your whining, you big baby. Don't you remember what we were getting ready to do before you passed out? Did you really think Tempess would sit and wait for me to take care of you? Come on! I really just didn't think you'd want him going down there without at least one of us. By the time we came out, it was almost twilight, so I figured I'd just let you wake up on your own in the cool of the night."

Sitting up, Fox remembered the hole. Excitedly he asked, "Oh! Right! I'm sorry, man, I completely spaced. What'd you find?"

Lowering his head, Wolfe responded dejectedly, "Nothing. Nada. There wasn't anything down there." Looking up with a slight twinkle in his eye, he continued, "Boy, I can tell ya, Tempess was fuming. In fact, as soon as we climbed out of the hole, he hailed a chopper and split. Needless to say, we're canned."

"Empty? Nothing?"

"Hey. Sorry, man. It was a blow to all of us."

"And that slime just left? I swear, if he thinks he's gonna renege on our deal, he's got another thing coming. I've spent over half a year looking for some stupid lab, baking in the hell-like heat of this godforsaken desert. I find some kind of freaky temple, and he thinks he ain't gonna pay up? Oh! I can't wait to get him alone in a room. I'll rip his teeth out. I'll break his lying jaw. I'll—"

"Cool it, man! The guy just left. He's sending choppers back tomorrow for us and the equipment. Dang! You're going crackers. Get over this thing you're harboring against the man."

"What are you talking about? Since when do you come down on his side? I'm starting to think the heat is getting to you too."

"Sorry, brother. You're right. I've been waiting for you to come to all evening and half the night. I haven't gotten any sleep, and I'm wiped. Why don't we go get some grub and drink? You look parched."

Calming down, Fox realized how hungry and thirsty he was. "Yeah. Sorry, man, I guess a day of sleeping in an oven knocks your senses off, plus you're right. I'm starving."

As they entered the mess tent, Fox noticed no one else was around. "Hey, Rich. Where is everyone? The camp looks deserted."

"Like I said, Tempess left and took everyone with him. I mean, would you want to hang around for nothing? Anyway, he was just gonna leave you here to wake up alone. I guess it shouldn't have surprised me, but even I didn't think he could be such a jerk. Anyway, I told him I'd stay behind and let you know what was going on."

Between bites of sausage and cheese, Fox questioned, "So you really think he'll send back a chopper?"

"Well, I tell you, at first, I wondered the same thing. Then I figured he may leave us out here, but he'd never leave his equipment. So unless his greed goes away by, say, now, he'd never leave all his stuff here." Stretching and yawing, he said, "Look, Jay, I'm really wiped. I'm gonna go catch some z's."

As Wolfe got up to go to the sleeping quarters, Fox took a large gulp of bottled water and said, "Okay, man. I'll see ya in the light. I think I'll just hang out for a while."

After finishing his meal, Jason Fox decided to have a look in the abyss, as Tempess called it. Taking a large flashlight and an extra bottle of water mixed with electrolyte powder, he strolled out to the site. As he approached the portico, a feeling of dread began to creep up his spine. By the time he had entered the cavern, the strange sensation of screaming out that he had felt at the moment of awakening pounded him again. Being better in control of his emotions now, he took a deep breath, counted to ten, and let go of it. As he approached the place where the stone had lay, he notice the fetid smell still hung slightly in the air. At the edge of the hole, he lay down on the ground and used the flashlight to illuminate the interior. The terrible odor made him wish he had gotten an oxygen mask before getting this far, but decided he'd come too far to go back now.

A ladder still occupied the cavity, and Fox descended it rapidly. The hollow was only about ten feet down and opened into a large underground cavern. The walls were covered with strange deep grooves that looked like animal claw marks, although Fox couldn't fathom what kind of animal. Standing amidst these claw marks, a vision of huge bats permeated his mind. Looking deeper inside himself, though, he saw a vision not of bats, but of the very creatures adorning the obelisks above. Once again, fear washed over him, dragging him down into the depth of insanity. He heard someone screaming and wondered who it was until he realized the scream came from him. Like a bat out of hell, he ascended the ladder and rushed out into the desert still screaming.

After catching his breath and getting a grip on his fear, he fell to the desert floor and began gulping the fresh air while crying and hugging himself. A few minutes later, after he regained control of himself, he tried to ponder the extent of what he saw. He couldn't comprehend what was happening, but he began to wonder what he had released into the world. As he began to stand up and walk toward the tents, he noticed out of the corner of his eye Wolfe running toward him full speed. Before he had a chance to react, Wolfe slammed full force into him, knocking him hard to the desert floor. Wolfe jumped on top of him and punched him in the jaw.

Stunned, Fox cried out, "What the—" He didn't get a chance to finish as his best friend once again pounded his face with his fist. Getting his bearings, Fox managed to avoid the next blow and head-butted Wolfe as hard as he could. Momentarily stunned, Wolfe rolled off him, giving Fox a chance to jump to his feet and take a fighting stance, fists out. Fox screamed, "What are you doing? Have you gone mad! Wolfe, man, what is happening?"

In a gruff animalistic voice, Wolfe replied, "There is no Wolfe. We have him. He is with us. He is dead!" Wolfe leaped toward Jason Fox, barely missing him as Fox countered with a blow to his friend's back.

"Who or what are you! And what have you done to my friend?"

"Don't you remember? Why, you set me—us free."

"What are you talking about? Set who free? Wolfe, man, come back! What? Are you under hypnosis? Wake up!"

Enjoying its little game, the thing spoke again, "Yessss, Fox. Hypnosis. Ha! Ha! Ha! I tire of this game, so I will tell you what you seek. We are the vision you saw. Our time has come on this earth, and we will *not* be defeated. The master has won! The awakening has begun."

Remembering the bats and the pictographs engraved on the obelisks, Jason Fox finally realized what the pictures portrayed. For the first time in his life, he believed in demons and maybe even hell. Knowing he would either live or die in the next few minutes, he decided to go out fighting. In a confident angry voice, he quipped, "I have to say—I guess I'll call you demon thing— you have messed with the wrong man this time. I've had a crappie day, and the last thing I need is some ugly, bat-like, people-stealing thing messing with me." With a burst of adrenaline and all his strength, Fox struck out blindly with his fists. Instead of connecting with the demon, though, he fell down as his once–best friend quickly moved to one side.

Laughing as Fox struggled to get his feet back under him, the demon said, "Why fight it? I have your friend. The only way to destroy me is to destroy him. You're too weak to do what you must."

Standing up, Fox sarcastically shot back, "Why not take me? Why was I spared? You think you're so strong! Well, why can't you do your own dirty work? Ha! You're the weak ones! Having to take a human form to accomplish anything! I spit on you!"

"You were lucky, Mr. Fox, but no matter. We are free. We will have all we want and more. Now I will destroy you." Before Fox could maneuver out of the demon's reach, it grabbed him by the throat. "You are nothing. You cannot beat us. We will take you and your world. Humans think they and their God are invincible, but we will show you! The time is now. Good bye, Jason Fox." As it spoke, it lifted him off the ground and threw him across the desert into the camp.

Momentarily stunned, Jason Fox forced himself to his feet and ran to the sleeping tent. Hurriedly, he rummaged through his suitcase, finding exactly what he needed. His 9mm pistol lay tucked safely into a pair of shorts. Grabbing the magazine that was hidden in a pair of socks, he made sure it was full and slammed it into the gun. He checked that the safety was set and slid it into his waistband, hiding it under his shirt. He ran out the back flap of the tent, hoping to surprise whatever his friend had become.

Running to and hiding behind the mess tent, Fox peered out into the desert and listened intently for any sound—human or other. It only took a few seconds to spot Wolfe. He was staggering and holding his head, moaning. Cautiously, Fox called out, "Wolfe, man, is that you?"

Looking dazed, Wolfe called back in his own voice, "Who else would it be? Man, what happened? My head feels like a ton of bricks, and I don't know what I'm doing out here." In midsentence, he fell to the desert floor, whimpering. Concerned, Fox stepped out of his hiding spot and began walking toward who he hoped was his best friend. As he approached Wolfe, Fox examined his mannerisms. Wolfe seemed genuinely in pain, and friendship overcame caution as Fox ran to his longtime friend.

Looking into Richard Wolfe's usually bright green eyes, compassion flowed through Jason Fox. Wolfe had a haunted faraway look. When Fox tried to speak to him, all he got in return was a blank stare. His friend since the fourth grade was stuck in some kind of catatonic trance. Seeing his best friend this way brought fury into his heart. He silently cursed everything he could think of and swore vengeance on Tempess for bringing them here and especially for leaving them here. As Fox was lost in his thoughts, the demon returned, prepared to take advantage of his vulnerable state. What it didn't see was Fox remove his gun and click off the safety. As the demon attacked, Jason Fox silently called out to whatever god would hear his prayer and asked Richard Wolfe to forgive him. He proceeded to unload the magazine into his best friend, killing him and sending the screaming demon back to hell.

In the quiet of the morning, Jason Fox buried Richard Wolfe, said a quick prayer, gathered up supplies, and set off toward the east to reap his revenge.

* * *

A few weeks following the congregational meeting, Resurrection's congregation had begun to grow by leaps and bounds. Numerically, it actually had continued to decrease. Spiritually, though, it seemed there could be no stopping the movement that had begun. Still, it seemed that something was lurking beneath the surface of the church. The spiritual growth, while increasing every day, seemed hampered by some unseen force that Pastor Stone couldn't quite place his finger on. He continued to pray for guidance and understanding and knew that in God's own time, he would be able to find and eliminate the undetected virus he knew to be there.

Pastor Stone, Miriam Matiska, Bob Johnson, and Scott Abrams worked diligently at keeping the small group of believers close and focused. Following the abdication of Burke Smith and the other leaders in the church, an emergency voters meeting was called to install new elders and a treasurer. Bob Johnson was voted the new head elder. The new treasurer, whose honesty and loyalty to God and the community were unimpeachable, was Kevin Davies, a tall muscular African American accountant who sported a shaved head and intelligent brown eyes. He proceeded to balance the books that were left in shambles by the previous administration. The five of them, Andrew, Miriam, Bob, Scott, and Kevin, having met once previously, decided it was time for another board meeting to assess the church's situation.

"…Amen. Okay, people, let's get this meeting underway," said Pastor Stone, calling the board meeting to order after saying the opening prayer. "Let's begin with the minutes from the last meeting. Mir?"

"Okay, last meeting, Pastor Andrew voiced his concern over some congregates still seeming to live more for the church than for a personal relationship with God. Bob informed us that members had been seeking spiritual help from the elders. Scott let us know that while the youth group had significantly decreased in number, the kids left—Zac, Kara, Eryn, Peter, Kat, and Josh—were renewing their commitment to God and intent on learning more about their faith. Kevin let us know that the ledgers were a mess and that only with the help of God would he ever get through it all." Everyone laughed. "He did promise us an update tonight."

"We'll hold you to that," snickered Scott.

"Ahem! Thank you for your insightful interjection, Mr. Abrams," interrupted Miriam playfully. "But back to business. Finally, I informed everyone of the sixty percent drop in membership. On that thought-provoking note, I'll turn the meeting back over to Pastor."

Dejectedly, Pastor Stone began, "Well, hopefully you guys have better news than me. I spoke with our synodical council this past week, and it seems that Burke put in a call to them, letting them know how we threw out over a third of our congregation and how another quarter left soon after—"

"What!" exclaimed Scott. "That's an outright lie! How can he—"

"Cool off, Scott. Getting worked up over this is not going to make it better. In fact, that's probably what Burke wants— for us to be at each other's throat. Remember, a house divided cannot stand."

"Sorry. It's just with the synod on our backs, we could stand to lose everything if we don't go along. And we can't turn around now."

"Yeah, this is crummy," said Bob. "So what *did* they have to say, Pastor?"

"They said I either change my judgmental attitude or else I can find myself another church."

An uncomfortable silence fell over the group until Miriam quietly asked what everyone else was thinking. "Can they do that? I mean, those people left on their own accord. I don't understand. The church voted for you."

"Yes. I know, but you have to remember only half the congregation voted for me. The others only abstained from the vote or voted in Burke's favor. And like you pointed out at our last meeting, sixty percent of the original congregates have left due directly to the change in policy."

Breaking his silence, Kevin chimed in glumly, "I hate to add coals to the fire, but without the synod's backing, we can't even afford to keep the church going. Burke's bunch had been embezzling money and fudging the books. Not to mention all the money they spent on all the renovations they made. You won't even believe how much that new sound system cost."

"Sure I do," answered Miriam. "It cost roughly fifteen hundred dollars…Oh no, don't tell me they lied about the price? I thought that was high. What did they spend?"

"Oh, about ten thousand."

Everyone in the room openly gasped at the amount.

"Ten thousand dollars!" yelled Bob unintentionally. "What on earth! Is it made of gold? Ten thousand dollars! I-I-I'm astounded."

"Well, I knew everyone would be as shocked as I was, so I decided to check on the system. Turns out a company called Techne-Corp built the system. I also discovered that a place called New Life Foundation, a New Age complex, helped develop the speakers and soundboard. There's some kind of microchip inserted in the mixing board and subwoofers that heighten the hearing sense. They really didn't go into details, but it started me wondering about maybe it's some kind of subliminal device? You know, once the new sound system was installed, that is when the congregation started going off the deep end. I wouldn't put it past that crowd to try brainwashing."

"Did you say New Life Foundation?" queried Miriam.

"Yeah, have you heard of them?"

"Yes, I have. I remember Pastor Stewart telling me that he attended a few retreats there, when he was working for Uni-Tech. Oh Lord! I forgot." Turning to Pastor Stone, she asked, "Do you remember when we first met and I told you about Pastor Stewart changing? You asked if anything changed, you know, after he got those phone calls?"

"Yeah, I remember."

"Well, it was someone from the New Life Foundation that called. I can't believe I'd forgotten. It's just that when Kevin said their name, it rung like a bell. Don't you see? Pastor Stewart changed after the foundation got in touch with him. Pastor, you told me you thought spiritual warfare is going on here. Well, isn't it possible that in his past, Stewart was into all that New Age spirit stuff?" Beginning to cry, she said, "I remember the last thing he said to me was that he was going to fight it. Why didn't I understand?"

Stunned at this revelation, everyone started talking among themselves while Pastor Stone tried to comfort Miriam. Suddenly and without warning, Scott stood up and said, "After all these revelations and not really even getting into the business meeting, I think we should abandon the synod and start fresh. As long as we have Christ on our side and people who need the truth and a place to worship, we have a church. I think we should have another congregational meeting and let the church know what's going on."

"I have to agree with Scott," said Bob. "If we stay, then we'll be compromising the truth and letting down the congregation. I believe God will bless us whether or not we have a beautiful building or just someone's home." Turning to face Kevin, he asked, "Kevin, if we were to leave the church and ultimately its debt, would we have enough to begin a new building or even rent one?"

"In actuality, yes, we would. People's giving has stayed the same or improved. Beginning fresh might actually be a very good idea."

After composing herself, Miriam responded, "I agree with your thoughts, but I think some prayer would be in order. This is a big decision, and I think God should be a part of it."

Everyone agreed and proceeded to the sanctuary. Kneeling before the altar, they joined hands and prayed, one after the other, beseeching God's will in this decision.

*   *   *

After finding Michael Damious and relaying Adder's request for more converts and the releasing of the captive spirits, Isabelle decided to practice some relaxation techniques. Not that she needed practice, but she wanted to empty herself so as to be able to better focus on her conversation with Adder. She knew she must have done something wrong and that perhaps in her relaxed state, the truth might be revealed. However, try as she could to relax, it just wasn't working. She found herself doing something she had not tried for years; she tried to contact her mother. After hours of trying, Isabelle finally broke down and began to cry. For the first time in her life, she felt alone. Afraid to reach out to Adder, her comforter, she curled up on her bed and drifted off to sleep.

Michael Damious already knew of the spirits' release. William Tempess had contacted him and told him of the success of the mission and the plan to kill Jason Fox. Unknown to Tempess, Fox had been a thorn in Damious's side for years. And while feeble little Tempess believed the untimely death of Mr. Fox was just good fortune on his part, Damious had planned it from the very beginning. Pleased the operation had proceeded as planned, he decided to escort Isabelle to dinner. As his mind raced with images of him and Isabelle, someone knocked on his door.

Annoyed at the interruption, he answered, "Come in." To his surprise, William Tempess entered. "Well, William, welcome. I wasn't expecting you. I thought you were returning to Techne-Corp to clean up our…little mess."

"Well, Michael, we have a small problem."

Damious's eyes narrowed, and he traded a smile for an angry grimace. "And what might that be?"

Suddenly, Tempess's mouth went dry. In a high-pitched voice, he said, "Well…" Lowering his tone, he mumbled, "Well, somehow Fox escaped. I don't—"

Backhanding Tempess hard enough to send him falling to the floor, Damious screamed, "What do you mean he escaped! How did this happen!"

Squinting his eyes to keep tears from falling, Tempess rose to his feet and timidly answered, "He shot him."

"Who shot who?"

"Fox shot Wolfe."

"Fox shot Wolfe?" he asked incredulously. "This is both good and bad. Yes, on the one hand, we can have him hunted down like a dog for murder. However, on the other hand, he has proven to be stronger than I thought, and more cunning, which makes him unpredictable…which makes him dangerous." Damious, still musing over this, had completely confused Tempess over his infatuation and knowledge of Jason Fox.

"How do you know so much about Fox, and why do you care?"

Instantly, Tempess knew he had overstepped his bounds. Damious slowly walked toward him. Stopping directly in front of him, Damious bent down to face him eye to eye. In a controlled but damnable voice, he said, "Lowly little man, don't ever question me again. Fox and I go way back. You think you're so clever. Well, surprise! You're not. I own you. You have no ideas. You have no thoughts. You do as I say, or someone may find you scattered all over, say, the northeastern seaboard? Get my drift? In answer to your infantile question about Fox, did you ever think that he might, I don't know, tell someone? If you ever mess up like this again, they may not find you at all." Damious picked him up by the throat, yelled for his guard to open the door, and proceeded to chuck him out the door. In his anger, Damious picked up a statue of a bull and threw it across the room, shattering it. Destroying things always made him feel better.

Returning his thoughts toward Isabelle, he said, "Now what was I thinking about? Oh, yes. Miss Zenn." Picking up his phone, he called Isabelle's room.

*   *   *

Isabelle woke from her nap to the beeping of her global phone. She climbed out of bed, walked to her desk, and noticed Damious's name on the caller ID. In a sleepy voice, she answered, "Hello, Michael...you want to go to dinner?" Not really wanting to go but knowing better than to say no, she answered, "Yes, thank you...Sure, seven will be fine. Yeah...Okay, bye." After hanging up the phone, she noticed that even though she knew what Damious had in mind, she felt a little at peace. Getting undressed and stepping into the shower, she thought about the dream she had. It was about her mother, not as a goddess ruling over some spiritual realm, but as a simple woman in a place of joy. She heard a small voice calling to her, a voice she didn't recognize but one she knew she wanted to know. Somehow, deep down, she knew she could never find this voice, although she truly longed to know what else it had to say. All she heard was, "Come to me as you are. Someone is praying for you. I have heard their prayer, but the next step is up to you. All are welcome." As the hot water poured over her, she felt a peace she'd never known and a presence she sensed she knew from the past. She thought, *Is there something more?* Suddenly, she felt a presence she knew all too well. Once again, Adder had come to her instead of her calling him.

"Is everything okay, child?" Adder asked sweetly.

"Yes, Adder. I'm sorry for whatever I did. I'm fine." Knowing her date with Damious would please it, she inserted, "In fact, Michael is taking me out tonight."

"Yesss. Good, child. That pleases me greatly. I too must apologize for my unforgivable outburst. Truly, child, it was my fault, not yours. I do need you as *you* need me. Are you sure nothing is troubling you?"

"No. I'm just a little tired. I have a lot of recruits coming next week, and I must prepare."

"Very well, I will let you get back to your shower." He left, and she finished showering. While drying herself, she thought back to her dream and wondered why she didn't tell Adder about it. For the first time, she had a secret, and she had decided to keep it to herself—for now, anyway. As she dressed, she unknowingly began humming the song "Amazing Grace," something she remembered from her mother. Then she thought, *How could my mother have sung that to me?* While she mused over her mother, a knock came at her door. It was Damious.

"I'll be there in a minute, Michael." Looking in the mirror, she tied a colorful scarf around her hair and left for dinner. Meanwhile, in a little cabin in the Colorado Mountains, a man prayed for Isabelle Zenn and a little church that was beginning a new journey.

Chapter 3

The aim of life is to live, and to live means to be aware,
joyously, drunkenly, serenely, divinely aware.

—Henry Miller

But the Spirit explicitly says that in later times some will
fall away from the faith, paying attention to deceitful
spirits and doctrines of demons.

—1 Timothy 4:1

After putting some distance between himself and the dig site, Jason Fox found a shady spot to rest for the day. He could scarcely believe the events that had led up to his self-imposed exile. Yesterday, he was working on the most exciting discovery of his career, and today, his life was turned upside down. He could not believe his best friend was gone forever. Looking toward the sky and speaking out loud, he asked, "What happened? I know I'm not the greatest person in the world, but I'm certainly not the worst. And, Rich, what did he ever do?" Screaming and shaking his fist, he cried, "If there is a god up there, I want an answer!"

Waiting for an answer he knew wouldn't come, Jason Fox fell into a deep sleep and dreamed of a tree covered mountain and a small cabin. An old man he did not recognize called to him. As he listened to the man calling his name, a shadow fell over the land. He turned to look at the sky and saw a huge red dragon flying through the air calling out to him. He recognized the face of the dragon but could not recall the name to which it belonged. Instantly, though, he recognized the voice—Tempess.

As the dragon saw him, the old man's call became more urgent. Fox sensed safety from the man and began to run toward the cabin. As he ran, he turned his head and yelled at the dragon, "I'll find you, Tempess! I'll get you!" The dragon narrowed its eyes and swooped down toward him. The gigantic talons grabbed for him, but he reached the cabin and slammed the door. The last thing he heard was a horrible scream from the dragon in the distance.

Started awake, Jason Fox found himself covered in sweat, his heart pounding. Opening one of his packs, he removed a bottle of water and took a large gulp as he tried to calm himself. He couldn't remember a time when a dream seemed so vivid. Even though he had no desire to eat, he knew better than to allow his strength to fall. Getting ahold of himself, he took out a piece of jerky and began to eat. After his small meal, he packed up his few belongings. Ensuring his gun had been reloaded, he set off again. Dusk had fallen, and Fox was grateful for waking before nightfall. His eyes gradually adjusted to the dark, and even though the moon was partially covered by clouds, he had acute night vision and had no trouble seeing his way.

For a few days and nights, he continued his routine of sleeping in the day and walking at night, always with the same dream of the cabin and dragon. Extremely low on water and food, Jason Fox held onto consciousness only through his desire for revenge.

Finally, he stumbled upon a highway and followed it. Shortly before dawn, he came to a diner/gas station with a little apartment above. Realizing his appearance would be off-putting, he found his way to the bathroom and did his best to clean up. After removing his shirt, he washed his face, upper body, and especially his armpits. Taking a comb from one of the packs, he attempted unsuccessfully to tame his hair. While pulling his shirt back on and staring in the mirror, Fox still considered himself to be unpresentable. Having no other choice but to enter the restaurant, he reached for the door and was pleased to see a little shop with clothes for sale gracing the entrance to the restaurant.

He approached the counter to pay for a pair of jeans and a T-shirt. The cashier, an attractive, pleasant, full-figured woman named Grace—probably assuming he was a vagabond—offered to let him clean up in her bathroom upstairs. He gratefully accepted, giving the woman a sob story about his girlfriend breaking up with him and leaving him on the road to suffer on his way home to Albuquerque. Thankfully, she accepted his story and left him to clean up, giving him a new razor for a shave.

After washing up and putting on clean clothes, he returned downstairs to the restaurant. He ordered bacon, eggs, pancakes, sausage, hash browns, toast, juice, and strong coffee. He and Grace had a pleasant conversation about the weather, relationships, and the restaurant. It turned out that her husband had died a year earlier, leaving her the gas station and restaurant to take care of alone. She told him that even though she was at a remote location, truckers knew it to be good food and good prices. Come eight o'clock, the patrons would start flowing in. She suggested that maybe he could catch a ride with one of the truckers heading east. He announced that was his plan and added that hopefully he might be able to stop back in someday.

As they were talking, a trucker came in, ordered breakfast to go, and paid for a full tank of gas. Grace introduced the trucker as Jack, and he generously agreed to take Fox to Albuquerque since it was on his way. Fox accepted gratefully, even though he had much farther to go. His main goal of causing great bodily harm to William Tempess would just have to wait a few more days. Thanking Grace for her hospitality, he paid the bill and left a generous tip. Jack gave Grace a long kiss before returning to the truck.

"She sure is a great gal," Jack offered.

"Yeah, she's one of the nicest people I've ever met. You guys a couple?"

"Yup! Sure are. I'm hopin' we'll get hitched soon. She still gots lots of love for her first husband, but I can wait."

"I think she's definitely worth the wait."

Happily, Jack respond, "You betcha!" After they both climbed into the cab, Jack shifted into gear, and Fox shifted back into dreamland.

This time, Fox only dreamed of the old man and the cabin. He had no idea about the man's importance, but he knew that he was important. The man walked him all over the woods. He showed him landmarks and kept saying, "Come to the mountains. Come to the cabin." He radiated peace and hope. Fox desperately wanted to speak at length with him, but all he would say was, "Come." As Fox continued to dream, he woke to Jack's voice saying, "Bathroom and food break."

Walking to the bathroom, Fox thought about how real this dream had become. He understood the dragon dream. After all, his subconscious was trying to tell him that even though he searched for Tempess, Tempess more than likely searched for him too. This dream, though, had nothing to do with anything. He didn't even recognize the man, and yet he felt that somehow he needed to see him.

After using the restroom and buying some snacks and drinks, Fox climbed back into the cab and waited for Jack to pay for the gas. He insisted on pitching in for the gas, but Jack wouldn't hear of it. He just kept saying any friend of Grace's was a guest in his truck. Fox decided not to argue and instead offered Jack some chips and cola. Jack turned on the radio, picking up a soft-rock station, and both men talked about politics, women, and football. When it came time to say good-bye, they both regretted their parting. Fox had enjoyed Jack's company immensely. Jack had driven him to a gas station and wished him luck with his girlfriend. Fox responded in kind, wishing him and Grace happiness in their life.

After Jack was out of site, Jason Fox stepped into the station and asked the attendant where he could catch a bus out of town. After a short conversation, the attendant informed Fox he would need to call a cab since the bus station was located halfway across town. Fox thanked him and used the pay phone to call a cab because he didn't want to take the chance that his cell phone would be tracked. As he waited, he began to contemplate where he should go. No matter how great his need for revenge on Tempess was, he knew that it would be better to lay low and feel out the situation. After all, he had killed a man, his best friend, and knowing Tempess, he would be on a manhunt. Then again, Tempess had a lot to lose, not to mention the environmentalists would be all over him for *desecrating* the desert. Even though he had managed to acquire approval to dig on government protected land, those little environmental nutters could cause him and his company plenty of trouble. The thought of that brought a delighted smile to Fox's lips.

While he was lost in thought, his cab came. After entering the cab and asking to be taken to the bus station, he decided on his destination. An old friend of his just moved to a remote little town in Colorado. That would be the perfect place to lay low.

After purchasing his bus ticket and taking his seat, Fox again fell asleep. Jostled awake as the bus pulled over for a bathroom break, Fox groggily hurried to the facilities. After relieving himself and stepping out of the bathroom, he looked around, taking in the scenery of the mountains and the town. He was shocked to see the very mountain from his dream towering high above him. Jason Fox never believed in visions or prophesies, but within the past week, he had seen his best friend turned into an evil demon thing, and now his dream of a mountain he had never seen was staring him in the face. With his curiosity piqued, he decided to enter the woods to see whether or not the cabin and the man existed. However, since night would soon be falling, he decided to wait until the next day to pursue his eccentric idea.

After being assured by the ticket master that he could use his ticket at any time to attain his destination, Fox placed it into one of the backpacks, walked down the street to a small motel, and purchased a room for the night. After tossing the soiled backpacks on the floor, he decided to buy camping gear. He counted his remaining cash and was disappointed to see only three thousand dollars left. He and Wolfe had always carried large sums of money on expeditions for just such emergencies. They had learned long ago that when they needed to get out of a bad situation without being found, cash was the only form of untraceable currency, especially with all the new tracing technology the global government had come up with.

Thinking about Wolfe caused him to run to the bathroom and throw up. This was the first time since the shooting he had consciously thought of his action. Remembering his best friend shake as the bullets pierced his body and then fall bleeding to the ground was the worst experience of his life. He remembered hearing the demon scream obscenities at him as, he hoped, it flopped back to hell to pay for its failure. He had felt no remorse at the time, just numbness.

Reviewing the week's events, he could no longer deny the actuality of some kind of spirit realm, but if a god really existed, he hated him as much as Tempess. A god that could let this travesty happen was not one that Jason Fox wanted to know, except maybe to spit on. Getting back to his task, he decided to buy only a sleeping bag, new backpack, hiking boots, a few disposable cell phones, a compass, a canteen, and food for his little trip into the mountains.

After waking, he remembered the urgency in the man's voice and started on his trek. Entering the woods, he felt a shiver up his spine and turned to look at the sky. This time, however, there were only blue skies, puffy white clouds, and bright sunshine above. No giant Tempess dragons flew through the air, and he thought, *Jeez Fox, I really think you are losing your mind.* Taking a deep breath, he entered the forest and began his journey into a reality he did not know if he could face.

* * *

After hours of prayer and searching, the five leaders of Resurrection Church decided unanimously to leave the synod and begin a new church for the believers who would choose to follow them. Miriam printed letters to all the congregants who had left the church with and after Burke, as well as the current members, telling them that Pastor Stone had an announcement that would affect them all and asking them if they would please come after services on Sunday. Bob informed the other elders of the situation personally at their weekly meeting and was disappointed to find that some were not ready to leave the established church to begin a new one. Scott met with the youth group and let them know the situation. Happily, all the youth were prepared to follow the church when it made the break. Kevin informed the synod that the previous administration had left the church tens of thousands of dollars in debt and sent them a detailed report of the fraud and waste which went on. Finally, Pastor Stone sent a letter of resignation to the synod informing them that he would not compromise his integrity to enjoy their financial help and that they had better keep a close eye on the goings-on there because the next pastor voted in would more than likely be as corrupt as Pastor Stewart in his final year.

As Sunday morning rolled around, Pastor Stone felt sick over what had to be done. More than that, he feared for the salvation of those who would remain behind. Miriam entered his office and offered to pray with him before service. Together, they prayed for strength and guidance, peace and comfort, and God's help in the trying times that were ahead. After the prayer, Pastor Stone quietly said, "Thank you, Mir. You have been a great source of strength for me since I came here." With a quick chuckle, he said, "I still remember the first day I met you. You came in here all headstrong, telling me I shouldn't be here."

"Yeah, I guess I came on a little strong, but that was probably one of our most interesting conversations. You know, at first I got the feeling you were hiding something from me. Sometimes I still think you are. When all this gets settled down, I want to hear all about your past."

"Hmm. Yeah, maybe. There's a lot there." Changing the subject, he said, "Well, back to the point at hand. This is a lot harder for me than I thought. I just wanted you to know how much you've meant to me."

"As much as you say I've helped you, you have helped me. It's hard for me too." Taking his hand, she continued, "But together with the others and especially with God, we can and will make it through this. We just have to keep the truth in mind. Well, I guess I should let you get on with preparing for the service." Letting go of his hand, she lightly kissed his cheek. "Good luck! And remember Psalm 27." As Stone watched her walk into the sanctuary, he thought of her words and the scripture she offered and felt strong enough to give it his best.

As the acolyte lit the altar candles, Pastor Stone walked up the aisle to the altar. As he bowed before God, he whispered another quick prayer. After the hymns were sung, the confessions absolved, and the readings read, Pastor Stone began his sermon.

He preached about following Christ with all of one's heart and how simply saying you believe in Jesus isn't enough if your life doesn't show his presence, and likewise, just because you live a good life, even righteous to man's eyes, if you haven't confessed a faith in Christ, it's all for nothing. He talked about Timothy and the fact that Paul told him to fight the good fight, to be strong and courageous and not to compromise the faith or the truth of the faith. He talked about Paul's letter to the Hebrews and his warning that even those who had tasted the heavenly gifts, received the Holy Spirit, and had been enlightened could fall away. He counseled them to be careful about what they follow and what they believe so that they too don't fall away. As usual, though, Pastor Stone left everyone with the hope and assurance that no matter what they may do, Christ is always there to forgive if they will repent, and He will forget their sins, never to be brought up again. His final note was from Psalm 27: 'The Lord is my light and my salvation; whom shall I fear? The Lord is the defense of my life; whom shall I dread?'

After the sermon, the offering was collected and the Lord's Prayer prayed. After the final hymn had been sung, Pastor Stone invited everyone to stay for the congregational meeting and asked Bob to let Burke and the others into the sanctuary. The current members were surprised and puzzled to see the former members at the meeting.

Pastor Stone began the meeting by asking Burke Smith to come forward. Haughtily, Burke approached the altar. Not bothering to bow, he smugly turned and faced Pastor Stone. "So, Andrew, what is the problem here? Are you asking us to come back?"

"No, Mr. Smith. I called this meeting to inform the congregation that the synod has asked me to step down as pastor or fall in line. Needless to say, I can't in good conscience change what I believe or feel to be best for the church, so I've decided to turn in my resignation." Facing the congregation, he finished, "The church is now in Mr. Smith's hands since he felt compelled to call the synod and inform them of his concern. That is, until you call a new pastor." Turning back to face Burke, he asked, "Well, do you accept?"

"I'm willing to take over as minister until a new one can come, but what about you, Andrew? I thought you were so gung ho over your intolerant ways."

"Actually, Burke, that's why I asked the whole congregation to come back. Miriam, Bob, Scott, Kevin, and I have together decided to begin a new congregation without synod aid. I wanted to let the old congregants know that if they wish to return here, I will be leaving. Anyone who wishes to come with us is welcome. It won't be easy at first, and we won't have a building, but if we have Christ on our side, we will be strong." Turning to Kevin, Pastor Stone asked him to come forward and share his findings.

Burke protested, "What on earth does he have to say? He only just took over as treasurer."

With a slight smile on his lips, Pastor Stone answered, "Oh, but, Burke, there is plenty for him to say, and since this administration is here until we leave today, anyone who wants can speak." Looking back to Kevin, he said, "Come on up, Kev, I'm sure the congregation eagerly awaits your report."

Pastor Stone and Burke took seats in the front pew as Kevin began his report. "I thought it only fair to inform everyone of where their money has gone under Pastor Stewart and Burke Smith's administration. I have printed out enough copies of my report for the whole congregation. You can pick them up to read after the meeting. To begin, there has been fraud. Several leaders were skimming money from the offering for their own benefit. Close to five thousand dollars were stolen over the year before Burke took a third of the congregation away. Also, the new sound system cost a whole lot more than fifteen hundred dollars. The actual price was ten thousand dollars."

Audible gasps came from the congregation.

"The worst is yet to come, though, I'm afraid. The sound system was purchased from a corporation with ties to a New Age foundation that installed a microchip which supposedly enhances hearing. However, I believe that it was used to implant subliminal messages to the congregation to alter your loyalties from God to the Church. There is no actual proof of a conspiracy to alter your minds, but you need to think about how and when things changed in this church. If you look closely, you'll see it happened with the new sound system when Burke and his cronies took over."

Angrily, Burke stood up and scolded, "How dare you speak about me that way, and without any proof! Needless to say, how stupid your conspiracy theory is. I ought to sue you for slander!"

"Just go ahead. With the evidence I have, you could go away to prison for a very long time."

Burke flopped down dejectedly in the pew.

Pastor Stone stood up again and said, "Okay. Thank you, Kevin." Speaking to the congregation, he said, "A couple months ago, you voted me to stay, and Mr. Smith took part of the congregation with him. Well, now it's my turn. I'm walking out of here today. Anyone who will come with us, come now. Anyone who chooses to follow later will be welcomed with open arms. Just remember, in the true Church, we put God first and man second." Finished with his comments, Andrew Stone walked down the aisle and out the door followed by Miriam, Bob, Scott, Kevin, and about a quarter of the congregation. Their parade followed down Main Street to Kevin and his wife's home for a time of celebration and direction. The congregation had a new beginning, and everyone was very excited.

At the door to Resurrection, Burke watched the little parade stroll down the street. He flipped open his global Internet phone and made a call to the New Life Foundation to inform Michael Damious of another hiccup in the plan.

On the first Monday of every third month, Isabelle and Damious welcomed new recruits to the New Life community. "Greetings!" cheered Damious. "Welcome to New Life Foundation and the beginning of your new and wonderful life. Here at the foundation, you will not only live in harmony without outside interference, you will experience your true selves through study, meditation, and love." Turning toward Isabelle and the other leaders, he continued, "While you will see me from time to time, Isabelle and the rest of the enlightened ones will be your primary guides." Turning back to his audience, he raised his hands and said, "Peace be with you all." Waving farewell, he handed the microphone over to Isabelle and strolled to his office. As he walked, he thought, *This is the largest crowd yet. Soon we'll move to the next level.* With a smile on his lips, he opened the administration door, picked up his messages, entered his office, and closed the door.

Isabelle continued the assembly easily, a task she had performed many times in the past. Usually, her spirit soared when seeing the new recruits eagerly awaiting their enlightenment. However, since the dream about her mother and the small voice calling to her, Isabelle had been confused and unfocused. Remembering her duty to Adder and his request for new converts, though, she pushed aside her thoughts and welcomed everyone with open arms.

Humbly, Isabelle addressed the crowd, "Greetings, seekers of knowledge, and welcome to your new home. Mr. Damious said that we would be your primary guides when, in truth, we will simply show you how to find your own personal guides, spirits who will show you where your destiny lies. I know your walk with us will be rewarding and fulfilling. I myself grew up here at the foundation and can tell you there is no more peaceful place on this planet. I know many of you have already begun your path to the light and that many of you are eager to begin, but with any beginning, there are rules that must be followed."

Regaining her enthusiasm, Isabelle continued, "As you know, we dress very relaxed here at New Life. You will find clothing in your rooms. Ladies, you must always remember that we see inner beauty here and makeup is not allowed. All of us must realize that the potential within us is our main focus. After your initiation period, you will either be chosen to continue on your path here, or you will be trained in a skill to take to the outside world to help bring others to the light, just as your teachers, friends, and family helped bring you here. The rules we follow here are simple. Respect all life and all thoughts of inclusiveness."

Concluding her speech, Isabelle explained, "After changing and taking the evening meal, everyone will begin their journey in the Great Meditation Garden. We will begin every day at six in the morning by emptying ourselves and seeking our guides. Likewise, after morning, noon, and evening meals, we will meet to meditate as one united mind. During the day, you will attend yoga, meditation, relaxation, and a number of other classes. In the evenings, you will be free to wander the campus, search yourselves, meditate, or engage in any other activity we have available. Please remember that during the initiation months, you must not speak to outsiders, even family. We find they can block your energies with negativism. However, after the initiation period is through, you will be free to contact whomever you wish. It truly is my hope that your life here at New Life will be fruitful for you and the world."

Following her speech, the other leaders took turns explaining their classes and functions in the foundation. After the assembly concluded, the initiates found their rooms and prepared for their journey into a new life.

* * *

Entering his office, Damious flipped through his messages. Finding one marked urgent, he looked it over. The message simply said, "We have another problem," with a phone number at the bottom. Recognizing the number, Damious's eyes narrowed, and he let out an angry sigh. Reaching for the phone, he crumpled the note and threw it on the floor. As he punched the speed dial, anger began to swell in him like a tidal wave rushing to shore. Walking around his desk to his chair, the line began to ring. As he sat at his desk, someone on the other line answered, "Burke Smith here."

Trying to sound calm, Damious asked, "What's the problem there, Smith?"

"Well, the good news is that we have control of the church again."

"And the bad news is?"

"Stone left and took the others with him."

"Well, that's not a complete loss. We still know where he is, don't we?"

"Well, yeah. We know where he is, but their new treasurer discovered the discrepancies in the books and also found out about the sound system." Sitting silently on the other end of the phone, Damious waited for Smith to speak again. With trepidation in his voice, Smith said, "Well? Are you there?"

Silently cursing to himself and envisioning Burke squirming on the other end, Damious replied, "Is that all, Smith? I have a feeling there's something more. I'm very much hoping that you're going to tell me that that's all there is to it. Well, Smith, is that it?"

"Actually, the treasurer, Kevin Davies, wrote a report about the foundation and the chip in the sound system and passed it out to the congregation, as well as sending a copy to the synod, but hey! No one believed it except the fundamentalist nuts that were with them in the first place. I mean, while they were leaving, most people were joking about it and making fun of their stupid conspiracy theories."

"Burke, you've got to be one of the most ignorant people I have the nonpleasure of knowing. I swear, between you and Tempess, I don't know which is more brain-dead! Have you not thought that just maybe somewhere down the road, someone else might see that report and begin snooping? I'll tell you what. You had better start damage control because I'm on my way, and if this is not taken care of by the time I arrive, you don't even want to try and imagine what I will do to you." Damious slammed the phone back into its cradle, called his secretary to make flight arrangements to Colorado, and left his office to find Isabelle and tell her she'd have to take care of the new recruits' affairs by herself.

* * *

In Jason Fox's dream, the woods had appeared to be dark and sinister. Even though the man had radiated peace, the woods had always been strange. In real life, however, the woods exuded beauty and charm. The thought that some Tempess dragon thing could even invade his dreams in such a place seemed silly to Fox. He thought, *What a beautiful morning!*

When he first entered the woods, he was nervous. For one thing, he feared his sanity was slipping away. What kind of idiot goes for a hike in the woods based on a dream? More so, he feared that the dream was true, and perhaps he wouldn't remember the woods clearly enough to find his way to the man. However, his fears diminished almost immediately. Once he began the journey, it was as if a map had been imprinted in his mind. Everything seemed natural and familiar to him.

Instead of searching his mind for directions, as he thought would be the case, Fox found himself enjoying the scenery and taking in the splendor of the forest. Tall pine trees and aspens towered above him dappling the sunlight and creating interesting little dots on the trees, wildflowers and other vegetation growing beneath the inspiring canopy. As he tramped through the underbrush, he endeavored to be as quiet as possible, listening to the forest's sounds. He also found himself smelling the air, noticing the freshness of it. He began to think, *Even if I don't find this old guy, I can build my own cabin and live out here for the rest of my life.* Being so caught up in his thoughts, Fox hadn't even noticed that he had maneuvered through the woods and come upon the first of the major landmarks that the old man had shown him: a gnarly old tree with a hollow at the base. He marveled at the immensity of it. Not being up on botanical knowledge, he had no idea what kind of tree towered above him, but he decided that it must be an oak. Feeling a little tired, he decided to sit and rest. Leaning against the ancient tree, he began pondering the immensity of the world and the smallness of his life. Placing his hands behind his head, enjoying the filtered sunlight on his face, he closed his eyes, and for the first time since his dreams of the old man began, he slept peacefully without dreaming.

Fox awoke with a start as a brown squirrel skittered across his leg. Looking at his watch, he noticed that he'd only slept for about an hour. Still enjoying the coolness of the woods and the warmth of the sun dotting his body, he remembered why he was here in the first place and began collecting his hiking gear to continue his trek. *Strange*, he thought, looking at his pack, *I don't remember putting this over here.* As he reached for his backpack, he noticed a small glint coming from the hollow in the tree. Looking around, he began to feel uncomfortable. Once again, chills ran up and down his spine. With clammy hands shaking, he reached into the hollow and, to his surprise, found a small brass key. Examining the key, he noticed the letter *S* engraved in it. He wondered who S might be. *Perhaps the old man.* Placing the key in his shirt pocket, he finished gathering his things and proceeded through the woods.

Feeling apprehensive now, Fox noticed that the woods no longer looked as beautiful as before. Everything looked veiled in gray. The sun began to feel uncomfortably hot, and Fox almost passed out. Suddenly, he had the feeling he was being watched. Looking around in all directions, he feared that perhaps the Wolfe demon thing was going to jump out at him, but of course, nothing happened. As quickly as his panic attack had begun, it was over. Shaking his head and regaining control of himself, he once again pondered the possibility of insanity. *Get it together, man!* he thought. Looking to the sky, he called out, "I've never believed in a god of any kind. But if you're there, I need your help now. I ain't gonna make you any promises. If you do exist, I don't get you, but if the old guy needs me or if I need him, I'd appreciate it if you'd just get me there without giving me the creeps anymore." Beginning to look ahead again, he looked back up and said, "Thanks."

After walking for a while, he came to the next landmark that the old man had shown him: a path with a fork in the road. His mind began to jumble as he tried to remember which path to follow. Not bothering to be silent anymore, Fox began questioning himself, "Now which way did the old man want me to go? This day sure is beginning to go down the toilet in a hurry. Think, man, think." Looking around, Fox noticed one path led deeper into the woods and the other to an open meadow. Closing his eyes, he took a deep breath and began to see a vision unfold before him.

The old man was here now. Taking his hand, the man began to lead him into the woods. Fox began to follow but then stopped. The old man turned to look at him, seeming to question why he had stopped. *What's wrong?* he thought. *Just follow the old guy.* Then he realized where the hesitation came from. Always before, the man had spoken his direction, never touched him, and this cold grip wasn't what Fox imagined his touch would feel like. Pulling his hand away, looking at the man in front of him, he jumped back as the face changed into that of the dragon. *Where have I seen this guy before? I know him, I just—aye! I can't remember.* The dragon man reached out to him, again speaking in Tempess's voice, "You can't hide from me. I will find you, and when I do, you'll pay."

Anger began rising in Fox's throat at hearing Tempess in this man. "Don't even threaten me, you freak! You'll only kill me if I don't kill you first! And if you think I've given up, man, you are sadly mistaken!"

The dragon-faced man just laughed. "You still don't have a clue, do you?"

Fox balled up his fist preparing to clobber the thing. Suddenly, the vision was over, and his eyes popped open. He was alone on the path. Breathing deeply and collecting his thoughts, he now knew what direction to take and turned toward the meadow of wildflowers.

Walking again, he heard a voice. It was not Tempess but the one he knew went with the dragon's face, "Don't worry, Jason, you'll remember me. All in good time."

The woods became quiet again, except for the wind in the trees and a bird's song high above. *Who is that guy?* he thought. As Fox began to cross the field, the memory of the vision faded as once again he began to enjoy the scenery around him. Deciding that the meadow would be a great place to picnic, he sat down, opened his pack, and took out an MRE. Opening the pack of mystery food, he was disappointed to see pork and beans. *Well, serves me right. I should've labeled the darn things.* As he ate his meal, he looked around at the natural plant life growing all by itself with no human interaction in this dry climate. The colors amazed him: yellow, purple, blue, pink, and green. The delicacy of the small and large blooms was far better than any city garden he'd seen. Finishing his meal, he made sure to put all his used items in a plastic bag and back into his pack. "No need to ruin this place." He was becoming more comfortable with his own voice, although he hoped when he returned to civilization, he would remember not to continue the habit.

Wanting to lay back and enjoy the fragrance of the meadow but not wanting to fall asleep and dream anymore, he thought better of it and reluctantly stood up. Shouldering his pack, he began to ramble again. Coming to the edge of the meadow and the beginning of the woods again, he began thinking of his latest vision, which brought chills up his spine. Thoughts of the mystery man were bombarding his memory. Where did he know that guy from? Granted, he'd ticked off a lot of people in his time but not to the point of wanting him dead—minus a few angry husbands. Even Tempess, for all his stupidity, got what he wanted. "Why am I such a threat?" He queried to no one in particular. "What's going on here? I did my job. I got heat sickness. Wolfe got possessed and shot. I go on the lam and start having psycho visions, ones that come true, mind you, and I'm the one who needs to be killed? Yeah right! That makes a lotta sense." Thinking about the past week and a half finally brought Jason Fox to his knees. Crying out of anger, exhaustion, and loss, Jason Fox fell to the ground. He punched the dirt and screamed expletives, questioning God, life, and the purpose of everything. He let his rage run out in a stream of tears and bitter words.

After what seemed an eternity of being out of control, Fox managed to regain his composure and continue on his way. Feeling drained and disheartened, Fox began to wonder about going on. "Maybe I should just go back. I don't even know if the old guy exists. Maybe, I'm cracking up." As he pondered quitting, he caught the sound of running water. "Well, I'll be," he said, realizing he was approaching the final landmark. Pushing through the underbrush and clearing the woods, he stepped out onto a small riverbank. "I guess I'll set up camp here! I must be cracking up, talking to myself. Who cares? I'm a goin' fishin'."

After setting out his sleeping bag and finding a good stick, Fox pulled out some string and a hook and proceeded to make himself a fishing pole. Congratulating himself on always having bits and pieces with him just in case, he said, "Just like in Boy Scouts!" After digging up some worms, he set to the task of catching dinner.

After about fifteen minutes of casting and pulling in, he decided next time he'd bring a fishing rod and reel. While contemplating the difficulties of fishing without a reel, he got a bite and was surprised when he had a nice-sized trout on the end of the line. "Hotdog! Maybe there is a god!" Looking toward the sky, he said, "Hey, I said maybe." After cleaning the trout, he built a small fire and cooked it on a stick. Nothing could've tasted better. After eating his dinner and making sure the fire was still nicely burning, he crawled into his sleeping bag and fell instantly asleep.

Waking to the sunrise, he was pleasantly surprised that he had not dreamt at all. "It's gonna be a glorious day!" Stripping down to his birthday suit, he took a quick dip in the river. "Aayyeee! Whoa! That's cold!" After quickly dunking his head and rubbing his pits, he jumped out of the water and got dressed. "Ahhh! Refreshing!" After rerolling his sleeping bag and fastening it to the pack, he pulled out a banana and ate it for breakfast. Taking a swig of water from his canteen and making sure the banana peel was stored in his plastic bag and the fire was completely out, he set off on his way, following the stream that he knew would lead him to the man.

After a couple hours of walking up hill, Fox finally came to the place he was waiting for: a path veering to the right which would lead to the cabin. He crossed the river on a fallen tree and practically ran the couple hundred feet to where he knew the cabin would be. Catching his breath and beginning to walk again, he followed a bend in the path to a plain log cabin sitting among the pines and aspens just waiting for him to knock.

*   *   *

After the congregation had fellowshipped for about an hour, people slowly began to file out of the house in small groups. The excitement of beginning anew had begun to fade as the reality and finality of their decision to leave the established church set in. There had been quite a lot of discussion about services and when they would be held. For now, everyone had decided that Kevin's house would be adequate for services until another place could be found or built.

As the last of the congregation left, Pastor Stone thanked them for standing with him and encouraged them to remember to pray and support one another. Words that were meant to comfort them as well as himself. He prayed silently for God to lead his steps and help this small part of His church grow. As he stared after his flock, Scott walked up to him and squeezed his shoulder, reminding him that this was the right decision and that God would guide them toward His plan. Stone closed the door, and the two men proceeded to the living room where the rest of the leaders were waiting.

The living room was spacious and bright as the late summer sun shone through the bay windows and skylight above. The windows looked out onto a beautifully kept garden. Mostly xeriscaped, it had many wildflowers and herbs growing heartily around a stone path leading to a newly built gazebo. A stone fireplace adorned almost the entire connecting wall. The oak mantle held family treasures: photos, knickknacks, and a small wooden cross with the "Footprints in the Sand" poem etched in it. The hardwood floor was partly covered by a simple rope rug placed in the middle of the floor. A matching overstuffed couch, love seat, and chair were placed neatly around the rug. Also in the room was a recliner and antique rocking chair covered with a quilt hand-sewn by Kevin's wife, Yvonne, a tall thin dark-skinned woman who spoke with a slight French accent. All in all, the room was pleasant and comfortable; the small group was beginning to feel like a real family.

"Well…" breathed Stone, falling onto the couch next to Miriam, "I can't believe we made it through this day."

"Yeah, I know what you mean." Bob sighed, resting in the recliner. "This has been one crazy week, and I for one am lookin' forward to starting fresh without the synod, and especially without Burke around."

"Come on, man," Scott interjected, sitting on the chair. "If you really think Burke is going to quietly fade away, you've gotta be crazy. Didn't you see his face? Granted, I think we took him by surprise, but I just have a feeling that there's a whole lot more going on here then we know."

"What do you mean?" asked Miriam. "We're nothing. Just a little group of people wanting to do our own thing. I would think Burke should be glad to be done with us."

"That's just it," Scott answered. "He had his chance to be done with us, but he did everything in his power to try and force Andrew to turn around. No. He has something up his sleeve, and I bet it has something to do with that foundation."

"Well, I have to agree with Scott," Kevin said. "This thing is bigger than all of us—the money they funneled, the sound system, the change in the service. I think we have to acknowledge that something else is going on. I think this is just the beginning. I've also been thinking about what Mir said about Pastor Stewart. He said that he was gonna fight something, right? Maybe he did, and that's what's freaking out Burke. After all, no one knows what happened to him."

Getting frustrated, Miriam quietly spoke, "Come on now. Granted, a lot of stuff has come out recently and it's tempting to try and find something to bring it all together, but if you're right, I don't understand why we're such a threat. We haven't gone out destroying anything or stirring up trouble. We've just been minding our own business."

"Yeah, but we're preaching the truth," Scott said, getting excited. "The truth will set you free! Burke knows that. The devil knows it. And I'll guarantee that the foundation knows it. God is in control, and I think it's getting through to the higher-ups that something is messing up their little plan, and that would be us!"

A silence fell over the group. All of them, even Miriam, had thought about the possibility of a larger conspiracy. The silence had become uncomfortable and pierced their souls with a reality that no one was prepared for.

Breaking the silence, Yvonne quietly asked for Pastor Stone to pray and ask for guidance. Everyone agreed and turned toward Andrew, who prayed for a long time. By the time he finished, there wasn't a dry eye in the room. Not because of anything sad that had occurred, but for the loss of a piece of themselves that had been taken with the realization of a conspiracy that was about to engulf their world.

* * *

As Damious sat comfortably on the foundation's private jet enjoying a Long Island iced tea, he began to relax and concentrate on the task ahead. He was going to enjoy confronting Burke Smith, the little worm that he was. He couldn't decide who was more pathetic, Smith or Tempess. For both of them to have messed up so egregiously couldn't be tolerated.

Tempess had the seemingly simple task of disposing of Fox, but nooo, he let him slip right through his fingers. It was a mistake, though, that could not have been foreseen. Who would've thought that Fox would actually kill his best friend?

With the knowledge Fox held, Damious had decided not to get the cops involved. Jason Fox had proven to be a worrisome adversary.

I never saw it coming, Damious thought. *Why didn't I see it coming?* Picking up his global Internet phone, Damious dialed the number for Isabelle. The phone rang several times until finally she picked up, "Hello."

"Hello, Isabelle. I have a favor to ask of you."

"Sure. What do you want?"

"I need you to contact Adder."

Pausing for a moment, she replied with a slight tremor in her voice, "Why don't you just contact Angelous?"

"I don't need Angelous now. What I need now is for you to *not* question me and to just do what I say! I need you to ask Adder about the plan and how it is proceeding." Trying to sound conciliatory, Damious continued, "You know, Isabelle, that Adder's mission and Angelous's mission are different, as is yours and mine. Please, just do as I say."

"All right, Michael, I will. Just to let you know, the new recruits are getting along well, and we'll be awaiting your return. What time would be best for me to call you back?"

"Eight o'clock Denver time will be fine."

"Very well, Michael. Will that be all, or is there something else?"

"No, Belle, that will be all."

In an annoyed tone, she replied, "Fine then, I'll call you at eight." Without saying good-bye, she hung up the phone.

Returning to his ice tea, Damious closed his eyes and began to leave his body to meet Angelous, his guide. The difference between Damious and Isabelle was that Damious knew completely what he was dealing with, or so he thought. Seeing the spirits in their true form never bothered him and, in some strange way, gave him a feeling of power. For in Damious's mind, he was in control, never realizing that he was the one being controlled.

When Damious visited his guide, there were no facades: no beautiful fields, no clouds, no peace, just utter chaos and pain. Where Damious went, he could see tortured souls, those damned to the worst hell had to offer. The Greek myths and their portrayals of pushing boulders up a hill or having food just out of reach were fairy tales compared to the carnage that was hell.

Souls have no body to torment, but from their prison, from their mind, they relive their worst nightmares over and over. New and ever more intricate tortures await them. Always dark, as if they are in a deep narrow hole, the soul reaches with unseen arms for a pinprick of light above. In the end, when the reunion of body and soul, occurs the light will be opened and they brought into it. Awaiting them, however, will not be safety, but fire and brimstone, a raging inferno—the lake of fire. Their screams of pain and the torturous knowledge of what could have been will fill eternity.

Damious loved coming here. He loved the power of feeling in control of it all, knowing that in his death, he would be elevated above such desperate souls and spared the ultimate fire. The demons, the devil, whatever humans call them, had already given him such power on earth that he had no fear of death. If only he knew what they had prepared for him, he would run. For now, though, he came to see Angelous.

Angelous, unlike Adder, was one of the more powerful spirits and controlled many more, including Adder. Angelous often thought of how easy ensnaring humans had become in the past century. The death of the one true God had turned out to be a marvelous plan. Of course, the demons knew that God still reigned, and they feared Him because they knew of the fall and what was lost. Still, they had followed Lucifer, angel of light, to the pit and reigned with him in the face of God. But humans, dumb humans, were always willing to follow a lie: God is in you. You must choose to follow God. You must be good like God. You must live like God. It was always a focus on themselves and their goodness instead of on God. Angelous's very favorite lie to suck in so-called Christians was, God is in all religion, and all gods are the same god. Oh, how it delighted in the lies. Of course, a little truth made the lies all the better.

Damious, however, was not a believer. He was a humanist, the easiest of prey, one who believes he controls his own destiny. While thinking about human arrogance, Angelous spewed out a hideous laugh and slew a nearby demon for the pure enjoyment of it. Even though demons were cast out of heaven into hell, there was an even worse place for them to go, and Angelous had no qualms about sending a peon away. While Angelous enjoyed its thoughts, Damious entered its lair.

In his strongest voice, Damious bellowed, "Hello, Angelous!"

Bored with him already, Angelous growled, "What is it, Michael? Have you any good news? Because all I've heard is bad. You don't want me to punish you now, do you?"

In a nervous but confident voice, Damious replied, "No. Not yet. I'm on my way to Denver to clean up this church mess. Trycon has not been leading his charges well. Both Smith and Tempess have managed to screw up."

"Trycon has failed? More than once? Hmmm." It scraped its talons, making a harsh screeching sound. Letting out a high-pitched squall, Angelous called for Trycon. Turning to Damious and grotesquely grinning, it said quietly, "Do you want to see what I do to those who fail me? Well, watch this."

A streak of red vapor streamed into the room following the spirit called Trycon. In a sniveling voice, it asked, "You called, Your Greatness?"

"Yes. I've heard some disturbing news about you." Angelous turned and gestured toward Damious, who wore a devilish grin. "Michael here says that you've failed on your mission with the two humans I charged you with." Leaning in toward Trycon and raising its eyebrows, it asked, "Is that true?"

Knowing what was about to come, Trycon cowered and began making excuses. "No! I mean, yes! I mean, it wasn't my fault. I wasn't told how strong the adversaries were."

Angelous grabbed Trycon and ripped off its wings. With a horrible scream of pain, Trycon struggled in vain under the harsh grasp of its master. "Strong adversaries! They're only humans! You are a pathetic excuse for a son of Lucifer, and since you failed me, you failed him!" Lifting the smaller demon over its head while drawing its black sword, Angelous laughed and brought the sword arcing down through Trycon's neck, severing its head. Only a wisp of red vapor remained as Angelous sent it to the abyss.

Turning to Damious, Angelous narrowed its snake-like eyes and quietly said, "That, my dear Michael, is what I do to those who fail me. Don't fail me!" Being tired of Damious's presence, it picked him up and flung him away.

Damious jolted awake to the pilot's voice as he announced their descent into Denver. Drenched in sweat, he downed the rest of his ice tea and began to prepare for his meeting with Burke Smith.

*   *   *

Back at New Life, Isabelle did as instructed and contacted Adder. Ever since it abruptly ended their session a few weeks ago, tension had been building between them. Not so much on Adder's part, it did apologize after all, but Isabelle couldn't shake the harsh feelings it had bestowed on her. When Adder would visit, she pretended everything was fine, and it was, at least the foundation was anyway, but her inner turmoil, the struggle growing within her, had begun to wear her down. Often, she found herself searching for her mother, but she had no luck and was beginning to wonder if her dream was true. Occasionally while meditating, she could hear the small voice calling her, telling her someone was praying for her. She did not understand this because she knew of no one who prayed. It was to her a silly Judeo-Christian habit that served no function except for people to hear themselves talk. True seeking came from within, from emptying one's mind and seeking calm—not filling yourself with a lot of words in a book, but finding your guide and receiving truth. Lately, though, she found herself trying to pray, but found no satisfaction from it and gave up on it quickly.

Finding her favorite spot in the gardens, she lay down and began to call Adder. She had no trouble, of course, because of their bond. Immediately, she was transported to her spirit world. Once there, she found Adder sitting in a tree enjoying a freshly plucked peach. It smiled when it saw her and bade her to come to it. Naturally, she obeyed. As she neared the tree, Adder jumped down and sat on the green grass surrounded by mums of every color and variety. Isabelle joined Adder, and it gently stroked her hair. This always relaxed her, and she began to forget Adder's strange behavior.

"What is it that you need, child?" Adder crooned softly.

Her reply was relaxed and quiet. "Michael wanted me to ask you how everything is going."

"Well, my dear, as far as I know, things are going well. Of course, my only dealings are with the foundation and new members." Pausing for effect, it continued, "And you, Isabelle, are doing a magnificent job."

Finding herself blushing, she replied, "Yes, well, the search for truth is universal. All those new souls just waiting to be brought into the light, I very much enjoy being a part of it."

"And you are so important, my child. I must tell you, I feel very fortunate to have been chosen as your guide. You have never let me down, and I am so grateful for that." Its true scaly self grimaced as it spoke to her. It really was pleased to have her. After all, Adder had never met the back of Angelous's hand or sword; Isabelle was so trusting and naive, so easy to control. Still, to put on such a facade for a human was unbearable for any self-respecting demon. It longed for the day it could reveal its true nature to her. *Won't she be surprised?* it thought happily. Continuing with their conversation, it said, "You are like a daughter to me."

Suddenly getting a chill up her spine, she tried to excuse herself, "Um, Adder, I need to get back now. I have some stuff to do, and then I have to call Michael and tell him everything is okay."

As she started to stand up, it gently grabbed her arm and said in a cool voice, "Wait. What's the rush? You haven't been visiting me lately. I've always had to come to you, and I feel that if Damious hadn't asked you to come, you wouldn't have."

"I'm sorry, Adder. It's been very hectic lately. I think I've just been running myself down. Plus, you visit me so much now that I don't really ever feel alone."

"Yesss, I suppose I have been coming to you, haven't I? Well, then I guess you should be getting back."

Isabelle walked back to her spot and lay down. Before she returned to her body, she turned her head to look at Adder. It had once again climbed its tree and had returned to its peach. She closed her eyes, and when she opened them, she was back at the foundation.

Slowly sitting up, she felt her heart pounding in her chest and again heard the voice calling. As she stood up, Tamara, a small slightly plump woman with long red hair and blazing green eyes, came up to her and asked if she was okay.

"Yeah, I'm fine, Tamara. I just came back from visiting Adder."

"You've been pushing yourself kinda hard lately, Izzy." Tamara was the only person who called her that. "I think when Michael gets back, you should see about taking a vacation."

The idea of a vacation hadn't crossed Isabelle's mind before, but now it struck her as a brilliant thought. "You know, maybe I will. I haven't left the foundation for a very long time. Not since—"

"Now never you mind about him. That is the past, and you just need to put it behind you."

"Yeah, Tam, I know, but I'd just really like to see him again."

"I know, sweetie, but you need to relax not get yourself into trouble. Michael would have a fit if you went looking for him. Promise me you won't do anything stupid."

Wanting to placate Tamara, Isabelle agreed, but she knew it was a lie. Andrew Stone was the only man she'd ever loved, and she intended to find him. Leaving Tamara in the garden to do her own meditating, Isabelle crossed the foundation and returned to her room. Isabelle finally started to feel like she hadn't in years— full of purpose. Waiting for her clock to strike ten o'clock, eight o'clock Denver time, Isabelle began to remember her lost love.

Chapter 4

Do not participate in the unfruitful deeds of darkness,
but instead even expose them.

—Ephesians 5:11

As a man is said to have a right to his property, he may
be equally said to have a property in his rights. Where
an excess of power prevails, property of no sort is duly
respected. No man is safe in his opinions, his person, his
faculties or his possessions.

—James Madison

Dateline September 2020
Global News Network

Amanda Wright

Today the United Global Heath Administration (UGHA)
has acknowledged a strange uptake in sterility cases
among childbearing age women and men. According to
administrative minister Catherine Sunsteen, the epidemic
seems to be related to complications from the H1N1
vaccines that were given ten years ago at the height of the
swine flu scare of 2009. UGHA scientists are currently
studying the problem.

Sunsteen stated, "While this is certainly sad for those
women and men desiring children this is actually a positive
thing. We've overpopulated the earth for generations, and
now perhaps through this sad side effect, we can begin to

keep the human population in check. This will be seen as a positive thing by future generations."

Short and to the point, exactly what any good reporter should do, thought Amanda Wright, a statuesque blonde Valley girl. It was her first assignment for the new news organization Global News Network (GNN), and she intended to give it her best shot. While writing newsfeed for arrogant news anchors wasn't her dream job as a veteran investigative journalist, it was a great honor to be chosen to be a part of the initial phase of the global press corp. Who would've thought after all the upheavals of the early part of the century that the world would actually mobilize as one united planet, a dream not shared by all, especially Americans and Middle Eastern countries, but nonetheless a reality. After the fall of the American dollar and the collapse of Western markets, not to mention the failed attempt at Islamic world rule, there really wasn't anywhere to go except into global oneness.

"Amanda! Hurry up and get that copy sent so we can get out of here," called Rachel Vecler, a five-foot-seven tomboy with midlength auburn hair and brown eyes.

Oh, Jeez! I forgot to hit Send, thought Amanda as she punched the key. "Sorry! I'm just so excited to be a part of all this! The interview with Catherine Sunsteen was awesome."

"Come on, don't you think it's kinda creepy? All those women and men being sterile? If you ask me, that's a story worth digging into."

"What are you talking about? Minister Sunsteen said that they were looking into it. Besides, it is good that the world will be less populated, don't you think? You science types always read too much into stuff."

"Science type? Since when don't investigative journalists read too much into stuff? I really don't understand how you can't be more curious. Why should we be deciding how many people is too many? If you ask me, I keep wondering how the world is going to keep functioning with less people. Granted, we don't need as many people in charge as we used to, but we still need people to work."

"Well, with the implementation of the updated version of the old United Nation's Agenda 21, I think people will be able to produce all they need in a smaller area, so no, I don't think we'll need too many more people. Heck, as an anthropologist, I'd think you'd be all for population control. After all, isn't that how nature has always taken care of itself? By reducing the number of people living in overpopulated areas?"

"Okay, you got me there, but was this nature taking care of itself or a human mistake or plan to cause sterility in the population? And you know, when populations dwindled in the past, they were built up again. What happens if we don't have enough of a population to sustain society?" Pointing to the poster proclaiming the wonders of the new global government initiative, Rachel continued, "With the United Global States of the Earth set up as the world government, it should be easy enough for the sustainable development provisions to be implemented, but there are still pockets of resistance, and if not enough people are born, we will have a hard time having enough workers in one hundred years. Sustainable development won't be sustainable without workers." Folding her arms across her chest and shaking her head, she continued, "There are too many unanswered questions, and I'm afraid very soon there'll be another war."

"Another war! The global meltdown of 2015 is something that will never be allowed to happen again. First, guns have been made illegal except for the military, and hate speech is illegal. Second, people seem to have accepted the new government and constitution and have settled down. Of course, all the religious zealots are being taken care of everywhere—"

"Except America and the Middle East."

"Well, soon enough, I think they'll fall in line. My father says things are coming together much better than anyone expected, some kind of thing going on in the desert of California and the

New Life Foundation. I guess they merged with Techne-Corp and are planning to help affect the changes coming with total sustainable development. Believe me, the people at the top know what they're doing."

"And who's going to be watching the people at the top?"

"Ummm…I'm not sure. How about we quit talking and think about going out on the town. I heard there is this new band playing at the Music Bar tonight, something like Windy or the Wind or something that has *wind* in it! You up for it?" questioned Amanda in her usual ADD way.

"Yeah, why not. I've got nothin' better to do!"

"Great! I'll see you at ten!" Skipping away, Amanda added, "Later!"

"Yeah, later!"

* * *

The cabin was exactly as it had been in his dream. A small rectangular log house with smoke curling up out of the chimney and three steps leading up to a porch that ran the entire length of the house sat in a clearing surrounded by pines and aspens. A small barn graced the edge of the clearing, and a chicken coop leaned up against one side of the house. An SUV and a pickup truck were parked at the back of the clearing covered by a carport. Jason Fox pinched himself to make sure he was actually awake. *Ow!* he thought. *I guess I am.* A cow lazily chewed its cud while chickens pecked at the ground. *Well, here goes,* he thought. He walked up the steps and knocked on the door that had been painted red.

"Come on in," a voice called from inside the house.

Jason Fox turned the knob and found it locked. Looking at the keyhole, he noticed a familiar symbol: the letter *S*. Taking the key he'd found near the ancient oak tree out of his pocket, he inserted it into the lock, turned it, and pushed open the door. *Cool,* he thought. The inside was not at all what he expected. For one thing, it looked like it was twice the size as the outside revealed, but the really amazing thing was the computer equipment and small arsenal that occupied two adjacent rooms. The room he walked into was nicely furnished. A large area rug filled the center of the great room and was surrounded by couches, recliners, and an obligatory rocking chair. Against the wall was a huge fireplace, one like you'd see in a medieval castle, complete with a nicely burning fire and black pot filled with some kind of soup or stew. Through an archway toward the back of the house was the dining room and kitchen area. This is where Jason Fox got his first view of a gray-haired Donald Stewart.

Turning from the sink where he was washing some dishes, the man introduced himself, "Hello, Mr. Fox. My name is Donald Stewart, but you can call me Don. I've been waiting for you."

"Waiting for me? How could you have been waiting for me, and how did I find this place, and—"

"I know you have many questions Mr. Fox. Why don't you sit down at the table and we'll have something to eat, and then I will answer your questions, at least the ones I can."

"Yeah, I guess I could eat. Is there somewhere I can wash up first?"

"Sure, the bathroom is the small room to your right."

"Thanks," answered Fox as he turned and opened the door to the bathroom. After washing up, he came out to see the table set with two bowls filled with the stew from the pot in the living room. Also, Stewart had placed a basket of cut-up French bread on the table.

"Would you like a beer?" asked Stewart. "Or something else?"

"A beer would be great," replied Fox, still not sure whether or not he was dreaming.

The two men sat down at the table, and after Donald said grace, they ate and drank in silence. Jason Fox hadn't realized how hungry he was and said, "Thanks for the food, Don. I guess all the walking around made me hungrier than I had realized."

"No problem. Have as much as you like. There is plenty."

"I have so many questions to ask. I don't know where to begin. I guess the hows and whys of our meeting are going to take a very long time, so I'll start with, what's with the arsenal? Are you planning to take someone out? Your computer equipment is top-of-the-line, not something I would assume a man living out on a mountain would have. How do you get a signal out here? There can't be any cable, and the forest seems pretty dense to get a satellite signal out."

Chuckling after swallowing a mouthful of stew, Stewart answered, "Well, start with the hard questions, why don't you? Where do I begin? I guess I'll start at the beginning, but I think it would be more comfortable to do the question-and-answer time after we eat, huh?"

"Yeah, I don't see why we should get indigestion. Let's enjoy our meal and then get into the deep questions."

The two men finished their meal in silence, not the uncomfortable kind where no one knows what to say but the kind of silence shared by people who've known each other for years. After dinner, the men washed up the dishes and put the extra stew in a container and into the fridge. Donald Stewart poured each of them a glass of scotch-whiskey, and the two of them settled down in the living room for a conversation that would take them late into the night.

* * *

After the meeting finished, Andrew Stone walked slowly through the town park toward his soon-to-be-ex home, mulling over the revelations made by the small band of saints. Of course, he already knew about the New Life Foundation and their plans to lead people subliminally. After all, he was one of the engineers who designed the system. *How could I have been so blind?* he thought to himself.

Looking around the park, he tried to imagine what it was like before the great environmental disaster of 2012 and the war of 2015. All the things he had believed so strongly in as a young man had turned out to be nothing more than lies created to gain power over the masses. Sadly, most people fell for the fiction created over so many years. It's hard to blame the public. They'd been filled with global, eco, and social misinformation since infancy, all the way back to their favorite cartoons.

Things looked so normal, but every now and then, if you looked hard enough and knew what to look for, you could see the modifications. Colors were a little more vivid than nature should allow. The air also had a slight burnt smell to it. Again, not all the time, but every now and then, if you took a deep breath at the right time of day, it was there in the background. The Global Ecological Administration had done a good job fixing the environmental collapse, or perhaps there never was a collapse and it was all just a scam sold to the world public to get a result. Who knew? Andrew Stone knew. The lies permeated all the way to the top of every government in the world and now to the new United Global States of the Earth. To Andrew Stone, the concept of a real global government was always just the imagination of the kook fringe until it finally happened and he found himself an unwilling accomplice.

Sitting on a bench, Andrew placed his head in his hands and began to pray, "Dear Lord, I have given my life to you. I have received your wonderful grace and forgiveness, but now I need you to help me to forgive myself. Help me to find the path you have for me and this congregation." Lifting his head and speaking toward the sky, he said, "I've done such evil, and now because of my pride, even the people of this small town, my congregation, are embroiled in a mess bigger than they know. I'm praying for help, Lord. I cannot do this alone. Give me the strength to confess my sins to these wonderful people. Most importantly, help them to be able to forgive me." Making the sign of the cross, Pastor Stone finished, "In the name of the Father, Son, and Holy Spirit."

Getting up from the bench, he felt utterly defeated. As he walked home, a bird, a black-capped chickadee, landed right on his shoulder and began chirping its little tune, *chick-a-dee-dee-dee-dee, chick-a-dee-dee-dee-dee.* Watching this little bird reminded him of the scripture 'Look at the birds of the air. They neither toil nor sow, but your father in heaven feeds them. Therefore do not worry about tomorrow.' As the bird flew away, Andrew Stone felt a calming presence and thought, *Thank you, Lord, for showing me your goodness. I will wait upon you.*

His mind wandered back to thoughts of where he was going to live now that he'd have to leave the parsonage, and as he stepped up to his door, put his key in the lock, and turned it to enter, a voice from the past spoke to him from the shadows, "Hi, Drew. Long time no see. Boy, do we have stuff to discuss."

Andrew Stone turned to see his old friend, Jason Fox, standing with a goofy grin on his face.

* * *

Michael Damious hated airports. Too many people milling around like stupid sheep just waiting for someone to come and tell them what to do. Well, soon they'd have their wish and they'd be in little pens where they belonged. It used to be that people who flew on private jets could get picked up directly from their hangers, but since 2017, when the leaders of every major nation were assassinated by homicide bombers dressed as chauffeurs, everyone who was not a head of state had to go through the airport to reach their cars. Diplomats were flown out by helicopters. *Like that's going to make a difference if a homicide bomber decides to fly a helicopter, but what can you expect from people? They overreact to everything,* thought Damious. Even though private jet patrons got to use a private area of the airport, Damious hated spending any time with those he deemed worthless, but he understood that it was a means to an end, so he put up with it. After getting through the airport and into his non-eco-friendly limousine, he took out his global Internet phone and called Burke Smith. "I'm at the airport and will be in your little town in a few hours. I have some business to attend on the way, so just be ready. I will meet you at your church, and I expect an update!"

"Sure, boss, but I don't have a lot more to add."

"Well, then we'll just have to figure something else to do, won't we? Do you really want to do something besides give me an update?"

"No, sir. I'll have an update and a plan."

"That's what I want to hear, a little go-getter spirit! Don't let me down." Finished with the conversation, Damious pushed the off button, threw the phone onto the seat, poured himself a drink, and sat back to let his thoughts go toward world domination.

Burke didn't know what to do. How was he supposed to know a handful of misfits would be able to figure out at least part of the plan? Resurrection had simply been a testing facility for the subliminal infiltration system. No one was supposed to figure it out. Stupid Donald Stewart and his disappearing act. When he thought about it, this whole mess was Damious's fault. After all, he picked Stewart as his point man. Was it Burke's fault that he went AWOL? He didn't think so, but nevertheless, Damious wasn't about to take responsibility for it, so he had to come up with a plan.

He had already called the synod and told them that Kevin Davies was a kook who was looking to make trouble for the church. After all, subliminal messages in a speaker? That seemed to make them happy, but the embezzlement was a bigger problem. There was no way to get around that. Luckily, though, Burke had come up with a plan, one that Damious would have to finance.

He figured he could place the missing money in a safe in the church and say Stewart must have put it in before disappearing without letting anyone know about it. He could have the lock picked, and all the money would be there. No one would be able to prove embezzlement or fraud because Stewart wouldn't be there to explain it. *Heck, he might even be the one accused of the embezzlement.* That thought put a wicked little smile on Burke's lips. If asked, Burke could just say that he came across the safe while looking for the missing money because he just couldn't believe anyone would actually steal from the church. Hopefully, Damious could get some of his spirit friends to influence the leaders at synod. After all, they were already corrupt in their own ways. He knew very few people in power that were not corruptible.

With his plan in place, all Burke had to do was sit back and wait for Damious to show up. He walked into the pastor's office and sat down behind the desk, preparing to put his plan into effect as soon as Damious gave him the okay and the money.

* * *

An hour later, a little electric car pulled up in front of the church, and Damious stepped out and walked into the church. He wore jeans and a T-shirt with a baseball cap that fit snuggly on his head. He needed a disguise in case Stone was around anywhere. He didn't want to take the chance of being recognized—not yet anyway.

"Hello! Anybody here?" he called out with a slight Southern drawl.

Burke walked out of the office clearly expecting to see a random stranger. He almost fell over when he recognized Damious under the disguise. "What the—" he spat.

"Hello, are you the pastor here?"

Finally catching on, Burke said, "Yes, sir. I'm the temporary pastor. How can I help you?"

"I'd like to find out some information about your church. Do you have time to talk with me?"

"Yes, of course. Why don't you step into my office and we can talk."

Once behind the door, Damious's facade came down. "Now, you little worm, you had better have a good report for me."

"Y-y-yes, sir."

As Burke lay out his plan, Damious's demeanor changed. He even displayed a wicked little smile when thinking about Stewart getting the possible blame for embezzlement. "Well, Mr. Smith, you have pleased me. Who would have thought you could come up with such an ingenious plan?" Reaching into his backpack, he pulled out his checkbook, signed a blank check, and passed it over to Burke Smith with an actual smile. "Fill in the appropriate amount and get the job done. And just because you have redeemed yourself doesn't mean I want another mistake like this again. Do you understand?"

"Yes, sir. I won't fail you again."

"I certainly hope not. I will not be so kind the next time. And keep an eye on Stone and his little band of renegades. I don't need any more surprises. Good-bye, Mr. Smith." Damious stood up without shaking Burke's hand, walked out the door, climbed into his car, and drove away. He didn't notice the man hiding behind a tree across the street watching.

* * *

After calling Damious, Isabelle retreated to her private garden. Even though it was dark outside, the moon cast silvery light on the abundant flora planted there. Isabelle enjoyed the fragrance of the sweet autumn clematis and the cool breeze on her face. Although nature's beauty had been altered since 2012, Isabelle's garden was all natural. Adder had told her that the higher spirits had spared her garden the disease that over took the rest of the planet because she had always been so faithful, and of course, she believed it unquestionably. Truthfully, there was no disease, no environmental disaster, just a cleverly planned wag the dog of sorts set up to help the global powers that be gain control over the population. Planting seeds of environmental fear had been going on for decades, and 2012 seemed like an appropriate time to set off a disaster. After all, the Aztecs had predicted an end of an age and beginning of a new one. The global elites just created their own.

Lying down on the grass and staring up at the stars, Isabelle traced the constellations that she recognized. Staring up at the moon, she let her mind drift back ten years to the day she met Andrew Stone. It was the first Monday of December, and a new batch of recruits was welcomed to New Life. Andrew Stone was a part of that group. The first moment that Isabelle saw him, she was smitten. Dating between leaders and recruits was supposed to be against the rules, but Isabelle got permission both from Damious and Adder to be with him. After her introductory speech, when the recruits were given time to change and go to dinner, Isabelle made sure to introduce herself to Andrew. He was twenty-five and had just left a career in archeology to pursue higher enlightenment and hopefully work with the foundation to make a better world. He was utterly intoxicating to her. He told her that he had a falling out with one of his best friends over his sister. It turned out that his friend, a real ladies' man, had decided to marry Andrew's sister. While he loved his friend very much, he did not approve of the marriage. He just didn't believe he would be able to be faithful to her. He decided that he wasn't going to stay around and see her make the biggest mistake of her life, so he left the dig they were working on and came here. Isabelle found that to be absolutely enchanting.

For the first month, recruits were not allowed physical contact with anyone, except for hugs or holding hands during mediation times. During this time, Isabelle and Andrew had time to talk and really get to know each other. He was astounded at her ability to reach Adder and other spirits. He had trouble with it and never actually connected to the spirit world, but he loved nature as much as she did. His knowledge of botany, astronomy, and history fascinated her. They grew very close and spent almost all their free time together.

After the first month, Andrew had become well established in the agriculture group and hoped to continue working with the landscaping of the huge New Life campus. He and Isabelle began to date on a regular basis and began to fall in love. They had been taking their relationship slowly and had not even kissed after six months of dating.

On the eve of the summer solstice, they planned a picnic and left the campus to go out to a local lake where Andrew wanted to show her a very special flower that only grew in this one spot. Isabelle spread out a blanket and proceeded to prepare the food that she had brought. The two finished off the picnic basket and lay down to rest. While they were lying there quietly, Andrew took her hand and led her down to the edge of the lake. Gently, he pulled back some brush that grew along the edge, and Isabelle saw what he brought her there to see. The most beautiful flowers she had ever seen grew in a little heart shape under the brush: dainty daisy-like flowers in every color imaginable. It was like looking at a rainbow growing from the ground. As he replaced the brush and stood up, he took her face gently in his hands and bent over and kissed her. It began as a gentle brush, just his lips fluttering over hers. Then as he pulled her closer, their lips pressed together, gently opening ever so lightly, their breath mingling. As quickly as it had begun, it ended. As he pulled away, they looked deep into each other's eyes and, at the same time, whispered, "I love you." The moment was eternally etched in Isabelle's mind. After their kiss, they went back to the blanket and laid down, him on his back and her resting her head on his chest. She still remembered his breathing, his chest rising up and down, up and down. When the moon was at its highest point, he took her hand again and led her back to the flowers. This time, when he pulled the brush back, the moonlight shone on the flowers, and they glowed like magic gems. The sight took her breath away. As they walked back to the car to return to the foundation, he made her promise to always keep the flowers a secret. He promised that as long as they bloomed, his love for her would last.

As she came back to reality, she realized that she had been crying. The loss of Andrew Stone had almost destroyed her, and she wondered if she really wanted to begin a quest to find him. While thinking these thoughts, she noticed the moon was at its highest point, and she walked over to her garden pond, pulled back some brush that she had planted, and stared at the very flowers that Andrew Stone had shown her glowing like gems in the moonlight. After he left the foundation, she carefully dug up the flowers and transplanted them. Gazing on them, she felt that first kiss and knew that she would seek and find Andrew Stone no matter what.

*   *   *

After catching a bus home to her small apartment building, Rachel undressed and stepped into a steaming hot shower. Letting the water run over her body, she laid her head back and ran her fingers through her hair, pushing it back. Showers always rejuvenated her, and with Amanda's plans for the night, she figured she'd need to be on her A game. Amanda liked to party hard, and it was usually left to Rachel to get her home. After toweling off and drying her hair, she removed her brown-tinted contacts to reveal stunning peridot-green eyes. She dressed in a midthigh faux leather skirt with a body-hugging tank top layered with an off-the-shoulder red T-shirt. She thought she looked sexy enough to go clubbing without saying "Come and get me" to every red-blooded male out trolling for the evening. Before leaving the bedroom, she returned to the bathroom and reinserted her contacts. After slipping her feet into a pair of high-heeled red pumps, she walked out through the living room into the kitchen and filled a round wineglass with white zinfandel.

She let her mind run back to her first meeting with Amanda and her father, Justin Wright. Amanda and Rachel had met at a retreat held at the New Life Foundation. Amanda was a recruit preparing to leave and continue life as a journalist for the newly formed global government, while Rachel was a social anthropologist who had decided to leave fieldwork to try and help construct the outline for a new global society. Working for the United Global States of the Earth (UGSE) seemed like the best way to achieve both of their goals. The New Life Foundation was intimately involved in the new government and allowed part of the campus to be used for training purposes. Recruits from the foundation were easily moved into positions of influence. The best and brightest from outside of the foundation in their perspective fields were initiated in on the most basic level. The foundation had spiritual ways of discerning those who would serve without question, which was the purpose of the retreat.

Rachel was introduced to Amanda and Justin Wright because she was one of the most promising social anthropologists in the field. Since Justin Wright's mandate was restructuring global social structure, Rachel's field of expertise would be most useful. Amanda and Rachel were placed together as global sisters, mostly because Amanda was firmly planted in the foundation and Rachel needed to be monitored. To Rachel's great fortune, though, Amanda was a bit of a flake, and the monitor became the monitored.

As the buzzer to her door sounded, Rachel put down her half-finished glass of wine, grabbed her purse, and opened the door. "Hi, Rachel! Are you ready to go? Whoa! I guess I don't have to ask. Girl, you look hot!" exclaimed an already-buzzed Amanda.

"You look pretty hot yourself," replied Rachel, knowing that the night was going to be full of adventure. While she had tried to tone it down, Amanda had pulled out the stops. Her skirt was so short you could almost see her panties, and her top was so sheer, it was good she had a bra underneath. "Let's get going," sighed Rachel.

After only two hours at the club, Amanda had done so many shots and drank so much she could barely walk. Rachel was getting concerned. She had never seen her friend so wasted before. "What's going on with you tonight?"

"What do you mean? Can't a girl have fun?" Amanda answered while eyeing the guy in the seat next to her.

"Fun is one thing, this is another. Your dad will flip if he finds out you're this out of control," exclaimed Rachel, looking around for any minders Justin Wright might have sent out to watch his daughter.

"What do I care what he thinks? He just wants to control me. If you only knew half of what he's planning, woooo, you'd just die!"

"Like what?"

"Hello, girls," a voice spoke from behind Rachel.

"Oh great! Daddy's here!" spat Amanda. "Say hi to Daddy everyone!" she said to no one in particular while waving her arms around.

Rachel spun in her chair. Blushing, she said, "Hi, Mr. Wright."

Justin Wright was the epitome of high society, well dressed and highly polished. His boyish good looks, well-styled blond hair, and striking blue eyes gave him the appearance of a man ten years his junior. "Hello, Ms. Vecler. Where does that come from anyway? Surely it's not your given name."

"It's just a name I came up with." Rachel stumbled over her words. "I-I thought Vecler sounded kind of mysterious. My given name is Stone—you know, like a rock. I think it just sounded boring, so I go by Vecler."

"Boorriinngg," slurred Amanda before she passed out in Rachel's arms.

Forgetting their conversation, Justin Wright called over a couple of big guys to take his daughter to the car. Turning back to Rachel, he said, "I must be going now. I hope in the future you will not allow my daughter to get in such a state!"

Preparing to protest but thinking better of it, Rachel replied, "Yes, sir. I'm terribly sorry. I tried to get her home—"

"I'm not interested in excuses, Ms. Vecler. I value your work at the UGSA, but I think your behavior needs to be improved."

Biting her tongue, Rachel replied, "I'll do better."

"Of course you will," he said, changing his demeanor back to polite. "Good night, Ms. Vecler." He turned away and walked out the door, leaving Rachel to stew in his admonishments.

Downing the rest of her drink, she threw some money on the bar, walked out the door, bought a disposable cell phone, and punched in a number she'd not called in two years. As the phone rang, a voice on the other end answered, "Hello?"

Rachel sighed and said, "Hi, Jason. It's Rachel. I think I need your help."

* * *

Justin Wright was the owner and CEO of Wright Master Builders and the head administrator for the newly formed United Global Society Administration (UGSA). He was looking for people in the socioeconomic and ecological fields to construct a plan of sustainable development. In the year 1992, the United Nations had formed an action plan called Agenda 21. Agenda 21's goal was to be a comprehensive plan of action to be implemented globally, nationally, and locally by organizations of the United Nations System, governments, and major groups in every area in which humans impact on the environment.

The world community at the time was not ready for global control, which was why the word *locally* was placed in the definition. In small towns all over the world, *sustainable development* had been the buzz words. Strategically placed crises had people clamoring to give up their freedoms to save the planet. Local governments brought the very logical ideas of building only around already-developed towns, utilizing farming regulations to clean the water and air and implementing mandatory conservation easements to their citizens with the caveat "If we do nothing, the town, county, state, even country will be devastated by environmental disaster." Allowing citizens to will their properties to conservation areas and nationalizing public lands in order to save them from evil developers in the future further strengthened the plan of getting all people pushed into small localized living areas and giving governments control of all public lands. With the scientific data they manufactured, why would anyone question such a common-sense plan?

Farmers and American constitutionalists were the first to spot the inevitable landgrabs by big government, as they called it, and fought hard against implementation in the years leading up to 2012. However, when the environmental disaster hit, the United States Congress, as well as most other Western governments, fell into the old trap of creating a government program to protect the citizens, and it was done. Sustainable development had become a new reality.

The US president gave the head of the Environmental Protection Agency (EPA) the power to do whatever was necessary. Farmers either capitulated to the new government regulations set up for running their farms or were relocated and their farms taken over by government-sanctioned farmers who would tend them according to strict environmental directives. The farmers who fought relocation just disappeared with their families. Towns and cities were overrun with refugees from the farms, so draconian measures were implemented. Anyone with more than one vehicle had to give up their other vehicles to those without and carpool to and from work. For bedroom communities, this became a nightmare since so many people worked in different parts of the cities. Families with multiple incomes, unable to get to work, began to lose their jobs. Foreclosures skyrocketed, and there was nothing to do but have the government once again come in and fix the problem. The Department of Housing and Urban Development (HUD) came in and placed multiple families into large foreclosed homes. Each family received one room and shared bathrooms and kitchens. It was like a scene out of the movie *Dr. Zhivago*.

In 2015, people got fed up with the status quo and started a resistance movement. No one knew how so many people all around the world attained weapons, but the citizen uprisings were global and well organized. Government offices all over the world were attacked. Unprepared governments began rounding up citizens and placed them in reeducation camps, whether or not they were in the resistance. The rebels started strong, and the war of 2015 raged, citizens against government.

When the world's governments finally mobilized to repel the plot, over half of their soldiers deserted rather than kill innocent citizens, but those remaining were ruthless. Unlike the wars of the twentieth century, cities were not bombed. Instead, biological and chemical weapons were dispersed. They were not toxic enough to kill but strong enough to empty out the big cities. Soldiers entered the cities and killed everyone who stayed behind: men, women, children, the elderly, and sick and dying people in hospitals. It was a government-sanctioned holocaust. The United Nations declared that it was a necessary evil. Not only did it purge much of the Western world of the sick who were using far too many resources, it reduced the populations of cities all over the world enough to restore order.

In 2016, a truce was called. National leaders from every country decided that since the population problems that had caused the need for the governmental intervention had been removed, society was ready to go back to the way it was before the war. It didn't. The governmental ruling mechanisms put in place by sixteenth- and seventeenth-century reformers were given lip service only. The populace, already accustomed to the ideas of sustainable development and environmental regulation, was more than happy to accept the new freedoms they were allowed.

They worked in employment fields that were available to them and close to home so the one-car rule wouldn't have such dire effects again. City communities began to rebuild with stores, businesses, and schools within walking distance of people's homes. If people lived too far from work, public transportation was made available. Everyone's paychecks were put into a community chest to help pay for all the necessary upgrades. People had become accustomed to the government withholding taxes before they received their pay, so the fact that most of them only saw 30 percent of their actual earnings didn't bother them. The government was taking care of the basic needs: jobs, housing, food, medicine, and transportation. People became grateful to get any extra money for themselves.

Being tired of war and fighting, they just gave up and withdrew into their shared homes, becoming slaves of the new world government under the guise of individual nation states. All the history books were rewritten for school children. References to individual freedoms afforded to past generations were expunged and replaced with false memories of a socialist utopia disrupted occasionally by troublemaking rebels who had caused all the miseries and wars in society. Soon even the adults in the communities forgot the freedoms which had stood in the West for over two hundred years.

As with the decline of any civilization, there was a small group left behind to remember and fight to bring it back. The resistance, while small, was global, very powerful and full of gifts and talents. Their main plan was to keep and store as much true history as they could. Before the beginning of the reorganization of the cities, the resistance found and hid as many books as they could. People filled journals with the facts and memories of their lives in the hope of being able to share it with future generations. Most of the resistance blended back into society, taking jobs and infiltrating as much of the new government as they could manage. The key to survival would be to disrupt as many of the new initiatives as possible.

The plan was progressing well until Michael Damious became aware of the plot. Together with other globalist leaders, a scheme was hatched. The scheme would allow them take complete control of state governments and destroy the credibility of the resistance. A summit of all major heads of state was set to take place in the spring of 2017. While the dignitaries were being taken to their private jets, homicide bombers detonated explosives, killing all the heads of state and throwing every major government into instant chaos. The fledgling global government being set up to replace the ineffective United Nations sprung to action by replacing all the dead leaders with their own people. The resistance was blamed for the attack, and thousands were rounded up and executed, whether or not they were actual resistance fighters; the mob simply needed examples. The global elites believed that they had completely destroyed the resistance movement, and the leaders of the resistance that weren't killed went into hiding. That was the beginning of the United Global States of the Earth or UGSE.

* * *

"What in God's name are you doing here?" asked Andrew Stone in total shock.

"What? No tearful hug? No 'great to see you, man'?" joked Fox.

Too stunned to speak, Andrew Stone reached over, grabbed Jason Fox, pulled him close, and gave him a huge bear hug. Fox responded with a hug back and said, "Whoa, hold on there, man. Let a brother breathe!"

Releasing his old friend, Stone replied, "Again, I have to ask, what are you doing here?"

"Well, invite me in, and we'll discuss it."

"Sure. Come on in."

The two men entered the house. Stone guided Fox toward the guest bedroom to put down his bags and then showed him to the shower. "Here, man, take a towel and clean yourself up. You stink! Take a shower, and I'll get us a couple of beers, and you can tell me the whole story."

"The whole story? That will probably take a case."

After cleaning up, Jason Fox and Andrew Stone got comfortable in the living room and Fox began to tell his story. "Well, I guess I'll start back two years ago when your sister left me to make the world a better place."

"What? She left you? What did you do?"

"Yeah, I forgot how you always thought I wasn't good enough for your sister. Well, it turns out you were wrong. I didn't break her heart. She broke mine."

"I'm so sorry, man. I don't know what to say. Did she leave for someone else? Did she cheat on you?"

"God no, like I said, she just decided that she didn't want to do fieldwork anymore. She said she wanted to take her knowledge and apply it to saving the world. Can you believe it? Rachel wanting to save the world? I always thought she'd be happy just digging in the dirt and figuring out the past forever. Such a waste."

"So you're still together, just apart?"

"Honestly, man, I don't know. If you're asking if I've been faithful, then yes, but as far as she goes, I have no idea. I keep my old phone with me, hoping she'll call, but so far, nada."

"You're still carrying a traceable phone? Are you crazy? You know better than that."

"Heck no. I modified the tracking system. Well, actually, Rich did, and you know how good he was with technology."

"Wait a minute. Why are you talking about Rich in the past tense? Where is he anyway?"

"He's still out in the desert." It wasn't actually a lie. He just wasn't ready to tell that part of the story.

"Why didn't he come back with you? You guys have always been inseparable. Did you have a fight?" It wasn't a really unusual question. Fox and Wolfe were always arguing about something. The discussion usually ended with Fox getting punched out.

"I'll get to that later in the story. I'm not ready to talk about it." Fox choked back tears as he spoke. Stone sensed the conflict in his friend, so just sat back and let him finish the story.

"Anyway, she left to go to the New Life Foundation. What it is with your family and that place?"

"What do you mean she's at the New Life Foundation? I thought you said she wanted to save the world? They do nothing but destroy it."

"Yeah, well, you can say that now. I remember a guy not too long ago who went there to save the world himself."

"Whatever. Keep going."

"Well, needless to say, I was pretty ticked off, so as usual, I found a job. It sounded really cool, lots of field work, although in the desert—you know how fond I am of the desert. Anyhoo, Wolfe and I did the usual research. I couldn't believe they actually got permits to dig. It was right in the middle of Death Valley, and you know how those environmental nuts are. Anyway, we got permission and set out."

"What were you looking for?"

"Some kind of secret lab set up in the 1970s. Who cared as long as it got me away from thinking about your sister? Anyway, back to my story. Wolfe and I researched it. The information we found said that the US government was building a secret lab to test bad stuff, and Techne-Corp, that's the company we worked for, wanted to use it for their own ends. Normal stuff. Big evil corporation wants to take over the world, whatever. The story went that the lab was deserted by the government because of mysterious deaths and industrial sabotage. I'll tell you more about that later."

"It sounds like you don't believe the research. Did you think it was fiction?"

"Not at first, but once we got out to the desert…well, let's just say, I've been to a lot of digs, and this didn't look like any government anything. Can I continue now?"

"Sure, sure. Sorry."

"Well, we get there and start looking around where the GPS led us, and I find this protrusion at the edge of a mesa. So we start digging…"

By the time Fox finished the story, he was shaking with rage. Remembering the death of his best friend didn't seem to get any easier, and why should it? He shot him after all. Stone put his arm around Fox to comfort him. For a while, they sat in silence. After Fox pulled himself together, he said, "Andrew, you got anything stronger than beer? The next part of the story is the wackiest part, and it's what led me here to you."

Stone got up and walked over to the kitchen. "What do you want? Scotch-whiskey, vodka, tequila? What's your poison?"

Teasingly, Fox said, "Gee, Drew, I thought priests were supposed to abstain from such sinful beverages."

"Ha-ha! Everything in moderation, brother. It's overindulgence that's sinful, not partaking. Even Paul told Timothy to have a drink to calm what ailed him."

"Whatever keeps your conscience clear, man. Give me the scotch, on the rocks with water."

"Is there any other way?"

After Stone prepared the drinks and sat down again, Fox continued the story. His journey to the cabin fascinated Andrew Stone. "I can't believe you followed a dream. It's so not like you. And you met the very man that I replaced. I guess God has some kind of plan for us."

"You have no idea. Wait until I finish the story." The two men sat back, and then a phone rang in the bedroom. Jason Fox looked over at his friend and said, "That's my phone. That's Rachel." The two men jumped up and ran to the bedroom. Fox flipped open the phone and said, "Hello?"

On the other end of the line, Rachel Vecler asked her husband for help.

*   *   *

"Well? Are you there?" asked Rachel.

"Yeah, yeah, of course. Where else would I be?" asked Fox incredulously.

"That's a stupid question," teased Rachel. "How are you? Where are you? What's going on?"

"Don't you think those are questions I should be asking? You just up and leave and join that cult, and I don't hear from you in two years and—"

"Yeah, okay, shut up! I need your help. I think I'm about to be in a whole world of trouble. Look, I'm sorry for being so direct, but I need you to come out to LA and help me."

"LA? What are you doing in LA? I thought you were at the New Life Foundation?"

"I was only there for a short time. I told you I wanted to work for the UGSE. It just so happened that their introductory retreat was at New Life—a creepy place, if you ask me. I'll be happy to never go there again. But let's get back to my problem. Can you come out here or what?"

"Well, babe, I'd love to come out there, but I'm pretty sure that I'm being looked for by some psychotic people, and I just got to Andrew's where—"

"Andrew? You're with my brother? How is he? I lost track of him. How did you find him? Where are you guys?"

"We're in Colorado, but I'm afraid we have our hands full here. Can't you come out here? What are you involved in?"

"Not a chance," Rachel whispered. "I'm working for Justin Wright, the minister of societal change. His daughter was set up to be my watcher, although she's not too good at her job. Anyway, tonight she got totally wasted and was about to tell me about some kind of plan, and then he showed up and whisked her away. I made a mistake, Jason. I used an alias like you taught me, but he asked me about it tonight, and I slipped. I don't know exactly why, but I told him my given name was Stone."

"Wait a minute. What are you doing working for the Global Society Administration? What on earth would they need you for? And how could you have been so careless to let your name slip?"

"Well, Jason, I am a social anthropologist. I study society and culture for a living. Why wouldn't I be an asset in planning the future of society? Look, I can't keep talking on the phone. Even though it's disposable, I don't know who could be listening. *Please*, can't you come out here? I need you." Rachel was almost in tears.

His heart breaking, Jason Fox answered, "Okay. I'll try and get there. Give me your real number, and I'll text you with my flight info."

"Thanks, Jason. We can meet at the airport. I love you."

After hanging up the phone, Fox turned to Stone and said, "It looks like the rest of my story is going to have to wait. Your sister has gotten herself into some trouble and needs me to go out to LA."

"If you think you're going to LA alone, you're out of your mind. I'm coming. You can finish your story on the plane."

"Are you crazy? You've got your own mess to take care of here. I won't be gone that long, and if you haven't forgotten, I could be wanted for murder. I wouldn't put it past Tempess to sick the cops on me."

"Wait a minute. Don't you think there would be bulletins out if they were looking for you? The Global News Network would've had your face all over it if they were looking for you. I think this Tempess guy probably has other plans for you. Obviously, someone is behind him. The dragon in your dream is a sign for you. This is personal to them. Let me help you and my sister. I just need to call my congregational leaders and tell them what's up. We can use my credit card to buy the tickets so you won't be traced." Grabbing Fox's arm, he finished, "You know I'm going."

"Fine, whatever, but I'm not going to be responsible for you. Do you have any money set aside?"

"Of course I do. I came up with the rules of engagement, remember?"

"Yeah, right. Let's get ready and go. It should take about an hour and a half to get to LA from Denver. Let's book a flight and get going."

Andrew Stone booked the first flight from Denver to LA and called Miriam Matiska to get everyone together within the hour to have a meeting.

"But it's the middle of the night," complained Miriam.

"I know it's late," Stone said, "but it's important. Do you think you can get them together and over here?"

"Sure. We'll be over there within the hour. Bye." Miriam hung up the phone.

Forty-five minutes later, Miriam, Scott, Kevin, and Bob joined Stone and Fox in the living room. After introductions were made, Stone informed everyone of Jason's meeting with Donald Stewart and told them that they had to fly out to LA to help his sister, Jason's wife.

Miriam was the first to speak. "Can you tell us what you talked with Pastor Stewart about?"

Fox replied, "I'll be happy to share everything he said with all of you when we get back, but there isn't enough time to do it now. Just know that he had to leave. Your church, your old church, is going to be key to the future of the global community. I think Andrew here has some stuff to share as well, something that will be able to shed light on some of what's going on."

Everyone turned to look at their pastor. As he looked guiltily at the floor, he said, "Jason's right. I have a confession to make to all of you, but it needs to wait until we get back. Why don't we pray, and then you guys can get back to bed and Jason and I can get to the airport."

The small group prayed for each other, Fox and Stone's trip, and the upcoming confrontation that they all feared. As Stone saw everyone to the door, Miriam turned to face him and, blushing, said, "Andrew, please be careful. I'd hate it if anything happened to you. I've become quite…fond of you." Before he could answer, she kissed him lightly on the lips. She turned, hurrying out into the early morning darkness.

*   *   *

Justin Wright had his daughter taken to her room and dumped on her bed. He often wondered why his Amanda had to embarrass him so much. Didn't she realize that he was in a position of power and the way his family behaved was a reflection on him? Then there was her friend Rachel. While recognizing her talent in the field of societal development, there was always something unnerving about her. Discovering her real name this evening might just be the key to finding out what she was hiding, if she was hiding anything.

She always did a good job, and her work was very impressive. Her plan for utilizing sustainable development outside of the cities was genius. Removing all malls, department stores, restaurants, and other freestanding businesses from open areas and moving all commercial business within walking distance of suburban and rural home developments would help the planet in substantial ways. People could work, shop, and live within a single communal unit.

Industrial business would be built outside of towns to minimize noise pollution on the community, and public transportation would be used to transport workers out to the factories. It would be wonderful for each area to be self-sustaining. No more need for trade agreements. True, many people would be hesitant to give up careers they'd worked years to develop, like when the cities were transformed, but when they were told it was for the good of society, they would relent.

Individual homes would become a thing of the past. Row-house apartments would replace single dwellings to fit more people in a manageable area. When demolition of outlying businesses and single-family homes began and the building of sustainable communities took control, jobs would be plentiful for all. Both men and women would work in the community while the children would be taken care of in community day cares and schools.

Everyone would watch the same news. Television and radio programs would be approved by the UGSA, regulating speech so that no unacceptable ideas could be inserted into society. Peace would be achieved when people gave up their free will and subjugated themselves to government leaders, those who knew and understood how things work. The average person just couldn't understand complicated issues. Rachel seemed to understand this. He just couldn't put his finger on why he distrusted her so much. Maybe it was because she asked so many questions. Well, today his questions about her would be answered.

After getting a few hours of sleep, Justin awoke at five thirty. He went for a jog, had a shower, ate breakfast, and read his daily reports. At eight thirty, he placed a call to the New Life Foundation.

"Hello, how may I help you?" Michael Damious's secretary, Tania, asked.

"This is Justin Wright. Is Michael available?"

"One moment, Mr. Wright." Hitting the intercom button to Damious's office, she told him Justin was on the phone.

"Thank you, Tania. Put the call through please."

Tania pressed the button to connect the two calls and hung up her phone.

"Well, Justin, what is it?"

"I'd like you to run a background check on my associate Rachel Vecler," Wright said matter-of-factly. He was one of the few people not intimidated by Michael Damious.

"Why? We ran a background check on all of the recruits. She turned up clean. Do you have some new information for us?"

"Yes. Yes, I do. In the course of a conversation we were having yesterday, I found out that her last name is not Vecler but Stone. I'd like you to check into it. Seems strange to me that her alias was not in the initial report."

"Stone? Did you say Stone? Interesting. We have an Andrew Stone giving us problems in Colorado. I wonder if there is a connection."

"Wondering? Wondering? Are you telling me that I may have a spy in my organization? A spy that's been planning the next phase of the mission? How could this have happened? You had better hope this is just a coincidence, Michael, because heads will roll if we have a problem with this."

"Just who do you think you're talking to, Justin? Don't think you can intimidate me. I can squash you like a bug, destroy your whole little dynasty. If you think the plan can't go ahead because of some silly little girl, you are sadly mistaken. Besides, I thought you were supposed to be watching the outsiders. It seems to me that you're the one with the problem. She's been working for you for how long? Two years?"

"Just check it out, Michael. I'm sure everything is fine. I'm just being cautious, is all. We don't need any delays." Changing the subject, Wright challenged, "When you say there is a problem in Colorado, it has nothing to do with the prototype does it?"

"That's none of your concern right now, is it? Just keep an eye on the girl, and I'll get back to you. Good-bye."

Pushing his intercom, Damious asked Tania to get William Tempess in his office at one o'clock this afternoon.

Justin Wright knew that he had pushed Damious's buttons and felt good about it. His interest in the UGSE was genuine, at least genuine in the fact that he wanted control over a large group of people. He really did believe that average people were too dumb to be able to take care of themselves without guidance from a more educated group of people. He believed he was one of those people. Getting up from his desk, he retired to the oversized couch in his den and lay down to contact his spiritual guide. Unlike Damious, he did not know he was working with demons. Like Isabelle, his spirit guide used a disguise. As he fell into the spirit realm, he found himself in a medieval castle seated in a king's throne. As he sat there admiring the tapestries hung on the walls, murals of faraway lands, dragons, and knights arrayed for battle, a beautiful woman dressed in royal medieval robes walked toward him. As she curtsied low to him, her long braided golden hair fell over her shoulder. Keeping her sapphire blue eyes turned to the floor, she spoke, "My lord, how good it is to see you."

"Arise, Jezeel, and come. Sit next to your king. I require your council," said Justin arrogantly.

Jezeel obeyed and sat meekly at the king's side. Underneath the facade, the demon Jezeel seethed. It hated using this pretense. It was so beneath a demon lord to belittle itself by pretending to be a human woman, let alone one who must cater to this fool. Regardless, it used its best English accent to answer. "How may I serve you, my lord?"

"I need to know if you've spoken with Angelous lately."

At the mention of Angelous's name, Jezeel visibly flinched and answered, "No, my lord. He has been much involved with his charges of late. May I ask why you inquire of him?"

"I spoke with one of his charges today, a Michael Damious, and he seemed distracted. He mentioned possible trouble in Colorado, a major piece of the initial plan. It concerned me, and since any possible failures on anyone's part can mean…unpleasant things, I just wanted to see if there was anything I could do."

The absolute arrogance of this human made Jezeel want to rip out his heart and feed it to him. *Why do humans take such little notice of the importance of names? Angelous should not be spoken of so casually, certainly not by a human.* Not that Jezeel had any love for Angelous, but demons knew their place in things, and while they were both demon lords, Angelous had seniority and therefore deserved respect. Trying to control its anger, Jezeel answered, "If you would like, my lord, I can see what I can find. Would that be acceptable?"

"Of course, my dear. Now come and serve your king as you should."

"Yes, my lord."

The two of them went to the king's chambers. If only Justin knew what his illusion really looked like. It was something Jezeel was going to relish—the time when it could reveal its true self.

While Justin lay seemingly asleep, Amanda entered the study to wake him. "Father, wake up," she spoke as she gently shook him.

He floated back to his body and slowly opened his eyes to his daughter's voice. She was a lovely girl. She wore her blonde hair long and had it pulled back in a loose ponytail this morning. Her blue eyes were rimmed in red from the night of drinking she had pursued. "Father, I am sooo sorry for my behavior last night," she cried as she fell to the floor and held his hand in hers. Keeping her eyes focused on the floor, she continued, "Please forgive me. I was just so tired of everything. I needed an escape. I just wanted to forget."

He gently reached down and lifted her face up so their eyes met. "My darling daughter, what am I to do with you?" Looking into his eyes, she saw only malice, and as she averted her gaze, her father's hand met her cheek with such force that she was knocked backward to the floor. While she scooted back against the wall, he stood, walked toward her, and laughed. "You are so pathetic, you know that? What are you so tired of? Having all the best things? Having everything given to you? Just what is it you want to forget, daughter? How much I've done for you? The place of honor you'll have—may have in the future?" Reverting back to his public persona of control and benevolence, he gave his hand to Amanda, and she took it. He helped her up and gently touched her now-red, soon-to-be-bruised cheek. He gave her a gentle kiss and sent her to the kitchen to put ice on it. With tears streaming down her face, Amanda got the ice and returned to her room. She knew she had to get out of the house but also knew her father would never allow it. Wondering what to do, she thought of Rachel and hoped she was okay. Would her father ever hurt someone else? She didn't know. What she did know was she had to go, so she picked up her phone and dialed Rachel's number hoping she would pick up and be able to help her.

* * *

At New Life, things were moving at a very quick pace. Spiritual activity was spiking, and Isabelle was very pleased at the new recruits' ability to meet their spirit guides. Since Fox and Tempess had released hundreds of demon lords, New Life Foundation's impact on the new global government had increased tenfold. Michael Damious was talking with the leaders of the UGSE almost on a daily basis. His power base strengthened with every mind a demon possessed. Between phone calls and his daily responsibilities at the foundation, he found himself stretched to his limits, but he wouldn't have it any other way. His plans of world domination were coming to fruition, and he was enjoying every minute of it.

"William Tempess is here to see you, Mr. Damious," reported Tania.

"Thank you, Tania. Show him in."

After his last meeting with Michael Damious, William Tempess tried to be confident, but as he spoke, he just came across like a sniveling worm, "Hello, Michael, what can I do for you?"

"Where do I begin?" Damious asked, leaning back in his chair, his hands laced behind his head. "Where are you on finding Fox?"

"Well, I'm having trouble on that end. It's like he dropped off the face of the earth. Obviously he's in hiding, but we can't ascertain where."

"That's very disappointing, William. I would have thought that with all the resources available to you, you might be able to find one insignificant man."

"Insignificant is not a word I would use to describe Jason Fox," said Tempess as he cringed, waiting to be struck. "He's proven to be a very difficult adversary. I can't even believe he made it out of the desert the way he got heat sickness every five minutes, but as it is, he's eluded us. I don't know what else to say, so if you're going to kill me, do it quickly!"

Damious was surprised at William Tempess's bold attitude. He laughed out loud and said, "Well, William, you never do cease to amaze me. You come in here as a failure and have the guts to assault me verbally. What am I to do with you?" As Tempess stood a little taller, preparing to take his punishment, Damious surprised him by saying, "I have a new assignment for you."

"What! I mean, what's the assignment?"

"I need you to follow a man named Andrew Stone. I need you to trace his movements, both now and in the past. I want to know what he's been doing for the past five years. Also, I need you to look into the past of a woman who works for the UGSA. She goes by the name Rachel Vecler, but her given last name is Stone. Check back into her past and find out exactly who Rachel Vecler-Stone is. Tania has the file on both of them. You can pick it up on your way out, and find Fox. I don't want any more excuses. He's somewhere, and I need to know where."

"Of course, Michael. Should I be looking for a link between Andrew and Rachel Stone?"

Exasperated with such an obvious question, Damious backhanded Tempess and hissed, "Do I need to answer such a stupid question? Now get out of my office before I do something you might regret."

Getting his bearings, Tempess spun around and bolted for the door. After getting himself together, he asked Tania for the file on the Stones and walked to his car. At times like this, he regretted ever getting involved with Damious and the foundation. Thinking back to his first meeting with Michael Damious, he wondered why he wanted so badly to be a part of the organization. Tempess had no delusions of world peace or making the planet better. He knew from the very beginning that Michael Damious had big plans and that benevolence was not part of it.

Tempess had been raised in a good Christian home. His parents went to church every Sunday and made sure he and his sister went to church, Bible studies, Vacation Bible School, and youth group. Their whole life revolved around the church. He thought church was cool, except everyone involved in it were hypocrites. It had been his dream to be a missionary and help people, but after seeing the backbiting, lying, scheming, and all-around hypocrisy of the congregation, he decided the whole concept of a good, loving God was nothing more than mythology, stories told to make people feel good about themselves. He'd met a few people who he believed really had faith, but he thought most were just weak-minded people who needed to belong to a group, just like everyone else in the world. Why were faithful Muslims, Buddhists, New Agers, or atheists any different? They were all just groups of people who wanted to be together. Good for them. But he wanted more.

He wanted power and prestige, so he decided to become involved in the world of political intrigue, a world that didn't hold to togetherness or friendship. It was a dog-eat-dog world. Sadly, by the time he realized he'd hitched his wagon to the wrong star, it was too late. He was in too deep and he knew too much to ever switch careers, so he accepted his role as whipping boy to Michael Damious. He went about his business, but sometimes he found himself trying to get back to the place he was as a young man, a place where the world could be good, where people wanted to be good and God was all-knowing and loving. *Yeah right, William. Get over it. You're the only person you can depend on.* With that thought, he put his car in gear and drove to his office to begin his search for Andrew Stone and finish his search for Jason Fox.

* * *

"Hey! Ms. Isabelle, wait up!" called Jerry Holmes, an enthusiastic twenty-one-year-old recruit sporting a mop of curly brown hair and friendly bright golden eyes.

"Oh, hi, Jerome! How are you? We missed you at meditation this morning. Were you skiving?" she asked with a wink.

"No way, Ms. Zenn." He called her that when they were joking. "I wasn't feeling well this morning and had to go to sick call." Noticing the look of concern on her face, he quickly added, "I'm okay, it was just a headache." Lowering his voice while looking around, his tone got serious, and he whispered, "I need to talk with you in private. Would that be okay?"

Lowering her voice, she replied, "Sure, but why are we whispering?"

Returning to a normal vocal level, he said, "Sorry, it's just that I had a dream last night, and it scared me. I need to talk to someone about it, and you were the first one to come to mind."

"A dream, huh? That's not really my area of specialty. Are you sure you wouldn't like to talk to Henry? He's a great dream therapist, you know."

"No, I really don't need the dream interpreted. I think I understand it perfectly. That's what scares me. It's about my spirit guide, Lucius. And before you tell me to go to him, I can't! I just can't!"

"Okay, calm down. Of course I'll talk with you. Would you like to meet in the East Meditation Garden after dinner?"

"Could we meet in your garden? I just want it to be private. No one else can know."

"Well, I suppose so, but this is very unusual. I'll see you around six thirty, okay?"

"Sure, six thirty. Later!" Jerry hurried away, and Isabelle looked after him and wondered what that was all about.

Continuing on her way, she entered her room, closed the door, and pulled out her laptop. Her searches for Andrew Stone had turned up nothing. She had no idea how many people were named Andrew Stone or some derivative of it. She had come to the conclusion that she needed to start when he left New Life and follow from there. Laying back on her bed, she remembered the last time they saw each other.

Five years ago, just before the war started, Andrew Stone rushed into Isabelle's room in a panic. "Izzy! Izzy!"

"What! What is it?" Isabelle called, rushing out of the bathroom.

Grabbing her and pulling her close, he gasped, "I just found out that my work, my research, has all been a big scam. The environmental disaster was faked. People from New Life and its subsidiaries actually planned it to get people to let the government regulate farms, industry—everything—so they could get control. How could they do that!"

Pushing him away, she took a deep breath and said, "What are you talking about? No one at New Life causes harm. We are all about making the world better, about peace and love. How dare you accuse New Life—me of something like this? What proof do you have?"

"Make the world better! At what cost? This place is willing to kill hundreds of creatures, plants, and people just to get their idea of utopia! Are you okay with that? Proof? You want proof? Here's your proof." He threw down a file filled with correspondence, charts, computer models, statistics, an outline for a global takeover of governments, and a plan—a plan he'd created to fix it, to bring life back.

With her hands shaking, she picked up the folder and leafed through it. With tears in her eyes, she cried, "I didn't know, Andrew, I swear! But it's done. Don't you think things are on a road to being better? Isn't the sustained development plan happening the way we always wanted? I know the cost was dear, but shouldn't we look toward the future now? Please, Andrew, what are you planning?"

Tears of anger flowed down Andrew Stone's face. "I can't believe you're saying this. How can you possibly be all right with this? I don't even know you." Pulling her close again and gazing into her eyes, he said, "I intend to bring this place down. I intend to tell the truth. Isabelle, I love you. I love you more than anyone or anything." Bringing his lips to hers, he kissed her passionately. Letting their lips linger, not wanting to let it end, he slowly pulled back and said, "I'm leaving. I want you to come with me, but I will leave without you."

Taking the folder from her hands, he turned and walked out the door, leaving Isabelle in tears, broken and confused.

As usual, when Isabelle had a problem, she called upon Adder. Not wanting to take the time of going to a meditation garden, Isabelle lay on her bed, closed her eyes, and let her consciousness float away to Adder's place. Adder was lying in a meadow surrounded by wildflowers of every color. Just coming here had a calming effect on her.

"Well, hello, my child," cooed Adder. "What brings you to me today?"

Isabelle strolled over to where Adder lay and responded, "I have a problem."

Curious, Adder rolled over onto its elbow and looked up at her. "Sit down, my dear, and tell me. What problem could you possibly have?"

Obeying and sitting among the flowers, Isabelle took a calming breath and told Adder everything that Andrew had accused New Life of being involved with.

Considering its words carefully, Adder responded, "Well, Isabelle. What do you think? And I want you to search your heart." While saying this, Adder adjusted its claws ever so slightly in her brain to bend her to its will.

"Well, now that I think of it, I just can't believe it," replied Isabelle, feeling a twinge in her head.

"Even with the evidence he produced? How can you explain that?"

"Well, I bet someone planted the evidence to confuse Andrew and pull him away, but who?"

Trying to keep her on track, Adder pushed her thoughts back to his agenda. "Now don't worry about who might have done this. Concentrate on Andrew and what you believe."

"You're right, Adder. I have to get back to Andrew and tell him." Smiling, she got up and said, "Thank you so much, Adder. You are so wise, and I am so blessed to have you!" Returning to her bed with a slight headache, she got up and hurried to talk with Andrew.

Rushing through the foundation, Isabelle finally came to his door and knocked.

"Come in," Stone called through the door.

When Isabelle entered, he assumed she had decided to come with him and pulled her into a loving embrace and kissed her. She returned his kiss with more passion than she could remember. As they stood there holding each other, he closed the door behind her and lowered her to his bed. Not remembering a time when he wanted her more, he let his hands move to her hair and pushed it back from her face. As he looked into her eyes, he noticed a distance in her stare, even though her eyes were lingering on his. Without thinking, he pulled himself back and asked her, "What's the matter?"

Still in the euphoria of the feeling of his love, she answered, "Nothing really. I just came to tell you that you don't have to go. The file you found is obviously a fake, something left for you to find to confuse you." When she tried to kiss him again, he fully pulled away and sat up next to her.

"What are you talking about? I thought you came here to leave with me. How can you doubt me?"

Surprised and hurt, she caressed his cheek and said, "I talked with Adder and—"

"What!" he almost yelled, jumping to his feet. "You went to your little spirit friend? You actually believe him over me? Are you freaking serious?"

Sitting up, she replied, "Of course I did! He's like my father. Do you really think I would leave my home, my life without consulting him?"

"Your life? I thought I was your life. Isabelle, one of the things I love most about you is your innocence, but I don't see how you can be so blind about this. You have been lied to. Damious is using your foundation to destroy society. Even if it is rebuilt in a way we think would be good, who are we to decide? You have to choose what you want. It's me or this place. I'm leaving in an hour. If you're not here, this is good-bye. Can you live with that?"

Standing up, she asked, "How can you expect me to make a decision like this in an hour? If you love me, you will stay."

Lifting her gaze to his, Stone kissed her for the last time and said, "I can't live with myself knowing I was a part of such unforgivable destruction. I can't. I will always love you, but one person is not more important than the whole world." Not giving her a chance to answer, he gently pushed her out the door and closed it.

With her heart broken, Isabelle slowly turned and walked back to her room with the folder she had stolen from Stone's bed safely tucked under her shirt.

* * *

One of the few positive things to come from the global restructuring was the fact that since the government banned weapons after the war and confiscated as many as they could find, airport security had become a breeze. Where Jason Fox may have been placed on a no-fly list before the war, he now had no problems getting through security and onto a plane with his

9mm safely tucked in his carry-on bag. Once safely on the plane, Fox leaned over and whispered to Stone, "I still have trouble getting used to not being basically strip-searched before getting on a plane. If there is one thing that will bring down the UGSE, it will be their overconfidence."

"Yeah," whispered back Stone while placing the backpack hiding his Walther PPK under the seat. "Unless some idiot such as yourself talks too much and gets them suspicious."

Feigning hurt, Fox winked and said, "You're right, someday my mouth is going to get me in more trouble than I can deal with. Pride goeth before a fall, right?"

"Right, so shut up and try to look like every other average Joe."

"Joe? Joe? Who's Joe? I thought I was Jason. Shouldn't I look like every other average Jason?"

Stone rolled his eyes. "Whatever, smart aleck."

Enjoying the game, Fox continued, "Alec? Alec? Who's—"

Not allowing him to finish, Stone smacked him upside the head with the in-flight magazine, and the two shared a laugh while getting comfortable and buckling their seat belts.

The flight from Denver to LA was relatively smooth and took only the allotted hour and a half. After disembarking, the two friends scanned the airport for Rachel but were surprised when an auburn-haired girl with brown eyes came up behind them, placed her arms around their shoulders, and said, "Hey guys! What's up?"

Expecting to see Rachel with her normal strawberry-blonde locks and peridot-colored eyes, the two men pulled quickly away. Getting his bearings together first, Andrew, seeing through the disguise, pulled his sister in and gave her a big hug. "Hey yourself, little sis. What's with the new look?"

"Don't ya just love it?" Rachel spun around. "It's all the fashion in espionage these days, you know."

Finally understanding the situation, Jason Fox clumsily said with a tinge of sarcasm, "Espionage? I thought you were saving the world."

Feeling the hurt in his voice, she leaned over and kissed him gently on the lips. "Good to see you too, Jay." Remembering the situation, Rachel nervously scanned the area and said, "Come on. We need to get somewhere more private. Follow me."

Still stunned at her clandestine behavior, both men followed without question. After exiting the terminal, they walked to the temporary parking lot and found her car. Not being able to resist, Fox teased, "So, you're driving green these days huh?"

"Still the little boy, Jay?" she teased back, pleased for the change in his demeanor. "Don't you know that all members of the UGSE drive environmentally friendly cars? We are, after all, the example for the rest of you."

Stone interjected tersely, "Can we get away from the fiction of the UGSE please, and just tell us what is going on!"

Getting serious, Rachel started the car and pulled it out of the parking lot. "All right, boys here's the story. Jason, I really did leave to make the world a better place. At first, I really did believe we could build a perfect society."

Both men cleared their throats in unison, with the word *bullcrap* encased in one of the coughs.

"Very nice, guys. Come on and give me a chance to finish. Like I told you, I've been working for the Global Society Administration since I left you." Fox cringed, and immediately she felt guilty. "With my scientific credentials, I had no problem getting a job with the UGSE, and after the retreat, you know where, I was placed at the UGSA. My roommate from New Life, Amanda, was named my global sister—so stupid—and basically became my watcher. Lucky for me, she's a space cadet. Don't get me wrong, I love her to death, but honestly, when common sense was passed out, she was obviously absent. It's a wonder she's won so many awards for journalism, probably her father's doing.

"Anyway, after working on the plan for sustainable societal development for about a year, I began to wonder why I thought I had any right to tell other people how to live. Granted, it made the most sense to live, work, and shop in a cohesive area, but what if someone wanted to live somewhere else? Why shouldn't they be able to?" Taking a moment to clear her throat, she continued. "I started asking questions around the office. Nothing major, you know, just what other people thought, but I guess it was the wrong thing to do because I was called into Mr. Wright's office for a talk. He was polite, but I always felt an underlying darkness around him. He asked me about my concerns and tried to answer them. Basically, he spouted all the right words, all the phrases that I had used a hundred times. You know, like, regular people just don't understand the issues, regular people needed guidance, we should use our knowledge for the good of everyone, blah-dee-blah-blah. But I just wasn't buying it now. I couldn't get past this fierce independence I felt.

"I kept thinking about Jason and me starting a family. We would have the option of living out of town because of my position, but what about our children when they grew up? According to my model, the government would decide where they would work and what they would do. They wouldn't have the choice we had. Also, under my plan, we wouldn't have any control over our children's lives. Basically, the government-run schools would teach our kids everything." Getting angry now, she proceeded, "And have you seen the new history texts? They're atrocious! It's like something out of the book *1984*, which, by the way, has been banned, rounded up, and burned. The UGSE has rewritten everything."

Interrupting, Fox said, "You and me? Children? You thought about that? I thought you didn't want anything to do with me. Why didn't you ever get in touch with me?"

"Well, at first, Jason, you were so angry with me for wanting to do this that I didn't think you would do anything but belittle me if I called, and as time went on, I began to wonder if you would want me back. I mean, I didn't know what you were up to."

Not being able to contain his hurt and anger, he raised his voice, "You didn't know what I was up to because you didn't get in touch with me. You want to know what I was up to? Let me tell you. I got involved with Techne-Corp, now a partner of the New Life Foundation, went to the desert, dug up some kind of demon cave—yeah, I know how crazy that sounds—and ended up shooting my best friend, so forgive me if I don't get all sympathetic for your plight!" Breathing heavy and trying to keep tears from coming, Fox turned his face to the window. Stone sat quietly in the back while Rachel veered off the road and turned off the car.

Grabbing Fox's arm, she pulled him to face her and said, "What do you mean shot your best friend? Rich? You shot Richard? How...why...what? I-I...just don't know what to say." Taking hold of her in a desperate embrace, they held each other in silence, weeping for the time lost and the loss of their friend.

Once they composed themselves and returned to driving, they sat in silence until Rachel pulled off the exit ramp and stopped at an out-of-the-way diner. Everyone got out of the car, entered the diner, and sat at a booth. After ordering drinks, they sat in silence looking at the menu. When the waitress came back with their drinks, Andrew and Jason ordered cheeseburgers and fries while Rachel ordered a chicken salad sandwich with sweet potato fries and a side salad. Rachel excused herself and went to the bathroom while Stone and Fox stayed at the table talking quietly.

"Well, this is a fun outing, isn't it?" said Stone sarcastically. "I've had more fun at a funeral."

"Well, what did you expect? Balloons and a band? Party steamers and a cake? Rachel's in trouble, I'm in trouble, you're in trouble, heck, the whole stupid world is in trouble, and what are we going to do about it? Nothing, just sit back and talk."

"I'm not talking about our situation. I'm talking about you and Rachel. Look, I know the separation has been difficult for both of you, but she's in serious trouble, and you have to get past your hurt feelings so that we can move on. You need to forgive her, or we're never going to be able to help."

"When did you get so grown-up?" Fox then acquiesced. "You're right, brother. I'm being selfish. There's plenty of time for the two of us to work out our problems. I'll apologize when she gets back."

"Speak of the devil." Andrew smiled.

Amused, Rachel asked, "What? What'd I do?" She sat next to Fox.

"Nothing," answered Fox. "I need to apologize for my outburst in the car. I'm trying to deal with the situation, and it's not fair to blame you. I promise to hold my tongue until this whole thing is over, okay?"

Leaning over and kissing him on the cheek, Rachel replied, "It's okay, Jay. I know I hurt you, and I can't say I'm sorry enough, but all we can do now is move forward."

All three of them engaged in small talk until their food arrived. Once they started eating, Rachel continued her story.

"After Wright dismissed me from his office with the promise that I would stop asking questions because I understood the importance of our mission, I returned to my office and made myself look busy until it was time to leave. Not surprisingly, Amanda called to see if we could go out clubbing, so I said yes and left to go home. As I expected, she quizzed me about my conversation with her father. I assured her that I had towed the line and was back on track—it never took much to convince her of anything when she wanted to go out—so she accepted my story, which she passed on to her father, and I wasn't bothered by them again." Taking a bite of her sandwich and a couple of fries, she kept going.

"Starting the next day, I sought out the resistance. I knew that they still existed, but wasn't sure where to begin. After a few weeks of searching, I got in touch with our old friend Marcus Daedalus—"

"Daedalus?" Fox asked while he and Stone stared stunned at Rachel. "I thought he was dead. How did you find him?"

"Yes, Daedalus. Now let me finish. I found him through Internet chat rooms. He used various aliases, but always something to do with his favorite Greek myth, so I pressed my luck and sent an e-mail to a man called Perdix—you know, Daedalus's nephew in the story. He remembered me and set up a meeting. Of course, he asked about you two, but I just said we had lost touch. I joined the resistance that day and have been working to give them information ever since." Pausing, she interjected excitedly, "Did you know the resistance is still in every country in the world? We have spies in every agency that is part of the UGSE. Undermining their plans is our top priority."

"Yes," said Stone, "I know the resistance. I've been working with them for four years, ever since my conversion."

Gobsmacked, Fox and Rachel just stared at him. Getting over the shock, Fox said, "There's something I didn't know. Since when do priests belong to the resistance movement?"

"Since forever, I guess. All armies need men of God to be available for confession, absolution, counseling, and communion—any and every duty that we do—so there it is."

"Does your congregation know?" Fox questioned.

"No, of course not. The resistance is completely underground. You could have two people in the same room together, and neither of them would know who the other was, like me and Rachel," responded Stone, still stunned by his sister's revelation.

After finishing their meal, they all ordered coffee and pie. Rachel concluded her story, which brought them to this moment. "After I realized what I had done, revealing my name, I knew I couldn't go back, but I need to get my research, and that will take some doing."

While the three of them sat there discussing possible scenarios, Rachel's UGSE phone rang. Amanda Wright was calling for help.

* * *

William Tempess's office was across town from the New Life Foundation, which suited him just fine. The farther away from Michael Damious he could be, the better. He'd have his office on the other side of the country if it was possible. Sitting behind his desk, he turned on his computer, typed in his password to the secret foundation files, and began his search for the Stones. His initial search showed Andrew Stone's life at the foundation up until he left and then nothing until he showed up in Colorado as the pastor of a church. He saw the name Burke Smith and a contact number and wrote them down.

Rachel Stone was another matter entirely. He found loads of information on her. In her file were her college transcripts, fieldwork on ancient societies, numerous papers on societal engineering, her name change to Vecler, and a fascinating fact that would put him back in the good graces of Michael Damious: she was married to Jason Fox.

Before reporting his major find, Tempess decided to call Burke Smith to find out any new pieces of information on Andrew Stone. Using his office phone as opposed to his cell, he dialed the number and waited for an answer. Getting the answering machine, he left a message for Burke to call him and decided that the news about Fox and Rachel Stone couldn't wait. Wanting to drop the bombshell in person, he jumped into his car and drove back across town to New Life.

While William Tempess was busy looking up information on the Stones, Burke Smith rang up Michael Damious and reported that Andrew Stone had left town and flown to LA with a man named Jason Fox.

"What action would you like me to take, Michael? Should I stay in town and watch the congregation or fly out to LA and try to locate Stone?"

"And how exactly do you plan to find them, Mr. Smith? Do you have some kind of radar that finds missing people? Do you have any concept of how large Los Angeles is? No, Burke. Stay in your miserable little town and get ready for the next phase of our plan."

"Yes, sir. I'll get right on it."

Hanging up his phone, Damious wondered why he surrounded himself with such useless idiots. "Tania!" he called into his intercom.

"Yes, Mr. Damious. What can I do for you?"

"I need you to get Isabelle on the phone for me. I'm not sure where she is right now, but I need to talk with her as soon as possible."

"I'll get right to it, sir."

Picking up his phone, Damious hit the speed dial for William Tempess. He got Tempess's voice mail and left a message for him to call back immediately. Leaning back in his chair, Damious let his mind take him to Angelous.

In the smoky darkness of Angelous's lair, Michael Damious breathed in the acrid air and reveled in the cries of agony. Sensing the human presence, Angelous soared toward Damious and stopped inches from his face. "What is it now, Michael?" spewed the demon impatiently.

"We're almost ready for the next phase of the plan. I wanted to let you know that the demon lords seem to be handling their charges well. Trycon's replacement has both Burke Smith and William Tempess well in hand," replied Damious a little more arrogantly than Angelous cared for.

Bored with Michael Damious, Angelous hissed, "Is there anything else, Michael?"

"No, I just like coming down here to soak in the atmosphere."

Grabbing Damious by the throat and lifting him off the ground, Angelous rebuked him, "Watch yourself, Michael! This is my province. I am a prince of demons, and as such I demand respect. How do you think my minions will react if I allow a human to treat me with such familiarity? You will only come here when summoned or when there is a serious incident. I grow tired of your arrogance! Leave here now!" Throwing Damious backward Angelous let out a gruesome scream and shot back up into the darkness.

Gasping for air and clawing at his bruised throat, Damious fell forward, hitting his head on his desk. While trying to get his breathing under control, Tania informed him that William Tempess was waiting. Furious that Tempess would show up without calling, Damious croaked, "Tell him to come back in a half an hour."

"Yes, sir. Are you all right, Mr. Damious?"

"I'm fine, Tania. I'm just busy at the moment."

"I'm sorry to bother you, sir, but Mr. Tempess says it's very important. Something he found out about a Rachel Stone."

"I told him to wait. Whatever he has to say can wait for a half an hour. Don't bother me again!"

Walking over to his office fridge, he bundled some ice in a towel and held it to his throat, while he pour himself a glass of water. While sipping the water, he thought back to his confrontation with Angelous. *How dare he treat me like that. Next time, I'd like to rip off his wings, cut his throat, and turn him into a red vapor spot!* Managing a weak smile at the thought, Damious returned to his desk and sat down. Leaning back in his chair, he closed his eyes and tried to come up with a plausible explanation for his throat. Not coming up with a suitable explanation, he decided to go with a turtleneck sweater to cover the marks. As he pulled the shirt over his head, Tania beeped again. This time, Isabelle was on the phone.

Damious picked up the receiver, "Hello, Isabelle. Thanks for getting back to me so quickly."

"No problem, Michael. What can I help you with?"

With a slight crack in his voice, he asked, "I have a question for you on a sensitive subject. I'm sure you haven't forgotten Mr. Andrew Stone."

Sitting in her garden, Isabelle tried to hide her excitement. Catching her breath, she answered, "No, of course you know I haven't. I loved him. I've spent the last five years trying to forget him, but if you need something, I will do my best to answer your question."

"It has come to our attention that he might have a sister named Rachel who works for us in Los Angeles. Since we have no information about his family, I was wondering if he ever mentioned a sister to you."

Knowing that her words could have dire consequences, Isabelle took a moment to think about her answer. Knowing Damious, if she told the truth, a young woman might be in trouble, but if she didn't, she might never find Andrew. Deciding she would deal with whatever Damious had in mind for the girl, she answered truthfully, "Yes, Michael. He did. He told me that his sister wanted to marry a friend of his who he didn't feel was worthy of her. Instead of watching her make a huge mistake, he chose to leave them and come here. That's all I know. He never told me her name. Why do you need to know about this girl? Has she done something?"

"It's not your concern, Belle. You worry about things at the foundation and leave everything else to me."

Furious that he called her Belle but determined not to let him know, she replied coolly, "Fine. Is that all, or is there something else I can help you with?"

"No. That's all, Belle. Perhaps we can do dinner again soon."

"I don't know, Michael. I have an awful lot on my plate these days. Maybe some time, but not now. I have to go. Bye."

Setting the receiver back into the phone base, Damious felt concerned by Isabelle's unusual abruptness. However, he did not have time to ponder over questions regarding his love life. Taking another sip of water, he allowed his thoughts to turn back to Tempess. "Tania, please show Mr. Tempess in."

Seeing the unusually large grin on William Tempess's face when he walked through the door, Damious knew his luck was changing. "So, William, what do you have for me?"

Giddy with excitement, Tempess sat down in the chair opposite Damious and said, "I didn't find anything new on Andrew Stone, but I did find out that Rachel Vecler-Stone is married to our good friend Jason Fox!"

Sitting up straight in his chair and folding his hands under his chin, Michael Damious did something very rare: He smiled, genuinely happy. "This is good news, Mr. Tempess, very good news."

"What are we going to do with it, sir?"

"We're going to LA, my annoying little friend. We are going to LA."

* * *

Isabelle looked at the clock. It read twenty after six. Jerry's dream had piqued her curiosity. Walking out into her garden, her global Internet phone began ringing. Noticing the name on the caller ID, she thought about not answering, but he'd keep bothering her until she did, "Hello, Michael. What can I do for you?"

"I just wanted to let you know that I will be leaving for Los Angeles tonight, so I'll need you to keep things in order here." Damious sounded excited, which sent a shudder up her spine.

"Does this have anything to do with our conversation earlier?"

"As a matter of fact, it does, and I might just be bringing a surprise back for you, my dear."

"Well, that's very thought-provoking, Michael. I look forward to seeing what you bring me, I think."

"Good. I don't know how long I'll be away, but only a few days at the most." He hung up, and Isabelle sighed in relief.

A knock on the door introduced Jerry's presence. Isabelle walked across her room and opened the door, "Well, hello, Jerome! Right on time, I see. Come on in."

Entering nervously, Jerry was surprised to see that Isabelle's room was very similar to all the others on the campus. "Wow. I thought you might have a fancier room than everyone else, Ms. Isabelle."

Smiling, she replied, "Well, I feel that no one should be above anyone else, but I must confess having my own personal garden is a treat."

"A treat you definitely deserve."

"Now let's go outside and discuss your concerns. You have me a little worried, Jerome."

Walking out among the gorgeous blooms of late summer, Jerry's breath was taken away. "This is gorgeous, Ms. Isabelle! I think it might be the prettiest garden I've seen."

"Well, I've been cultivating it for many years." Sitting on a small bench, she motioned for him to sit next to her, and the conversation turned serious. "Now tell me about this dream you had."

Sitting down, he began, "Okay, but promise me you won't get mad." She assured him she wouldn't, so he continued. "It started a few weeks ago. At first, whenever I met with my spirit guide Lucius, I would get a feeling in my stomach. I don't know how to describe it. I guess it was kinda like butterflies—you know, like you get before going on stage?" Isabelle smiled and nodded. "Since last week I've had some weird experiences. It's like while I'm awake, there'll be this voice in my head saying, 'Someone's praying for you.' It like totally fills me with peace."

At this piece of news, Isabelle took special notice, although she kept her surprise to herself.

"Anyway, I keep hearing this old hymn my grandma used to sing, "Amazing Grace," do you know it?"

Isabelle nodded.

"And I don't know…" Lowering his voice, he whispered, "I started questioning the stuff we do here." He looked at her, hoping she wouldn't throw him out and was surprised to see understanding in her eyes and an almost haunted faraway look. "Ms. Isabelle, are you okay?"

"Y-y-yes, of course, it's just that I recently experienced a similar thing. Have you spoken to anyone else about this?"

"No. No one. What do you think it means?"

"I don't know, Jerome. Why don't you tell me about your dream?"

"Well, last night before bed, I got down on my knees at my bed and said a prayer, like my grandma used to show me. Please don't get mad. I know we're not supposed to, but you always teach us to follow our heart, and that's where my heart led me."

"I'm not angry, Jerome," she replied, a little jealous that she never felt led when she had tried to pray. "Just finish your story please."

"Well, after I fell asleep, this really cool spirit came to me, maybe an angel or something. Anyway, it took me to Lucius's workshop—you know, where I usually hang out with him?— but while we stood there, the whole place changed. It wasn't a workshop anymore but a dark smoky chamber with horrible screams. The smell was like one of those cemeteries after the war, where the bodies were rotting and the blood was everywhere, and then I saw Lucius flying around with a wicked flaming sword. I turned to look away, to run away, but the angel spirit wouldn't let me. It touched me, and I felt safe. Then it whispered in my ear to open my eyes, and when I did"—he had his hands over his face, breathing hard while shutting his eyes as tight as possible, and as Isabelle watched and listened in horror, he lowered his hands and opened his eyes—"I saw him or it...whatever it was. A dark creature with black leather-like wings and sharp curvy teeth and claws where his hands and feet should be. Then the angel spirit covered me with its wings, and I was back in my bed."

Shaking, with fear in his eyes, he looked over at Isabelle who was herself shaking, and he started crying. Isabelle enveloped him in her arms and hugged him, assuring him that he was okay. After a few moments, she held his face with her hands and looked into his eyes. "Jerome, I don't know how to council you on this matter. I feel conflicted and need some time to think. You will be all right. Even though we don't encourage prayer, if it gives you peace, please continue it. I need you to listen carefully to what I say. Don't tell anyone else about this dream, even Lucius, especially Lucius."

Glad for her understanding and words, he replied, "But what if he comes to me?"

"What do you mean, Jerome? Spirit guides are only supposed to come when you call them. Are you telling me that Lucius has actually contacted you?" she asked, surprised that any recruit could have such a connection with a spirit.

"Well, yeah. He started coming to me a few weeks ago, right before all this started. He said something about a big event and that we needed to get ready. Is that not normal?"

"It's not unheard of, Jerome. It's just not something that happens often. It's nothing to worry about. If he comes to you, just listen and do your best to get back quickly, okay?" she said with more confidence than she felt.

"Okay, but what if he looks like the angel spirit showed me. I don't think I can deal with that."

"Calm down. First, you don't know that what you saw wasn't just a dream. Maybe your mind is playing tricks on you. Second, you know there are many spirits. This angel spirit, as you call it, may be trying to trick you. I want you to go to one of the meditation gardens and just rest your mind. Take some time for yourself."

He hadn't actually thought about it that way. Maybe the angel spirit was the bad one, but he didn't think so. With no intention of meditating, he lied, "Okay, Ms. Isabelle, I will."

Before he walked out the door, Isabelle spoke one last time. "Jerome." He turned and listened. "Trust yourself and do what you think is best. I'll be here if you need me at anytime, day or night. Do you understand?"

Smiling, he replied, "Okay, Ms. Isabelle, I will." He turned, walked through the door, and closed it gently.

Thinking back to all the things she had been experiencing the last few weeks, Isabelle determined she was going to find out exactly what Damious and his partners and even Adder was hiding. With him gone for a few days, she intended to do just that.

Chapter 5

A free people claim their rights as derived from the laws of nature, and not as the gift of their chief magistrate.

—Thomas Jefferson

The Lord is far from the wicked, but He hears the prayer of the righteous.

—Proverbs 15:29

The congregation was being led in intercessory prayer for Pastor Stone, the Church, the country, and the world. Everyone felt the spiritual pull, the unseen battle that they all knew was going on around them. The urgency was palpable, and everyone was wondering how it would manifest in the real world.

Bob, Miriam, Scott, and Kevin decided to get together at Kevin's and try to figure out the strange meeting they had attended at Andrew Stone's house earlier that morning. Yvonne joined them with a carafe of coffee and a plate of cookies that she had baked earlier in the day.

Bob began, "Well, I didn't think anything could confuse me more than Burke and his gang, but last night takes the cake. I mean, who is this Jason Fox guy, and how did he find Pastor Stewart? Did anyone even know Andrew had a sister?"

Scott joined in, "What about this confession he needs to make? That Fox guy made it sound like Pastor Stone knows what's going on. I mean, how much do we really know about Andrew Stone? We've made a huge decision, and he might be behind it all."

"Oh, be quiet, Scott," interjected Miriam. "You're acting crazy. We all felt the changes happening before he even showed up. The changes made to the church were done by Pastor Stewart and Burke, not Andrew. Even if he has some background knowledge of this crazy stuff, it doesn't mean he's in anyway a part of it." She sat back, pouting.

"Miriam's right," Yvonne jumped in. "Pastor Stone has done nothing but lead us spiritually. I defy any of you to show me one thing he's done or said that isn't scriptural. All he did was take a stand against an evil man—I mean, group of men and women— and showed us what we already felt in our hearts."

Taking his wife's hand and squeezing it lovingly, Kevin agreed, "We need to stay strong, not fight against each other. After all, isn't that what the enemy wants?"

Scott and Bob both agreed and apologized for their disbelief. As the small group sat together enjoying the cookies and coffee, a knock came at the door.

"Who could that be?" Kevin asked as he walked to open the door.

"Hello, Kevin." Burke smiled as Kevin pulled back the door. "May I come in?"

Standing to the side, Kevin answered, "Sure, why not."

Scott started to stand up and said, "What do you want, Burke? Don't you know that you're not welcome here?"

"Sit down, Scott," said Bob. "Everyone is welcome here. What can we do for you, Burke?"

Taking the chair that Kevin had been sitting in, Burke got right to the point. "As you all know, I am chairman of the local town council, so I wanted to invite you to a special meeting set up for Wednesday night at seven o'clock. Our town has been chosen by the UGSE to be a part of the initial phase of their new global initiative. They are calling it Sustainable Societal Development. Since you are the leaders of a new business, I thought you'd like to come and listen. By the way, where is Stone? I stopped by his house first, but no one was home. I assumed he'd be here."

Miriam, furious at his arrogance, answered, "First, Mr. Smith, we are not a business. We are a church, and second, why is this the first anyone has heard about this initiative? Doesn't the council have to publish a public hearing two weeks in advance? This is a public hearing, isn't it? And as for Pastor Stone, he's gone to LA to see his sister, if it's any of your business."

"Ooohh, tsk, tsk, tsk, Ms. Matiska. I don't remember you being so rude before. No matter. I came by to tell you what I wanted, and now, if you all will excuse me, I will be off." Standing up, Burke prepared to leave.

Scott stood up and grabbed Burke by the arm, spinning him around to face him. "Wait a minute, Burke. What gives you the right to think you can just treat people like little pieces of lint?" Staring him directly in the eye, he demanded, "Answer Mir's question. Is this a public hearing or not?"

"Mr. Abrams, I came here in good faith to give you a heads-up. To answer Ms. Matiska's question, no. This is not a public hearing. It is a matter of fact. The world has changed, and we are under global rule now. The UGSE has decided that we will be a part of their initial phase, so we will. End of story. If you'd like to have a say in it, please show up. If not, deal with it. Good morning."

Leaving everyone in stunned silence, Burke showed himself out. Pleased with his little display of power, he called a friend of his at the Global Credit Headquarters and asked about Stone's recent credit card purchase. He found out that Stone had booked two tickets to Los Angeles.

After arriving back at the church and sitting behind his desk, he called the Denver airport, used his UGSE passcode, and found out that Mr. Stone had booked a seat for himself and someone named Jason Fox. A smile played across his face as he called Michael Damious.

* * *

On the foundation's private jet, William Tempess continued his research on Andrew Stone, while Michael Damious placed a call to Justin Wright.

"Hello, Michael. How's it going? What can I do for you?"

"Are you at the office or at home?"

"I'm at home. Is there a problem?"

"No. No, problem. I just wanted to let you know that I looked into that girl Rachel Vecler and found out that she has a very interesting background. Now I'm not sure whether or not she is a spy, but she has some very shady characters in her past. Were you aware that she is married?"

"Married? No, I wasn't aware. Is this man a spy?"

Laughing out loud, Damious continued, "Spy? Fox? No. He *is* dangerous, though, and I intend to use your little Rachel to catch him."

"Okay, what do you want me to do?"

"I need you to get her to a private place where we can pick her up. Can you do that?

"Why, yes, Michael, I think I can get her to a very secluded place. I assume when you say 'we can pick her up,' you are on your way here?"

"Yes. I am on my way there. We should be landing in about two hours. Where should we meet?"

"When you reach the airport, go to the UGSE office and request a car to my home. I should hope Ms. Vecler, I mean, Mrs. Fox, will be here by the time you arrive."

"Your home. Very good. I'll see you then."

Placing the phone on the seat next to him, Damious asked Tempess if he'd managed to find anything interesting on Andrew Stone. As he expected, Tempess was at a loss. *What a waste of space,* he thought. Damious leaned back in his chair and closed his eyes for the remainder of the flight.

Excited to be able to help Damious in his quest, Justin Wright called for his daughter to come to his study. Entering the room with an herbal poultice pressed to her bruised cheek, Amanda asked her father what she could do for him.

Walking over to her with concern on his face, he asked, "How's that cheek, dear? You know I didn't mean to hit you. It's just you make me so mad when you let me down."

"I know, Father, and I'm sorry. I'll do better in the future. I promise."

Perking up, he pointed her toward the couch and said, "Well, you can redeem yourself right now. I need you to call your friend Rachel and invite her over. I have some colleagues who would like to talk with her, friends high up in the organization."

Concerned for herself as well as her friend, she replied very carefully, "What do they want to talk with her for? Are they planning on promoting her?" Pretending to be excited, she continued, "I'm sure she'll be excited. When should I ask her to come?"

"As soon as she can. I'm expecting them in a few hours."

"I'll go upstairs and call her now. Excuse me, Father."

He stared after her as she climbed the staircase, wondering how he could ever have been so angry at her earlier. *Oh well*, he thought, *I'm sure she deserved it*. He walked over to his desk, sat down, and busied himself with the plans for the initial phase of the new society.

In her room with the door closed, Amanda dialed Rachel's global Internet number and prayed that she'd pick up. After three rings, Rachel picked up and said, "Hi, Amanda, I'm really busy right now. Can I call you back later?"

"No! Please don't hang up," she cried, surprising Rachel. "I need your help, and I think you might need my help."

"What are you talking about, Amanda? I really don't have time for this. Are you really in trouble?"

After a stream of expletives, Amanda said, "Yes! My father is up to something. He smacked me so hard this morning that he left a bruise, and this evening, a few minutes ago, he asked me to invite you over here to meet with someone who is, to quote him, 'higher up in the organization.' Please! Rachel, if you don't come, I don't know what he'll do to me, and I want to leave—forever."

"Who, who wants to meet me? And why at your house? Why not at the office?"

"I honestly don't know, Rachel, but I think it could be dangerous for you. He said the people will be here in a few hours. Will you come?"

"Amanda, listen to me. I'm with some people right now, and it's not a good time, but if you really need me, I'll see what I can do. Let me call you back in a half an hour. Would that be okay?"

"You'll call back in a half an hour? Okay, but will you come?"

"Yes, Amanda, I'll be there. Later." On the other side of town, Rachel pushed the off button on her phone, looked at her brother and husband, and said, "Guys, I think we've got some more trouble."

*   *   *

Stunned at Burke's announcement, the little band of Christians sat in silence, letting his words flow over them. Breaking the silence, Scott Abrams recited the preamble of the US Constitution.

Looking at him like he'd lost his mind, Bob spoke, "Why are you quoting the Constitution?"

"Because I refuse to accept what Burke said. We are Americans, and even though things are bad, we cannot just accept a global takeover," Scott protested.

"Come on, Scott. America ceased to be in 2015," Miriam said sadly. "Even before the war, people had given over their rights to the government. It started way back at the beginning of the twentieth century. By the time people decided to take a stand, it was too late. Our last chance was in 2012, but after the environmental disaster, the Congress went back on their promise to restore the country. They gave all legislative power to the president, who, in turn, gave our sovereignty over to the United

Nations and the plan for global society. You know as well as the rest of us that our government is a sham and our president is a pawn of the UGSE. The globalists finally got their wish. The Constitution is now a worthless piece of paper. We need to try and find our way in this new world, and we need to do it with prayer and the Lord. If Burke is involved with changing society, you can bet things for true believers are going to get really bad. The hate speech legislation has already affected our rights. When you think about it, Pastor Stone was lucky that he didn't get fined or thrown in jail for his sermon a few weeks ago, only by the grace of God."

Bob said, "Mir is right. We can't look back to the past. Scott, if you want the country back the way it was, it's going to be a battle. We've lost our Constitution. A whole generation of children has been and is being brought up to depend totally on the government rather than God or even their parents. People are tired of fighting. They've been beaten down, and most of those with the will to fight were executed after the war."

"I refuse to accept that," Scott spat. "If we're here and Pastor Stewart is out there somewhere, there must still be people all over the country and all over the world that want to fight. We just have to find them."

Having taken in all the words exchanged, Kevin finally added his two cents, "You're all right. We have to accept that the world is different. If we only try to keep the past alive, we'll never be able to move forward. We need keep the spirit of the past alive while living in the now. We can't focus on all the bad happening and forget that there is good. Scott is right about others being out there. I think the time is coming when we are going to have to go out and find the others that agree with us and join with them. Otherwise, Burke and his lot will make all true Christians criminals."

Sitting in silence again, they all began praying for guidance and faith. The quiet of their prayer was broken by the doorbell.

"Again?" asked Yvonne. "Can't Burke take a hint and leave us alone? I'm not going to answer it. Maybe he'll just go away."

The bell rang again. Silence. It rang again. Silence. It rang again, and Yvonne had enough. She marched over to the door and flung it open, ready to tell Burke to take a flying leap, and gasped, "Pastor Stewart!"

Everyone turned to look at the door and said as one, "Where have you been?"

Hurrying in through the door and closing it behind him, Pastor Stewart's face beamed with a huge smile. "Hello, children. I'm back, and it's time to get ready to stand."

After the initial shock, everyone walked over to Pastor Stewart and patted him on the back or gave him a hug. His first question was, "Where's Jason Fox?"

After telling him the story of their quick meeting with Jason Fox and Andrew Stone, Pastor Stewart became very agitated. "I need Stone's phone number. I have to speak with him at once. He and Jason are in great danger." Miriam took out her phone, pushed the speed dial for Stone's phone and waited for his answer. On the fourth ring, he answered, "Hello, Mir. Is everything okay?"

"I have someone who needs to talk with you," Mir said, handing the phone over to Donald.

"Hello. Is this Andrew Stone?"

"Yes. Who is this?"

"Mr. Stone, this is Donald Stewart. I need to ask if you know a man named Michael Damious."

Stone remembered Damious all right and wasn't very excited to have this question put to him, "Yes, I know who Damious is. Why?"

"Because he was here at your old church yesterday meeting with Mr. Burke Smith, and today, Mr. Smith found out that you and Jason Fox are in Los Angeles looking for your sister. Now from what I know about Mr. Smith, if he knows, Damious knows, so watch yourself. May I speak to Mr. Fox please?"

Stunned by this revelation, he handed the phone over to Fox, who asked, "Hello, who is this?

"It's Don, Jason. I'm at Andrew's friend Kevin's house waiting for you. We'll be getting things together. When you guys get ready to come back, give me a call on Andrew's phone, and watch your back. 'Til then, good-bye."

Handing the phone back to Stone, Fox asked, "What on earth is going on?"

Confused, he answered, "I wish I knew, man, but I think we're all in big trouble now."

*   *   *

"What's with all the phone calls?" Marcus Daedalus questioned.

"Bad news, my brother," quipped Stone, "bad news."

After finishing their meal at the diner, Rachel had contacted Marcus and set up a meeting, something he was not pleased about, but he saw no other option. Marcus Daedalus was not what most people would assume a leader of the resistance would look like. Standing five foot seven inches tall, he had a lean, muscular build. His skin was almost as black as an onyx stone. His eyes were a rich chocolate brown surrounded by flecks of gold that gave him a mystical aura. His kind, friendly demeanor had been distorted by the ruthlessness he encountered during the war. He was a man not to be underestimated. He was as agile and fast as a hawk and as powerful as a tiger. His greatest asset, however, was his mind. Like his namesake, he was a master at invention.

Jason, Andrew, and Rachel had met him on a dig they were undertaking in the jungles of Africa. Marcus was the point man. Being ten years older than both men and twelve years older than Rachel, he seemed like an archaeology god to them. His knowledge of the history of the region, as well has his botanical and zoological familiarity with the living things of the area, was astounding. Their quest was for a missing civilization rumored to have existed thousands of years in the past. For Rachel, the possibility of being the first to study an unknown society was intoxicating. Jason, Andrew, and Richard Wolfe were hoping to stumble on an adventure to rival their movie hero. However, with all the upheaval on the African continent at the time, their dig was cut short by governmental bureaucracy, basically meaning, they didn't have enough money to grease the palms of all the corrupt politicians.

Having spent the better part of a year preparing for their adventure, the group had grown very close, and their parting was bittersweet. They kept in contact until 2017, when the news reported that the head of the African resistance, Marcus Daedalus, had been executed for his part in the attacks on world government leaders. Each had mourned him in their own special way. Jason fell deeper into his work, Rachel began feeling the tug to do something more for society, and Andrew started down his new path of faith.

Marcus had set up the meeting in an abandoned building downtown that he had kitted out with the latest known and unknown technologies: computers linked to UGSE terminals all over the world, devices for blocking and redirecting incoming and outgoing signals, many different kinds of communication devices, as well as a tech geek's paradise of half-finished inventions in various states of completion littering tables along the far wall. There was an arsenal that would please any military general from anytime in human history. Not only did he have all the newest and best weapons available, he had weapons that could only be categorized as ancient: crossbows, longbows, any kind of bow you could imagine, cannons, maces, battle-axes, swords of every possible variety, slings, etc. Marcus believed that an army or a soldier should be prepared for every eventuality. He thought that the UGSE was so overconfident in their military might that they wouldn't know what to do if a group of soldiers came at them with not only guns but swords, maces, and axes ready for close-combat skirmishes. The greatest treasure he possessed, though, was in a side room filled floor to ceiling with books saved from the all-out assault on history and unapproved knowledge.

The small group of old friends sat together around a foldout card table waiting for Andrew Stone to explain the phone call. Everyone recognized Michael Damious's name except Fox, who asked, "Who is this Damious person, and why did all of you turn pale when Drew mentioned his name?"

"You know him too," Stone said, "except you knew him when he was called Michael Davis."

Trying to stifle a laugh, Fox said, "Michael Davis? From our first dig? That little freak who thought he was going to be the most powerful man in the world? What a dweeb." Understanding the situation, he continued, "I'm assuming he's still a freak, but is the most powerful man in the world now?"

"Bingo!" said Marcus. "But not the most important yet. He's an arrogant, powerful, and evil dweeb these days."

Thinking back to his dream, Fox's eyes grew large with the realization that the face on the dragon was Michael Damious.

Noticing the look on his friend's face, Stone asked, "What is it?"

He replied with sigh, "You remember the dragon in my dream? The one whose face I couldn't place?"

"Dragon? Dream? What?" Rachel interrupted.

Ignoring Rachel, Stone finished Fox's thought, "It was Damious's face, wasn't it?"

"Yes," Fox said.

A little annoyed at her brother, Rachel repeated her question, "What dream are we talking about with a dragon in it?"

Marcus looked over at Fox, interested in hearing the answer too.

Fox told his story from the point where he shot the demon in Wolfe, all the way up until he got the call from Rachel. Rachel and Marcus were stunned at the revelation Stewart had told Fox. While they had both heard of Donald Stewart, neither of them were prepared for his plan. Only one person in their group understood what Donald Stewart was saying, and it was up to Andrew Stone to explain it.

* * *

Isabelle had never been in Michael Damious's office without him present before, and she thought how strange it was that she still felt his icy presence all around her. Before she could change her mind, she sat at his desk, turned on his computer, and began to search for any clue as to what was going on. It didn't take very long.

Damious was clever, but not as clever as he supposed. He told everyone that his spirit guide was the archangel Michael, but Isabelle knew his master's true name and used it to get through his security. *Amateur,* she thought as she typed in Angelous as the password. She was not ready for what she discovered. His desktop was set up with individual files: UGSE, UGSA, GNN, along with every other global organization she had heard of. Other files were titled 2012, War, Resistance, and various names she recognized, including her own. The one that stunned her the most was simply titled Demons.

As she clicked on each file, she copied it onto a smart drive without reading the material—until she came to the demon file. She had to know what it contained. At first she didn't understand it. It was nothing more than a random list of names, names she recognized as spirit guides, but when she saw Adder and clicked on it, she sat as still as a statue. The file was filled with years of meetings she had had with her guide, things that no one except she and Adder could have known. She realized that it was a report written by Adder through a surrogate. Reading some of his personal comments made her have to run to the bathroom and throw up. Her whole life had been a lie. Her mother's death, her mission, and her mentor and best friend were fictions created to keep her doing what she did best: guide innocent people to their spirit guides or, as she now knew, demon masters. With tears flowing down her face, she copied the final file, turned off the computer, and left Damious's office.

Once she had returned to her room, she downloaded the smart drive onto her computer. Sitting back on her bed, she read with horror all the things that Michael Damious had been doing. Of course she already knew about the environmental disaster being a set up, but reading the scope of the planned operation was astounding. She was amazed at how far back this plan went and the actual purpose behind it. She had always thought that the human desire for power was the base of every government plot to take over the world, but she noticed a pattern while reading through the various files, a pattern of spiritual activity. It seemed that the desire men had for power came from the original desire of the spiritual master known as Lucifer.

She had always been taught that Lucifer was, as his name implied, a spirit of light. In fact, she had been taught Lucifer was the highest ancient master, the first to overcome the deception of power—power being the desire one had to be above another. The story talked about Lucifer realizing that all beings were equal and could achieve a higher state of being when they gave over their mortal concept of ownership. He tried to overthrow the spirit that believers call God, the all-powerful. Lucifer led a group of spirits against God, and as everyone knows, they lost. Because God won, the story got spun into the myth Judeo-Christians believed. Isabelle had always been taught that all spirits were good but that some had been led astray, such as those called angels, and like man, the spirits had to work out their karma through birth and rebirth. Those who ascended the earthly plane were freed from their mortality and became higher spirits who would then guide those left on earth. It was such a beautiful concept for Isabelle. The belief that everyone was good and could attain their higher self was something she had dedicated her life to, and now she was finding out that perhaps her beliefs were the fiction. Could Jerry's dream be true? Was Adder a horrible creature too? She just couldn't believe it, but here it was right in front of her.

Damious's personal diary was full of descriptions of a place just like Jerry had described. Angelous was a deceitful, evil, and power-hungry spirit controlling demons that, in turn, were controlling humans instead of helping them. The leaders of the UGSE all seemed to be like Damious, working with the spirits for control of the world. The average person was like Isabelle or Andrew, either being deceived by spirits or just wanting to be the best that they could be.

The symbiotic relationship between world governments and demonic forces was nothing new. Getting people to trust their governments to take care of them over family, churches, or communities was the culmination of generations of societal and demonic experiments. They had tried this all throughout history. Every major civilization started as a handful of honorable people wanting to create a place to be free and work and live. After years, decades, and centuries of success, a charismatic figure would take power and spiral the society into destruction. With every death of society, the demons took their previous knowledge and applied it to the new society being born and reborn—a karma of its own.

After millennia of wars and endless destruction, the demonic leadership had realized that the downfall of man would come not through might, but through knowledge and peace. Knowledge had exploded in the twentieth century. Ideas conceptualized centuries earlier had actually been invented. Egyptians, Babylonians, Medes, Greeks, Romans, and even Aztec and Mayan civilizations in the new world had created magnificent buildings, aqueducts, gardens, medicines, roads, and more. This was nothing compared to the building projects and medical advancements of the past two centuries. Skyscrapers, airplanes, automobiles, supercomputers, satellites, and space travel were things the ancients only dreamed about. Doctors could do anything, from healing infertility to bringing people back from the dead. God had been reduced to a buddy you might want to take out for a beer, instead of an all-powerful loving, and righteous ruler who takes care of those in need. Lucifer, or the devil as he was called, had actually almost accomplished a feat never before possible—the death of God.

Isabelle didn't understand why, but the thought of the death of God made her feel sick. A few weeks ago, the idea of people giving up on God or killing God would have given her pleasure. She had always seen the concept of God as a wall keeping people from attaining spiritual enlightenment. Isabelle had begun to see that it was actually she who had been the wall keeping people from true spiritual enlightenment. She kept going back to the still-small voice in her head that said, 'Someone is praying for you' and her mother singing "Amazing Grace."

She had one last file to open, the one she feared and desired the most, the one labeled Isabelle Zenn. After reading it, tears streaming down her face, she knew she would never be the same again, and she fell on her knees and began to pray. She prayed like never before in a language she didn't know but could understand. As she knelt praying, a peace that she had never felt before enveloped her. She fell to the floor dreaming the most wonderful dream ever, the dream of her salvation.

*   *   *

Pastor Stewart's plan didn't make sense to Rachel or Marcus because neither of them were people of faith, but still they listened carefully. After Fox described Stewart's small arsenal, Stone explained, "While Pastor Stewart understands the need to arm ourselves, he also understands that this is not just a war of men, it is a war of spirit—angels and demons, God and Satan. This war has been waging since God threw Satan and his fallen angels out of heaven. Satan has been trying to turn man away from God since the garden of Eden, and he hasn't changed his plan much. What did he say to Eve in the garden?"

Rachel spoke up, "Didn't he say Eve would be like God?"

"Very good, little sis." She made a little curtsy as he smiled and continued, "He said that she and Adam would be like God, knowing good and evil. Well, that's pretty much what he's telling people today. The leaders of the UGSE think they're going to be gods, ruling the world. The average person thinks they know good from evil. As long as they work for the betterment of the world, they will be like gods themselves because they believe they are in control of the environment of the world. Once the UGSE enforces the hate-speech rule, anyone who says there is definite truth will be put in jail or killed. After all, anyone can be offended by another person's beliefs. The scriptures say that faith comes through hearing the Word, but how can they hear the Word if there's no one to preach the Word? Sis, you should know better than anyone what will happen when the government stifles free speech. You've studied society for most of your adult life. Civilizations fall when people aren't allowed to question authority." Taking a breath and letting a little smile play across his lips, he finished, "Just think, all the world thinks God is too limiting, both in what you can say or do, but God gives man the right to choose what to do and what to say. It's men who limit other men."

"Yeah, really funny," Marcus injected. "What does this have to do with Stewart's plan?"

"Give me a minute," Stone teased. "I've got to lay the groundwork first. It's like the resistance. You have people all over the world ready to take up arms, punch in computer viruses, or do whatever to disrupt the UGSE. Well, Stewart has set up an army of his own, an army of prayer warriors. They are just as important in this war as your weapons over there." Stone motioned toward the armory. "Whether you want to believe it or not, there are forces outside your realm of understanding that are in a battle. New Life Foundation has been possessing people for decades. I've seen it firsthand, and so have you, Rachel, if you'll open your eyes to what happened while you were there. Didn't you say it creeped you out? That was the Holy Spirit protecting you through prayers. I pray for you every day."

"Come on, bro," replied Rachel. "Sure, I saw some weird stuff there, but I never saw any demons or spirits or whatever. Just a bunch of fruitcakes living in the fantasy land of their minds. Thanks for the prayers, though. It's nice to know you care."

Growing tired of the small talk, Fox interrupted, "Look, Rachel, you know I never went in for any of this stuff before, but something happened to me up on that mountain, not just the visions and the fact Stewart was there. God actually revealed Himself to me out there. I got saved up there. I even got baptized in the river. You just have no idea how awesome it all is!"

Everyone looked at him, stunned by this revelation. He hadn't even shared this with Stone.

"I'll tell you all about my conversion later, but you have to have faith now. Otherwise, we all might as well go home and get ready to bend over and take it." Pausing, Fox looked over at Stone. "Go on, Drew."

Still stunned by Fox's profession of faith, Stone closed his mouth and finished, "Stewart has churches all over the world ready to pray against the forces of the devil. He wants to link up with the resistance armies around the world so that each group of intercessors can pray for specifics: names, missions, time—"

"Wait a minute," Marcus interrupted. "You basically want me to give all our plans away to a man I don't know just because you and Fox have found God? Are you serious? If you believe in God so much, why can't you just pray for the cause? This is too crazy for me!"

Rachel chimed in, "I have to agree with Marcus. If I had known you were going to come up with all this nonsense, I wouldn't have called you. My god, what happened to you?"

Angry now, Stone stood up. "Look, I know what I'm asking sounds crazy, but you both know me. I'm asking you to have faith. We have to fight on all fronts in this war. There is a spiritual battle going on. Yes, we can pray in general, but let me ask you, if you have the best fighters in the world armed to the teeth but with no specific directive, are they going to be effective? Yeah, they may kill some people, and they may even win a battle, but what is their mission? What is their goal? Will they win the war?"

Sitting down again, Stone looked over at Marcus and Rachel, who were both thinking about the question. After a few moments, Marcus looked Andrew and Fox in the eyes and said, "I just can't give that information out. I'm a realist, and I have to think of my people first. You must understand."

"What if I can prove it to you?" asked Stone hopefully.

"How? These are pretty out there things, man. What? Is God gonna just hit me over the head or blind me like that dude on the road to wherever from the Bible?"

Laughing at his basic knowledge of Apostle Paul's conversion, Stone answered, "I don't know how, but I do know that God has a plan, and it involves you. So if you'll give me a phone to call Stewart on, I'll get my little congregation praying for our meeting over at Mr. Wright's house."

Interrupting, Rachel said, "You mean *my* meeting over at the Wright's house. You guys aren't part of the meeting."

Getting up and walking over to his wife, Fox helped her out of her chair, pulled her close to him, and kissed her passionately while dipping her low. Bringing her back to a vertical position breathless, he looked in her eyes and playfully said, "Now come on, Rach, you know us better than that! We're full of surprises, and if you think we're letting you walk into the snake pit alone, you don't know us very well at all."

Enjoying the fact that her husband acknowledged her in such a sensual way, she returned his affection with a hug and smaller kiss, looked at the other men in the room who were smiling like schoolboys, and said playfully, "Well then, husband, brother, and Mr. Daedalus, let's get going."

* * *

Since separating from the corporate church, Stone's congregation had become one in Christ, but guided into different groups composed of people led toward different spiritual gifts. Pastor Stone had shown them that God doesn't call everyone the same. Each person has individual gifts to share with everyone else. He told them that the congregation comes together to worship and be filled and refilled by the Spirit. Then they go out into the world to share the gospel as God leads them.

Some gathered as teachers and some as hospitality. The youth formed a group of evangelists and worship teams. Others worked together in different areas of ministry. A small group, including the four leaders, formed an intercessory prayer group. With Pastor Stone, they prayed together for unity and the guidance of God, but Pastor Stewart opened a whole new way to pray: pray with a mission. Pastor Stewart gave the small group homework. They were to find scripture relating to battle. He said it didn't matter whether it was physical or spiritual battle.

Unsure of how finding scripture was going to help with their prayer mission, Scott asked, "I thought prayer was supposed to come from within the person praying and listening for the Holy Spirit to guide them? I know scriptures show us how to live, but what will we do with them after we find them in regard to prayer? I hope that's not too stupid a question."

Pastor Stewart patiently instructed the whole group of intercessors which included four other congregants: Thomas Amos, Doris White, James Rickman, and Debbie Cardinale. "Listen as I read from Isaiah 55. 'For as the rain and the snow come down from heaven, And do not return there without watering the earth, and making it bear and sprout, and furnishing seed to the sower and bread to the eater; So shall My word be which goes forth from My mouth; it shall not return to Me empty, without accomplishing what I desired and without succeeding to the matter for which I sent it.' Taking a moment to let the scripture sink in, he said, "We will be praying scripture because scripture is the word of God. We don't need to trust our words. We need to trust God's Word. We will take the scriptures you find, read them, and let the Spirit pray the Word through us. We will let God use us for His will. Does that make sense, Mr. Abrams? Everyone?"

Everyone nodded their head while they sat quietly for a moment to let his words sink in. Awed by the concept, Miriam spoke, "Why haven't we been shown to pray this way before? Is this a new idea?"

Smiling, he replied, "Well, what are you talking about, Mir? We pray scripture every week during the worship service." Looking guilty, he continued, "At least we used to before I let Burke change up the service."

"What are you talking about? We've never prayed scripture that I know of," she challenged. Scott, Bob, Tom, and Debbie all nodded in agreement while Doris, James and the Davies smiled knowingly.

Stewart continued, "What is the liturgy if not scripture? Every time we sing or speak the liturgy, we are praying scripture. How could you not know that?"

Like a light turning on in their heads, they all walked over to the hymnals and checked it out. Tom asked, "How is it that I never noticed the scriptural references before?"

Scott chimed in, "Well, I noticed the references, but it never struck me that it was showing where the words came from. I just thought they were someone's interpretation of scripture. This is awesome!"

Doris joked, "Don't you ever *read* the Bible? How could you read the Psalms or the story of Jesus and not realize it was the same words you had sung your whole life?"

They looked a little ashamed until Pastor Stewart interjected, "You'd be surprised at how many people do not realize that they are praying scripture during the service. Sadly, it is why so many liturgical services have been reduced to touchy-feely phrases or removed completely. People have been taught that church should be fun and geared toward the people as opposed to being a place to come acknowledge our sinfulness and need for forgiveness before God, a place to receive that forgiveness through the Word and sacraments." He looked wistfully at no one in particular. Then remembering the purpose of the meeting, he continued, "So now that you know about the importance of scripture in prayer, let's get to work."

Everyone picked up their Bibles and diligently went to work. Pastor Stewart watched his little army of intercessors and couldn't help but smile as he watched them search the scriptures, highlight their Bibles, write down verses, and show excitement at learning new scriptures that they had never realized before. *God is truly good*, he thought. While mulling over his plan, Miriam's phone rang. Everyone froze. Miriam reached over, hit the talk button, and said, "Hello?"

"Hey, Miriam! How's everything going there?" questioned Andrew Stone.

"Great! Pastor Stewart is teaching us about praying scripture, and we've all just been searching the Word. I never realized how exciting it could be just reading the Bible, but it is!"

"Great, Miriam," he replied, feeling a little jealous for his congregation. "Can I speak with Donald please?"

A little disappointed that he didn't want to talk with her longer, she handed the phone over to Donald Stewart and went back to looking through the scriptures. Stewart took the phone and asked, "What's up?"

After explaining what they planned to do, Stone asked Pastor Stewart for prayer cover and for God to reveal to Rachel and Marcus the truth. Stewart agreed and reminded him that God would not give him anything he couldn't handle, and for every trial, He would give him a way out. Stone thanked him for his word and for the prayers and hung up.

Pastor Stewart gathered the small group of prayer warriors and explained that Pastor Stone and his friends were about to step out in faith and meet the enemy head-on. "I want each of you to take a moment and listen to God. If you feel that He is speaking to your heart, and if one of your scriptures would be pertinent to the task at hand, please share it with us."

After a few moments, James reminded everyone of the story of Shadrach, Meshach, and Abednego. "Wouldn't those be good scriptures to focus on?"

Pleased with James's boldness, Stewart answered, "Yes, James, I think that will do excellently. Everyone, let's gather together in the middle of the room."

Everyone moved to the furniture in the center of the room and looked to Pastor Stewart.

"Now, James, could you tell us where in Daniel to turn our Bibles?"

Speaking nervously, James replied, "Sure. It's in Daniel 3:13–30."

Everyone turned to Daniel and waited for Stewart to continue.

"Now I want James to read the verses aloud. After, we will sit quietly and let the Lord speak a prayer through us. You may reread a scripture that seems significant and pray for our friends. You may feel a word coming. Speak it out. A song may come to your mind. Lead us in it. Just focus on the Word of God. Focus on the predicament our friends are going into. Like Shadrach, Meshach, and Abednego, our friends might be thrown into the fiery furnace, and we need to give them coverage through our prayers. Is everyone ready?"

Everyone nodded.

"Then James, begin."

Feeling unsure and uncomfortable, they began. As they prayed, sang, and read, they could feel the Lord's presence all around them. Their prayers became bold, and each one felt the power of the Holy Spirit speaking through them. They prayed continually for the next four hours without even realizing the time. Pastor Stewart encouraged them to take rest in small increments. Like in regular war, they had at least two people keeping watch or praying at all times. When people had to leave for work, those left behind kept the pace. The prayer went on for three days, and they read various scriptures as a focus. The small group of intercessors kept faithfully to their task until the time had come to see the fulfillment of Pastor Stewart's original scripture in Isaiah: 'So shall My word be which goes forth from My mouth; it shall not return to Me empty, without accomplishing what I desired and without succeeding to the matter for which I sent it.'

* * *

Not pleased with the plan but willing to go along, Marcus said sarcastically, "Okay, so you guys walk in there like three warrior smart-mouths, talk to these very hospitable evil dudes, get Rachel's friend, and walk out with happy, happy smiles on everyone's face." Marcus looked each of them in the eye as they grinned back at him. He continued with his derisive review. "Now if by some crazy chance things don't go to plan, I'm supposed to wait out here and save the day while not getting caught myself. That's the plan."

With his normal smart-mouth comeback, Fox answered, "Hey brother, have we ever let you down before?"

Rolling his eyes, Marcus simply smiled and shook his head.

Rachel interjected, "Okay, so if we're done with all the chitchat, can we get moving?"

Serious now, Marcus asked, "Does everyone have their earpiece set?" He had developed a new kind of listening device that would sit inside the ear completely undetectable by the naked eye and send as well as receive sound. Marcus was a genius with technology and would probably have been a multimillionaire if not for the fact he was a resistance fighter.

Stone answered for everyone, "Yes, they're in. This is incredible, Marcus. How does this thing work? There's no microphone or wires or anything."

Answering in his best covert voice, he replied, "Everything is inside the device. I could tell you how it works, but then I'd have to kill you, wouldn't I?"

Laughing together, the four friends gave each other a hug and allowed Stone to speak a short prayer before Marcus returned to his car and the other three walked up to the front door.

Even before Rachel had a chance to knock, Amanda swung open the door and embraced her friend. Noticing the two men with her, she stepped back into the entryway, mouth open.

Before letting Amanda speak, Rachel said, "Hi, Amanda, let me introduce my brother, Andrew." Stone smiled and waved with a stupid look on his face. "And this is my husband, Jason."

Fox threw caution to the wind, stepped forward, and kissed Amanda full on the lips, saying, "Hi, Amanda! Pleased to meet you!"

Still stunned and now blushing, Amanda invited the small group into the house. Once inside, Rachel noticed the bruise on Amanda's cheek and gasped. "Oh my gosh! Is that what your dad did?"

Amanda kicked her foot nervously, looking at the floor with shame on her face. Breaking down into a flood of tears, Amanda replayed the violent attack by her father. "Th-th-that's why I called you. Please take me away. We need to go before my father realizes—"

"Realizes what, dear?" Wright asked as he turned the corner to meet his guests. Amanda almost jumped out of her skin, afraid of what her father was going to do. "Amanda, why haven't you invited our guests into the parlor for drinks? I have to say, I was only expecting Ms. Vecler-Stone, or should I say Fox?" The three friends looked nervously at each other, stunned that Wright could know her name. "I can guess that this must be Mr. Stone and Mr. Fox?"

Offering his hand to Wright, Fox said cheekily, "Well, sir, I think we're at a disadvantage. You seem to know our names, but we don't know yours. I'm Jason Fox, and you are?"

Shaking Fox's hand firmly while challenging his eyes, Wright replied haughtily, "Pleased to make your acquaintance, Mr. Fox. I'm Justin Wright, and I have some colleagues who will be most happy to find you here."

Not pulling back his hand, Fox returned his stare and replied more impertinently, "Friends like, say, Michael Damious?"

Stunned by Fox's knowledge, Wright unconsciously pulled his hand away. "Touché, Mr. Fox, but it really doesn't matter that you know his name. You did not expect him to be here, which he should be in about fifteen minutes. So please, won't you and your friends join me in the lounge for a drink?"

Not wanting to give him any satisfaction, Stone jumped in and replied, "I hope you have scotch, Mr. Wright, and not some cheap brand—the good stuff."

Concerned at the two men's bravery but not wanting to show weakness, Justin Wright led the three visitors and his daughter to the lounge. Taking seats on the comfortable furnishings, Fox and Stone both accepted tumblers of twelve-year-old scotch, each choosing a chair opposite the other while Rachel and Amanda drank glasses of chardonnay, choosing to sit on one of the two couches gracing the room. Justin Wright sat in a refurbished leather chair watching the group. While the ladies nervously chatted with each other, Fox and Stone stared down Wright while feverishly trying to figure a way out of the situation.

Right on schedule, the doorbell rang, and Michael Damious and William Tempess were shown into the room. Without allowing Wright the chance to greet his guests, Jason Fox sprung from his chair, jumped on William Tempess, and began beating the man senseless, yelling about demons and Wolfe. Everyone in the room was taken by surprised by Jason Fox's attack, but Andrew Stone wasted no time in jumping to action and took a swing at his nemesis, Michael Damious. Connecting his fist to Damious's cheek, he silently prayed for God to help them overcome the enemy, or at least stun them enough to make a dash for the door. While Fox continued pummeling Tempess, Damious was not about to go down without a fight, and fists flew between Stone and himself.

Finally coming to his senses, Wright hit the intercom button on his chair and called in his security. The fight, which seemed to go on forever to the girls, was cut short by four large security guards. Two attacked the men fighting, pulling them apart, while the other two trained their guns on Fox and Stone.

Wright spoke in a parental tone, "Now, Mr. Fox and Mr. Stone, it's time to stop your fighting and sit back down. Mr. Damious, are you all right? It looks like your associate is unconscious." Looking at the two security guards that broke up the fight, he continued, "Please see to it that Mr. Damious's associate is seen to."

"Yes, sir," they replied while removing Tempess from the room.

With fire in his eyes, Fox spat, "I'm going to kill Tempess for what he did, you piece of—" Before he could finish his sentence, one of the armed guards pistol-whipped him in the mouth. Spitting blood from his split lip, he looked at the guard and seethed, "Yeah, you're a tough guy, hitting a guy with your gun. I'd like to see what you'd do in a fair fight, you big sissy." Just as the guard was preparing to hit Fox again, he was stopped by Justin Wright.

"Now, now, Mr. Jasper. I think Mr. Fox has had enough. Just sit him back in his chair and keep an eye on him. I'll give you leave to tie him up if he becomes unruly again. Does that work for you, Mr. Fox?"

"Do I have a choice?"

"No, I guess you don't."

As Mr. Jasper indelicately tossed Fox in his chair, Rachel dashed to his side, grabbed a tissue from an end table, and dabbed his bleeding lip. Gently kissing him, she asked, "Are you okay?"

Not wanting to give Fox any peace, Wright motioned for Mr. Jasper to place Rachel back next to Amanda.

Slapping Jasper's face after he indelicately replaced her on the couch, Rachel spat, "Don't you touch me, you big ape."

Stunned, Mr. Jasper, after assessing the situation, let out a huge bellow as his colleague and Justin Wright followed in evil laughter at her outburst.

Andrew Stone was replaced in his chair by the other guard while Michael Damious straightened out his suit, ran his hands through his hair, and excused himself to go to the bathroom to clean up. A few minutes later, Damious returned to the room looking no worse for wear, but anger flashed in his eyes as he looked over at Stone.

Trying to get the meeting back on track, Wright offered everyone another drink. Fox, Stone, Rachel, and Amanda refused while Damious accepted a snifter of brandy. After downing his drink, Damious smiled wickedly and revealed his plan, "Well, well, well, I couldn't have planned this better. I came here intending to use Ms. Vecler as bait to capture Mr. Fox, and here I have both of you and a bonus in Mr. Stone."

"Well, Michael, aren't you special?" Stone mocked.

Trying to buy time, Rachel asked, "What is it you want with us, Mr. Damious? I've done you no wrong or Mr. Wright. Hasn't my work ever been anything but the very best?"

Wright stood up, walked over to Rachel, and looked her directly in the eye. "No, Ms. Vec—Mrs. Fox, your work has always been very good, at least as far as I know, but you lied. There must be a reason, and honestly, I've never trusted you. Your questions and discussions about people's reaction to the UGSE's plans disturb me." Bending down to within inches of her face, he continued, "Perhaps you're part of the resistance." Standing again but keeping eye contact, he asked, "Are you, Rachel? Are you a part of the resistance?"

Getting tired of his games, Rachel stood up, bringing her face within inches of his, and spoke coolly, "And if I were, Mr. Wright, do you really think I could be intimidated by a worm like yourself?"

Sending her flying back onto the couch with the back of his hand, Wright turned away from her, walked over to Damious, and said in a controlled rage, "Michael, you have what you wanted. Take them and leave my house." Turning back toward Amanda, he narrowed his eyes wickedly. "I need to deal with my daughter now."

Amanda, who had been comforting Rachel, shrank back into the couch and began to cry while Fox tried to rise. He was restrained by Mr. Jasper. "You're a rat," hissed Fox. "And one day I *will* get you."

Not taking the bait, Wright picked up his drink and sat back down in his chair. "Michael, feel free to use my men to remove these wretches from my house. This is Mr. Jasper and Mr. Trax. Gentlemen, do whatever Mr. Damious requests of you and then return."

Damious, annoyed at Wright's arrogance, ordered the guards to tie and gag Fox, Stone, and Rachel. As they left the room, William Tempess, face swollen, walked up to Jason Fox, who struggled against his bonds. Intending to pay him back, Tempess grabbed Fox's shirt, but before he landed a punch, Damious snapped at him, "William, there will be time for your revenge after we get back to the foundation." Seeing Andrew's eyes widen, Damious smiled, saying, "Yes, Mr. Stone we will be returning to New Life, and I think Ms. Zenn will enjoy seeing you again, or maybe not!"

Tempess stood down, and Mr. Jasper and Mr. Trax manhandled the prisoners through the door and into the waiting car. As they stepped onto the porch, the sound of a girl screaming could be heard just before the door closed. Rachel's eyes filled with tears as she wondered if she'd ever see her friend again.

*   *   *

Waiting outside in the bushes, Marcus was getting bored listening to the quiet murmurs going on inside when a limousine pulled up to the front entrance and two men exited the car. He assumed the tall evil-looking one was Michael Damious, but the squat bald man was a mystery. Sizing them up, he didn't think it would be very difficult to take them out. He didn't notice anyone else besides the driver, so he returned to his vigil under the shrubbery.

It didn't take long to realize something had gone terribly wrong when he heard Fox's voice screaming something about demons and Wolfe and many *oofs* and *oowws* as someone else began fighting. It wasn't until Wright called in the cavalry that Marcus knew he'd been right. A plan B was going to be needed. No one knew that Wright had security, and Marcus didn't know how many were inside.

Stealthily edging his way out of the bushes and back to the car, he kept listening. Thankfully, Rachel was using her communication device and was feeding info to Marcus in whispers. "Marcus, I hope you can hear me. There are four unfriendlies here—two troll-looking brutes and two hired guns, also pretty troll-like. I don't see anyone else, but I have a feeling we're going to be going for a ride. Get ready to follow us. Gotta go. Don't let us down."

Great. Think, Marcus, think. Marcus was trying to come up with a viable plan. He knew the foundation was on the other side of the country, so somehow he was going to have to get on their plane—easier said than done. Opening his personal laptop that was kitted out with all his security, he contacted his inside guy at the airport. After several back-and-forth texts, it was settled. Someone at the airport was going to poison the copilot, and Marcus would set himself up as the replacement. His years flying get-away planes in Africa afforded him enough knowledge to be able to play the part. Someone on the ground crew would steal a uniform from the New Life Foundation's section of the airport and have it ready for him. Putting his car in gear, Marcus raced toward the airport. Trying out Stone's idea, he said a quick prayer. "Dear God, I don't know if You're up there, but my friend says You are, so right now I'm going with him. I pray that You will get me to the airport and on the plane with no problems. Umm… thanks and amen. Yay, God!" He hoped it was good enough. Almost as soon as his prayer was done, he received a call on his global Internet phone. "Hello. Yes, this is Jake Kapinti. You need a copilot to go out to the foundation? Sure. When do you need me? Within the hour? We leave in an hour? Yes, I can make it. See you soon. Bye." Pleased that his cloned phone worked so well, he prayed again, "Well, if that was You, thanks, God, but now I need to get there, so please help me. Later."

Twenty minutes later, he pulled into the foundation's parking area at the airport. He felt like he almost skipped part of his trip. It should have taken at least another fifteen minutes. Not one to look a gift horse in the mouth, he hurried to the prearranged rendezvous spot, got his uniform, dressed, and walked to the concourse to board the plane.

A very happy Foundation administrator came up to Marcus and thanked him for his prompt reply to the call. "Mr. Kapinti, you have no idea how grateful we are. This flight was requisitioned by Michael Damious himself!"

"No problem, Ms."—he looked at her name tag—"Castle. That's why we're on alert, to be here to serve the community."

"Well, I'm still grateful." After showing him to the boarding gate, she walked off, getting busy with some other kind of business.

Thinking this whole thing was too easy, he put up another prayer and boarded the plane.

"Hello, Captain," Marcus spoke.

Looking up and not recognizing Marcus, the captain asked, "What happened to Murphy?"

"I heard he got some kind of food poisoning. I'm not sure, but they called me, and here I am. Name's Kapinti. Jake Kapinti," Marcus said while extending his hand.

Taking his hand and shaking it briefly, he introduced himself as Captain Erikson. After the introductions, the two men went through preflight and waited for their passengers to board. About ten minutes later, the flight attendant notified them that their passengers had arrived, five in all. The two pilots began getting the plane ready to pull away when Michael Damious poked his head through the door and said, "Okay. We're all ready to go."

"Yes, sir," the men replied in unison.

They pulled away from the boarding gate, taxied to the runway, got clearance to take off, and up they went. After being in the air for twenty minutes, Marcus stood up and walked to the cabin. Talking to the flight attendant about mundane things, he peeked through the curtain and saw Jason, Andrew, and Rachel asleep. *More like drugged*, he thought. Damious and Tempess were sitting in silence. Tempess was working on his laptop, and Damious was nursing a drink, deep in thought.

Pleased that plan B was going according to plan, he told the flight attendant to keep up the good work, and he returned to the cockpit to prepare for plan C.

* * *

In her dream, Isabelle found herself completely enveloped in darkness, darkness so deep that she actually felt a part of it. The air felt cold and clammy, and she sensed a presence that was angry and full of hate. She wanted to escape but was unable to run. As she lay on the floor, she heard the familiar voice saying, "Someone is praying for you" and the song "Amazing Grace" being sung. Listening to the lyrics, "I once was lost, but now am found, was blind, but now I see," the darkness began to lift, and she felt the hateful presence being pushed away from her. As the light grew stronger, Isabelle shaded her eyes, but then she realized the light didn't hurt, so she lowered her hand and watched the light grow and fill her whole room, except it wasn't her room. She sat up and looked around to find that she was surrounded by a mist, like a veil. A voice sounded, one she did not recognize but felt safe with, and called, "Come up here."

Immediately, the mist parted, and she saw a door standing open, with steps leading up to a throne surrounded by a rainbow, but a kind of rainbow she had never seen before. She obeyed the voice, entered through the door, climbed the stairs, and was astounded by the sight before her. Around the throne were twenty-four other thrones, with beings clothed in white with crowns on their heads. In front of the throne were seven fiery lamps burning and four strange creatures, each with six wings and different faces: one like a lion, one like a calf, one like a man, and one like an eagle. The eyes seemed to see everywhere at once. The creatures continually were saying, "Holy, holy, holy, is the Lord God Almighty, who was and is and is to come." As the creatures spoke, the twenty-four beings fell down before the throne, removed their crowns, and threw them at the foot of the throne while giving glory to the one sitting on the throne, saying, "Worthy are You, our Lord and our God, to receive glory and honor and power, for You created all things, and because of Your will they existed and were created."

Stunned, she spoke, "Where am I? What does this mean?" Not being a stranger to spiritual things, she had no fear, just a genuine curiosity.

The same voice that called her to come spoke again, "I am a messenger of the one true God, sent by Him to share His Word with you." As the voice spoke, the vision before her shimmered and changed to a familiar place, Adder's place, and a young man stood before her smiling warmly, holding out his hand for her to take, which she did.

"Are you what they call an angel? What is your name?"

"I am an angel, a messenger from God. My name is unimportant. I am only here to tell you God's will for you. If you need to call me a name, you may choose one that makes you comfortable."

"I see, you want me to focus on the message and not the messenger. Since you're going to share truth with me, I'll call you Veritas. Is that suitable?"

Smiling at her cleverness, he replied, "Veritas will be fine."

"Why have you brought me to Adder's garden? I have been here many times before."

"I have brought you here to see the truth. Are you ready?"

Remembering Jerry's dream, she nervously answered, "Yes. I think so."

While they stood together looking at Adder's tree, the strange mist began to swirl around them like a veil. Suddenly, Veritas extended his arms with his hands pushing outward, and the mist parted. Isabelle finally saw the truth. Instead of a lush garden, she stood on a ledge in the middle of an endless pit. The smell of smoke and sulfur assaulted her nose, and as she peered out into the void, she noticed Adder floating around in space. She began to call out to it, but Veritas held his finger to his lips, and she was struck dumb. While Isabelle watched the scene unfold, Veritas pulled a brilliant white flaming sword out of nowhere, holding it up like a shield. Adder seemed to acknowledge some kind of unseen change in his surroundings and began to look around. A mist appeared around him, and as it dissipated, Isabelle finally saw Adder's true form. Instead of floating, she saw that he was actually flying around on leathery black wings, and his beauty had been transformed into the hideous form of a demon. Tears streamed down her face as she realized again that her whole world had been a lie. Knowing he had shown her what she needed to see, Veritas brought the mist back, and when it cleared, he and Isabelle were standing in a crowd of people dressed in the garb of Middle-Eastern Arabs.

Isabelle knew she and Veritas were invisible, but she still tried not to jostle the people near her. Looking around, she noticed that they had been transported two thousand years into the past, to a place where Roman soldiers were preparing to crucify three criminals. She watched in horror as the Romans lifted the men into the upright position. Immediately, she realized what this place was and what was happening—Jesus, the Savior of the Christian Church, was being crucified.

She had read and heard the story, but actually living it was a whole new experience. There were women wailing at the foot of the cross while other people were yelling curses and making fun of Him. As they stood there for hours, she saw soldiers casting lots for His clothes and offering Him sour wine to drink. One of the men being crucified next to Jesus started insulting Him, encouraging Him to save Himself and the other man being crucified. Then to her surprise, the other man admonished him and asked Jesus to remember him when he came into His kingdom. Jesus told him they would be together in paradise.

She asked Veritas to take her away from here, but he said she had more to see. Watching the agony of Jesus took her breath away. The blood flowing down His face from the crown of thorns on His head and the blood pooling under His feet as it ran down His back where He'd been scourged made her want to throw up. Him pushing up on His nailed feet to gasp for breath before falling back down in agony made her want to bring Him down and comfort Him. The taunts and evil nature of the people in the crowd yelling at Him caused her to wish them dead.

Just before He took his last breath, He called out, "Father, forgive them, for they know not what they do." She knew Jesus forgave, but to see the love for this hateful group of people in His eyes broke her heart. For the last time, the mist enveloped her and Veritas, and she found herself before the throne again, except this time, in the midst of the twenty-four beings and the four strange creatures was a Lamb standing, as if slain, having seven horns and seven eyes. She realized this represented Jesus and that He truly did rise and still lived.

Falling on her face before the Lamb and the throne, she called out to Jesus to save her. She gave glory with the elders and cried "holy!" with the creatures. As she did, the Spirit of God fell upon her and filled her until she cried out in joy and fell asleep again. When she opened her eyes, she was back in her room at the foundation, sweaty and exhausted but strangely invigorated.

After taking a shower, dressing in clean clothes, and drying her hair, she sat back down in front of her laptop. Clicking back to her file, she noticed a subfile marked Gabriella, her mother's name. As she read the file, tears began falling down her face again because she finally found out the truth about her mother's life at the foundation.

* * *

Captain Erikson announced they would be arriving in twenty minutes, giving Marcus time to check on the passengers again. "Excuse me, Captain, I'm gonna use the head before landing."

"Sure thing, Kapinti, just make it quick," Erikson stated.

Instead of going straight to the toilet, Marcus walked over to talk with the flight attendant and took a quick look through the curtain to the passenger section. All three prisoners were alert and looking annoyed, especially Jason Fox. He eyed Tempess with a look of malice that could've melted steel. Saying a friendly good-bye to the flight attendant, Marcus entered the small toilet, locked the door, and replaced his earpiece. Whispering, he said, "Hi, guys!" hoping their earpieces still worked. "I'm playing copilot on this flight, so I hope it's been a pleasant trip for you."

In the other room, the three prisoners sat a little taller and then resumed their annoyed stares, trying to hide their excitement. They rolled their eyes at Marcus's attempt at humor.

"Okay, so here's the deal. I'm gonna have to do postflight with the captain to keep my cover. Once I get off the plane and through the airport, I'll get in touch with one of my people inside the foundation and try and find out what's going on. These communication devices have a range large enough for us to communicate anywhere from inside the foundation, and even in the parking lot. Keep pretending to be annoyed and obnoxious, and we'll find a way to get you out." Turning on the faucet to give the appearance of finishing in the bathroom, Marcus said one more thing. "Stone, send a prayer up to God for me."

Fox quietly responded to Marcus's comment about pretending to be annoyed with his typical flippancy, "Yeah, like I need to pretend."

The other two gave him stern looks as Tempess turned and said, "No one cares what you have to say Fox, so just shut up!"

Not being able to hold his tongue, Fox replied tersely, "Why don't you come over here and make me, you bald imbecile. Do you need me to define that for ya, Willy?"

Tempess started to undo his seat belt when Damious interjected, "Now, William, let's not play into Mr. Fox's little games." Tempess let his belt sit back against his lap as Damious continued, "And, Mr. Fox, unless you would like a little more of the sleeping drug we gave you earlier, please behave."

Preparing to shoot back a snide comment, Jason looked over at Rachel, who was shooting daggers at him with her eyes, so he thought better of it and kept quiet.

"Very good, Mr. Fox," oozed Damious. "I knew you'd see things my way."

Marcus resumed his seat in the cockpit, and the plane landed with no trouble. While he and Captain Erikson went through postflight, the others departed the plane and climbed aboard the foundation's helicopter and took off toward New Life.

"Good-bye, Mr. Kapinti, it was a pleasure flying with you," declared Erikson.

Marcus replied, "Yeah, good flying with you too." As the two went their separate ways, Marcus pulled out his cell phone and called his contact at the foundation. It turned out that no one knew anything yet, except that Mr. Damious was returning with some visitors. She promised to call him back if she found anything out. She told him to rent a car and drive out to the foundation and wait in the parking area. Marcus, never one to use money if he didn't have to, pulled out an ID card identifying him as Perdix Talos, a play on his namesake's possible apprentices. He walked over to the UGSE's help desk, showed his ID, and received a Foundation car. Pulling out of the parking garage, he smiled at the thought of deceiving the all-powerful world government and drove an hour to the foundation. As instructed, he waited in the parking lot for any information. Thankfully, the earpieces were doing their job, and it wasn't long until he had a front row seat at the events taking place inside.

*   *   *

During the short helicopter ride, the captives and captors sat in silence, but scenarios of every sort were running through their minds. Both Fox and Tempess were thinking about throwing the other out the window while Rachel just hoped she wouldn't fall out. Damious and Stone both had their thoughts on something else: Stone on the fear of seeing Isabelle again and Damious on the excitement of putting the two together. *Won't Isabelle be surprised*, he thought wickedly.

After landing at the helipad on the roof of the New Life Foundation, Damious instructed the four guards that he'd radioed for to take the prisoners to his office and to keep them bound until he joined them. Mindlessly, they obeyed and roughly jostled the small group through the corridors of the foundation, ending at Michael Damious's office. "Get inside and sit down," ordered one of the guards.

Fox politely quipped while bowing toward the door, "Please, after you."

The guard smiled and then punched him in the stomach, pushed him through the door, and said, "No. After you." The rest followed, rolling their eyes at the gasping Jason Fox sprawled on the floor, and took their seats.

As Fox got to his feet and sat down, Andrew looked at him and said, "Well, I guess they don't appreciate your kind gestures."

"Yeah, but they sure offer a great punch."

The guards closed the door and took up sentry duty, two on either side of the door, both inside and out. Rachel, being tired of the boys' tomfoolery, spoke to the guards in her sweetest flirty voice, "You know, Mr. Damious only said we had to come in here, but he didn't say we had to be quiet, so if I can get these two buffoons to watch their tongues, do you think we could please speak to each other?"

"Well, I guess. As long as you all don't try anything," the smaller of the two guards replied.

"Thank you so much…ummm, what's your name?"

Blushing and smiling like a teenage boy in love, he replied, "My name's Johnny, ma'am."

Incredulous, Fox leaned back in his chair, looked at his wife, and asked, "Did you really bat your eyelashes? Geez, how on earth did I ever get tangled up with you?"

Playing along, giving him bedroom eyes, and blowing him a kiss, she replied, "How do you think I got you?"

Stone jumped in, "Come on, you two. No one needs to watch you making googly eyes at each other. Save it for the bedroom."

Marcus chimed into the conversation, "Dang, it's good you've got Rachel with you. If it was up to Fox, they'd have you all gagged. Thanks for getting the conversation going, Rach."

"You're welcome," she replied to no one in particular, making Johnny and the other guard look at her like she was crazy.

"I guess I spoke too soon," Marcus replied, laughing. "I'm in the parking lot waiting to see what happens. I can hear all your conversations, so if you get split up, try and get to the D parking lot. I'm in a red UGSE electric toy car. It's not surprising they had to force people to buy these. Who on earth would choose to?" Remembering he was talking to his friends, he got back on track. "Sorry, just had an ADD moment. I've got a small network of spies on the inside, so if you get into too big of a jam, I'll try and get help to you, but mostly you're on your own. If you're clear on this, nod your heads at Rachel, and, Rach, tell Johnny, 'Thanks again for being so nice.'"

Both men nodded at Rachel, and she did as Marcus said. While they were sitting and having small talk, Jason let out a stunned yell, causing everyone to look at him.

"What's wrong with you?" guard number two grunted at him.

Looking ghostly white while turning his head in every which direction, he answered, "N-n-nothing. I just had a pain shoot up my leg." Getting his bearings, he continued sarcastically, "You know, that's what happens when you make people sit too long."

"Shut up and be still, or I'll have to gag you," answered the guard.

Mouth hanging open in awe, Jason replied, "Yeah, sure, whatever."

Rachel, concerned for her husband, whispered, "What's really wrong, Jason?"

Still stunned and looking around, he asked, "You don't see them, do you?"

"See who? The guards? Jason, you're scaring me. What do you see?"

"Angels. Big, huge, shiny, serious-looking angels holding flaming swords. Four standing around each of us."

The two guards broke out laughing, thinking he was having a negative reaction to the drugs he'd been given earlier.

Rachel looked around her chair and the room and then looked at Jason and said, "Honey, I don't see anything."

Stone, who had been sitting watching the whole scene with amusement, leaned forward and whispered, "They've been with us since the house. They're the answer to my congregation's prayers."

Rachel and Fox stared at him, dumbstruck. Jason, still looking around at the heavenly host, whispered back, "You mean, you've seen them all along? If they're guarding us, why did we get caught?"

"We got caught because it's what God wants, but we're under His protection, so just have faith and keep your wits about you."

Before Rachel could speak, the door opened and Damious walked in. Looking smug as usual, he dismissed the guards. "Well, how are my detainees?" Fox started to open his mouth, but Damious cut him off. "I have a visitor for you, Mr. Stone." Opening the door wider and stepping to the side, he continued, "Isabelle, here's your surprise."

When Isabelle saw Stone, she ran to him, hugged him, and kissed him passionately. It was a kiss which he reciprocated. When their kiss had finished, she whispered in his ear, "I'm sorry. You were right."

Damious, disgusted by the whole display of affection, pulled Isabelle back, leaving Stone confused and furious at Damious. "Isabelle, you may leave now. Mr. Stone will be leaving us soon, but I wanted you to be able to say good-bye—for good."

Isabelle began to protest, but one look from Damious stopped her cold, and she sadly left the room.

"Why did you do that to her, Damious?" Stone spat through clenched teeth. "You didn't need to hurt her like that."

"Of course I did, Mr. Stone. She's going to be my wife one of these days, and I need her to know that you are truly gone."

Laughing at him, Stone said, "She'll never marry you, Mikey—"

Stopping him midsentence with a fist to the mouth, Damious, smiling evilly, said, "Yes, she will, *Andy*. She doesn't have a choice."

"I'm going to kill you, Damious. I will," Stone spoke weakly through the blood trickling from his split lip.

"Now, Andrew, I thought you were a good Christian man. Isn't it against your beliefs to kill someone in cold blood?" He left the room laughing like a madman as the two guards reappeared.

Stone dropped his head in defeat while Rachel and Jason watched in awe—Rachel, because she never knew her brother had such deep feelings for Isabelle and Jason because while the two men were battling, the angels that were standing guard around Stone began fighting with what he guessed were their evil counterparts. He couldn't help wondering if Stone's scrap with Damious would have been worse without the angel's protection.

Leaning forward toward Andrew, he asked, "Did you see the angels fighting?"

"No. I took my eyes off the things of God. I got swept up in my hatred of Damious." Looking at his friend, he asked, "Were they really fighting? What were they fighting?"

"Yeah, they were fighting! It looked like two giant bats, like the creatures I released from the desert."

Rachel interrupted, "Look. I don't know what either of you are seeing, and I don't understand all this God stuff. Heck, I haven't been to church since I left home, but I do know that if all this stuff is real, then we have to give our troubles over to God, don't we, Andrew? You're the priest. How do we do it?"

Looking at his sister with sadness in his heart for her unbelief but joy for her faith, he answered with a little more strength, "Well, little sis. Jason and I have already given our lives to God. I see that you have faith, but you've pushed God away."

Taking over, Fox continued, "Pastor Stewart told me that there wasn't anything I needed to do. He said Jesus did it all on the cross and through the Father and Spirit in the resurrection. All I had to do was quit denying and pushing Him away, so that's what I did. I just quit fighting, and His spirit came into me and filled me with a feeling I can't even describe. Pastor Stewart baptized me in the river and spent about a week showing me scriptures that applied to my life and praying with me. Then he sent me off to find Andrew."

Changing the subject, he went on, "I always heard Christians talk about God's will for them and what they could do to show

God to the world, but it always rang hollow. One minute, they would say something was God's will, but then when it didn't work out, they would say that they misunderstood or that God had a new plan for them. Pastor Stewart told me that I didn't need to worry about what I needed to do because God would show me in His own time. All I had to be ready for was to go when I was called. Thankfully, he also said that if I mess up, God will forgive me. I guess he was right because I didn't do anything to be able to see angels fighting demons, but I am."

Still not sure, she looked at her brother and asked, "Is that right? I don't have to do anything? What about changing my life? Don't I have to be perfect? I just don't think I can be what a Christian should be."

Feeling renewed by his friend's testimony, Stone prayed in his spirit for the Lord to speak through him and answered, "He's right. You don't have to do anything. God will convict you in areas that need changing. You just have to be willing to let Him change you. Rachel, I can tell that God's convicting you, but you're pulling away. It's scary—believe me, I know—but once you let go of the fear, you'll just be changed. Just give up your will."

With tears in her eyes, she looked away from the two men she loved most in the world, and simply said, "I-I-I'm just not ready."

Jason's heart wanted to burst as he fought against his bonds. He wanted to comfort his wife. "It's okay, Rach. When it's time, you'll be ready."

A knock came at the door. Johnny opened it, surprised to see Isabelle instead of Damious. "Hello, Ms. Zenn. What can I do for you?"

Finding strength she didn't realize she had, Isabelle said, "I've come for one of the prisoners. I need to see him alone in my room."

"I'm sorry, Ms. Zenn. Mr. Damious said we were to keep them here."

"Excuse me, *guard*, but am I or am I not the owner of this foundation? If I say Mr. Stone will accompany me to my bedroom, then you will make it so, won't you!"

"Yes, ma'am." Johnny walked over to Andrew and escorted him to the door. "Would you like me to untie his hands, Ms. Zenn?"

"No. I think I'll feel safer with his hands bound. Thank you." Noticing Andrew's two companions tied up as well, Isabelle spoke to both guards, "I don't want these two left here in Mr. Damious's office. Take them to the Orchid Meditation Garden, untie them, and bring them some food. Then stand guard outside the door. The Orchid Garden is far more secure than Mr. Damious's office, and there are no sharp items for them to use in an escape attempt, which I'm sure they've been plotting." Looking Andrew in the, eye she said, "Now, Mr. Stone, will you please follow me?"

Stunned at her boldness, Stone could do nothing other than nod and follow.

* * *

In the pit, Angelous had been getting reports about the forces of the enemy infiltrating the foundation. First, Lucius reported an actual intrusion by an archangel, and then Adder had said he felt a powerful presence near his fake garden, not to mention the short skirmish two of his own demonic guards fought in Damious's office. Trycon's failure must have been greater than he realized. The human, Stewart, should never have been allowed to escape.

He convened a meeting of his demon lords, twenty-four in all. Calling the meeting to order, he growled, "Attention! We are more powerful than ever before! The great awakening has brought many of our imprisoned brothers back to us. We have deceived much of the human world, but the enemy still has a small remnant left. We are tasked by the Great One to destroy those remaining loyal to the Way. You must give the humans loyal to us ideas and dreams of the destruction of the Church and the chosen race. The time has come!"

The demon lords laughed and, as one, shrieked, "Glory and honor to the highest one, Great Lucifer, the first of all against the One!" As the cry went up, demons, from guardians to the lowest imp, joined in the celebration of the awakening. A swirling mass of leathery wings and claws mixed with red and orange flaming swords whooped and hollered as the demonic parade tortured lost souls captive in their hell.

Suddenly, a blinding white light broke the darkness, throwing the reveling into chaos. Black demons shot up out of the abyss into the night sky above the foundation. Angels of The One battled the lords of the damned. Swords of red flames thundered against swords of white flames, each causing a burst of lighting and a deafening boom. Angels slashed demons, sending red tendrils of smoke back to the abyss. Demons slashed angels, sending white streams of light up to the heavens. The battle raged for two hours until the legions of the damned were thrown back into the abyss and the victorious host of the heavens disappeared back to the throne. Only one was left to guard a little red car sitting in the parking lot.

Listening intently to the conversations going on in Damious's office, Marcus was taking stock of his own life. He was not raised in the church, but he had always had a great respect for it. Most of the small villages he worked with on his travels through Africa were aided by various churches. They brought food and clothes but also a sense of respect and love. He had always wondered how a god that was supposed to be full of love and mercy could allow the evils of genocide, not to mention regular murders, rapes, mutilations, and all around-destruction, but listening to Stone and Fox talk about the choices men make, it all started to make more sense. Maybe it wasn't God's fault.

He knew enough about the Bible to know that God gave mankind free will. God created a perfect world, and man chose to destroy it. It was man and not God responsible for the evils. It made so much sense. Those who claimed the one true God, Christians and even Jews, were the ones who ministered selflessly. They came with no motive other than to serve and share their message. They spread the love; they lived the love. It was always the evil hearts of men that moved others to violence and malevolence. One needed only to let God do it. He was determined to talk with Stone more about this when it was all over.

While mulling these thoughts over in his head, the sky above the foundation suddenly opened up, and Marcus saw a sight he would never have believed possible: dark beings and light beings fighting. He realized they must be angels and demons, just like Fox was describing in the office. He watched the battle, enraptured at the sight. Just as suddenly as it had opened, the sky closed again, and there was nothing but stars and the moon. Marcus had had enough. He opened the car door, fell to his knees, lifted his hands to the sky, and called upon God to fill him like He did for Fox. Marcus was not disappointed. Like Fox said, it was an indescribable feeling. Marcus rose to his feet, climbed back into his car, and continued to listen to the conversations going on within the foundation, all the while praying for Rachel to receive the gift, the most precious gift in the world.

* * *

Johnny and his partner each grabbed a prisoner and escorted them to the Orchid Meditation Garden as Isabelle had ordered, stopping at the cafeteria to get them some food. Sitting them in the middle of the room on the floor, Johnny untied their hands as the other guard set their food on a bench on the far side of the room. "Now you enjoy the time you have left," Johnny said. "We'll be right outside the door."

Rachel reached out, took his hand, and squeezed it gently. "Thank you, Johnny. We will, and I hope you know we don't hold any of this against you. We know you're just doing your job."

"Yeah, like the Nazis," Fox inserted.

Rachel elbowed him in the ribs. "Forgive my husband's behavior. He's tired and angry about the situation."

Fox went to say something else, but Rachel put her hand over his mouth. Johnny looked at them with sadness in his eyes and then smiled at Rachel, saying, "I really am sorry, ma'am, but if this is going to be your final hours, you really couldn't have gotten a nicer place." Turning, he walked to the door, closed and locked it, leaving the two alone.

The room was very beautiful. The floor wasn't a floor at all, but a carpet of well-tended grass. The ceiling and the far wall were made completely of glass, like a conservatory, and the waning moon and stars sparkled high above them. Benches were scattered around the room in various places for meditation and just pure enjoyment. However, the thing that made the room spectacular were the planters filled with hundreds of orchids of every color and species. The air in the room was almost intoxicating with fragrance. Each bench had one or two blankets folded neatly next to them for anyone wanting to lie or sit on the grass. The temperature and humidity were regulated, so the room felt tropical but not uncomfortable.

Walking over to retrieve the food, Fox said, "What was that all about? Telling the kid it was okay what they're doing. It's not okay, Rach."

"Like you said, he's just a kid. Anyway, when we do try our escape, wouldn't you rather have him sympathetic to our plight, just in case we need him?" Accepting her meal gratefully after spreading out one of the blankets, she sat down to eat.

Sitting down next to his wife, Fox agreed, saying, "Yeah, I guess you're right. I just have a problem bringing myself to be nice to a man who is keeping me prisoner."

They ate their meals in silence, and after putting the trays next to the door, Fox called on Marcus. "Hey, Marcus, you still out there?"

"Reading you five by five, buddy. What can I do you for?"

"I don't know. You heard we're in the Orchid Meditation Garden? Can you get someone to get us out?"

"I'll try. FYI, those glass windows in there are made of a special polymer that is unbreakable. I checked out schematics for the room, so you're not getting out that way." Teasing them, he said, "You two better be careful. Orchids are a flower of love, you know. Two married people who haven't been together for two years in a room full of orchids...dangerous!"

"Thanks for the warning because of course that is what's been going through our minds. Come on, Rach, let's get it on!"

They all had a good laugh together, and then Marcus excused himself to call his contact. Walking over to her husband and gently walking her fingers up his arm, she smiled and whispered in his ear, "Well, Jason, what should we do?" Turning her face to his, she couldn't help giggling at his expression. "Is that a look of confusion, terror, or both?"

Changing his demeanor, he grabbed her by the waist and pulled her close. With a wry smile, he brought his lips to within millimeters of hers, pausing just a moment to move his mouth to her ear, whispering, "My dearest Rachel, the thought of making love with you right now both excites and terrifies me, but if you insist"—he pulled back quickly, surprising her, and in his best frat-boy yelp, with a flourish of his arm, said—"let's get it on!"

The two began laughing uncontrollably at the joke and fell into each other's arms as they slid to the floor. Kissing Fox quickly on his lips, she chuckled. "You know, I knew there was a reason I married you, Jason Fox! I have missed your sense of humor." Getting a little more serious, she continued, "I really am sorry that I left you for such a waste of time. Who was I to think I could change the world?"

Touching her chin and lifting it so they looked in each other's eyes, he said, "Rachel, this is going to sound lame, but God has a plan for everything. You had to leave so I could go work for Tempess and release those creatures. You needed to contact Marcus so he could be here to help us. Whatever plan you concocted for the UGSE was in the works decades earlier. You weren't the one who came up with the idea of sustainable development. You just took it to the next level. Even if we stop this mess now, someone else is going to come along eventually and take it to the next level until it's completed. We all just play our parts, but I really believe that in the end it will all work out. I know I only just started learning about the Bible and about prophecies for the end of days, but it seems that the UGSE may be the final piece of the puzzle. Then again, the world may go on for millennia. All we can do is tell the truth about what's going on and hope enough people are still awake enough to hear and fight for change."

Looking deep into his eyes, into his soul, Rachel leaned forward and kissed him. "You're right, Jason, I don't understand all this, and it does seem lame, but I believe you, and if you believe it, I believe it."

Unable to control the feelings that had been budding in them, they embraced each other, and Fox gently laid his wife on the ground, continuing to kiss her softly, slowly. Placing one of her fingers to his lips, Rachel quietly said, "I guess Marcus was right."

* * *

At first, Damious was furious that Isabelle had subverted his orders, but on a second look, he decided he couldn't have planned things better himself. Everything seemed to be falling into place. With Isabelle's plentiful charms, Andrew Stone would not be able to resist her, and his feeble attempts at stopping him would be thwarted. After all, Damious knew Stone's real weakness. Also, sticking Fox and his estranged wife together in the most sexually charged room in the place should take their focus off their mission.

While Isabelle and most of the other mindless plebes in this place believed they were here to help each other overcome their weaknesses, Damious knew that this place thrived on getting people to embrace their weaknesses. Encouraging people to believe in and live out their fantasies was the real power of this place and the UGSE. Love, peace, patience, goodness, joy, gentleness, faithfulness, and self-control had been usurped from the enemy and made into a worldly mantra. When people believed they could bring about all these fruits by their own abilities, they gave up their need for God and turned to their governments. The leaders of the world would give them their desires and make them believe they were good, but really, they were just slaves to those pulling the strings. It was a glorious plan, and so simple. Throughout history, the poor had been forced into slavery and subjugation, but now they just lined up to give up their freedom and join the peasantry. It truly was an amazing thing to watch. Damious loved it.

Taking stock of the events of the past two days, finding Fox and Stone and capturing them, he felt excitement at the prospect of putting the plan into effect. *If Burke pulls off phase one tomorrow, we'll be on our way*, thought Damious. Checking that he and Tempess were scheduled to fly out to Denver tonight, he thought of contacting Angelous, but after their last meeting, he thought better of it. *Let him come and speak to me for info if he wants it.* Thinking about Angelous's outburst filled Damious with a fiery rage and thoughts of breaking something. Instead of breaking things, he let his mind wander to Isabelle and Stone. The thought of what they were getting up to helped alleviate the anger. He decided to get some sleep even though it was nearly four o'clock in the morning. Turning off the lights in his office, he closed the door and walked to his room, intending to get a good night's or, as it was, a good day's sleep.

After being asleep for about two hours, Damious was transported to a part of Angelous's lair that he'd never seen before. Instead of the normal hustle and bustle of demons torturing human souls, it was the demons screaming in anguish. Shocked at the sight and sounds, Damious wondered what was going on. Suddenly, out of nowhere, Angelous attacked him like a kamikaze pilot targeting an aircraft carrier. Too fast for Damious to dodge, the demon hit him full force in the chest, causing him to double over in pain, gasping for breath.

"What the—" Damious wheezed before Angelous cut him off with another blow to the mouth.

"Shut up, Michael! Don't you dare to ask me what is going on. I am asking you! What's going on up there? We have been attacked by the One's host and have accumulated many casualties! Don't make me ask you again!"

Stunned and seeing double from the attack, Damious tried to get to his feet, stumbling back to the ground. Unable to speak, he looked into Angelous's murderous eyes for the first time with fear. Trying to make sense of the demon's rant, Damious again tried to stand, this time managing to wobble on his feet. "I don't know." Damious tried to sound contrite, but his anger was flaring, and his words were laced with malice. "We brought Stone and Fox to the foundation like you asked. They have been neutralized. Both are experiencing carnal pleasures, just as you desired. Believe me, they are not praying or casting spells or whatever the miscreants do." Standing up straight and looking the demon in the eye, he continued, "And I'm getting tired of you attacking me!" As a demon flew by, Damious grabbed the flaming sword from its hand and struck Angelous with it, causing red vapor to mist from the wound. "There! How's that, you psychotic piece of crap?"

Stunned at Damious's boldness and incensed at his disrespectful attack, Angelous first swung its sword at the demon that Damious had disarmed, turning it to red vapor, and then struck Damious. Being human, Damious did not evaporate or die. In this realm, the living could only be tortured, but the scream that proceeded from his mouth would have made any demon lord proud.

Spewing yellow sulfuric vapor, Angelous screamed at Damious, "You insignificant fool! You belong to me! I do not belong to you!" Lowering its voice to a normal snarl, it continued, "I thought I had settled this with you at our last meeting. I am the master, and you are my slave!" Narrowing its eyes, it continued through Damious's whimpering, "If we have the two here, then it must be Stewart. Your incompetence in that matter is inexcusable. He must be stopped! Your plans are secondary to ours. Once the One is defeated, then all your plans can fall into place, but as long as we're under attack, you will fail!"

Being finished with Damious but not wanting him to be done suffering, Angelous called one of his elite demons, Morpheus, after the god of nightmares. Bowing low, Morpheus asked, "Yes, my lord, how may I serve you?"

With a malicious gleam in its eye, Angelous instructed, "Take Mr. Damious to one of your special rooms and give him a nightmare to remember."

Smiling wickedly with its pointy black teeth extended, Morpheus replied, "Yes, my lord. Gladly, my lord."

Before allowing Damious to be taken away, Angelous explained where they were. "This, Michael, is the abyss, the place even demons fear to come, the place they are sent to heal after being vaporized. Time spent here is torturous for them. You are one of the few humans we've invited here. I hope by the time I see you again, you will have learned your place. Morpheus here is very good at his work."

Pleading with Angelous to let him go, Damious promised to never act that way again; however, Angelous was not a merciful master and wasn't about to let one of its slaves behave so insolently. Morpheus willingly grabbed a screaming Michael Damious around the throat and dragged him off to its special place.

Around two o'clock in the afternoon, Damious awoke with a scream in his throat and drenched in sweat. After getting his heart rate under control, he got out of his bed, climbed into a hot shower, and scrubbed himself almost raw trying to wash away the memory of his torture at the hands of Morpheus. He dried off and got dressed in a pair of jeans and a polo shirt, with a wool sweater as the top layer. Combing his wet hair back off his forehead, he looked at his reflection in the mirror. He'd never looked so haggard and pale before. He hoped after a cup of coffee and lunch he'd get some color back in his face.

Damious took a moment to remember the conversation with Angelous and allowed the rage to fill him. Feeling renewed in his spirit, Damious opened his door and limped toward his office. Even though a sword strike in the other world couldn't kill him, it left its scar on this side. Once in his office and sitting at his desk, he called Tania to bring him some coffee and get his car ready to take him out to meet with Tempess for lunch before their scheduled trip to Colorado.

*   *   *

Isabelle and Stone walked in silence to her room. Without looking at him, she unlocked her door, opened it, and allowed Stone to enter first. After closing her door, she untied his hands and walked around to face him. Rubbing his wrists to get the blood circulating freely, he looked her in the eyes and asked, "What's going on, Izzy? Why did you bring me here?"

Averting her eyes to the floor, she replied, "I need to talk with you. I need to apologize to you." Returning her gaze to his and reaching her hand to caress his cheek, she continued, "I need you to forgive me."

Placing his hand over hers, he confessed, "Isabelle, I forgave you years ago. It was too much for me to ask you to leave on such short notice. I know you did what you felt you had to, just like I did what I felt I had to." Placing his hands around her waist, he pulled her close. "I never stopped loving you, but I can't just pick up where we left off. I've changed. I've moved on."

Resting her head on his chest, she asked, "Why? You kissed me back in Michael's office. You didn't seem to have any trouble picking up where we left off." Looking into his face, trying to read his eyes, she continued, "I have dreamed of this moment since you left, and it never ended with you telling me you moved on. Have you? Have you really?"

Lowering his gaze and releasing her, he said, "Yes, Isabelle. I gave my life to Jesus Christ. I became a Christian, and I'm not about to give that up. If I give in to my desire—and yes, I really want to—I'll be returning to a place I don't want to go back to." Walking through her room and into her garden, he was startled to see the plant life. "Isabelle! These are unmodified plants! How on earth did you keep these after I left? I thought those cretins had destroyed everything." Turning in every direction, mouth open, he took in the splendor of the room. "This is so awesome!"

With tears in her eyes, she walked over to him, took his hand in hers, and led him over to the pond. Kneeling down and motioning him to join her, she whispered, "I have something else to show you." Gently, she moved the brush back, revealing the flowers he had shown her so long ago. Even though the moon was waning, the flowers sparkled like jewels.

Stunned at her revelation, Stone looked at the flowers and then at Isabelle, and all the walls he was trying to build came crashing down. He kissed her, softly at first, and then their hunger for each other took over, and their kiss became deep, long, and passionate. Slowly they stood, continuing their kiss. Andrew gently drew her into his arms, carried her back into her room, and laid her on the bed. She entwined her fingers in his hair, pulling him down to her, and continued to kiss him. She whispered to him, "I love you, Andrew. I love you so much. Promise me you'll never leave me again. Promise me you'll take me with you."

Rolling onto his side, resting his head on his elbow while she unbuttoned his shirt, he reached his hand down and stopped her. Looking into her confused eyes made his heart melt. He wanted to take her and love her and keep her safe. Gently touching her cheek with the backs of his fingers, he said, "Izzy, I will take you with me, but this time, it's not going to be as easy." Sitting on the edge of the bed, rebuttoning his shirt, glad of the fact they didn't take this moment to its conclusion, he continued, "Michael wants me dead, not to mention Jason and my sister. I can't leave without them. I've also got to get some information about what's really going on," Stone paused for a moment and then continued, "his plans. I need to get back into his office, Isabelle."

Still lying on her back, surprised that he stopped, she returned his gaze, and a mischievous grin grew across her face. Sitting up next to him and reaching across him to her bedside table, she picked up a tiny smart drive and held it in front of him. "You mean, something like the entire contents of his hard drive on something like this?"

A look of wonder spread across his face as he realized what was in her hand. Leaning over and kissing her again, he said, "You never cease to amaze me! What else have you been up to, Isabelle?"

She began telling her story—about the voice, about her mother's singing, about Jerry, about her search for him, and finally, about her vision. "Andrew, I asked Jesus to save me, but I really don't know what that means. I mean, I felt a change, an indwelling like I never have before, but after the vision was over, the euphoria wore off. I still feel different, but I'm so afraid of Adder coming to me, and there's one more thing I have to tell you. It's about my mother." Changing her voice to a whisper, although not realizing why, she leaned in close to him and said, "My mother didn't die in childbirth. My father had her killed." Tears filled her eyes. "It turns out that my father wasn't really my father. My real dad's name was Donald Stewart, and I think Michael is looking for him. I mentioned his name to Adder a few weeks ago, and he got angry at me. He'd never been angry with me before."

Shocked by this revelation, Stone held her close and said, "I think getting out of here is going to be way more difficult." Taking her by the shoulders and gently pushing her back so she could see his face, he continued, "I know Stewart. I know where he is, and that's where I'm going to take you when we leave."

"What?" she asked, confused. "How do you know him? What's going on here?" She pulled abruptly away from him and backed away.

"Izzy—"

"D-don't call me that. Are you a part of this? Is this all some kind of plot?" Without warning, she swooned and fell to the ground.

Stone bolted over to her and cradled her head gently in his lap, calling out her name. She just lay there, still. He checked for a pulse and breathing, both of which were present, so he did the only thing he could think of—he prayed for her. While he prayed, he felt a presence in the room. Looking up, he saw a demon searching for something or someone. He assumed it must be Adder. When he looked back at Isabelle, he noticed a shimmering shield over her held by two angels. Amazed, he looked back up at the demon. It was pretty much the way Jason had described it, except this one looked furious. He kept trying to penetrate the shield and reach Isabelle, but the angels held fast. Suddenly, he heard a voice reminding him that he had the power to command the demon to depart. The angels looked at him expectantly, so he stood up and spoke the demon's name. "Adder!"

Adder looked at him with shock and began snarling.

"Adder! I command you in the name of our Lord Jesus Christ to leave here!"

Adder, stunned at being commanded by Stone, replied, "I don't think so, man of The One! You have no authority over me!" It drew its sword and swung it toward Stone.

Stone flinched as Adder's sword was met by another angel, one guarding him. Adder screamed in anger.

"Adder! I command you in the name of our Lord Jesus Christ, *leave here!*"

"No!" Adder swung his sword, but each time, it was parried by the angel.

"In the name of Jesus Christ, I command you to leave!"

With one final scream, Adder shot up through the ceiling. The angels looked over at Andrew with approving smiles. Exhausted after his bout with Adder, Andrew melted to the floor and continued cradling Isabelle's head until she finally awoke. She looked up at him, smiling, and sat up, pulling him close, hugging him, and loving him with everything she had. "Andrew, you won't believe this, or maybe you will after what you just went through."

"How, how do you know what just happened?"

"You remember the angel I told you about? The one I called Veritas? Well, he came to me and said I wasn't ready to battle Adder and that you had to do it. So he brought me out of myself, and I watched you battle with Adder. You saved me, Andrew." She kissed him, and he kissed her back. "Veritas told me that someday God will use me too. Do you think so? Do you think I'll ever be worthy to be of use to Him?"

Looking into her eyes, he answered with levity in his voice, "Well, since Veritas means truth, and he is a messenger from God, I think he probably spoke the truth."

"But I've worked against Him my whole life. How can I make up for that? Why does He even want me? Why did He forgive me?" She started crying.

Standing up and pulling her to her feet, he kissed her tears. He walked her out to the garden again, sat with her on one of the benches as the dawn began to break, and said, "Let me tell you my story, Izzy, after I left here. Believe me, if God could forgive me, He can forgive you."

* * *

Fox and Rachel just couldn't seem to get enough of each other. Both knew they needed to find a way to escape, but they couldn't seem to pull away from each other. Exhausted, they fell asleep in each other's arms as they watched the sun rising through the ceiling. Rachel began to dream. Vague images and shapes came into her mind until they formed an image. It was a place she didn't recognize, but it was familiar to her nonetheless.

She walked toward a cabin in the woods, tall aspens waving in the breeze, leaves preparing to fall. She walked up the steps to the porch and knocked on the door. When no one answered, she tried the doorknob. It turned, so she opened the door and walked in. She realized this was the cabin Jason had told her about. She recognized the armory and the room filled with computer equipment, the fireplace, the living room, and the kitchen/dining area. As she looked around, she noticed a crown sitting on one of the chairs. Curious, she walked over and examined it more closely. She noticed a name imprinted on the inside: Rachel Fox. She picked up the crown, running her fingers over the beautiful jewels encrusted all around it, and she wondered what it could possibly mean. Then she heard a voice. "Rachel." She looked all around for the person who spoke but saw no one.

Setting the crown back on the chair, the voice returned. "Rachel."

Becoming annoyed at being called, she answered back, "Who's there? What do You want?"

"I want you to let Me place the crown on your head."

"Why? I'm nothing special. I'm certainly not royalty. What possible use could I have for a crown?"

"Do you know who I am?

"Well, I assume You're my subconscious trying to convince me that God is talking to me. Am I right?"

"Almost."

"What does *almost* mean? What! Is this really God?"

"Yes, Rachel, and I'm waiting for you to let Me help you."

"How do I know You're not one of those demons Jason and Drew talked about? And why do You have to wait for me? Can't You just zap me or something if You're God?"

"I don't do *zapping*, Rachel. Your parents already brought you to Me at your baptism. You are My child, but you keep pushing Me away. I'm here simply waiting for you to stop pushing. I'm waiting to give you your position in the kingdom of God."

Picking up the crown, Rachel placed it on her head. "Well, God, I already placed it on my head. It's here. Now You can leave me alone."

"That's not how it works, Rachel." The crown appeared back on the chair, and Rachel touched her head where it had sat. "The King crowns the heir. There is nothing you can do but quit pushing. I'm waiting."

Wanting to say "Yes, do it" but not being able to say the words, Rachel waited for the voice to say something else, but it was gone.

Rachel sat on the floor and wondered what was wrong with her. Her surroundings changed, and she found herself back lying with Fox on the floor of the Orchid Garden. She thought how amazing it was that she could smell the flowers even in her dream. Suddenly, a light brighter than the sun appeared, momentarily blinding her. As her vision cleared, she noticed the angels surrounding them. After the initial shock, she became embarrassed, thinking of them being there the whole time. One of the angels spoke to her, "Rachel, it's time for you and Jason to leave. Wake him and get dressed."

Stunned but not exactly surprised, she asked, "Are you going to show us how to get out?"

The angel answered, "Something like that, yes."

Shaking Fox awake, she told him what the angel said, and he obediently followed.

"Okay, babe. I'm dressed. What's this angel saying now?" Fox yawned.

"Can't you see them?"

"Of course I can see them. I've been seeing them since Damious's office, except when we were"—he winked—"you know, but they have yet to speak to me, so what're they saying?"

"They aren't saying anything right now, but the one that talked with me is motioning us to follow. Can't you see it?"

Looking at all the angels, he answered, "Nope. All I see is eight angels with swords drawn looking ready for a fight. I guess since it's your dream, only you can see it. Don't worry, though, I'll be a good boy and follow your lead." He saluted her, making her giggle. "But you know, it would be more fun to stay here a bit longer...wink, wink."

Walking toward him and kissing him, she agreed, "You're right. For some reason, I just want to stay."

The angel spoke loudly, "No! You must fight! This room is full of spells and potions. You were put here to keep you from your mission. You need to leave now!"

Jason was the first to come to his senses, shaking his head like he was clearing out cobwebs and said, "Wow! I heard that. I guess that explains last night." Returning to his normal gibes, he prattled on, "And here I was thinking I was all that. Bummer!"

Her head clearing too, she laughed and joked, "Yeah, and I thought I had such a stud muffin. I guess I'll have to go back to plain old Jason."

"Hey! What about me? Here I was thinking I had a hot cross bun, and I'll have to go back to a plain old muffin."

"Oh well, we'll just have to deal!"

The angel rolled its eyes and sighed. "People! Always oblivious to the danger of their situation. We need to go."

"Fine," Rachel said, taking her husband's hand. "Touchy angels."

They followed the angel to the door, and it walked right through it. "Well, this is a dream. I guess we should walk on through." She took a step forward. "Ow!" she cried as she hit the door. Touching the door, she looked at Fox and asked, "This is a dream, isn't it?"

Reaching out for the door, Fox knocked on it. "Feels pretty solid to me. Maybe we are awake. Freaky."

Punching him lovingly on the arm, she was about to speak when the door opened and the angel motioned them through. They walked through the door expecting to see the guards sleeping or knocked out, but they were standing tall and alert.

Leaning toward his wife, Fox whispered, "Why are they just standing there? We must be dreaming."

"I don't know, Jason. This is really creeping me out. I hope I wake up soon. I'd hate to think what they'll do to us if they notice us, even in a dream."

The angel held its finger to its lips, shushing them and motioning for them to continue forward. They walked in silence through crowds of people who seemed oblivious to the fact they were there. The angel stopped in front of a door and told Rachel to knock and trust the boy on the other side. Confused at this dream, she did as she was told. When the door opened, a smiling young man said, "Hello, Mr. and Mrs. Fox, my name is Jerry. I was told you'd be coming. Hurry inside before someone sees you."

Amazed that this young man knew their name they entered his room, closed the door, and asked together, "How do you know our names?"

"An angel named Amicus came to me and told me you'd be coming. Are you Christians?"

Fox answered for both of them, "Yes, we are, but why are you so excited about it?"

"I just came to know Jesus personally, and I want—no, need someone to talk with about it. It's just so awesome! Isn't it awesome to you?"

"I'm new at the whole thing too, so I get what you mean about awesome, but I don't know how much help I can be to you."

"Just being with others who believe like me is enough. Are you going to take me with you? Amicus said you would."

"Well, I guess if your friend said we would, we will, but we'll need your help. Do you know Isabelle Zenn? She's got our friend, and we have to get him out with us."

"I know Ms. Isabelle. She's my friend. I can go see her if you want me too."

"Yes, Jerry. That would be great," Rachel added. "Is this real or a dream? We walked through the guards and the campus without anyone so much as acknowledging our presence."

Laughing, Jerry answered, "Well, Ms. Rachel, I guess this is real because I'd never be asleep at this time of the day. And as for people not seeing you, well, I guess God can do anything He wants to." Clapping his hands together, he finished, "Too cool!" Then he left to find Isabelle.

Remembering their earpieces, Jason called out to Marcus, "Hey, Marcus. You out there?"

"You know I am, man," the voice on the other end spoke.

Rachel asked, "Marcus, what have you found out. When can we get out of here?"

"The word around the foundation is that Damious is taking a plane out to Colorado to be a part of some experiment. I'm making arrangements to get us on the plane, but it's only gonna happen if you guys get out of there, and now you're bringing someone extra? We might have to stuff one of our extra guests in the trunk of this battery-operated toy. Have I mentioned how much I despise these cars?"

"Yeah, you've mentioned it once or twice," Stone chimed in.

Marcus, surprised and angry, said, "Whoa, man, I was wondering if you'd been killed. I lost your signal once you entered your girlfriend's room. What's going on?"

"Sorry, brother, I took it out once I got situated in here. We had some crazy stuff going on in here. Anyway, what's that you said about Colorado? Damious is going out there? It must have something to do with my church. I have to get back."

Fox jumped in, "I have to get to Colorado too. Stewart is expecting me, but for some reason, I feel that Rachel and Marcus need to get back to LA and get their people together."

Shocked that her husband would want her to leave him again, Rachel protested, "Wait a minute! I'm not going anywhere without you, Jason." Her eyes started filling with tears.

Seeing Rachel cry broke Fox's heart, but he steadied himself and held fast to his thought. Hugging Rachel tightly, he said, "Rach, stop. You and Marcus have a job to do in LA. Andrew and I have a job to do in Colorado. We'll be back together. Heck, we've spent two years apart! What's a little more?" Touching her chin and raising it so their eyes met, he kissed her and continued, "God will protect us. With all that we've seen today, you must believe that, even if you don't yet accept it."

Looking down and then in her husband's eyes again, she agreed, "Okay. I'll go with Marcus, but if you go and get yourself killed, I'll never forgive you. What's the plan? Anyone?"

Marcus jumped in, "I'm on it, just give me a little more time. Are you all okay where you're at? Because the longer we can go without making a scene, the better."

"As long as Damious keeps away from me and Isabelle, we'll be good here. What about you and Rachel?" Stone asked.

"I think we'll be fine for now, but the sooner we're out of here, the better. We're both kinda freaking out in here," Fox responded.

"Right then. Keep your pants on, and I mean that literally, Foxes," Marcus joked. "And I'll get back with you in thirty minutes. Cool?"

Everyone answered in unison, "Great," and then Marcus set to work.

* * *

Before Stone began his tale, Isabelle walked into her room, retrieving a blanket to sit on, "I'd prefer to sit on the ground, if you don't mind, Andrew." Spreading out the blanket over the grass of her garden, Isabelle sat down, grabbing Andrew's hand and pulling him next to her. "Okay, now I'm ready to hear your story."

Lying on his back looking up at the sky, Stone began, "After I left here, I flew over to Europe. I had some friends working on a dig in England looking for Druid artifacts, so I thought I'd just pop in on them. They were happy to have me there, and I stayed with them for a few months, drinking, partying, hooking up, and working in between hangovers. I was just happy to be away from all the stupid political stuff going on and trying to forget about the part I played in the environmental crisis."

Turning his head to look at Isabelle, he continued, "You know, it was strange being out on the British Isles watching the modified plant life taking over. Even after three years, the changes were occurring. It was like one day the native plants were dying, and the next they sprang to new life, albeit slightly different. No one else seemed to notice the changes except me. I guess that's because I knew what to look for. I just couldn't stand to be around it anymore, so I went to Paris, France. I figured if there was one place I could go to get away from my sins, it would be a city, and Paris seemed like as good a choice as any. Then the war broke out."

Looking back at the sky, he mused, "Who would've thought the French would have the will to fight? But I guess if you take away enough freedom, you can get anyone to rebel."

Laughing, Isabelle added, "Yeah, after the Islamic takeover failed, you'd have thought all of Europe would've had enough of fighting, but when it comes to taking away a European's right to have sex or drink, watch out!"

"Yeah, the UGSE is much more lenient in those areas. Anyway, back to my story. After the resistance blew up the embassies and overpowered the police, there was chaos everywhere. It was like you join the resistance or hide away. Well, you know me, I'm not one to hide, so I got in touch with Marcus Daedalus, a guy I met years ago in Africa. If anyone was going to be resistance, it would be him, and sure enough, he was the head of the African resistance. I made my way to the coast and stowed away on a ship bound for Nigeria where Marcus had set up our meeting point. He flew us in a small Skyhawk to various safe locations until we arrived at his headquarters. I'm still not even sure where we were. I didn't join the resistance right away even though I was working with them. It's not like you can just leave. Once you're in, you're in. I was just happy to be fighting against the PTBs.

"Marcus was amazing. He had all this technology in the middle of nowhere running on solar, wind, and oil power. He had even figured out how to use sand as a power source! The man is a freakin' genius. His computer network was extensive, and he was in touch with people all over the world, commanding the troops from his little hideaway. I never knew anyone's name, mostly because I hadn't committed, but I worked on keeping all the equipment up to snuff while he managed the people and developed new weapons and electronic toys—you know, stuff like listening devices and untraceable phones. He was even trying to create laser weapons like in *Star Wars* or *Star Trek*. I still get excited just thinking about his creativity."

Isabelle lowered herself next to Andrew on the blanket and said, "I'd like to meet him someday. Is he still around? I know they killed a lot of the resistance leaders at the end of the war."

Turning his head to look at her, he answered, "He's still around, still creating, still fighting." Looking back at the sky, he went on, "About a year after I got there, he received an emergency call saying that we had been made and needed to get out of there, so we packed everything up in his truck. It was a big truck, and we drove out to a different airstrip that had a big military transport waiting and ready for us. About twenty men came and helped us unload the gear into the plane, and then we took off. God must have been with us even then because as the wheels lifted off the ground, a small army of global militia burst on the scene. I swear, if we'd taken off two minutes later, we'd have been toast."

Sitting up and turning to face Isabelle who was still lying on the floor, he hugged his knees to his chest. "Once we landed, he told me that we had to part ways. He had a commercial airline ticket for me to Australia. I asked him why we had to split up, and he just told me that I could do more in Australia. He had to meet with other leaders of the resistance, which was top secret. When I tried to protest, he apologized, then knocked me out. By the time I came to, I was halfway across the Indian Ocean with a black eye. Furious at him, I decided I was just gonna get off the plane and disappear. To you-know-where with him and the resistance. I was done with them—until I stepped off the plane."

Sitting up, Isabelle curiously asked, "What happened when you got off the plane?"

He took her hand, kissed it, then released it, and smiling, he joked, "Well, if you'd quit interrupting, I'll get to it."

Smiling back, she said, "Sorry. Go on."

"We landed in Canberra, and when I stepped off the plane, I was stunned. What should have been a bustling airport was a giant morgue. Bodies were everywhere—men, women, children, old people, and even babies just stacked side by side. The smell was unbelievable, but they said it was the coolest place they could put all the dead until they could take care of them. You see, the global militia had been through. After gassing the city, they came in and shot anyone left. They went through the prisons, hospitals, schools, homes, and businesses, killing everyone who hadn't fled. I was angrier than I had ever been. I found the commander of the resistance forces and told him Marcus had sent me. That was good enough for him. He geared me up with a uniform, weapons, and comms. I joined a group of fighters on their way out to take care of the murderous global militia, and when we caught up with them, we did just that."

Catching his breath and looking away from Isabelle shamefully while blinking away tears, the story went on. "The global militia was a group of mercenaries. From the looks of them, they were

from different countries, but their evil was from the same place—
the United Nations. We waited until they fell asleep and then
attacked. Some of my comrades had Special Forces training and
took out the guards pretty easily. They slit their throats or stabbed
them in order to kill them quickly, so as not to let them make
a noise. They were very good at their jobs. Then the rest of us
entered the tents." Choking up, he pushed Isabelle's hand away
as she reached out for him. "We forwent our guns and pulled out
our knives. With a pleasure that makes me sick now, I stabbed
a man through the back of his neck, severing his spinal cord.
Knowing that he didn't suffer made me not be so kind to the
next man. There were five more men in the tent. I knew that if
I wanted to make them suffer, then I had to start shooting to
disable them before they woke up. I guess the other guys had
the same idea because that's when all hell broke loose, and we all
started shooting. I think I killed three of the other men in the
tent because I only remember cutting up two people. We dragged
the few who survived out of the tents into the middle of their
camp, and we took our time. Hours of screams didn't deter us."

Giving Isabelle a haunted look, he asked, "Do you know that
when you cut someone, it doesn't spurt like you'd think? Unless
you hit an artery, the blood just kind of runs out. You can literally
watch someone bleed to death, and if you do it right, it can take a
very long time. Anyhow, by the time we were finished, they were
all dead, and we left them to rot. We didn't burn them, didn't bury
them. We just left them for the animals. We took their vehicles,
guns, food, and anything else we could salvage and drove back to
the city. We must have looked horrible, all covered in blood and
bits of gore, but everyone cheered us and patted us on the back.
We were heroes."

Isabelle looked sick and horrified but also sympathetic toward
the man she loved. "Do you want to stop now?"

Wiping tears from his eyes, he said, "No, I can finish. After I
got back to my room, I showered, but I just couldn't wash away

the blood. I scrubbed and scrubbed, but still I was red, mostly because I had scrubbed myself so hard. I got out of the shower, dressed, and lay down on my bed, numb. I fell asleep and had the worst nightmares—bloody bodies coming for me and trying to choke me. I woke up and ran to the bathroom to throw up. When I got back to my bed, I noticed the drawer was open a little and inside was a Bible. I remembered as a young teen going to youth group. The pastor told us a story about a soldier who had done some pretty bad stuff. He had nightmares, and his life had fallen into the gutter, but God forgave him and helped him stop having the nightmares. Well, I didn't know if I even believed in God at that point, but I couldn't live like this, and I didn't want to end up in the gutter. After all, I still wanted to help fight the global takeover, so I found a church and went in to pray."

Calming down, taking her hands, and looking into her eyes, he finished his story, "I met the most wonderful man there. His name was Pastor Timothy Mancina. He listened to my confession and asked me if I had been baptized before. I was confused because I had just finished telling him what I told you, and he acted like it was nothing. I told him I was baptized as a baby and was raised in the church. He asked me if I had ever confirmed my faith, and I said that I had. Then he asked me if I still believed what I had at my confirmation. Well, I was stunned. I hadn't even thought about it since the day, but I thought back and decided that yes, I did still believe all the stuff I had been taught. He told me that now I had to decide if I wanted to continue in that faith. I looked at him like he was crazy. Why else would I have come to the church? I asked him what I needed to do to make it up to God and what I could do for the church. What he said next amazed me. He told me that I didn't have to do anything. The fact that I had come there should tell me that God already was with me. He said that I needed to be still and listen to what God was trying to show me or say to me. He said the best thing I could do for the church was just to live my life to the glory of God, just to let Him work through me. It was just so simple. I'd never heard anything so easy.

"We walked up to the altar rail, knelt down, and then prayed the Lord's Prayer. As I knelt there, I felt the presence of God in a way I never had before, a kind of knowing and peace in my heart. I was forgiven. Pastor Mancina got up and brought me the Eucharist. After I took the bread and wine, he anointed me with oil and blessed me. Then he prayed scripture over me. 'The Lord is my light and my salvation; whom shall I fear…Wait for the Lord, be strong, and let your heart take courage, yes wait for the Lord.' I remember it clearly because I asked him where the words came from, and he told me Psalm 27. It's become my very favorite psalm.

"After that, I decided to become a pastor and went through a very short seminary course. They needed all the pastors they could get. After my ordination, I went to the resistance headquarters to join. They were happy to have a pastor, especially one they considered a hero, even though I had told them I would never do what I did again. I spent the next year traveling around Australia helping with rebuilding as well as helping people find and grow in the faith. After the so-called death of the resistance in 2017, I decided to return to England for a while and do missions there until I got a call to go to Colorado, which is where this story began."

After he finished, they sat in silence for what seemed like an eternity until Isabelle smiled impishly and spoke, "Well, it seems that you're right. If God can forgive you, then He can forgive me." Kissing him gently, she continued, "I'm glad you told me your story. I hope now we can start a new story of our own."

Returning her kiss but holding it a little longer, he was about to speak when a knock came at the door. Isabelle rose to answer it and was pleased to find Jerry. "Hello, Jerome, what can I do for you?" she asked, looking around cautiously.

Pushing his way into her room and closing the door, he said, "I'm sorry for being so abrupt, but there are two people in my room that are your friends, and they asked me to come and find you."

"Jason and Rachel are with you?"

Hearing his friend and sister's name, Stone walked into the room, placed his communication device back in his ear, and heard Marcus's voice on the other end. Smiling and shaking Jerry's hand, Stone jumped into the conversation going on between Jason and Marcus saying, "Yeah, you've mentioned it once or twice."

Both Jerry and Isabelle looked at him like he was crazy until he pointed to his ear and Jerry and the door, and they realized that somehow he was talking with Jason and Rachel. They both sat down waiting for the conversation to end.

* * *

Stone sent Jerry back to his room to wait with Jason and Rachel for more instructions from Marcus while he and Isabelle looked over the files. Stone clicked on the UGSE file and a list of subfiles appeared. Scanning the screen, he noticed the name Burke Smith, Colorado and clicked on it. He couldn't believe what he was seeing. Donald Stewart's name was everywhere. Even though his call hadn't been orchestrated by the foundation, they had used him to implement an experiment, the one Kevin Davies uncovered, but that wasn't the end of it. Stone now understood why it was so important for them to get to Colorado. There was going to be a town council meeting tomorrow night. The subliminal sound system was going to be used on the unsuspecting citizenry and business leaders to make them fall in line with the UGSE's new sustainable development program. Looking at Isabelle with horror in his eyes, he said, "If they get this right, they'll be able to control the whole world."

Isabelle drew on something she remembered from a movie, "Well, is everyone affected, or will it only work on the weak-minded—you know, like the Force from *Star Wars?*"

Blurting out a laugh at her movie knowledge, Stone answered, "Yeah, I guess it is kinda like the Force. The power only works on the weak-minded, but sadly, most of the population has given up and are weak right now. Our only choice is going to be stopping the implementation."

"But how can you do that?"

"Considering I helped develop it, I think I might just be able to mess with it enough to ruin Damious's little experiment. Our biggest problem will come down to Michael not realizing that we're gone."

"Leave that to me," she said while picking up her phone and hitting the speed dial, "Hello, Michael, it's Isabelle."

She heard Damious clear his throat before he answered, "Well, hello, Belle." She cringed. "I would think you'd be busy getting busy with Mr. Stone."

"Well, Michael, it is going well. He just stepped into the shower, so I thought I'd check in. I know you're probably angry with me for going against your wishes, but you really gave me no choice. You know how I feel about him. I just couldn't not be with him. You're not going to hurt him, are you?"

She could hear the arrogant condescension in his voice when he answered, "You know you can't keep him, Belle. He's trouble, and he must be dealt with, but you can enjoy him for now. I was disappointed that you moved the Foxes without my approval, although after thinking about it, you did place them in the best possible room to keep their minds and bodies occupied."

Happy that her ruse worked, she agreed, "Yes, well, I didn't like the way you were treating them, and I figured the Orchid Garden would be a good place. No one in love can resist it. I'm glad that you approve. I won't let you hurt Andrew, though. I'll do whatever you want if you just let him go. After all, how much trouble can he be now? The awakening has started, and you seem to have everything in hand like always." She made gagging motions as Stone smiled, surprised at how easily she was manipulating the man.

"Isabelle, you've shown yourself to be a useful if not bothersome nemesis, so you keep Mr. Stone occupied for the next couple of days, and we'll see what I can do for you when I get back."

"Are you going somewhere? Again? You just got back from Colorado. Where are you going this time?"

"Don't you worry, Belle. We're starting phase one of the new society. I think you'll enjoy it. All the higher spirits are preparing for their roles. It will be glorious!"

"Of course, Michael. I only want the best for everyone's spirit. I'll get things ready here as best as I can. Good-bye." She hung up and looked over at Andrew, who was still staring in awe. Walking over to him, she leaned down to kiss him, but he grabbed her, flinging her to the bed, rolled over, and kissed her.

Smiling he said, in his best Bogart impression, "This looks like the beginning of a beautiful friendship."

Laughing and throwing her head back, she said, "You know, he really believes he controls everyone. I can't wait to see the look on his face when you foil his plan, but"—her face got more serious—"do you really think your friend can get us there? Michael may be overconfident, but he's not stupid. How are we going to get on a plane to Colorado?"

"Don't worry about Marcus. There's no one in the world like him. If I believed in magic, like in books and movies, I'd say he was a wizard, but as it is, he's just a freaking genius." Changing the subject, Stone sat up and pulled the laptop back onto his lap, "Let's look at some more of these files."

As they clicked on another subfile, Marcus's voice crackled over the comms device. "Okay, boys and girls, are you ready?"

Everyone answered in unison, "Yeah."

"All right then. I'll need Isabelle and Jerry to get you guys to the kitchen. Once you get there, ask for Chef Daniel. He'll get you kitted out in serving gear and send you out the back. Make your way to parking area A, I've acquired a slightly larger ride, although it's still one of these stupid electric toys—"

"Yada, yada, yada." Rachel sighed. "Keep on subject. What will the toy car look like?"

"Hey, sorry, it's just I can't stand these things. It's a beige mini-SUV. The license plate is NLFRST4. I'm the only one here. We have to be moseying pretty darn quickly, so you'd better get going." After making a plan to get to the kitchen, Isabelle and Jerry got their friends ready to escape.

Isabelle closed the laptop, picked up the smart drive, and dropped it in her skirt pocket. She walked over to her closet and picked out a jumpsuit for Stone to wear.

"What? You want me to wear that thing?" Stone asked.

"Well, it used to be yours. I kept it as a memento. You don't look like you've gotten any fatter, although I must say you are definitely more well defined. Mmmm."

"Good lord. I forgot. Well, hand it over. Let me slip into it."

After zipping up the jumpsuit, he looked in the mirror and thought of how stupid he looked. Isabelle opened the door and escorted him out into the hallway. Dressed as a New Life scientist, no one gave him a second look, so they walked quietly to Jerry's door. He opened it with a silly grin pasted to his face, and for good reason. Fox was wearing a janitors overalls, and Rachel had on one of the long flowing skirts and peasant blouses that Isabelle wore. Isabelle was struck by Rachel's green eyes, commenting, "Wow! You're eyes are stunning!"

Blushing, she thanked her and added, "You should see me when my hair is long and reddish-blonde. I look like a fairy out of a fairy tale."

Annoyed with the girly blather, Fox interrupted, "If we're all finished complimenting each other, shall we get going?"

"Just because no one thinks you're beautiful doesn't mean we can't appreciate ourselves," Rachel teased, kissing him on the cheek.

All the men rolled their eyes, and the five of them tried to inconspicuously walk down the hall. Rachel and Isabelle walked together whispering quietly, Jerry and Fox tried to look like janitors while Stone trailed behind. Once they arrived in the kitchen, Isabelle asked for Chef Daniel and was immediately escorted to the walk-in freezer.

Daniel, with spiky blond hair and light blue eyes, didn't look like any of them expected. Looking at their shocked expressions, he smiled and said with a strong Australian accent, "Yeah, I know, you thought I'd look more mature. I've never heard that before."

Everyone laughed and shook hands. He pulled out three male and one female server uniforms. He told them they should be able to blend in with the other catering workers who were getting ready to go out to a big party in town. They would be walking to parking area B, which went by A, so they could just quietly peel off to meet Marcus. "That's all there is to it. I didn't get anything for Isabelle because everyone knows her. I figure she can just walk out and give everyone a blessing and then walk over to the parking area. Does that work for you, Isabelle?"

"Yes, Daniel, that will be very good." Then she leaned over and added, "I'm sorry for misleading you. I was misguided myself."

Taking her hand and kissing it like she was a lady of old, he whispered, "I've always known the truth, but I'm glad to know you're with us now. I've always liked you."

Almost crying, she kissed him on the cheek, and they began to carry out the plan.

*　　*　　*

Glad to be out of the freezer, the little band of adventurers checked over each other to make sure their uniforms were tidy. Isabelle told them that the New Life Foundation had strict rules about decorum. They needed to make sure they stood tall, and of course, no sarcastic remarks. She looked at Fox. Everyone laughed, and after calming down, Isabelle led them to the other servers and proceeded to speak a blessing over them. Once finished, she whispered into the ear of the caterer, shot a quick smile toward Stone, and gracefully walked away to the rendezvous spot.

Stone slapped his hands over his mouth in shock as four electric people movers pulled up next to the group. Lowering his hands and whispering to his companions, he said, "Okay, people, we're not walking. We're riding now. We've got to come up with plan B pronto!"

Assessing the situation visually, Fox replied under his breath, "There's four carts each able to hold six plus a driver. There's eighteen actual servers plus us, so if we hang back and get the last cart, we should be good at least until we get to our parking lot."

Trying not to look concerned, Rachel jumped in, "The drivers all look like men. I could do some girly flirting to catch his attention, and one of you can knock him out. I just don't see any other way."

Bringing his cart next to the small group, the driver spoke, "There's been a slight change in plan." As each of them climbed into the cart, surprise and smiles crossed their faces as they passed the driver casually waving them on. In the driver's seat sat none other than their friend, the punk rocker chef, Chef Daniel. "Good day, mates! Anyone need a ride?" he asked with a silly grin on his face. "When I heard they were bringing in the people movers, I acted quickly. Since I am the head chef, I thought it would be good for my assistant chefs to humble themselves and drive their servers! Clever, aye?" Following the other carts, he continued, "Of course, you know one of you is going to have to knock me out. I figure I can fall far enough behind so that when they turn the corner to the entrance to B parking, you all can make a run for it."

Stunned at this young man's willingness to be sacrificed, Rachel asked, "Why are you doing this?"

Smiling and quickly glancing over his shoulder at her, he answered, "Sweetheart, my name's Daniel. I've been living in the lion's den for over a year now, and God has kept me safe so far. I can't do much for the cause other than keeping my ear to the ground and sharing info. This is my chance to actually *do* something. I figure I was put here for a reason, and if I have to take a conk to the head, then so be it! Okay, the others are turning, so this is it." He hit the brakes, and everyone got off.

As Fox stood over Daniel, preparing to strike him, the Australian quipped, "Okay, I'm ready, but I do have a dinner to get on, so make sure you don't do too much damage."

Smiling and shaking his head, Fox replied, "I'll do my best."

That was the last thing Daniel remembered because as Jason prepared to punch him, Stone reached over and pinched the nerves in his neck, causing him to pass out and slump over in his seat. "Thanks, kid," he said, turning and walking away. The others looked at him, wondering how he knew how to incapacitate a man that way. Realizing their shock, he turned and said, "Just something I picked up in Australia. Can we get moving?"

The four of them immediately started toward the tan SUV sitting in the parking lot. Without stopping, they slipped into the open doors, Marcus turned the key, and they drove out of New Life Foundation.

*　*　*

After getting off the phone with Isabelle, Damious returned to his lunch with Tempess. He smiled and said, "Well, William, perhaps things are finally going our way. Isabelle has Stone under control, and the Foxes are safely locked away."

"Well, things aren't going my way. Fox is enjoying his wife instead of moaning in agony at my hand, and we have to fly out to Colorado and deal with Burke. I can't stand him!"

"Now, now, William, there will be plenty of time for you to deal with Fox"—he winked—"and his wife. Just let your imagination run wild with thoughts of how you'll punish him. He'll still be waiting for you when we return. I promise you can take him to the dark room and deal with him in any way you see fit, but for now, I need you to keep Burke in line. I don't trust him. He's got another agenda, and the fact that Stone's people are still capable of causing trouble is a problem."

"I don't get the deal with this Stone guy. I know he had a thing for Isabelle, but he's a preacher. What possible danger could he pose?"

"Stone is our biggest problem. True spiritual Christians can do more damage to us than any resistance army, idiot! That's why we need Stewart too. A large portion of our agenda works on the spiritual plane, and we don't need troublesome Goodie Two-shoes messing with us."

"What? You mean your little awakening? The thing we did in the desert? We released your captive spirits. I don't see how Stone or Stewart could possibly stop such an ancient power. I thought we were stronger."

If they had been alone in Damious's office, Tempess would be on the floor in pain. He could see that he had misspoken and was happy to be in a public place. Damious looked about to explode. "Of course we're stronger, but the One has power too, and it's through pesky praying Christians that his power rises. We thought we had taken care of most of them, but it seems there are still enough out there to cause trouble. We need all our forces arrayed against humans, not fighting the hosts of the One."

"Ah. I see now. What can we do, though? I mean, we've got Stone locked away with Isabelle, and Stewart is only one man. Do you think he's come out of hiding?"

Calming down and sipping his wine, Damious answered, "No one knows. He has yet to show up on any of our radar, but he's been a clever adversary, and I won't put anything past his abilities. If we can get the subliminal system online soon, we won't have very much more resistance. People have fallen into melancholy and are already pretty pliable. As long as we keep them relatively comfortable until it's online, we should have no trouble. I just have a feeling that the resistance is getting ready to pull something off, and we don't need the citizenry getting any patriotic fervor."

Answering his global Internet phone, Damious held up a finger to Tempess, indicating he'd only be a minute. After putting the phone away, he said, "Burke says that the people in his church don't know anything important about the sound system. Andrew Stone helped develop it, so we have to hope that he didn't share any information about it with his people. I can't imagine why he would have. He can't have a notion of what we're planning to do with it, but I just can't shake the feeling that something is going to happen." Taking out his phone again, he called the foundation and asked how the prisoners were doing. According to his people, the Foxes were still sleeping in the Orchid Garden and Isabelle was still with Stone. Satisfied that they wouldn't be a problem, he hung up, leaned back in his chair, picked up his wine glass, and toasted to the success of phase one.

* * *

Marcus pulled the car off the highway, and they made their way down back roads until they came to a small airstrip that was basically a field that had been mowed short. A small six-seat Piper sat at one end of the makeshift runway next to a large military-style tent. Marcus had everything ready, including changes of clothes for everyone. A young Asian man greeted them warmly as they pulled up and stopped, but he had an air about him that said, *Watch out*. Marcus introduced him as Phoenix and explained that he was his main contact for air travel in the local resistance. Phoenix was about five foot nine, with a lean frame that was all muscle. His eyes were a bluish purple, similar to Isabelle's, but his hair was jet black and hung straight to his shoulders. He reminded Marcus of a character out of an early-century video game, very strong and very ready for a fight.

"It's very good to meet you all. I have acquired passage for you on one of our small planes. It will take you to another unmarked airfield in Colorado. A car will be waiting to take you wherever you need to go." Turning to face Marcus, he continued with a smile, "And we made sure that it was a *real* car, not a toy!"

Gleefully, Marcus smiled and did a little jig. "Thank God! And I mean that in so many ways. I can't wait to tell you all what happened to me last night in the parking lot. Freakin' awesome! But now if you all will step into the tent, there is a change of clothes for you—unless you prefer to wear your little server suits."

Happily pulling at his tie, Fox replied, "I'll take the new clothes. I don't think I've worn anything but jeans and boots for twenty-some years." Looking at Rachel, he bowed and said, "Except of course our wedding. Got myself a nice penguin suit and everything."

Curtsying and laughing, she answered, "Yes, but only after my mom threatened to ruin our honeymoon if you didn't!"

Looking sad and wistful, Stone said, "Yeah, I'm really sorry I was such a jerk. I should have been there. I would have loved to see you in a penguin suit!"

Walking over and punching him in the arm, Jason said, "Yeah, you can laugh now, but if you'd been there, you would've been in one too!"

Stone put his index finger to his temple, pretending to think, smiled, and said, "Well, I guess I take it back. I'm glad I wasn't there."

Rachel jumped on her brother, pretending to beat him up, and they fell to the ground laughing. Jason joined the dog pile and pulled Isabelle down with him. As they all lay on the ground laughing, Jerry and Marcus looked at each other, shrugged their shoulders, and piled on.

After a few minutes of unbridled fun, Phoenix cleared his throat loudly and interrupted the jumble, "Um…I don't mean to ruin all the fun, but if you want to get out of here before it gets really dark, we really need to get on with it."

Getting up and dusting off their clothes, the little group entered the tent and changed clothes. As Isabelle and Rachel emerged from the tent, whistles and catcalls were heard all around. Rachel looked over at Isabelle, who was blushing. She rolled her eyes and then, in a playful voice, said, "Don't worry, Isabelle. The boys forget that we're about to go into the fight of our lives. They're ruled by a lower power!"

Everyone laughed and climbed into the plane. Marcus climbed into the pilot seat and Stone joined him as copilot. Mouths open in shock, Fox and Rachel asked at the same time, "You can fly planes too?"

"I spent almost a year in Africa with Marcus and longer in Australia as a missionary. Do you really think I walked everywhere? Jeez!"

After everyone buckled in, Andrew said a quick prayer for safety and stealth, and Marcus taxied down the faux runway and took off. The passengers fell asleep almost instantly while Marcus told Andrew about his vision in the parking lot.

"Do you think they were really there?" Marcus questioned while gazing out the window.

"Yes, of course. Why not? I know Stewart has my congregation praying. It's not called prayer cover for nothing. It would kind of explain how we all got out of there so easily. If the demons controlling things there hadn't been otherwise occupied, our escape might have been much more difficult."

Changing the subject slightly, Marcus lowered his voice, looking around the cockpit, "Are the angels still here? I mean, do you still see them?"

"Why are you whispering? If they were here, don't you think they could hear you? To answer your question, I'm sure they're around, but no, they aren't visible to me. I kind of think our eyes could see through the spiritual veil when we needed extra encouragement."

Smiling while banking the plane slightly to the right to adjust course, Marcus said in his normal voice, "Yeah, I guess having huge angels with flaming swords would tend to bolster ones confidence. I would have *loved* to see Fox's face when he first saw those angels. I can just imagine the shock."

"Yeah, it was priceless." Imitating Fox's reaction, he opened his mouth and eyes wide, looking in all directions.

The two laughed together until tears streamed down their cheeks. Getting control of themselves, Marcus told Stone the rest of the story, how he got out of his car, fell to his knees, and received the Spirit of God. "Man, it was so strange. All the negative thoughts I'd always had about the church and my enemies and everything just disappeared. It was like in that moment, I knew everything. I just can't describe it. You know what I mean?"

"No, I never had a moment like that."

"Well, how did you become so faithful then? How did you know?"

"Well, I was baptized as a baby and raised in the church. I really never had a time that I didn't know God loved me or Jesus died for me or that I was a sinner in need of saving. Obviously, there was a time when I walked away from the faith, even though I never stopped believing, but I think the Holy Spirit was always with me, pulling me back to the truth...like the prodigal son. It was probably the reason that I could never reach my"—he made quote marks with his fingers—"spirit guide when I was at the foundation. God kept me safe." Remembering his actions in Australia, he made the sign of the cross and continued, "It wasn't until I did—well, you know what happened in Canberra—that I realized how lost I was and how much I needed to repent. That was basically it for me. Granted, the Lord has shown me wonders since, but I guess my story isn't as exciting as some."

"No way, brother. You're lucky. I mean, I spent my whole life drifting from one place to the next, always on my own, looking for the next adventure to fill the void in my life, but you always had the knowledge. You always had someone looking out for you. I mean, I could've died without ever knowing. What would have happened? What will happen? I haven't really even thought about the next step. Do I need to go to some kind of class, or do I have to start wearing suits and stuff? I mean, I do some pretty wacked stuff to get information. How can I lead the resistance?"

"Whoa! Why does everyone think you have to do stuff?" Sighing, Stone continued, "You didn't have to do anything to receive the Spirit, did you? You just let Him come. Everything is like that. I mean, yeah, you need to go to church and read the Bible, and you need to get baptized, but the changes that need to be made in your life will come from God. He'll show you and lead you. Just like in the parking lot. You just have to be willing to let Him do it. That's the hard part."

"But why do I need to go to church? I mean, God didn't come to me in church. Why can't I just be open like now?"

Stone smiled and gently shook his head. "Wow. I've never heard that one before. Let me ask you. How did you get good at all the things you do? Did it just jump into your head?… Well, I know things just pop up in your head, but I mean, you had to learn it and practice, right? You don't just go into battle. You have to meet with others to plan for attacks, right?"

"Yeah."

"Well, church is like that. Anyone can read a book and learn how to do stuff, but until you meet with others who can use your knowledge or help you implement yours, it doesn't do anyone else any good. Church isn't supposed to be about feeling good or showing what a good person you are. It's supposed to be about receiving the gifts of God and sharing them with others. When the church works the way it's supposed to, you'll have people with all sorts of different gifts and talents working together to help each other and bring others to the truth. Just like the resistance coming together to win battles, to win the war."

"Hmmm. I never thought of it that way. I just thought it was a lot of good people or not-so-good people getting together to make themselves feel good. I think it would be cool to go to a church like you described. Are there any? I haven't come across any."

"Well, they exist somewhere, it's just a matter of finding them. It's like the resistance. Not everyone is like you. There are groups, like the one I got involved with in Canberra, which give us a bad name. I think if Damious and the UGSE get their way, the real church that you're looking for is going to be underground, like the resistance."

"Yeah…Speaking of the resistance, when I drop you guys in Colorado, Rachel and I will be taking off for LA. The car is for you. Couldn't have my buds riding in a toy!" Banking left, Marcus continued, "I'll get the names you asked for to Stewart at his bunker. I've written all my codes, at least the few that aren't totally secret, down here." He reached into his pocket and removed a small notepad, handing it to Stone. "Stewart will have to get in touch with me so I can get the names he needs." Biting his lip, he sighed. "I'm really stepping out in faith on this one. If the names I share get out, it could be disastrous for us." Taking a moment to get into leader mode, Marcus continued, "You know the drill. After he gets the info, he memorizes it and destroys it. I haven't gotten to do much research on him, but the little bit I found makes him out to be an exceptional ally on both the God front as well as the war front. The man knows his stuff."

Leafing through the notebook, Stone put it in his pocket and answered, "Yeah, I know how hard this is for you. I promise to do my best to keep as much on the QT as possible. You know that even though I messed up in Canberra, I'm still willing to do what I have to…in defense. If the Colorado resistance needs bodies, there are some in my church that I know would be willing to take up arms. Like I told you, some of us have gifts for prayer, but some of us have gifts in other areas, and we're gonna need everyone in this fight."

"I get it, man, but I don't want you to put yourself in the fray unless absolutely necessary. You have inside knowledge on too many of their plans to be taken out." Changing the subject again, Marcus asked, "What are your plans for this subliminal sound system?"

"Well, it works on the basis of getting a low frequency to calm areas of the brain, making them susceptible to suggestion." Putting his head in his hands, he continued, "I thought it would only be used with words and speech, but since learning of the spirit world and how it works, I think they are intending for demons to do the influencing as well. Those with no Christian background won't have a chance. Isabelle always used meditation to get people into a state to accept the spirit guides. Some people use drugs as a way of altering the mind's state. This does the same thing, but quicker and without the side effects. The implications are frightening, especially if this is carried out on a worldwide scale."

"What about Christians? Are you saying they can't be influenced?"

"No. Anyone can be influenced. True Christians should be safe from the demons. After all, the Holy Spirit doesn't share His home, but the mind can be open to many ideas. With all the pretraining people have had throughout their lives, like social justice, sustainable development, multiculturalism, government welfare, socialized medicine, and the like, they'll be easy to manipulate. Too many people have already given themselves over to indentured servitude in the name of peace. It won't be long until they become slaves. All the workers believing they're equal, while the people in control live in the lap of luxury. It disgusts me and angers me that people can be so stupid. I'm afraid the UGSE is going to win. All we can do is keep fighting and speaking the truth until they kill us or the Lord returns."

"Happy thoughts."

"Yeah."

Except for mechanical discussions, the two sat in silence for the remainder of the flight, thinking about the coming battles and the eventual outcome of the war.

*   *   *

Smiling about how well the plans were going, Burke called Damious to let him know that everything was on schedule, "Hey, Michael. Just checking in like you asked. Everything is set. We've got the system in the town meeting room, and we'll be hooking everything up tomorrow."

"Good. What about our little bumps in the road? Have they been making any trouble?"

"Surprisingly no. Since Stone left, they've pretty much just been going about their daily routines. They're having a lot of Bible meetings, but it's only a few at a time, so right now, I'd say, as long as Stone is out of the picture, we should be good to go."

"Very good, Burke. I don't think Stone will be a problem for us. He's safely ensconced at the foundation. See you later."

After hanging up, Burke leaned back in his chair and dreamed of his future in the UGSE. Like most people involved in the world government, he believed in the promise of a better world. He hoped that once fanatics on every side were shut down, the people who knew what was best for society, like himself, would be able to shepherd and contain the populace and put them in the places that they would be most useful. Whether it was called any type of socialism, communism, or democracy, it all meant the same thing: the elites who were highly educated and wealthy people taking care of the ignorant masses who weren't capable of understanding for themselves what was best. He was a part of the total reshaping of the world, and he liked it. Of course, it never occurred to him that those at the top, like Damious and Wright, were the ones that would shepherd the new society and people like him would be mere plebes. In his blissful ignorance, he went about the business of preparing for tomorrow's announcement.

Resurrection had been sent a new pastor to replace Burke as interim leader, so he no longer had to spend a lot of time at the church, which suited him just fine. In his government office, he called his secretary to make sure all the spokespeople for the UGSE were going to be there on time tomorrow. He had a small but powerful slate of speakers scheduled. This included Michael Damious, Justin Wright, and Catherine Sunsteen. He wanted to make sure that everything would be in place. Getting up from behind his desk, he left his office and walked down the two flights of steps to the town meeting room.

A banner had been hung over a podium that was standing on a stage at one end of the room with the phrase "A Plausible Reality—the Beginning of Global Sustainable Societal Development." The American flag stood to the left of the podium situated slightly lower than the UGSE flag on the right, an obvious display of the reduction of American influence in the world. Folding chairs had been placed facing the stage with an aisle left in the middle. On stage, two tables had been placed behind the podium, with two chairs each for the dignitaries to await their turn at the microphone. But the pièce de résistance was the subliminal sound system waiting to be hooked up. The soundboard was set up under the stage. Like a regular PA, the levers were set for volume and feedback control. A separate set of levers was labeled Deep Sound Filters, and those were the most important feature. They would be hooked up to special speakers and two different kinds of subwoofers to get the right frequency out to the masses. It would still be important to keep the volume steady. Any feedback would break the control stream, but the people from Resurrection who had been working the system for over a year were deft hands with it and would not fail. They would be controlling it via a remote device, a backup plan Burke had envisioned to halt any sabotage attempts on the night. Burke was almost giddy with the anticipation of pulling this off, and with the little band of renegades out of the picture, he was confident it would go off without a hitch.

He thought he should stop by Kevin Davies's house this evening to make sure they were all going to come. Granted, the system didn't seem to affect them while they were at the church, but the message had been filtered through actual scripture. Perhaps without the effect of church stuff, they would have better luck. Burke knew there was something to all the spiritual stuff. After all, Damious was totally freaked out about the church. Burke believed in humanity more than any god, so he just didn't worry about it much.

Around six o'clock, he knocked on the Davies's door. When Yvonne opened the door, he was stunned at the sight. The normally tidy living room was littered with Bibles and people sitting around praying, singing, and reading. A buffet had been set up in the dining room to his left, and those not participating were sitting and eating. Yvonne spoke to him without inviting him in, "Well, hello, Mr. Smith. What can I do for you this evening?"

"I was just wondering if you all were planning on coming to the council meeting tomorrow."

Looking over her shoulder, he saw Scott Abrams walking toward him. Scott touched Yvonne's shoulder. She said good-bye to Burke and walked into the kitchen to help Miriam finish up the dishes. In a friendly yet cynical voice, Scott said, "Hi, Burke! Is there something you need? I heard you all got a new pastor for your congregation. I hope he's preaching the truth, although if you've welcomed him, I will assume he's not."

"If you mean is he preaching that God doesn't want people who disagree with you, then the answer is no, but if you mean is he preaching love and tolerance, then the answer is yes. Stone is gone, and your little group will be history soon enough. I just wanted to know if you were planning on coming to the meeting tomorrow."

"Why, Burke? Are you planning on trying to brainwash all of us? Do you actually think your little sound system is going to fool us? We have the power of the Holy Spirit working in us and through us, and we don't fear you, so, yes, most of us will be coming to your little meeting, and we intend to speak against your socialist agenda."

"Typical, your kind always throws out the *socialism* word when you don't like something. Only you could be against the community coming together to work towards a better, more open society."

Getting right into Burke's face, Scott lowered his voice menacingly, "Burke, your idea of a better society is you being a duke or lord over a bunch of peasants doing your bidding. Yeah, I'm opposed to that." Standing back up straight, he continued, "The only good thing that could come from your new society is when you find out that you're going to be one of the peasants. I might even be able to enjoy living as a slave just to watch you grovel. As it is, I will stand for the Word, and I will speak against your treachery until we win or until God takes me home. You see, Burke, the others and I aren't afraid of you or your plan, so bring it on."

"Oh, I'll bring it on. Just remember, Mr. Abrams, that there are laws against hate speech, so you had better choose your words carefully because the people at this meeting will not hesitate to have you incarcerated." Turning away, Burke stepped down off the porch and ambled down the walk to his car parked on the street. Taking out his phone, he called the town's chief of police and told him to double up on security through tonight and tomorrow. Nothing was going to go wrong.

At the house, Bob and Kevin asked Scott, "What was that all about?"

Closing the door and turning to face them, he said, "Burke's agenda. He's got something up his sleeve and wants us all there."

Bob smiled. "Well then, we must not disappoint him."

Kevin chimed in, "Yeah, I just wish Pastor Stone were here. He always knew how to take Burke on."

Pastor Stewart walked silently up behind them and interrupted, "Well, he's got his own path to follow right now, but I have a feeling we might be seeing him sooner than we think."

Stunned, they all looked at him. Bob spoke up first, "Do you know something?"

"Perhaps," he answered and then walked away.

Looking after him, Scott sighed. "I wish he wouldn't always do that. Since we started praying, he's been so withdrawn. I'd like to know what he's thinking."

Miriam touched Scott's shoulder, making him flinch. "You know, he wasn't all that verbal before...at least since all this started. We have to trust that he knows what he's doing and just keep on keepin' on"—lightly punching him twice on the arm, she giggled—"and two for flinching."

Surprised by her humor, they all laughed together, and Kevin thanked her for lightening the mood. "Well, Mir, it's nice to know there's still some humor left in the world. Maybe, just maybe, we'll get through this okay." She put her arm around Scott's and Bob's waists, and they all walked back into the living room, picked up their Bibles, and continued their prayers, not knowing how soon they would find out the answers.

Chapter 6

The only thing necessary for the triumph of evil is for good men to do nothing.

—Edmund Burke

While they are saying, "Peace and safety!" then destruction will come upon them suddenly like birth pangs upon a woman with child; and they shall not escape.

—1 Thessalonians 5:3

After finishing lunch around four o'clock, Damious and Tempess drove to the airport to meet with Catherine Sunsteen in the foundation lounge. They had a New Life jet scheduled to take off at seven o'clock, which gave them a good hour and a half to two hours to discuss their plans. Walking into the lounge at ten after five, they noticed UGHA minister Sunsteen seated on one of the sofas drinking a screwdriver. She was dressed comfortably for travel in a pair of faded jeans, a white T-shirt with a daisy print on the front, and a pink hoodie zipped halfway up her lean torso. Her blonde hair, normally twisted and pinned back, hung softly around her face and cascaded halfway down her back. Looking up from the file she was reading, she waved them over, blue eyes sparkling. Damious and Tempess had never seen her so casual and were amazed at her natural beauty. Walking over, Damious said, "Hello, Minister. How has your visit been going?"

Sweetly, she answered, "Very well, Michael. I'm so excited about tomorrow! Finally we get to begin taking the world toward the path to enlightenment. Is everything in place?"

"As far as I know, everything should be good to go."

After ordering martinis for himself and Tempess, he joined Catherine on the couch while Tempess walked over to a table to sit alone with his laptop. Trying to keep the conversation light, Damious asked her what her topic would be tomorrow.

"Oh, I'm going to be talking about the health situations in the sustainable development complexes. I think people will really take to our model. Of course, it's based on the Chinese model of living and working in the same area, but our housing areas will be less congested. Since the plan to sterilize half the population by 2020 with our vaccine program has gone so well, we should be able to deal with the health issues of new populations very easily. And of course, once people become disabled or too old to be useful members of the community, we'll humanely put them down, so they won't drain the resources needed to keep the rest healthy and well."

"Are you really going to say that? Don't you think some people will resist such realistic but unpopular ideas?"

"Well, Michael, if your people have done what they promised, there should be no one to dissent. Am I wrong?"

Nervously, he sipped his drink. "Of course not, but you realize this is a test run. We don't know how it will affect everyone. Some people have shown an immunity to the system."

"Immunity? What people have shown immunity?"

"Well, the fundamentalist members of the church it was initially experimented on showed a remarkable ability to fight the changes our people introduced, but they were very set in their ways. You know, the religious teachings they had grown up with were ingrained in their way of doing things. The people we'll be dealing with at the Plausible Reality meeting tomorrow have been engineered their whole lives to accept your plans, which is why the eugenic stuff might be better left to another time. Even those ready to be controlled for peace aren't ready to have their life and deaths controlled."

Sipping her drink and mulling over his comment, she agreed, "Perhaps you're right, Michael. We do need to tread softly for our initial trial. We need to see how far we can push the envelope before breaking the barrier. I'm just so excited to see an end to all the subterfuge. If this works, we'll be able to implement all of our policies without all the interference of the uneducated masses."

Finishing off her drink, she continued, "Whoever came up with the idea of a direct democracy was obviously a fool. Now the idea of a democratic republic was fantastic. Giving poor, ignorant people the illusion of voting for a representative, which would only result with the election of educated, highly intelligent, wealthy people was sheer genius. It wasn't until average middle-class people realized that they too could get elected that the idea was ruined." Ordering another screwdriver, she frowned. "Just think of all the unworthy people that were elected at the turn of the century. A bunch of imbeciles who actually believed average people were capable of making rational decisions. You know, if it wasn't for our environmental disaster scheme, those right-wing lunatics might have ruined everything we had worked so hard to build? But now people are willing to work just to be taken care of. As long as we keep those fundamentalists at bay with our new constitution, we should be fine."

After tipping the waiter as her drink was delivered, she continued, "You know? For the founding fathers having been such enlightened people, they just had too much trust in the average man. I mean, getting rid of the Bill of Rights in 2018 was the best thing we ever accomplished. Convincing people that limiting speech for the peace and well-being of society was magical. Your manipulation of the war to our benefit, even after the cleansing, was beyond amazing. You actually convinced the world to give all national sovereignty to the then soon-to-be

UGSE and dismantled the United Nations in a month." Eyeing him curiously, she said, "I'd still like to know how you did it."

Enjoying her praise, he raised his glass. "Well, Minister Sunsteen, that is a secret. Let's just say that the foundation has many useful secrets and is pleased to be partners with the UGSE."

"Well, Michael, since you've convinced me to change my discussion topic, what would you suggest? What are you going to talk about?"

"Me? I'm going to talk about a global faith initiative."

"Isn't that a little dangerous? We're trying to clear out religious fanatics, not create new ones."

"Not at all, Minister. In fact, we've developed a very controlling faith experience at the New Life Foundation. We encourage people to empty their minds and focus their thoughts on specific mantras, much like Eastern-religions, except we provide thoughts and phrases that get people to desire our agendas: peace, love, no personal possession, etc. It makes them very pliable and open to a global society. Our main spiritual counselor is also the owner of the foundation. She is wonderful with the recruits and, best of all, believes everything we teach without any concept of the deceptions being set forth. There is no belief in God, only in self. It is, if I may say so, the perfect distraction for those who feel the need to have a higher purpose." Eating the olive from his drink, he finished, "After all, Minister, there will always be those who have a yearning for that sort of thing."

"I guess you're right, Michael. You know, it's so nice to talk with someone like yourself." Rolling her eyes, she continued, "Do you have to deal with Justin Wright very often? He is a complete pain. He never thinks out of the box. He just kisses butt and lets his employees do all the thinking. I swear, if he didn't have so much money, he would have nothing whatsoever to do with the UGSE."

"He's not my favorite person either, but he does have his uses—like you say, money, but also influence—so we must smile and act like performing monkeys and do our best to keep him in the background. As for what you might want to say in your speech, I would still talk about the sterilization situation, but from a sympathetic angle. Get the crowd to believe you feel bad for them. Then when you start talking about the changes in living conditions, you can use it as a transition to how less people will mean a better standard of living for those left or something like that. I've always felt you were very good at…what did you call it? Subterfuge?"

He held her hand. "I know you want all the secrets to be done and over, and very soon they will be. Once we get the system perfected, no one will be able to resist, and if by some strange chance they do, we will have the means of taking care of them, but we must be patient just a while longer."

Pulling her hand away, she looked him in the eye. "Mr. Damious, I know I may seem like a naïve young woman, but believe me, flattery will get you nowhere. I respect your ambition and mind, but I know what we're doing, and I know the stakes. I also know that we will eventually win, so please don't try and play me."

Sitting back, stunned by her harsh honesty, Damious folded his arms in front of him and stared at her. "I see you're not a woman to be taken advantage of, and I guess I can respect that, but, my dear, you only know what you need to know. There is more going on than your small brain can contemplate." Sunsteen's mouth dropped open. Damious went on, "If you don't want me to play you, then let me be blunt. You will say what I tell you to say, and you will do what I tell you to do. You are a pretty face, a nice spokesperson, but you can be replaced in a moment, so unless you want to be one of the people living in cramped little row houses, you'd better learn your place."

Smiling at her reaction, Damious ordered another martini and continued to stare her down. Composing herself, she answered with a hint of uncertainty in her voice, "I know enough about the whole plan to blow it wide open, Michael, so please don't think you can scare me with your threats."

Sitting forward, he took her hand again, more firmly this time. "Ms. Sunsteen, I never make threats. I make promises." Dropping her hand, he sat back again. "Mr. Tempess, could you please pull up Ms. Sunsteen's file and bring the computer over to show her?"

Annoyed that he had to stop playing the game that he was engrossed in, Tempess obliged Damious and brought the computer over to her. Trembling slightly, she accepted the laptop and read the screen. Eyes bulging, she looked from the screen to Damious and back to the screen several times. Pursing her lips, Sunsteen politely returned the computer to the waiting Tempess, who resumed his seat at the table. She turned to look at Damious and smiled sweetly. "Well, Michael, since we both seem to want similar outcomes within the global community, I will certainly be happy to work with you, but I think I'll go sit at the bar until our flight."

Standing up, she looked down on him and said, "You know, I think I was wrong earlier." She leaned down eye to eye with him. "You're just as big a pain as Wright." Turning, she walked to the bar, sat down, ordered a shot of vodka and another screwdriver. Damious simply leaned back, closed his eyes, and thought, *How good it is to be me.*

* * *

"Okay, boys and girls! Please place your seat backs in the upright position to prepare for landing," Marcus mocked in his best flight attendant voice. "We hope your trip was splendid and would very much appreciate you remembering us for any future travel needs. Now hold on, the landing could be very bumpy."

Jerry's eyes grew wide. "What do you mean bumpy landing? Oh, Lord, keep us safe."

Taking his hand, Isabelle soothed him with her calming voice, "It's okay, Jerome. Mr. Daedalus here is a good pilot and has many safe landings under his belt. Isn't that right, Mr. Daedalus?"

Using a drunk accent, Marcus slurred, "Welllll, Ms. Zenn, I don' know about that. I'm not…not…not feeling too well. I-I—"

Slapping him upside the head, Stone laughed. "Don't worry, Jerry. Marcus here has landed in far more difficult air fields and situations than this. It will only be bumpy because we'll be landing on grass and not asphalt."

Rubbing his head, Marcus whined, "Hey man! Ow, that really hurt." Smiling and taking his hands off the wheel, he joked, "I don't think I want to land the plane now. You do it."

Rachel spoke up when Jerry almost jumped out of his seat. "Okay, joke's over. Just land the plane and quit teasing Jerry. He doesn't know you morons like everyone else." Turning Jerry's pale face to look at her, she continued, "If you're gonna be a part of the resistance, especially with these jokers"—the three men feigned shock—"you're going to have to get a sense of humor. Sometimes it's the only way to deal with the reality of war. Do you understand?"

Calming down a little and getting color back into his face, he laughed weakly. "Yeah, I guess I'm just not used to all of this." Turning back to face front, he asked no one in particular, "Does it get any easier?"

Checking instruments while Marcus banked the plane to the right to line up with the runway, Stone responded, "The jokes get easier, the friendships get closer, but the worry and stress always remain." Turning to face Jerry, he continued, "And, kid, they're important emotions. When you aren't worried, stressed, or afraid anymore, that's when you need to get help. Fear will keep you alive as long as you don't let it rule you."

Marcus spoke into his headset. "Okay, Jenna, turn on the landing lights." Suddenly, the ground lit up with two lines of lights running parallel. The black strip in between was lined up perfectly with the heading of the plane. "Roger, Jenna. Lights visible. Preparing to land." Turning back to the passengers, he exclaimed, "Hang on, folks! We're going in. Yee-haw!" Turning back to the front, he placed his hands on the wheel and proceeded to land the plane with nary a bump for Jerry.

Smiling, the two pilots gave each other a high five after taxiing the plane into a large tent set up as a hanger. Unbuckling their seat belts, the two friends turned to their passengers and said, "Thank you, ladies and gentlemen. You've been a great bunch of travelers, but now get the heck out of the plane!"

Not needing any encouragement, Jerry opened the door and hastily slid out of the plane, followed by Isabelle, Rachel, and Fox. Marcus and Stone quickly checked over the cockpit. Pleased that everything was ready to go, the two climbed out of the plane.

Fox was unloading the bags alone, so Stone walked over to him. "Hey man. How's it going?"

"You know. It kinda stinks. I know I said Rachel needed to go with Marcus, but now that the moment is here, I don't want to let her go. I can't even bear to look at her." Choking up, he looked at Stone with tears forming in the corners of his eyes.

Taking a hold of his friend, Stone hugged him. "Jay, I'm so sorry for not believing in you all those years ago. I can't believe I couldn't see how much you loved her. I feel like such an—"

"Hey guys." Rachel sauntered up behind Fox and wrapped her arms around him. "Is this a private confab, or can anyone join?" Looking into her brother's eyes, she found her answer. Letting go of Jason, she said, "Oh, I guess not. I'll just go—"

"No, sis. You two need to spend some time together. I'll just be going over there." He pointed to the others, who were standing around talking. Taking his leave, Rachel walked around Fox and embraced him. Returning the hug, the two stood still for a few minutes until he untangled himself from her arms. Looking into her eyes, he didn't need any words.

She brought her lips to his and gently kissed him. "Jason, it will be okay. I don't want to leave any more than you do, but you were right. Marcus needs to get back to LA, and I can be more helpful there. Plus I want to see what happened to Amanda after we left and try to get her out if I can."

Pushing her hair off her face and running his hand through it to the ends, Fox agreed, "I know." He looked away from her. "I just can't believe that I got you back, and now we have to part again." Turning back to her and gazing into her eyes, "I want you to remember everything I taught you. No more mistakes." Reaching behind his back, he pulled out his 9mm. "Here, take this. Shoot anyone who even looks like they're going to mess with you."

Smiling at him and not accepting the gun, she said, "No, Jay. This is your gun, and I know you've had it specialized for you. Marcus has plenty of weapons that I can use." She put her finger over his mouth, so he couldn't interrupt. "I promise to carry a gun, okay?" Nodding, he looked at the ground again and tucked his gun back into his jeans. Touching his chin and raising it to look into his eyes, she thought about how much she wanted to forget the war and just stay with him forever. As they continued gazing at each other, a smile crept across his face, and he leaned forward and kissed her. Surprised and curious, she asked, "What's that smile all about?"

Getting his sense of humor back, he replied, "I know what you were thinking. You were thinking we should just run away and let everyone else fight this stupid war. Am I right?" Surprised he could read her so well, she nodded her affirmation. "Well don't even think about it. You and I aren't runners. We're fighters. We lost our way for a while, but now we're back, and nothing is going to separate us again. This battle is going to be over one way or the other tomorrow. We either stop Damious, or we regroup and move on from there. Either way, we will be back together in no time, agreed?"

Smiling, she nodded. "Marcus, Marcus! Get over here!"

Curious at her outburst, everyone walked over to hear what she needed. Marcus exclaimed "Yo, girl! What's all the ruckus about?"

"Well, I'll tell ya, Marcus. Listening to my husband drone on about responsibility and such, I had me a thought." Feigning hurt, Fox put his hand over his heart and quietly moaned. Punching him in the arm, she continued, "Since this thing at the town meeting is going to be over tomorrow one way or the other, why do we have to leave right now? Doesn't it make sense to have you"—she made a flourishing movement with her arm—"our wonderful, glorious, amazing inventor and brain around to help?" Marcus blushed and bowed at the acclamation. Rachel continued, "I don't think Marcus and I should leave until this is resolved. That way, he and Stewart can powwow and decide who should be going where. What sense does it make for us to go and then figure out that Jason and Jerry and who knows who else from Andrew's church should come with us? I want to stay."

Preparing to protest but thinking better of it, Fox looked over to Marcus and then to Stone. The three friends seemed to communicate through unspoken words and looks. As one, they said, "Okay."

Marcus continued, "If we do this, then we have to be smart about it. I can't just walk into a situation that might be monitored. I'm supposed to be dead, remember? Jason, you'll take me to the cabin first, and then the rest of you will rendezvous with Stewart's people." Stopping to think, mumbling to himself while walking in circles, Marcus let the wheels in his head spin before articulating his plan to the others. "Okay, Stewart is expecting one of you to call him and let him know we're coming, right?"

"Yeah," Fox answered.

"Great. You do that. Find out what they need or might need. From what I've read about your Donald Stewart, he's almost as brilliant as me." Everyone looked at him with shock. "I said *almost!*" The whole group laughed. "Let him know that we'll be at the cabin and can get anything that he can use and that you all should be there early in the morning." Holding his hand up to stop anyone from asking more questions, he took a moment and then said, "If his communication set up is anything like Fox described, I should be able to contact my people to let them know what's going on and then decide how everyone wants to proceed. It's been three days since I've been in contact, so who knows what's gone down. Everyone okay with the plan?"

Everyone nodded their assent and started talking amongst themselves. A new face emerged from a tent on the far side of the runway. Jenna Wallace, a spunky recruit from Scotland, sauntered over to the small crowd and addressed Marcus in a light Scottish brogue while eyeing the others suspiciously. "Marcus, the car is ready for you. As you requested, it's large and completely dependent on gas to get from point A to B. Are you and your mates ready to go?"

"Yes. Thanks, Jenna." Introducing her to the rest of the group, he said, "Everyone, this is Jenna. Jenna, everyone." Noticing Jenna's hesitancy to embrace his friends, he put his arm around her shoulder, reassuring her of their trustworthiness, and said, "Jenna has a problem with strangers. Her whole family was betrayed and slaughtered in the 2017 raids. I found her on a layover in Scotland when I was escaping the global militia in the Congo. She was a mess. I brought her out here because the people in the local resistance are very caring, and I knew they would help her." Looking Jenna in the eyes, he continued, "Jenna, these people are like family to me, and I trust them totally. I hope someday you will too." She smiled sheepishly and shook each person's hand. When she got to Jerry, her hand lingered.

Jerry held her hand and said, "It looks like we might be the same age. Maybe when we get our present situation figured out, I can come back here and we can work together." She smiled and then showed everyone to the car.

"How on earth can you afford to keep this thing filled with gas?" Fox asked. "It must cost an absolute fortune."

Affectionately hitting the hood of the car, he answered, "Well, brother, when one is a genius and an expert forger, he can get a gas card on the UGSE and not have to worry about it." Getting a worried look on his face, he turned to Andrew and asked, "Can I still do that?"

Smiling, Andrew said, "God's ways are not our ways. If the UGSE is not paying attention to who they're giving out gas cards to, then who are we to question the providence of it? Even King David broke the Law once or twice for his soldiers. Perhaps you should pray about it and then follow your heart."

"All right, everyone," Rachel chimed in, "let's get in the car and go." The small group piled into the car.

Jerry reached out for Jenna's hand, smiled, and said, "Goodbye, and see ya later!"

She smiled back and replied, "I'll hold you to it."

Isabelle promised Jenna that she would take good care of Jerry and to get him back if it was possible. "I think he might like to learn to fly airplanes, if you know how!" she said, winking at Jerry.

Turning pale, Jerry said, "No! I mean, I think I'd rather be on the ground crew."

"Well, that's good then because I only fly if necessary. My feet stay on the ground!" Jenna replied. Slapping the roof, she said, "Better get going."

Marcus waved, said good-bye, drove the car out onto a rutted path that was meant to be a road, and disappeared into the night.

* * *

Once seven o'clock rolled around, Damious, Tempess, and Sunsteen boarded the plane and took off for Colorado. Catherine Sunsteen chose a seat near the rear of the plane facing away from Michael Damious and nursed a very large vodka martini. Damious sat in his regular spot next to the window, reclined his seat, and asked the flight attendant to bring him a sweet tea. He'd drunk enough at the bar and wanted his head to be clear for his meeting tomorrow morning with Burke Smith. Catherine soon passed out and slept fitfully in her seat while Tempess closed his laptop, reclined his chair, and closed his eyes as he thought about the direction his life had taken since joining the New Life Foundation.

Damious had just closed his eyes, preparing to rest a little before arriving, when his phone rang. Annoyed, he answered, "This had better be good."

A nervous voice on the other end said, "Mr. Damious, this is Peter Baless, head of foundation security. I don't know how to say this, but somehow, Mr. and Mrs. Fox, Mr. Stone, and Isabelle are gone."

Trying to stand up but held in place by his seat belt, Damious howled into the phone, "What! How can this be? They were supposed to be under surveillance!" Calming down a little, he asked the flight attendant to bring him a large scotch on the rocks and said into his phone, "How did this happen? Are you sure they aren't there?"

"We have checked everywhere. We checked the CCTV and found nothing. It's like they just vanished."

"Mr. Baless, people do not just vanish. You had better find out where they went and how they escaped. I don't care how, but I think a good place to start would be with the guards. Take them to one of the dark rooms and find out what happened. And if you haven't found out by the time I get back, you will find yourself in a dark room." Preparing to hang up, Damious paused and added, "If anything goes wrong with our meeting tomorrow that has to do with Stone or the Foxes, I will kill every one of the people on your staff. Is that clear?"

"Yes, sir. I'll get on it."

Stunned by Damious's outburst, Tempess asked, "What is it?"

Downing his scotch and asking for another, Damious answered, "It seems that our prey has escaped somehow." Letting the alcohol take effect, Damious calmed down a bit. "William, call Burke and tell him we may have a problem. Tell him to watch out for Stone. I don't know how, but I have a feeling he'll be showing up."

"Sure thing, boss. I'll get right on it."

While Tempess called Burke, Damious placed a call to Isabelle. After hanging up, Damious picked up his empty glass and threw it across the cabin, shattering the crystal. Catherine woke from her alcoholic stupor and mumbled, "What the—" Then she immediately fell back into unconsciousness. Stunned, Tempess ended his call to Burke and made a huge mistake by asking Damious what had happened.

Eyes bulging, face red, Damious ranted about Isabelle and Stone and something about lying, with plenty of expletives thrown in, then more ranting about Fox and Stewart and back to Isabelle. From what Tempess could gather from the tirade, Isabelle had joined with the others, but was trying to convince Damious that they were still at the foundation. Tempess had never seen him so angry before and began to fear for his own safety. When Damious had finished his rant, he threw a look toward Tempess, daring him to speak again. Then he fell into his chair and seemed to pass out. Tempess, not daring to disturb his boss, picked up his laptop and joined Catherine in the back of the plane as far away from Damious as possible. *What in God's name am I doing here?* he thought. Opening his laptop, he began to search for various places that he might be able to escape to and just disappear.

* * *

Damious had not fallen asleep. He had been summoned by Angelous and transported to the demon's reality. Furious at having been dragged back here but mindful of what happened the last time, Damious held his tongue as he looked around for Angelous. He was pleased to see that he wasn't in the abyss but in the usual surroundings of tortured screams—human screams— darkness, the smell of sulfur, and demons going about their regular business of messing with damned human souls. Preparing to call out for Angelous, he thought better of it and just soaked in the atmosphere. While it still gave him a feeling of power, he now had a feeling of dread underneath that took some of the joy out of coming here. Suddenly a voice called out, "Michael!"

He wanted to disrespectfully yell, "What!" but he decided to simply turn around and wait for Angelous to continue. Looking up, he saw Angelous speeding toward him and stood his ground. Angelous came to a halt only inches from his face, stared directly into his eyes, and narrowed its gaze into a menacing grimace, daring Damious to move. As Damious stood firm, returning its glare in a kind of face-off, Angelous let a wicked smile move across his lips. Holding up a claw-like finger to his lips, it made a shushing movement that froze Damious in place. Suddenly, Damious felt a searing pain in his head, and an explosion flared across his line of sight. Willing his hands toward his head but unable to do so, he just stood screeching like a banshee, anger filling every pore of his body. Finally, after what seemed an eternity but in actuality was only a few seconds, Angelous lowered its claw, and Damious was released. He fell to the ground holding his head and swore under his breath.

"Was there something you wanted to say, Michael?"

Yeah, you psychotic pain in the— Damious thought but chose instead to say, "No, Lord Angelous. Why did you summon me?" as he got his feet back under him.

"Well, since you asked so pleasantly, I will tell you." Lowering its tone, the demon went on, "We have had some very unpleasant news down here. Adder has informed us that he has lost his control of Ms. Zenn. In fact, he says that he was rebuked by a man of The One, and she was protected by two very powerful angels." Backhanding Damious and knocking him to the ground again, Angelous screamed, "How did this happen!?"

Stunned at the revelation, he began to get a picture of how the group had escaped. "I don't know, Angelous," Damious answered with a little too much sarcasm. "Why don't you tell me? I thought you guys were the all-powerful. Why didn't Adder keep control of her?" Standing up, letting the rage fill him, he fumed, "It's kind of like Trycon. How did he screw up so bad with both Burke and Tempess? We actually wouldn't be in this mess at all if Tempess had dealt with Fox, and Burke had dealt with Stone and Stewart. It seems that it's your little demon buddies that have been screwing up." Fearing retribution but not caring, he continued, "I've done everything that you wanted me to. I've instituted the plan to perfection. You're the one who wanted Stone brought to the foundation, not me. You're the one who's lost control." Narrowing his eyes, Damious finished, "Maybe it's time for your higher-ups to deal with your incompetence, huh?"

A glimmer of fear passed across Angelous's face for a moment, and then its usual sneer returned. Grabbing Michael by the throat, it hissed, "Don't threaten me, Michael. I am the lord of my realm. You'll do well to remember that. Isabelle has escaped for now, but she will not remain strong enough to resist Adder for long." Releasing Damious, it settled its tone. "We control the spiritual realm. We have the power to implant thoughts and desires. We have the power to bring nightmares or bliss. What we don't have the power to do is physically harm. Oh, we can convince humans to kill or commit suicide, but it ultimately comes down to their will, which is why I need you, Michael. I need you to take care of these annoyances and keep the plan alive. We are symbiotic creatures, so you must deal with this"—it lowered its voice to a whisper—"or I might have someone deal with you."

Damious had never thought about Angelous turning on him. As he settled back into his body, he wondered what the breaking point would be. After all, Damious was premade for this job. He knew the complete truth and was still willing to implement all of it. He didn't have imaginary friends; he had a Lord, and he knew its will, and he knew he would fulfill all that was required of him.

Keeping his eyes closed, he reached for his drink. The ice had almost completely melted, and he downed it in one gulp. Setting it back on the table, he let his mind wander to tomorrow's meeting and implementing the sustainable development plans in all their various forms until his mind finally got to a place where it shut off, and he fell asleep, his first dreamless sleep in a very long time.

* * *

After bumping over rough terrain for what seemed like days, they arrived at Donald Stewart's cabin. Happy to be done with the ride, the six companions escaped the car with no time to waste. Marcus was the first to speak. After slamming the door closed, he exclaimed, "Now who wants to thank me for ordering a real car and not one of those ridiculous toys?" Everyone raised their hands, and Jerry began bowing with his arms extended in a juvenile attempt at what he called Marcus worship. Everyone laughed, and Fox led them up the steps to the door and into the cabin.

Rachel was gobsmacked when she entered because the place was exactly like her dream. She walked over to the table and gently touched the chair where the crown had sat. Stone, noticing her amazement, asked, "What is it sis?"

Coming to her senses and looking around the room, she answered, "Nothing, Drew, I guess it's just that it looks so much bigger inside than from the outside." Her excuse seemed to satisfy him, and he turned toward the arsenal to examine the weaponry. Jerry joined Stone, Isabelle walked to the kitchen to put water in the kettle to make tea, and Fox and Marcus looked over the communication room.

"Stewart does not disappoint!" Marcus gushed while caressing the equipment.

Laughing, Fox covered his eyes while peeking through a few fingers. "Jeez, Marcus, should I leave you alone in here?"

Smiling, Marcus turned toward the various monitors, computers, other communication devices, and tools, saying, "Now, now, babies, don't listen to Mr. Fox. He just doesn't get our love."

Feigning disgust, Fox patted Marcus on the back, shrugged his shoulders, and said, "To each his own, man. Let's get these bad boys up and ready to go, or should I say, bad girls?"

Marcus got an evil glint in his eye, grabbed Fox around the neck, and proceeded to give him noogies while laughing hysterically. "Say uncle! Come on, Fox, man, say it!"

"Okay! Okay! Uncle! Uncle!" After getting his breathing under control, Fox snickered. "I'll get you back, Marcus. You just wait."

Marcus put his fingers up to his mouth, pretending to chew his fingernails, and let his knees knock together. "Ooooh, I'm so afraid."

Fox punched him in the arm, and they got to work turning on switches, dusting off equipment, and opening Stewart's books. They talked quietly together, finally getting things going.

Isabelle and Rachel stared at the two men wrestling in the communication room, then they rolled their eyes and began getting to know each other. Rachel said, "Don't mind them. They have the mentality of third graders. Thankfully, they're also both incredibly intelligent…when they need to be."

"Yes, this has been quite a trip for me. Everyone at the foundation was always calm and respectful. We only ever touched each other gently, with love. I never knew violence could be so much fun, even loving."

"Really? You all never played around? Forgive me, but I just can't imagine my brother staying in a place like that for as long as he did. He must have loved you very much."

Blushing, Isabelle nodded while getting out two mugs and placing tea bags in them. "Yes. We were very much in love, but his conscience was stronger than our love."

Turning off the whistling kettle, Rachel poured water into the mugs. "What do you mean? Why did he leave?"

Surprised at her lack of knowledge, Isabelle told her the story of Andrew's discovery and departure from the New Life Foundation. Rachel was shocked to hear about the environmental deception and the fact that her brother had anything to do with it. "I don't understand. How could Drew be involved in something like that? Messing with genetics to the point of creating synthetic life?"

"Now that's not fair. Science had been genetically modifying plants for decades. He had no intention for his work to be used to destroy. He was taking worst-case scenarios and trying to find solutions for them. When he found out what they had done, he tried to let the world know, but—"

"But what?"

"But I took the proof before he left," she said, ashamed.

Stunned that her brother could forgive such a betrayal, Rachel stared at Isabelle. "And now? What are your intentions now, Isabelle?"

Feeling anger rising in her, Isabelle, not knowing how to control it, yelled at Rachel, "How dare you! What are my intentions? I left my whole world! I returned the documents and gave him the whole contents of Michael's computer!" Everyone else stuck their heads out of the rooms they were working in while she continued, "My intentions are to redeem whatever I can of my sorry life to help you stop the UGSE's plans if possible! My intentions are to love your brother and grow old with him!

"You've done your share of damage creating the whole scenario of societal sustainable development! How many people do you think died between 2015 and 2017 to bring your plan to fruition?" Covering her tearstained face, Isabelle apologized, "I'm sorry, Rachel, more sorry than you can ever know, but don't you think I deserve a chance at redemption? Your brother? Yourself?" She looked at Rachel with pleading eyes.

Feeling ashamed by her accusations and self-righteousness, Rachel walked over, hugged Isabelle, and together they cried. Apologetically, Rachel acknowledged her faults, "I forgive you, Isabelle, as if I have any right to, and I'm sorry for being such a sanctimonious hypocrite. Will you forgive me?"

Releasing their embrace, Isabelle and Rachel examined each other for a few moments and laughed. Isabelle gently punched Rachel on the arm, like she'd seen the guys do as a sign of friendship, and Rachel knowingly nodded back. Pleased to have their argument over, they looked at the men staring at them and as one said, "What?" The guys shrugged their shoulders and returned to whatever they were doing while the girls continued quietly chatting.

Before Isabelle's outburst, Andrew and Jerry had walked into the armory, and both whistled with amazement at the collection of weaponry that surrounded them. Pistols, shotguns, rifles, bows, crossbows, grenades, RPGs, dynamite, C4, wires, detonators, and like Marcus's cache, ancient weapons too.

Jerry commented, "I've never seen so many weapons. Are we going to be using them?"

"Well, do you know how to use any of them?"

Picking up a pistol, placing his finger on the trigger, and looking down the sight, Jerry asked, "How hard can it be? Point and click, right?"

Andrew quickly reached over and took the gun from him. Frowning, he said, "First, never put your finger on a trigger unless you intend to fire the weapon. Second, never point a gun when you don't know if it's loaded or not." After smacking Jerry lightly upside the head, he continued, "And third, guns are not toys. They're tools. In war, they're usually intended to kill an opponent, which is not something you should ever strive to accomplish. Killing a person is not easy, it's not fun, and it's not to be taken lightly. Do you understand?"

Shocked, embarrassed, and a little angry at having been spoken to like a child, Jerry answered, "Yes, sir."

"Yes, sir?" Andrew laughed. Taking Jerry by the arm, he chuckled. "Jerry, I'm not a drill sergeant. You don't have to call me sir. I just want you to understand the seriousness of the situation. Most people either consider guns as evil or fun when they're neither. They're a means to an end. I won't lie, shooting targets and hunting can be a lot of fun and very fulfilling as a means of showing skill, but taking a human life is not fun and never fulfilling. Guns aren't evil, only the people who misuse them. Most accidental shootings are the result of people not respecting them. If you'd like, I can show you how to use one properly. Like you said, just point and squeeze."

Jerry thought about his words and answered back, "I never thought about it that way. I guess playing video games and paintball growing up doesn't really prepare you for the realities of war. I guess I never thought of shooting someone as really killing them. Gosh, could I really be so stupid?"

"You're not stupid, Jerry. You're young and thankfully haven't had to deal with this kind of reality. I'm sorry you got dragged into this."

"It's okay, Mr. Andrew. Do you think Jenna knows how to shoot? Maybe she can teach me when I go back to the flight place."

"You know, Jerry, I think you may just be a little smarter than me! Jenna would probably be a great teacher for you, and maybe she'll be able to keep you out of the thick of things. For now, how about we put down the guns and—" Both men looked out the door when they heard Isabelle yelling. Once she calmed down, they returned to their inspection of the weapons.

Rachel and Isabelle had found a bunch of dehydrated food in the cabinets and put together a nice rustic meal for everyone. About an hour and a half after arriving, they had the table set and food waiting for the hungry group. Rachel sang out, "Dinner is ready! Come and get it!"

The guys lined up outside of the bathroom to wash their hands and then gathered at the table. "Boy, oh boy!" Fox exclaimed. "Dinner at midnight! It doesn't get better than that!"

Walking over and kissing her husband on the cheek, Rachel said, "Keep it up, babe, and there won't be any dinner for you."

Marcus was surprised at all the food. "Wow! All of this was dehydrated? Hey, Andrew, can we thank God for dehydrated food? Or only the fresh stuff?"

"Funny. Is this how it's gonna be? Hey, Andrew, what about this? Hey, Andrew, what about that? Sheeesh!"

Jerry interrupted, "Not to be rude, but how about we eat before it gets cold?"

Everyone laughed at the young man's appetite and sat down to eat.

* * *

Most of the prayer warriors had gone to bed for the night, but Miriam, Doris, Yvonne, Scott, James, and Donald had chosen to stay up to keep the overnight watch. Around eleven o'clock, Miriam's phone rang, and the prayer abruptly stopped while everyone looked at the phone like it was a holy relic. Pastor Stewart spoke, "Well, Miriam, are you going to answer it?"

Regaining her senses, Miriam quickly answered the phone. "Hello? Hello, Pastor Stone. How is everything going?... Here? You're in Colorado?... Yes, Pastor Stewart is right here...It's good to hear your voice too...Yeah, one minute." Handing the phone to Stewart, she smiled and said, "It's Andrew."

The small group huddled together in a group hug as Stewart talked with Stone. "Yeah...Oh, I see...Hmmm, let me think for a minute...Okay, the code to get into my computer is MmlJ12C12TjR. Make sure Marcus types it in correctly. He'll only get one chance. My computer is set to disable for four hours after a wrong code is introduced...Yeah, well, tell him too bad, that's how it is...Yeah, that is funny!...All right, now I need you to bring a couple of rifles and a variety of handguns…I don't care. Just bring 'em…Grenades? No, I don't think we'll need any for this…Marcus should be able to figure that out…Ask Fox. I showed him where everything is…Yeah, that's about it…Four this morning? I guess we can get you in…Yeah, we'll keep praying…What? She's with you? And she knows? That should be interesting…I see. All right, we'll get everything together here…Yup, see you later. Bye."

After hanging up, he turned to the others and said, "Well, folks, our prayers have been answered. Pastor Stone is fine, as is his sister and Mr. Fox. They should be here around four this morning, and they're bringing my daughter Isabelle and someone they rescued named Jerry—"

"Hold on a minute!" Scott blurted, "What do you mean daughter? I didn't know you had a daughter." Everyone nodded in agreement, tired of all the surprises cropping up in their lives.

"Well, to make a long story short, when I was at the New Life Foundation, I fell in love with her mother, yada, yada, yada, then came Isabelle. Her mother was married to the son of the founder of New Life, Warren Zenn. Needless to say, he didn't want me around, so he tried to have me killed, but I escaped and have been on the run ever since. The guy who took over after Warren, the guy in charge now, Michael Damious, got in touch with me and offered me my anonymity back if I helped them out, hence the sound system and changes at the church. It was only after I did some digging that I realized what was going on. By then it was too late to fix anything, so I went back underground and got Stone to replace me. I knew he was a part of the resistance, so he was the perfect person to figure things out and do the right thing, and I was right…well, sort of. I didn't expect Isabelle to be involved, but then again, I've been praying for her for her whole life. I guess God answers prayers in His own time."

Shaking her head as if to clear it, Miriam asked, "Resistance? Andrew is part of the resistance? You're part of the resistance? I thought they were wiped out in 2017. What is going on?"

Everyone started talking at once and getting upset, so Stewart spoke over them and told them to shut up. Stunned at his abruptness, they quieted down and listened. "Yes, we are part of the resistance. He didn't know I was resistance when he was called, and he didn't come here as resistance. He came to shepherd your church without an inkling of what was going down. Everything that he's done for you has been totally honorable and real. He's been thrown into this the same as you, but you are blessed to have him.

"I'm sorry to be so abrupt, but this is grown-up time, and you need to get onboard. Nothing has changed. When they get here, they will explain everything that is going on and will be going on. They have a plan, and it requires prayer as well as fighters. Stone has a list of who he thinks will be best suited to what tasks. He and Fox are going to be like our generals on this one. Now we have to get things ready here and figure out how to hide them until the meeting tomorrow night. Are you ready, or do we need more questioning?"

Yvonne answered for the group, "We'll get things ready, but when they get here, we all need the truth. No more waiting, no more *need to know*. We need to know everything. None of us signed up as resistance fighters, so we'll let you know how involved we want to be. I'll go get the others up to prepare a plan, and those of us still willing will be praying." Looking to everyone and getting approving nods, she added, "I think that's all. Is that okay for now?"

Surprised at the overall reaction, Stewart agreed but then added, "You're wrong about not signing up as resistance. The moment you stood up to Burke, whether you like it or not, you became a part of the resistance. Know this, the papers lied about us. We didn't assassinate those world leaders, the UGSE did. I'll leave that for you to think about. The others will fill you in on the rest when they get here."

With a heaviness of heart, a small group went about the business of preparing for their new guests, but the group of prayer warriors was being lifted high in the Spirit, and their hearts grew light and filled as they prayed. Finally, they would see the fruits of their labor.

* * *

"We'll be landing in approximately ten minutes," Captain Erikson announced as he made the final approach toward the runway. Catherine Sunsteen returned to her seat after having spent twenty minutes in the bathroom fixing her appearance. Except for the raging headache from too much drinking, she looked very fresh and felt invigorated. She smiled as she spoke to the flight attendant, "Excuse me, Dana. I wonder if you could bring me an aspirin or three and some water."

"Certainly, Ms. Sunsteen. One minute." She walked to the galley to retrieve the medication.

Tempess had returned to his original seat and was busy stowing his laptop when Damious spoke, "So, Catherine, did we have a little too much to drink?"

"You should know. You look like death warmed up. At least I took the time to make myself presentable. I thought you were going to stay away from the bottle last night. You look like you downed half a bottle of scotch."

"I'd watch your mouth, Ms. Sunsteen. We wouldn't want any information getting out about you now, would we?" She pursed her lips but said nothing in reply. Knowing he'd won the battle, he unbuckled his seat belt and sauntered to the bathroom.

As Dana returned with the water and aspirin, she reminded him that they were about to land and he should take his seat. As he passed by, he simply ignored her and proceeded onto the lavatory while she looked at him with anger flaring in her eyes. "What a rat," she said to no one in particular. Tempess looked up in horror at the bathroom door and was pleased to see it closed. Then he looked at Dana and nodded.

Catherine let out a hearty laugh and said, "You better watch your mouth around Mr. Damious. If he had heard you, you just might disappear, but bravo for pointing out a most exemplary point." Dana turned pale at her words as she handed over the medication and water, but quickly recovered, smiled, and returned to the galley.

"Please make sure your seat belts are fastened and prepare for landing," Erikson's voice rang out over the intercom.

Damious strolled out of the bathroom looking like a million bucks. He sat down, fastened his seat belt, and called out to Dana, "Ms. Flight Attendant, I'm in my seat now."

Annoyed at his childishness, Dana chose to ignore his comment and proceeded to strap herself in for landing.

Catherine couldn't help herself and commented, "Why don't you just grow up, Michael? Jeez." Tempess looked over at Damious, who was smiling like the fox who just looted the hen house.

After landing, the three disembarked and were greeted by Amanda Wright. Surprised that she looked so good after the screams that came from the house when they left, Damious bowed, kissed her hand, and greeted her, "Well, hello, Amanda. How's your father doing?"

Flinching at the mention of her father, she averted her eyes toward the ground, answering quietly, "He's very good, Mr. Damious. He's in the UGSE lounge. He wanted me to make sure you all get there. He has a car waiting."

Understanding the situation from Amanda's behavior and the healing bruise on her cheek, Catherine reached out, touched her arm, and comforted her. "Thank you, Amanda. Why don't you lead us, and we can sit and talk together."

Amanda lightly smiled, accepting her kindness, and led them through the airport, down an escalator, and to the UGSE VIP lounge. Her father sat reading a newspaper while drinking some kind of vegetable/fruit drink that he believed kept him healthy. Looking up from his newspaper, he stood and greeted his comrades warmly. "Well, hello, Michael, William"—he shook their hands, then turned and kissed Catherine on the cheek—"and, Catherine. Good to see you all." Turning toward Amanda, he reached out for her. She flinched noticeably but allowed him to pull her to his side. "Do you know my daughter, Catherine?"

"Michael introduced us when we left the plane. Amanda, right?"

"Yes, that's right. She writes for the Global News Network. In fact, she wrote the report on the sterilization cases. Perhaps you could give her an in-depth interview."

Hoping for any reason to get Amanda away from her father, Catherine answered, "Of course. I'm always pleased to give the press UGHA information. So much speculation and nonsense out there these days." Turning to face Amanda, she asked, "Would that be at all helpful?"

"Yes, ma'am, I'd love to have a personal interview. The network would probably even give me a bonus for it."

"It's settled then. Tomorrow after the kickoff of our sustainable development initiative, we'll sit down, and you can ask me anything you'd like."

"Excellent," Amanda gushed. She sat down, pulled out her phone, and called the Global News Network to find out what angle they'd like her to focus on.

While Amanda talked to her editors, the four colleagues sat down to discuss the day's events. While Wright sipped at his vegetable glop, Damious and Catherine ordered coffee, and Tempess decided on a soda with extra ice. Once their drinks were delivered, Wright laid out the agenda. "Okay, first we'll get to our hotel and get a good night's sleep. In the morning, we'll meet in the dining room for brunch at eleven o'clock. Mr. Burke Smith will meet us and have a schedule ready for our approval. After brunch, we'll drive to the town hall and inspect the meeting area and offer any suggestions we have. After that, everyone is free to do whatever they would like. Mr. Smith has arranged for us to be able to use his home to freshen up before the meeting, which is scheduled for seven o'clock. It's should be pretty easy"—looking over at Damious, he frowned a bit—"as long as there are no problems. Is everything good, Michael?"

Tired of Wright's holier-than-thou attitude, Damious snapped, "Actually, Mr. Wright, we do have a possible problem. It seems that Mr. Stone and Mr. Fox, as well as Mrs. Fox and Ms. Zenn have left the foundation. I must assume they will be showing up to cause us a bit of trouble. Burke, er, Mr. Smith is supposed to be doubling security, and of course, we have our *extra* security."

Catherine and Tempess had no idea what extra security he was talking about, but Justin seemed to get it. "Right then, Michael. Hopefully, there will be no problems."

Concerned, Catherine joined the conversation. "What exactly are we concerned these people could do?" She glared at Damious. "I know I'm not indispensable, but I can assure you that the people in charge at the UGSE will not be pleased if this doesn't go off fairly smoothly. Do I need to contact them?"

Wright looked at Damious. He appeared about to explode, but he calmly said, "No, Ms. Sunsteen. It won't be necessary for you to contact anyone. Things will be fine. If anyone is going to be talking to the powers that be, it will be me."

Staring each other down, Catherine and Damious dared the other to speak. Justin Wright interrupted their battle by stating that the car was ready and that they could go to the hotel now. Breaking eye contact, Catherine stood up and walked over to Amanda to get her attention while Damious, Tempess, and Wright began walking toward the door.

"Come on, Amanda, it's time to go," Catherine offered.

Hanging up her phone, Amanda took her hand and answered happily, "Okay, let's go."

The two followed the men out into the parking area, got in the car, and sped off to the hotel for the night.

* * *

After finishing dinner, the ladies washed the dishes while Stone and Jerry collected up all the weapons that they thought they would need in town. Fox helped Marcus finish getting all the communications systems up and running. Before the small group prepared to go, Marcus called everyone into the living room. He handed out the three earpieces they had used previously and showed them how the receiver worked. The receiver looked like one of those small computers that you could read books on; however, Marcus had tweaked it to receive sound as well as script. He gave a brief lesson on how a standard global Internet phone, as well as a cell phone, could communicate with the receiver. It worked as both a phone and text messenger. A simple programming protocol could sync up any device with his receiver, which would encrypt it and allow only his instruments to pick it up.

"What makes these earpieces different than a cell phone? Can't someone pick up the signal if they know what to look for?" Jerry asked.

Stunned that anyone would question his device, Marcus answered, "Well, it's kind of like a cell phone, except you can't see the phone because it is in your ear, and it's powered by the person wearing it. It doesn't run on a regular battery. The electric signals from the brain power it, so it's on when it's in the ear and off when it's out. The receiver and the other earpieces are the only things that can unscramble the signal, which is why I couldn't hear Stone when he was in Isabelle's room, so when you think about it, the signal moves like a cell phone's, but everything else is nothing like a cell phone."

Jerry had been listening with his mouth open in awe. "So it's powered by someone's brain? What happens if someone else gets it?"

"Well, if someone else gets it, then we're pretty much screwed, so"—he looked around at everyone—"whoever wears them needs to keep track of them. However, if the person wearing it dies with it in, it will short-circuit and internally destruct as the brain dies, so the enemy won't be able to use it." Everyone looked at him in shock. "Well, I always try to find a positive to end on." He smiled.

Fox interjected, "Yeah, hey, you're dead, but at least the enemy won't get our technology! Great!"

Everyone laughed. Once the weapons and technology were loaded into the car, Marcus said good-bye to everyone, one by one. When he got to Stone, he said, "I think I'll miss you most of all, scarecrow."

Stone answered, "There's no place like home, there's no place like home."

Rachel grabbed her brother by the collar, pushed him toward the car, and finished the conversation, "Come on, bro, we're off to see the wizard—the wonderful wizard of all things evil." Looking back to Marcus, she said, "We'll see you soon, Marcus." She climbed into the front seat with Fox, closed the door, and the small group drove off into the darkness.

As promised, they arrived in Andrew Stone's town right around four in the morning. About a mile outside of town, Marcus had one of his colleagues leave a small moving van hidden in the woods. Fox pulled the car off the road, and the group transferred the weapons and Marcus's devices into the back of the van, along with Rachel, Isabelle, Stone and Fox. The plan was that Jerry would drive the van into town. That way, if he was pulled over, he wouldn't be arrested since no one in town or from the UGSE knew him. Marcus had made sure there was furniture strategically positioned so that the little group could hide behind it with all their treasures and not be spotted if anyone requested to look in the back. It was a good plan because as soon as the van pulled onto Main Street, a red-and-blue light blinked behind it, and a siren sounded. Jerry pulled the truck over and acted surprised. "What did I do, Officer?"

Patrolman Johnson asked for his license and registration. Without looking up, he said, "Sorry to inconvenience you sir, but we have some VIPs coming to town for a very important meeting, and we've been authorized by a local judge to stop and search all unknown vehicles coming through town. Could you please step out of the van and open the back?"

Nervous but trying to stay cool, Jerry opened the driver side door, stepped onto the pavement, walked around to the back of the truck, and opened the rear door, praying silently the whole time. As Johnson shined his flashlight all around the interior, Jerry's mouth dropped open because inside the truck were four angels holding up shields. One winked at him and held a finger to its lips, signaling for him to be quiet. Continuing to pray and not being able to contain the smile creeping across his face, Jerry asked, "Is there anything else I can do for you, Officer?"

Shining his light one more time before seeming satisfied that nothing except furniture filled the van, he said, "No. That should do it. Like I said, I'm sorry about the delay, but orders are orders."

Closing the door, Jerry answered, "Oh, that's okay. I understand, you gotta do what you gotta do."

Patrolman Johnson returned to his vehicle without acknowledging Jerry again. Relieved, Jerry climbed into the cab of the van and drove to a local garage that was owned by a resistance member. He parked the van in one of the garage's work areas. After the owner, Jared Miller, secured the maintenance door, Jerry opened the back of the van and let his friends out.

"Jared Miller," Jared said as he held out his hand to Fox, "pleased to meet you."

Returning the handshake, he introduced himself and the others, "Hi, Jared, I'm Jason, Jason Fox, and this is my wife, Rachel. This crazy man here is my brother-in-law and partner in all things trouble, Andrew Stone. He is also the pastor of a local congregation."

"Yeah, I know who Stone is. Marcus filled me in, plus I've seen you around town," he said, shaking Stone's hand. "Pleased to meet you, and who is this other lovely woman?"

Isabelle blushed, and Fox introduced her, "This is Ms. Isabelle Zenn from the New Life Foundation and currently Mr. Stone's love interest." Stone punched him in the arm. "Ow! That's what I get for being honest." Walking over to and putting his arm around Jerry's shoulder, Fox finished his introductions. "This young man, the deceiver extraordinaire, is Jerry. Hey man, what is your last name? I never got it."

"It's Holmes, Mr. Fox, like Sherlock!"

"Ah, I see," Fox thought aloud. "Elementary, my dear Jerry. Now I see why you were so good with the cop. You have analytical skill in your blood. By the way, great job with the good officer."

Lowering his voice, Jerry said, "Well, Mr. Fox—"

"Jason," Fox interrupted.

"Jason," Jerry corrected. "It wasn't me. There were angels with you guys in the truck. Coolest thing I ever saw. Just standing there holding up shields so the guard couldn't see you. It was awesome."

Jared interrupted, not sure what on earth Jerry was going on about, "Ummm, good to meet you all, I think. Marcus had me get a car for you, very nondescript and local—my car, to be exact—so please take good care of it." He called Stone over to explain where he needed to park to keep the car out of Burke's line of sight. "Now Smith has people watching the front of the house but not the back. Kevin has private parking in the rear of his house. You have to go down a small alley from Aspen Drive. It opens up to the back of his property. No one ever goes down there, so it's very private. Take my car, unload your cargo, and then park it on Aspen Drive, where I'll pick it up later this morning. Got it?" Stone nodded, and then Jared handed him a disposable phone.

"Marcus told me to give you this to get in touch with Stewart. Good luck, guys. Now let's get this cargo into my trunk."

The small group of resistance fighters loaded the car, said good-bye, and drove away from the garage. Stone checked the mirrors regularly, and when he was sure that there was no tail, he turned onto Aspen Drive, found the alley, and turned the car down the narrow lane. After a short distance, the alley opened into a private area, just like Jared said. Once the car was parked, Stone called Stewart and let him know they were there.

About a minute later, four people walked up to the car: Scott Abrams, Bob Johnson, Kevin Davies, and Donald Stewart. Practically jumping out of the car, Stone hugged his friends and made introductions all around.

"Well, it's good to meet all of you, especially you, Isabelle, but we'd better get all this stuff and you guys inside before anyone notices us," Stewart ordered. Everyone took armloads of guns and electronics and hurried to the backdoor. Once everyone was inside, Scott left to take the car and park it on Aspen Drive.

While everyone was putting down the gear, Miriam walked into the room. When she saw Stone, she ran up to him, threw her arms around him, kissed him on the cheek, and said, "It's so good to have you back, Pastor Stone! It seems our prayers were answered!"

Returning her hug, he replied, "Whoa! Leave a couple-a ribs intact. It's good to be back." Removing her arms from his neck, he began introductions, "Mir, you already met Jason."

Fox grabbed her, dipped her, kissed her full on the mouth, and then stood her back up. "Enchanté, mademoiselle."

Breathless, Miriam blushed. Rachel popped Fox one on the arm. "Excuse my husband. He has such bad manners."

Laughing, Stone continued, "This is my sister, Rachel." Rachel took a little bow. "And this is Jerry Holmes, a friend from the New Life Foundation and a very clever young man."

Jerry interrupted, "Sorry, miss, I'm too shy to do what Mr. Fo—I mean, Jason did, so I'll just shake your hand."

"Pleased to meet you, Jerry," Mir said.

Walking over to Isabelle, he put his arm around her waist and said, "This is Isabelle, an old friend of mine from New Life and Pastor Stewart's daughter."

"Please to meet you, Isabelle," Miriam said, feeling a little jealous of Stone's affection toward her.

Sensing Miriam's discomfort, Isabelle replied with a hug. "It will be nice to have another woman around. Rachel and I have been dealing with nothing by guy silliness for too long." Releasing a surprised Miriam, she walked over to her father, looked into his eyes, and said, "Hello, Mr. Stewart, or should I say Dad? I think it would be nice to have a chat, don't you?"

All eyes turned to Stewart, who answered with a deep exhale, "Yes, you're right, and since Yvonne has demanded no more secrets, I think I should tell the story to everyone, if that's all right with you?" Isabelle nodded. "But for now, I think you all are probably exhausted. Why don't we all get some sleep, and we can discuss everything, including our plan, in the morning—or later in the morning, as it is."

Not realizing how tired they were, the small group agreed that sleep would be a nice change. Yvonne had Isabelle sleep in one of the guest rooms while Stone and Jerry shared another one. Jason and Rachel, not wanting to be separated, chose to sleep on the floor in the den. As soon as their heads hit the pillows, they fell fast asleep.

Stewart, Kevin, and Bob decided everyone else should go home to their own houses and apartments tonight. They all agreed to meet back at the Davieses' house around eleven o'clock for brunch. No one had to worry about work because Burke had set the day aside as a holiday in preparation for the big meeting that night.

When Miriam was out of earshot, Bob asked Kevin and Donald, "Did you notice some chemistry between Pastor Stone and that Isabelle woman?"

"Yeah," Kevin agreed, "I noticed, and I also noticed that Mir got a little tense about it. Is there something going on there that I don't know about?"

Yvonne jumped in, "Boy, you all are thick! It's obvious that Miriam has been crushing on Pastor Stone for a long time. I actually thought he was interested too, but I have to agree with you guys, there was definitely something between Pastor and Isabelle."

Stewart agreed, "I think the two of them were an item back when he lived at the foundation, and it seems that they might have picked up where they left off. If that is the case and, like you said, Miriam and Stone had something, we could have a potential problem brewing. We'll just have to keep an eye on the situation."

"What's everyone whispering about?" Miriam asked, reentering the room.

"Umm…nothing really," Bob lied.

"You were talking about that Isabelle, weren't you?" Miriam interjected. "I noticed the two of them." Everyone looked at her expectantly. "Don't worry. There was never anything between me and him, not really. Whatever happens, happens. I won't have everyone stressing over me. We need to focus on the task at hand, right?"

Impressed, Stewart nodded. "You're right, Mir. We need to stay focused and worry about the rest later. Why don't we say a quick prayer for a good night's rest?" The small group prayed quietly for a few minutes and then dispersed until their meeting for brunch.

Chapter 7

It is easy to go down into Hell; night and day, the gates
of dark Death stand wide; but to climb back again, to
retrace one's steps to the upper air—there's the rub, the
task

—Virgil

For God has not given us a spirit of timidity, but of
power and love and discipline.

—2 Timothy 1:7

Waking around nine in the morning, Catherine felt well rested
and decided to take a swim in the hotel pool before getting ready.
Dressing in her swimsuit, she grabbed, a towel, and her key card.
She left her room and walked to the elevator. While waiting,
she noticed Amanda peek out into the hallway and called out to
her. Amanda quickly shut the door. Surprised, Catherine walked
toward the door and knocked. "Hello, Amanda. It's Catherine
Sunsteen. I saw you look out a minute ago. Do you want to go for
a swim with me?"

Tentatively, Amanda opened the door slightly and said, "I'm
sorry, Ms. Sunsteen, I'm not supposed to leave my room without
my father's permission."

"Well, Amanda, I'm going for a swim, and I don't think your
father would mind you spending time with me. How about you
get your suit on, and we'll go together. I'll take the blame if your
father gets angry."

"No thank you, Ms. Sunsteen, I'm sorry, but I just can't. I'll talk with you later…okay? Bye." She closed the door, and Catherine was left stunned at the fear this young girl carried. Angry at Justin Wright, she walked to the elevator and rode it to the main floor. Not watching where she was going, she nearly knocked over an elderly man entering the small space. "Oh, pardon me, sir. I'm so sorry. I wasn't looking where I was going."

With a thick Caribbean accent, the man answered, "Don' worry, sista. Peoples knocking into me all de time." Smiling a huge white tooth-filled grin, he asked, "Are you plannin' on havin' a swim then?"

Smiling back, she answered, "Yes, yes, I am. Nice meeting you, and again, sorry for bumping into you."

"Tink nuttin' of it, sista." As the doors closed, he flashed his smile at her again.

Something's so familiar about him, she thought. Focusing on her swim, she put the thought out of her head and strolled to the pool to swim off some of her anger. After about three quarters of an hour, she climbed out of the pool and toweled off her hair and body. Lying back in a lounge chair, she closed her eyes and, in her mind's eye, remembered the man from the elevator. She wondered why he was so impressed on her psyche. She searched her memory for his face; just when she thought she had it, it slipped away.

After a few minutes of memory probing, she gave up and decided to head back upstairs to her room to get cleaned up for brunch. She was not looking forward to meeting anymore of Damious's or Wright's coworkers. From what she'd heard about Burke Smith, he had failed on numerous counts, and now the future of the sustainable social development plans were in his hands. *Why am I forced to deal with these people? I can't wait to get home to intelligent people who aren't so backward-thinking. Religion should just be done with. Why on earth are we going to encourage people to keep on with such nonsense?* Pushing the button to go back upstairs, she watched her step before getting on the elevator, but this time it was empty. Pleased to see that she was alone, she stepped into the box and pressed the button for the fourth floor.

As the elevator door opened, she heard banging and someone shouting. It was Justin Wright. "Amanda, open this door right now!"

Hurrying toward Amanda's door, anger flaring again, Catherine opened her mouth to yell at Justin when the image of the black man with the Caribbean accent shot into view. "Oh my lord!" she called out.

Surprised by her voice, Justin demanded, "What in the world are you yelling about?"

Banging on the door, she called out, "Amanda! Amanda! If you're there, open this door! Now!"

"What do you mean if?"

"Get on your phone right now and call the front desk to open this door! If I'm right, she's not in there. The resistance has her."

"What! What do you mean the resistance? How—why would you think that?"

Not having to wait for the front desk, a security guard rushed over to them inquiring what was wrong and why they were making such a ruckus.

Wright pulled out his UGSE credentials to show the guard while Catherine explained, "We're with the UGSE. Mr. Wright's daughter is supposed to be in this room, but I think she's been kidnapped by someone in the resis—I mean, someone I saw in the restaurant this morning. Never mind, we're with the UGSE. Open this door immediately!"

Not having to be told twice, the guard opened the door. Catherine and Justin nearly tripped over each pushing to get into the room. All the drawers were empty, and all of Amanda's personal items were gone from the dresser and the bathroom. "Oh man," Catherine said, running her hands nervously through her hair.

"What is it?" the guard asked.

Wright answered, "Nothing, nothing to see. You can go. But I'd like you to inform Mr. Michael Damious that Justin Wright needs to see him in this room ASAP. You can get his information from the front desk." Turning to face the shocked guard, he demanded, "I hope I don't need to tell you again!"

"No, sir. Right away, sir," the guard agreed as he turned on his heels and ran to the stairs.

Looking at a piece of paper on the dresser, Catherine paled and almost fainted. Justin took a few steps toward her while reaching out to steady her. "What does that mean?" he asked, pointing at the paper.

Picking it up, Catherine sighed. "Trouble. It means we're in trouble."

"Should I get a forensic team in here?" Wright asked, preparing to dial his phone.

Catherine shook her head. "No. He doesn't leave anything behind except his calling card." She held up the paper. "I know exactly who did this, but it just seems…I mean, I just don't get it. Why now? Why Amanda? What's the connection?"

As she mulled the questions over in her mind, Damious showed up, out of breath and only half-dressed. "What in the name of Hades is going on! Why did you want me to come down to your daughter's room in such a hurr—" Damious stalled as he looked at the picture on the calling card, which Catherine held up silently toward his face. "No way. No way! Where did that come from?"

Now it was Justin's turn to ask questions. "What is going on here? Who has my daughter, and why are both of you so— what's the word? Freaked out? What resistance? *The* resistance? I thought they were gone."

Placing the paper gently on the bed while sitting next to it, Catherine answered, "Marcus Daedalus."

"Daedalus?" Justin queried. "He's dead. We put him to death back in '17." Letting the reality wash over him, he stated, "We didn't. We made it up. You mean to tell me Marcus Daedalus is still around? With my daughter? Please don't tell me he's working with Stone and Fox. Please tell me that!"

Glaring at him while standing up with her blue eyes blazing, Catherine hissed, "You ignorant toad! Of course he's working with them, or at least Stewart! Why the heck else would he be here? The question is, why are they here? Obviously they know about the meeting and intend to disrupt it, but where does Amanda fit in?"

Damious entered the fray. "Okay, wait a minute. Let's calm down. We only know Daedalus was here and probably has Amanda. He's surfaced after three years for a purpose, and it isn't to stop our test. There has to be something bigger, although his involvement would explain a lot about how they escaped the foundation. Daedalus is a genius. He has eluded us from the beginning." Turning to Wright, he continued, "But he's never been a follower of The One, so I don't know if he'd be hooked up with Stewart or Stone. We don't even know if Stone is affiliated with the resistance." He turned back to Catherine. "You're right, though. Why now, and why Amanda?"

Wright asked, "Do you think he'll hurt Amanda?" He seemed genuinely worried.

"What do you care? It's obvious that you didn't treat her like a little princess. I noticed the bruise on her face and the fear she had of you. You're a pathetic little worm, and to answer your question, no, I don't think he'll hurt her. It's not his style. She's probably safer with him than with you. In fact, if you hadn't scared her so bad, she would have been in the pool with me instead of up here alone."

"Who do you think you are? What—"

Damious changed the subject. "Look, right now we need to get our heads together. Catherine, go and get dressed. Obviously,

I need to get myself put together too. We'll meet down in the dining room for brunch at eleven like we planned. That gives us"—he checked his watch—"about thirty minutes. We'll decide what to do then. Don't call anyone. Burke should be here soon, and we'll get everything worked out then."

Everyone agreed, albeit unhappily, and retired to their rooms until eleven o'clock.

* * *

By the time eleven o'clock arrived, the Davieses' house smelled of bacon, pancakes, eggs, muffins, and coffee. Kevin, Yvonne, Bob, Scott, Miriam, Donald, Andrew, Isabelle, Jason, Rachel, and Jerry served themselves buffet style before sitting down on an array of mismatched chairs around the table. Kevin said a blessing over the meal, and the group hungrily devoured the food set before them. After everyone placed their plates in the sink, the small group moved into the living room to wait for the rest of the congregation to arrive. Awkward silence enveloped them until Jerry said, "I know I'm new here, but you can cut the tension in this room with a knife. Can we please break the ice?"

Patting him on the back, Scott agreed, "Jerry's right. There is no reason that we can't take the time to get to know each other before everyone else arrives."

"Who all's coming?" Stone asked.

Bob answered, "Well, Tom, Doris, James, and Debbie are coming, and I think Scott has a few youth kids that were interested. Scott?"

"Yeah, Kara, Josh, Kat, Peter, Eryn, and Zac are ready to help out," Scott stated.

Rachel asked, "Sorry, but what are teenagers going to do?"

"First, they're not all teenagers. Some of them are early twenties, but as diversions go, you'll find none better. The kids, I mean, young people, love to—how can I say this? Push the envelope. Trust me. They'll be in the audience causing little bits of mayhem."

Concerned, Isabelle chimed in, "Do you think it's right to get such young people involved in this? Are they aware of the dangers?"

"These are the strongest, most faithful group of young people I've worked with. Not only are they strong spiritually, but they believe very strongly in freedom, and they want to fight." Lowering his voice, he added, "They'd probably join the resistance in a heartbeat if given the chance."

Stewart added his thoughts, "Well, if Marcus were here, I'm sure he'd sign them up, but for now we'll keep the whole resistance talk under wraps. All they need to know is that we're going to try and stop Burke using the mind-warp on anyone."

"Mind-warp?" Fox cracked up. "Who came up with that?" Almost falling off his chair in uncontrollable laughter, he continued, "No, no, please don't use the mind-warp!"

Enjoying the spectacle of his friend but wanting to get back on track, Stone pushed him to the floor, chuckling along. "Get over it, bro, we need to stay on track."

Rachel rolled her eyes as she helped her husband up. "Please forgive his childishness. Jason never did grow up!"

In his normal frat-boy way, Fox grabbed Rachel, dipped her, kissed her, let her back up, and joked, "Yep! That's me. Just call me Peter Pan."

Using a calm and authoritative voice, Stewart said, "All right, all right. We thank you, Mr. Fox, for breaking our uncomfortable silence, but we do need to get back on topic."

Miriam raised her hand in a schoolgirl attempt to get attention. "Umm, I have a question. If we're going to ask the kids to put themselves in harm's way, shouldn't they understand why? Why are they on a need-to-know basis?"

Stewart's phone rang, and he excused himself.

Andrew tried to answer. "Mir, there are a lot of things you don't know about me, about the resistance, basically about all of this. Joining the resistance isn't something you just jump into, usually anyway." Looking around, he added, "Right now, most people, including those in positions of power, don't know that we've regrouped. Since 2017, they've pretty much assumed that we're scattered and weak—"

"Not anymore," Stewart interrupted, rejoining the group. "Marcus is planning something either very stupid or over-the-top smart. He's going to get Justin Wright's daughter and bring her here." Looking over at Rachel, he asked, "You know her, right?"

"Yes, I—we know her. How on earth did Marcus find her? Save her?"

"I guess his genius flows over into master of disguise. He didn't give me many details, just that she's working for the resistance and he snuck into her hotel and helped her get away. He wanted me to let you know that she was safe and that you don't have to worry about her. She's helping us hack into her father's files as we speak. It's not going to take them long to figure out she's gone, and as usual, Marcus left his calling card." Taking a breath and returning the conversation back to the original topic, he said, "So now back to the need for secrecy."

Stone finished his statement, saying, "So, Mir, for now, for their safety and the safety of the resistance, we need to work on a need-to-know basis. Do you get it?"

"Yes, but I don't like it."

The doorbell rang, and Yvonne got up to answer it. One by one, the small group of prayer warriors showed up: Doris, James, Debbie, and Tom. However, the youth group showed up as one cohesive group, ready to cause mischief. "Hey, Scott! Troop trouble is ready, assembled, and prepared to cause mayhem!" Peter, the comical but able leader of the youth, spoke. He sported aquamarine eyes and a brown Mohawk with red highlights.

Fox walked up to him and shook his hand. "I like your style, man. I'm Jason, Jason Fox, adult mayhem causer!"

Peter shook his hand happily. "Pleased to meet anyone who enjoys my line of work!"

Rolling his eyes at the thought of Fox and Peter teaming up, Stone called everyone to the living room to get a briefing. First up was Pastor Stewart and the story of Isabelle.

Looking at the young people, he began. "This is the story of one of the biggest mistakes and blessings to ever happen in my life. So as I tell this, I want you to understand that adultery before, during, or after marriage is not a good thing, and you should save yourselves for marriage, as God intended. However, sometimes we break God's law, and this is where my story begins.

"I had gone to the New Life Foundation to find some meaning for my life. I was working for a company called Uni-Tech, and they often sent their employees to the foundation both for spiritual refreshment and to help with technological advances. After my first visit, I met with Warren Zenn, the head of New Life. He looked a lot like President John F. Kennedy and had an air of royalty about him. He was a very articulate and well-meaning man, at least I thought so at the time. He liked my work on the plans for his laboratory in the desert. I had helped to engineer blueprints for solar and wind power to run the whole place without any power from outside sources. At that time, that kind of technology was in its infancy. I took a lot of inspiration from the inventions and knowledge of Archimedes, Daedalus— the Greek inventor, not Marcus—and of course, da Vinci and Einstein. Anyway, Warren really liked my ideas, so he invited me to join his council of engineers. It was a great step up, so I quit Uni-Tech and joined New Life.

"After being there for about two months, Warren invited me to come to dinner with the heads of his various councils. You know, at that time, the PTBs—that's powers that be to those of you who don't know—were more discrete, and the world government was in the closet. The New Life Foundation Councils were kind of like the beginnings of the UGSE administrators. We were all from different countries working on different aspects of developmental plans. Since I was invited to this meeting, it was obvious that I had been promoted to director of the engineers.

"Anyway, at that meeting, I met the most beautiful woman I had ever seen, Isabelle's mom, Gabriella. She had the same lustrous dark hair and violet eyes that you do, Isabelle, and as her name suggested, she was an angel, not just her outer beauty but her spirit. When we first met, we became friends quickly." He laughed as he remembered. "She was interested in the use of solar power, but she didn't like the panels. She wanted something smaller that wouldn't take up so much room." Looking around at everyone and ending on Isabelle, he said, "She loved nature and didn't like things that disrupted its beauty. I think she'd probably have gone back to the preindustrial age if she could." Isabelle smiled. She had thought the same thing many times.

"Our friendship grew, and over the next few years, we became very close, especially once Warren started getting more involved in United Nation issues; he worked closely with the global elites that pulled the strings behind the scenes. It got to the point that he was gone more than he was around. I kept working on alternative energies but began to realize that something was very wrong with the big picture. I began wondering how the technologies I was working on would be used. It was just too cost-prohibitive for average societal use. Gabriella had the thought that perhaps they were just going to use the fear of running out of fossil fuels as a scare tactic to gain power over the populace, rather than truly wanting a cleaner environment. I, of course, thought that was a preposterous idea. At the time, the whole concept of world government and secret societies planning the takeover of the world was all conspiracy theory. She began to pull away from me because of my attitude. I think my dismissiveness reminded her too much of Warren.

"Without her around to talk with, I tried to join some of the foundation activities, but I just couldn't get the hang of calling on spirit guides, so I went outside the foundation for spiritual guidance. It bothered me because one thing that Gabriella was good at was contacting her spirit guide, but I just couldn't do it. That's when I went to St. Christopher's church. I just walked in and prayed. One of the pastors, Pastor Sirron, came up to me and asked if there was anything I needed. I told him that I didn't know and was just looking for something to fill my life. Well, he asked me the normal questions about what I believed personally, and then we just talked about life. It was the first time I ever just talked with a pastor like a friend. I went to church there for about five months, and one day, while I was listening to the sermon, I just got this feeling—a calling. During communion, while I was at the rail receiving the Eucharist, I just felt clean. I don't know any other way to describe it. It was just a feeling like being in a shower after a hot and sweaty day's work—clean, refreshed, and ready to move on.

"Anyway, I went back to the foundation, and Gabriella was waiting for me in my room. She had a bruise on her check and had been crying. I knew what had happened and immediately I turned around to find Warren and give him back what he'd done to her. She called out to me and told me to stay. Even though my desire to pummel Warren was strong, her need controlled me more, and I sat next to her, comforting her. She told me that he wanted her to have a baby but that she didn't want to bring a child into this place. She confided in me that she had recently become a Christian and feared what Warren would do with her child, and that that was why she had pulled away from me. Of course, I was stunned because I had only that day given my life back over to the Lord. She was so excited when she heard that she kissed me. Nothing overtly sexual, just a friendly kiss, but in our state of hurt, joy, fear, and excitement, we kissed again, but this time it led to…well, you know, a place it shouldn't have.

"After, while we lay together, she told me that she had been in love with me for a very long time. I just couldn't believe it. I mean, I had always been infatuated with her, but I'd never thought of love until that moment. It was then that I realized that I had loved her for a long time as well. We stayed there together for a little longer, and I wondered at how I could square what we'd just done with my newfound faith.

"After she dressed and left the room, I quickly returned to the church and spoke with Pastor Sirron." Looking at Stone, he commented, "You know, his name was Andrew too. Anyway, he set me straight. I had to not see her again, at least not in that way. And I didn't, but"—he blushed and turned his eyes to the floor in shame—"Isabelle had already been conceived.

"By the time I had returned to the foundation, Gabby had come to the same conclusion after spending time alone praying. We decided together that this would never happen again. Sadly, our friendship had changed, and the ease with which we used to talk had become strained as we both were trying to stay away from each other, you know what I mean." With a look of shame and sadness, he gazed at Isabelle. "Two months later, Gabriella told me that she was pregnant and that it was mine. We decided not to tell anyone and tried to come up with a plan to escape.

"Needless to say, Warren was over the moon about his wife's pregnancy. He treated her like a queen, but Gabriella knew that once the child was born, things would go back to the way they were, or even worse. We started spending a lot of time together. Our friendship was like it was before we...were together. Our friendship and love grew like a weed, and it wasn't long before Warren began noticing our close friendship and decided he didn't like it.

"In her eighth month of pregnancy, strange things began happening to me..." He made air quotes with his fingers and said, "Accidents. It became obvious that a hit had been put out on me. However, so as not to upset Gabby, they didn't want it to be an obvious murder. Their ineptitude made it easy for me to spot their attempts, and I foiled them at every turn. Finally, Warren came right out and told me that I needed to go or the accidents would stop and I'd basically get a bullet through my head." A few people let out audible gasps. "Well, after talking to Gabriella about it, we tearfully decided that I would leave and work from the outside to help her escape while she worked on the inside. We prayed together, and I kissed her good-bye." Eyeing the floor and trying not to cry, he said, "It was the last time I ever saw her."

Isabelle got up, walked over to him, and embraced him like a daughter would her father. It was then that the tears spilled. The two wept together for about five minutes before calming down. Yvonne gave them a box of tissues, and he continued his story. Holding Isabelle's hand, he turned to look in her eyes. "Your mom did have a rough delivery. It almost killed her, but the doctors managed to save her. Your father, or stepfather as it were, wanted to name you Tamara, but your mom and I had decided to call you Isabelle. Your father acquiesced after your mother agreed to use Tamara as your middle name. Did you know Isabelle means *my God is a vow?* We made a vow to God to keep you in Him. A friend of mine and your mom's told me at the funeral that she had baptized you in secret and read Bible stories to you, even though you were just an infant." Tears began to fall as he finished, "My friend told me that Warren heard your mom singing 'Amazing Grace' to you and confronted her about her faith. Your mom would not lie and told him that she had converted and that you weren't his child. She begged him to let her go with you. Of course, he refused. The next day, your mom was found dead in her room, an apparent suicide caused by postpartum depression. No one believed it. Anyone who saw Gabriella with you knew you were the joy of her life, but Warren had already become a powerful man, and no one dared to cross him.

"The only time I ever saw you was at her funeral. Warren was holding you. You were only about a month old and dressed in a little red dress with a bonnet on your head. I saw straightaway that you looked like your mom. You have her lovely eyes. After everyone had left, I walked up to the grave and promised Gabriella that I would always pray for you and someday get you away from there." Smiling, he said, "And here you are."

Hugging him close, she whispered in his ear, "And I've come to know the Lord as well."

Holding her at arm's length, he looked into her eyes, smiled, and thanked God for bringing her safely home.

* * *

In the hotel restaurant, the small group of globalists sat together trying to piece together the events of the morning. After ordering, Damious began, "Okay, now, Catherine, would you please go through it one more time. What exactly happened?"

"Fine. I was leaving the elevator when an old black man with a cane bumped into me, or I bumped into him. We had a short polite conversation. Then I went my way, and he went his. I went for a swim, and while I was going back to my room, Wright was yelling at Amanda's door."

"Hmmm…" Damious sighed. "All right, now, Justin, one more time."

Tired of going over the story, Wright exhaled as he retold his story, "I tried to call Amanda's room several times, and when she refused to answer, I went down to her room to talk in person. Then Catherine showed up."

Looking hopefully at Tempess, Damious asked, "William, what did you find on the hotel CCTV feed?"

Knowing his information wouldn't shed much light on the situation, Tempess gave his report. "The camera shows Daedalus come in through the front door. The rat even looked into the camera and waved. Like Catherine said, they bumped into each other at the elevator. Once he got to Amanda's floor, he dialed a number on his phone, walked to her door, and she opened it."

Wright interrupted, "Did he knock?"

"No. She just opened the door when he walked up to it. I don't know what went on in the room since there are no cameras, but she was expecting him. They were only in there for about two minutes before they came out. She had her suitcases and was wearing a brunette wig while he had changed his old-man look for a reggae-looking freak. They took the stairs down to the lobby and walked out the front door, and once again, he turned and waved at the camera."

It was Damious's turn to interrupt, "Did the outside cameras pick up anything?"

"Well, that is the weird thing," Tempess replied. "Once they left the lobby, it was like they disappeared. No trace of them at all. I don't know how they did it."

Wright and Damious said at the same time, "I need a drink."

Catherine sneered and sniggered at them. "You guys are pathetic! It's not doing any good going over all this stuff. We need to focus on the meeting today and worry about Daedalus and Amanda later, and I'll tell you right now, Mr. Wright, if your daughter has been involved with the resistance right under your nose, you *will* pay!"

Forgetting that he was in a public place, Justin stood up and began raising his hand as if to strike Catherine. She stood up, turned her cheek to him, and dared him to do it. He caught himself and lowered his hand immediately. Fuming, he stared her down. "Ms. Sunsteen, I don't know who you think you are, but let me tell you, if my daughter has anything to do with the resistance, I will hunt her down and kill her myself, but as the saying goes, she's not the brightest bulb in the pack."

Damious placed himself in the middle of the row and calmed the situation as best as he could. "Catherine is right. For now we have to go on with the plan." Turning to Burke, he said, "I hope you have some good news for us, Mr. Burke."

"Yes, I think I do. As you asked, I invited Stone's whole congregation." A demonic smile danced across his face. "In fact, you could say I made it almost impossible for them to say no…at least the leaders. With them gone, the rest will fall back into line."

"Why is this group such a big issue?" Catherine asked. Turning to face Damious, she continued, "I know you have this burning desire to keep religion alive for people, but what is the big deal with this group? Are they part of the resistance or something?"

Burke let out a loud bellow of a laugh. "Resistance? Ha! No, but they have shown that they're willing to stand against the church growth model that we've put forward. You know, we've been working since the '70s to get the churches to focus more on the personal aspect of worship, to make it all about feelings and fun. Well, this group isn't looking for that. Our sound system didn't seem to affect them, and the emergent, open, free-belief system we've been striving for doesn't seem to be touching them either. They have chosen instead to be poor and ignore community outreach programs for a more closed scriptural-based worship and lifestyle, something that is obviously anathema to the new sustainability plans the UGSE is putting forward. They must be stopped, and tonight is the night."

Smiling and feeling a sense of excitement for the first time since coming on this trip, Catherine asked, "Do you think so? You think the sound system has been tweaked enough to touch these dissenters?"

"Yes, yes of course. We've tweaked it enough."

Catherine felt a wave of peace wash over her at this news, and Damious leaned back comfortably in his chair, sipping coffee watching his plot unfold. As the waitress brought their breakfast, the discussion turned toward the meeting that night. Burke went over the agenda. First would be an invocation of peace through the new global government followed by a quick pledge of allegiance to the American flag—they had to keep up appearances, after all. Then Wright would be speaking about the sustainable building projects, both businesses coming to town, and housing and child care/school plans. Then Catherine would be speaking on the societal sustainability plans. Finally, Damious would be speaking on universal faith based sustainability and inclusiveness plans. There would be a brief question-and-answer time at the conclusion, followed by a reception.

The subliminal sound system would come online after the pledge, and the question-and-answer time would show whether or not it was successful. All of them knew that the plans would be implemented with or without wide public support, but it would be much easier if the majority blissfully went along with the plans. The last thing anyone wanted was another war.

Through a mouthful of eggs, Wright asked, "So is that it? Everything is set? Great, but we have the small problem of Daedalus. We have no idea what his plans are."

Catherine rolled her eyes. Wiping her mouth, she commented, "Justin, quit worrying about it. The meeting is seven hours away. If he has a plan, we'll be ready." Looking over at Burke, she asked, "You do have security all taken care of, right?"

"The one thing I'm sure about is that the security is tight. My men have been briefed and are well ready. Our town is relatively small, so we know most of the people and anyone that my guys don't know isn't getting in, plain and simple."

"Good, then I'm going to my room to get my bags together. What time are we planning to leave?"

Damious answered, "We'll be leaving around one o'clock, my dear."

"One o'clock. Very good. I'll be ready, and, Michael, I would appreciate it if you called me by my name because I am not and never will be dear to you." She stood up and excused herself from the table. The men stood in respect and sat back down.

"What a—"Justin began.

"Now, now, Mr. Wright, we mustn't be crude." Damious laughed cruelly. "Ms. Sunsteen has the right to her opinions. Just because she's always wrong is of no consequence to us."

The other men joined his laughter. "Now down to business," Burke began. "I take it Ms. Sunsteen doesn't know anything about our plans to get rid of Stone's people?"

Satisfied in his ruse, Damious answered, "No, she doesn't know a thing. It's always satisfying to take care of multiple business deals at once. We get to test the subliminal machine, and we get to remove a stumbling block all at once."

"We can only hope that Stone and Fox turn up too," Wright said, scowling.

At the name Fox, Tempess brightened up. "You mean, you think the Foxes will be showing their faces?"

Damious answered, "Why not? We can assume that they are working with Daedalus, although, how they got in touch with him I can't imagine. His last known location was Dallas, Texas, and they've not been there recently."

Tempess jumped in and said, "Well, we don't really know where Fox was between shooting Wolfe and showing up in LA. It's very possible he got together with Daedalus during that time."

Wright looked concerned. "Who's Wolfe, and what do you mean Fox shot him? Can't we get him on a murder charge?"

Wondering what this idiot was doing in their midst, Tempess answered with an annoyed tone, "No, Mr. Wright. We can't get him on a murder charge. It would put too much heat on Techne-Corp and the foundation. Could you imagine the fallout if the environmentalists got wind of the fact we were digging in the desert? Heck, it's practically sacred to the kooks! Anyway, whatever made Fox do it, the fact that he killed his best friend will haunt him forever. We accomplished what we set out to do, so why bring any light to it?"

"What were you trying to accomplish in the desert?"

Damious answered, "Not that it's any of your business, Justin, but we were trying to acquire some artifacts for our religious collection at the foundation. We found what we were looking for, so why not just leave it at that." Damious's tone showed that he meant the discussion was closed, so Wright let it go.

The three men staying in the hotel excused themselves from the table to go and get their luggage together while Burke stayed at the table looking over some charts and finishing his coffee. After Tempess exited the elevator at his floor, Wright spoke to Damious in a whisper, "That Burke guy needs to go."

"Don't worry, Justin, everything is under control."

The elevator doors opened, and the two men went their separate ways. At one o'clock, the small band met up at the front pickup area in front of the hotel. Burke had arranged a very nice-sized SUV to take them to town. After everyone was settled in the car, Damious announced, "Here we go, people, on the first of many adventures to come for the UGSE." The driver put the car in gear and sped away.

* * *

Amanda was pleased when Catherine gave up her attempt to get her out of the room. It would have been very awkward if Marcus showed up and she was there. After getting rid of Catherine, Amanda finished packing her clothes and set to work getting into her wig. Since joining the resistance two years ago, she had played her part excellently. Neither she nor Rachel knew the other was resistance. Both were giving information to Marcus, overlapping from time to time, but their different views had helped Marcus get a pretty good grasp on the United Global Society Association through Justin Wright's front company, Wright Master Builders.

Justin Wright had been on the forefront of the global government for decades, but he had only recently got the position as head of the UGSA. His ties to the green industry made him very wealthy once the global warming scare of the '90s took hold. His company got most of the governmental contracts available through congressional earmarks set aside for local Go Green projects.

Marcus's blood began to boil every time he thought about the misinformation relayed to the public through the corrupt media and education systems. Justin Wright was one of the most crooked salesmen of them all. He took his ill-gotten gains and poured them into schemes to bring about the end of capitalism and American constitutional governance. His greatest achievement came with the environmental disaster of 2012. Orchestrated to coincide with the Mayan prophecies of a doomsday, Justin and the foundation discovered a way to not really destroy but change nature enough to make people believe it was going to be the end of the world. Of course, they came out like knights in shining armor to fix the problem. Within a few short months, the incidents were corrected, and everything was put back to the way people believed it was supposed to be. Only those who knew the molecular manipulations could really detect the changes. A genetically modified world gave the UGSE total power over nature. They could manipulate any disaster they chose now with a few clicks of a computer keyboard, a secret that only a very few people were privy to.

Amanda had joined the resistance two years ago when she had had enough abuse from her father. Marcus frequently haunted bars and clubs looking for people who seemed to fit the profile for the resistance. People who wanted to fight for the ideals of freedom simply sought out the resistance, but the key to battling the UGSE came from insiders. Getting them to turn was always a delicate task. However, Marcus knew Amanda from Rachel's reports, and her intelligence would be highly profitable for the organization. He followed her for about four months before making his move.

He met her at a local club in downtown LA. It was obvious that she'd been in a fight with her father because not only had she been crying, but a huge black-and-blue bruise peeked out from under her short-sleeved blouse marking where he had struck her. After buying her several drinks, he began asking questions about her father and family, leading her toward thoughts of betraying her father. Marcus knew that manipulating someone took time and patience. He met with her over the course of a month before revealing that he was with the resistance and wanted to induct her in as a spy. At first, she was angry. Here she thought she had met a friend, and all along, he just wanted to use her. To her amazement, he agreed with her assessment. He admitted that he saw her usefulness and wanted to acquire it and added that it didn't change the fact that her father was a giant hemorrhoid who did not deserve her loyalty. He also played on her need to belong and be safe by letting her know that she could always depend on him. If she ever felt his plans were too dangerous, she could say no. She thought about it and decided that anything she could do to bring down her father was what she wanted. She put up with a lot to get the information out. Beatings were a normal occurrence for her, so allowing them to continue with the knowledge that eventually she'd get her revenge gave her the courage to endure.

After arriving in Denver, she managed to go through her father's papers, and what she found cut her to the core. She decided that once she passed the info to Marcus, her cover would be blown, so he needed to extract her as soon as possible. It was only by God's providence that he was just a few hours away and in the perfect position to help her. She put out an alert bulletin for him over the resistance network, the only means he gave her to contact him because he couldn't risk her father getting his direct line number.

Once they talked, he knew time was of the essence, so he put together the old-man disguise and moved the plan into action. He told her to get copies of everything she could get her hands on and any passwords and information on her dad. While he was driving out to the hotel, she sent everything she had via a secure line to Marcus's contact in Europe. Once her disappearance was noticed, Wright would no doubt get his people to change all access to his private records. Hopefully, by the time they arrived in Stone's town, all the information would be downloaded, and then they could try to stop Damious and Wright's plot.

Marcus's jaw almost hit the ground when he and Amanda emerged from the hotel. As soon as they exited the building, six angels surrounded them with shields, and he knew that the protection they provided would keep prying eyes from following their escape. They hurried around the side of the building where he had parked Stewart's SUV. Amanda was surprised at the car, and Marcus, reading her mind, said, "Yeah, I know. Not the most subtle of rides, but it's all I had at my disposal, so get in and let's get out of here!" Once they were on the road, Marcus began telling her the whole story of Fox, Stone, Rachel, and himself, their trip to New Life, and his conversion.

So much of the story seemed unbelievable, even up to the angels protecting them as they left the hotel, but the only thing that came out of her mouth was, "Rachel's been a part of the resistance all this time? I can't believe neither of us knew."

"Yeah, I bet Rachel's going to be surprised too."

Pulling off onto the side of the road, he told her to take over driving because he needed to contact Stewart and let him know what was about to go down. As she pulled back onto the highway, he realized that his battery was dead. Knowing better than to throw his phone but needing to release his frustration, he banged on the dashboard.

Surprised, Amanda asked, "What? What is it?"

"My stupid battery is dead, that's what! All the stupid technology in the world, and I forget to bring any batteries or a charger."

"Can't you use my phone?"

"No, Amanda. I can't. They'll be trying to track your phone. As a matter of fact, give it to me." She handed him her phone.

"Is there anything on this phone about me or the resistance? Any information that you can't live without?"

"No."

"Well then"—he threw the phone out the window—"we'll just get rid of it."

"What are you doing?"

"You said there wasn't anything you couldn't live without, and I couldn't take the chance that they would track it."

"But it had all my friends' numbers and stuff. How am I going to get in touch with them now?"

"What did you think was going to happen now? You're not allowed to talk with anyone you know from your past. You're gone now, nada, finished. We're going to have to get you a new identity, and we'll probably have to move you to another part of the world…at least another part of the country."

Her fate began to sink in, and she started tearing up. "No, I guess I hadn't thought that far ahead." Looking at him, she corrected herself, "I mean, of course I've thought about it. It's just that I guess I never let it be real."

They sat in silence for a little while until Marcus finally spoke up. "Well, we'll worry about that later. Right now, we've got to get to that meeting and try and help them."

Thanking God for the GPS and four-wheel drive of the SUV, Marcus tried to keep his eyes on the road. They couldn't take the main highways because they might be watched, so it was back roads all the way. Since devising the plan to help Amanda escape and implementing it, he hadn't got a chance to sleep and was beginning to feel the effects of sleep deprivation. Trying to keep his mind focused, he asked Amanda, "Back in LA, why did you call Rachel to get you away from your father instead of me?"

"Well, duh! Back then I just wanted to get away from my dad. He'd never hit me across the face before, and I just got scared. I thought if I called you to extract me, my mission would be over, and I wasn't ready for that to happen. Truth be told, I wasn't actually ready yet, but I knew as soon as I passed you this information, they would know it was me that leaked it, so I just didn't have a choice. I figured Rachel would have been able to talk my dad around." Taking a moment to think, she continued, "I had no idea Rach was in such trouble, and come to think of it, how long has she been married? I had no idea, although thinking back now. It would explain why she never hooked up with anyone when we went out—"

"Shush! Just shush a minute."

Surprised by his outburst, she slouched slightly in her seat and silently maneuvered the car. Marcus was studying her technique with the steering wheel and heard a quiet *thwapping* coming from under the vehicle. "Oh, snap!" he said, looking over at her, "How long have you been fighting with the wheel? Pull the car over."

Not understanding his comment, she pulled over to the side of the road and turned off the engine. "What do you mean fighting with the wheel?"

"You didn't feel the car pulling to the right?"

"Well, now that you mention it, yeah, maybe a little, but I just thought it was the road. What's it mean?"

He answered while opening the door, "Well, if you couple it with the *thwapping* noise coming from under the car, it means we probably have"—he kicked the right front passenger tire—"a flat."

"I'm sorry, Marcus. I'm used to taking cabs and town cars everywhere with a driver, I guess I missed it."

Opening the trunk to find a brand-new full-sized tire but no tire iron, Marcus let out a line of expletives that would've made a soldier blush. Feeling defeated, he slumped to the ground, put his head in his hands, and just sat.

Surprised to see her handler and mentor so dejected, Amanda tried to figure out what to do, but nothing sprang to mind. As she sat down next to him, she commented, "Where are those stupid angels now when we need them? If this is all about God's big plan or whatever, why isn't *He* helping us?"

Taking his head out of his hands, Marcus began laughing short broken laughs like a madman. Amanda felt fear rising as she thought Marcus was losing his mind. He reached over, grabbed her face, and kissed her cheek. "Amanda! You're brilliant! Of course, we need to ask for help."

Now she really did think he was losing his mind. "Uh, yeah, sure, Marcus. Let's ask for help as soon as a car comes by—"

"No, silly girl, not ask someone for help, but ask God for help."

"Come on, Marcus. I was just being obnoxious, just playing on your fantasy. God is not coming to help us. Get a grip, man."

But he had already fallen to his knees, raised his hands to the heavens, and was saying, "Now, God, I'm new at this, and I don't know exactly the right way to pray or anything, but You've shown me great things over the past few days, and I know You're watching over us. Please send us some help."

No sooner had the words passed his lips than over the horizon came a car cruising toward them. Amanda's jaw dropped open, and Marcus silently mouthed a thank-you. It was an electric car, what Marcus would normally call a toy, but today it was the most beautiful thing he'd ever laid eyes on. As it pulled over across the road from them, a woman got out and asked what she could do. Marcus asked if she had a tire iron in her car. She answered that she didn't and wouldn't know what to do with one if she did. Smiling, she offered him her phone to call for help. He thanked her, pulled up the world network on the screen, found a number to the nearest gas station, and dialed the number. A man answered on the other side and said he would be out to meet them with a tire iron in about an hour or two. While Marcus wasn't pleased with the delay, he knew it would still give them time to get to the meeting.

Amanda whispered in his ear, "Don't you think we could call them and warn them with her phone?"

Wanting to kick himself for not thinking of it himself, he asked the woman if she'd mind if he made another call. Being pleased to help, she told him to go ahead. After trying Stone, Stewart, and Fox, he realized her number wouldn't be recognized by their phones, and they weren't going to answer. He thanked her as he returned her phone, they said polite good-byes, and she drove away, leaving the two of them to chat.

"All right, I'm not saying I believe or anything, but tell me a little bit more about your God experiences," Amanda requested. "I don't know if that car was happenstance or an answer to your prayer, but I'd like to know more."

Pleased that God had opened this door, he sat down and told her everything that he knew and planted a seed that he hoped would take root and grow strong.

* * *

After Stewart had relayed the story of his infidelity, the small group sat quietly for a few minutes, pondering the awesome power of God and, sadly, how long it could take for prayers to be answered. The youth were quietly talking among themselves when finally, Kara, the youngest of the group, a girl with mischievous brown eyes and dark curly hair tied back in a ponytail, spoke up, "Well, Okay. Now what?"

Her boldness snapped everyone out of their contemplations, and Fox, looking over at Stewart, said, "Yes, now what?"

Everyone turned their attention to Donald Stewart, expecting a plan. "Well, don't look at me. Andrew is the one who came up with the theory of the mind-warp machine, and you all know this town better than me. I think it's up to you all to have a plan. I'm here for prayer support and, if need be, other kinds of help."

Scott spoke up, "What do you mean? Andrew came up with the theory of the mind-warp machine? When did this happen?"

Now everyone's gaze fell upon Stone, and his discomfort grew. "We don't have time to go into my past right now. Let's just say that I worked at New Life for a few years developing various technologies. I'll tell you all about the fake environmental disaster of 2012 that I was a part of another time too, but for now, yes, I helped develop the prototype for the subliminal machine. It was supposed to be used on world leaders. You know, if they weren't cooperating, they could just be mind-controlled." Everyone was staring in horror at the thought of the words coming out of their pastor's mouth. Noticing their looks, he defended himself, "Hey, I know it sounds bad, but at the time, I was not only not following God, I was also being indoctrinated by this kind of psychology. I honestly believed I was helping mankind. After all, I thought these people were right." Looking miserably at the floor, he added, "I was wrong."

Not being able to control her emotions, Isabelle crawled over to him and kissed him. Turning to everyone else, she said, "Andrew was and is a good man. He only did what he thought was right. Bringing the world into harmony and balance is a Christian ideal too, is it not? Damious, the spirits—I mean, demons, and the other leaders have learned to manipulate the language to fit their needs, and they have led many astray, so before anyone judges Andrew, you better judge yourself first." She turned back to him, hugged him, and looked into his eyes. He just stared back at her with a thankful gaze.

"No one here is judging him, Isabelle," Bob interrupted. "I just think we're all shocked, both by what he's telling us is and has been going on and the fact that he had a part in it. I think I can speak for all of us when I say that we love and support him as our pastor and friend." Everyone nodded their head in agreement.

"Thanks, you guys. That means more to me than you know. I have a hard enough time forgiving myself, but maybe God can use me now to stop their plans. Here's what I know about the machine. It works on the premise that our brains take in far more information than we comprehend…visually, audibly, and tactilely. The idea that I came up with and from what I've seen from Isabelle's intelligence has to do with undetectable decibels. Basically, they use a very powerful subwoofer that puts out deep bass tones. It puts the listener in a state of openness, for lack of a better term."

"It basically puts you in a hypnotic state," Isabelle chimed in. "Some of us can achieve it through meditation or drugs, but others need help or, like in this case, have no choice but to become open."

Eryn, an intelligent nineteen-year-old with light brown eyes and brown layered hair, spoke up, "Well, if this thing can control minds, then why are we going to go in there and get zapped? I mean, do we have some kind of immunity pill or something?"

Scott answered, "We have something better than that. We have the power of prayer and the Holy Spirit indwelling us. It's like the people at Resurrection. We all noticed and wondered at how people we've known forever could have accepted all the new programs put forward by Burke and his gang. Now we know. Burke had been using the subliminal machine, and those with a weak will fell prey to it. We were spared because we had the true faith and clung to it."

"That's right," Stone finished. "We were spared because God was protecting us. Prayer is our most powerful ally right now, and while we go to the meeting to stir trouble and stop this thing, Doris, James, Miriam, Stewart, Debbie, Jerry, Yvonne, and Tom will be praying."

"We'll also have people all over the world praying," Stewart interrupted. "I've been in contact with other prayer groups, and starting at six thirty our time, people will begin the prayers until I call them and let them know the outcome."

"Cool," the youth group said as one.

"Okay," Fox took over, "so here's the basic plan. Bob, Kevin, Scott, and the kids are going to go in and take their seats. The adults will be scattered throughout the room while you young people will stay toward the back. From what we've managed to gather about the agenda of the meeting, it will start out with an invocation and the pledge, and then the speakers will begin.

I don't know who's going to be first, but as soon as you all hear something you know to be wrong, which shouldn't take much time with these people, you start getting loud. Shout out 'liar!' or 'yeah right!' or whatever comes to mind."

"Except no swear words!" Miriam intoned. Everyone looked at her and laughed.

"Thanks for that break in the seriousness, Ms. Matiska," Zac, a high-spirited eighteen-year-old with spiked blond hair and deep blue eyes, jumped in. "Like the first thing out of our mouth would be cursing. I think you should be more worried about our phrases and insults." The other youth got mischievous grins on their faces, and Miriam threw up her hands in mock disgust.

"Back on track, everyone," Rachel guided.

"Now when Burke's guys are busy with you all," Fox continued, "we'll sneak over to wherever the PA system is, and Drew will try and disable it while Rach and I keep guard. Oh, and by the way, you can stick these in your ears"—he handed everyone a pair of earplugs—"just in case." Everyone took the earplugs and laughed. "This will pretty much be contingent on God's providence, so if anyone feels like things are going south, you need to get out as quickly as possible."

Yvonne interrupted the conversation, "Well, now that all the plans are out there, I think we should pray and let you all get out the computers and whatever you need to get your plans fixed in your minds."

"Yvonne's right," Stewart spoke. "It's time to pray, and then with the equipment Marcus sent, I should be able to hack into the CCTV footage at the Town Hall and get some idea of where things are."

Everyone gathered together, and after their prayer, they broke off into groups to plan their individual sorties.

Chapter 8

God is, even though the whole world deny Him.
Truth stands, even if there be no public support. It is
self-sustained.

—Mohandas Gandhi

Blessed is a man who perseveres under trial; for once
he has been approved, he will receive the crown of life,
which the Lord has promised to those who love Him.

—James1:12

When the small group of UGSE officials rolled into town, the streets looked like a major holiday carnival had been planned. UGSE bunting, flags, and signs of welcome lined the main street, and vendors had set up little shops of trinkets and food. Citizens mingled and chatted, wondering what exciting thing their little town had been chosen for to have such important VIPs coming to meet them.

As the car pulled up to the town hall, people milled around hoping for a glimpse of Catherine Sunsteen or Justin Wright, two of the most famous and popular politicians on the world stage. They were not disappointed because Sunsteen and Wright not only made an appearance but joined in the street party to talk and shake hands with everyone who came up to them. Many people wondered who Damious was because he made no effort to mingle with the little people, as he thought of them. He found Catherine and Justin's behavior beneath high-ranking officials of the global government. Burke joined the two politicians schmoozing the crowd while Tempess excused himself to get some food from one of the vendors. Damious asked Burke if he'd mind if he went in and looked over the setup. Burke pointed the way, returning to his politicking instead of showing Damious around, something that Damious would not forget.

Walking into the town hall was bliss for Michael. As soon as the doors closed, the din of the street party was silenced, and he walked noiselessly through the freshly waxed halls to the double doors of the council chambers. As he walked toward the doors, he could hear the technicians hooking up the sound system because the doors had been propped open. Damious strolled casually into the room. The space was adequate, and the stage had been set up nicely. He immediately noticed the disparities between the UGSE and American flags and couldn't help but smile inwardly as he thought about the ease of conquering of the American public. *Make enough of a crisis, and eventually they all come running for the government to help.*

Unconsciously looking over his shoulder to see if he'd been followed, he meandered his way through the chairs, up to the stage, and over to the men working on hooking up the speakers for the subliminal sound system. "Hello, gentlemen."

Surprised at the interruption, the two workmen grunted hello and turned back to their work. Not being used to people disregarding his presence, he cleared his throat loudly and waited for one or both of the men to address him. One of the technicians, a tall, lanky young man in his late twenties with intense blue eyes and short, spiky, bleached hair, ripped jeans, and a shirt with an electric blue guitar printed on it, turned to him, stood up, and spoke, "May I help you?"

Annoyed at his lack of civility, Damious answered in a very authoritative voice, "Yes, you can. I am one of the featured speakers tonight and also one of the developers of this system, so I'd like to inspect your work and have you walk me through what you've done—if you can spare the time!"

Shocked at his tone and awed by his presence, both young men stopped what they were doing and introduced themselves. "Wow! You're the dude who came up with this? Wicked! This is totally righteous! My name is Rick, and this guy here is Tony."

Tony, also lanky but not as tall, reached out his hand to shake Damious's and said, "Hi. Like he said, I'm Tony. This really is an extraordinary setup. Is this really the only one? I can't believe anyone wouldn't have another prototype ready to go."

Damious was surprised at the difference between the two young men. While Rick came across as an immature basement-dwelling geek, Tony, with his soulful brown eyes and matching well-groomed hair, dressed in clean hole-free jeans and a polo shirt, had an aura of quiet, thoughtful intelligence that Damious found intriguing. He wondered how someone like Tony could stand to be around someone like Rick.

"To answer your question, Rick, no, I did not come up with the idea, but I did help in the development of it and want to be sure that it functions properly. And, Tony, of course we have others prepared, just as soon as we make sure this one works." Taking out one of his business cards, he handed it to Tony. "Here's my card. I get a sense that you have a good mind. If you're interested in working on the development of projects like this, give me a call."

Amazed at his offer, Tony took the card with a polite thank-you. Rick expected a card too, but when Damious didn't offer him one, he just shook it off and proceeded to go over the system with Tony and Damious. After they had explained everything and he had made sure it was all hooked up properly, Damious told the young men that they were welcome to leave and go join the party. He would be following momentarily but needed to check something out first. Pleased to be given permission to leave, the two friends hurried out the doors and into the street. After he was sure they had gone, Damious slipped under the stage and approached the sound system. He opened the bag he'd been carrying and removed a small but very powerful explosive device. Opening a secret panel in the sound system, he placed the explosive inside, closed the panel, and imagined the surprise of the town, country, and world at the useless loss of life and devastation caused by the return of the resistance. He couldn't believe his luck in Marcus turning up now. Everything was on his side, and his plan for control of the world was becoming an ever-increasing reality. Pleased at the effortlessness of his task, Damious walked to the double doors, closed them, strolled through the hall, opened the door to the mirth in the street, took a deep breath, and joined his comrades in the party.

*   *   *

After waiting nearly three hours for the gas station attendant to send someone out to them and paying four times what a tire iron should cost, Marcus decided instead of paying extra for the grease monkey to change his flat, he'd do it himself. The act of changing the tire only took about twenty minutes, and they were back on the road, this time with Marcus driving. Annoyed at the time lost and about not bringing extra batteries, Marcus said, "I hope we get there in time. This is going to be very bad for everyone if Damious carries out his plan. How did you get this information when your dad didn't?"

"Well, a while ago, I had a friend of mine hack into my dad's computer, and he noticed that my dad could also access other people at the UGSE and its affiliates. He hooked my computer into their databases." Reaching into the backseat, she retrieved her inoperative laptop, which Marcus had already checked for bugging devices. "He said that my dad probably didn't even realize it was there, and it turned out to be a glitch, so very rarely did any information come across it. Jake, that's my friend, actually thought it was somebody's backdoor—"

"Amanda, stay focused."

"Right, sorry. Anyway, last night or early this morning, I was logging into the GNN site to let them know the details of my interview with Catherine Sunsteen when an alert showed up on my screen. I clicked on it, and it took me to Michael Damious's personal files, and it just opened on what I showed you. Interestingly, as soon as I printed it, it just vanished. It was like it never existed, but at least I copied it before it deleted. That's when I made the decision to get out."

Shocked into silence, Marcus just sat quietly to let the info sink in. "You know, Amanda, I think it was God or the angels or something. I mean, info just showing up at the exact time we needed it. It's just too coincidental."

Rolling her eyes and shaking her head, Amanda answered, "Come on, Marcus. I'll admit that everything you told me that happened this weekend is eye-opening, but don't you think this is a little far-fetched? I mean, God working over the net?"

"Is it any stranger than believing God came down as a man, took on the sins of the world, died, rose again, and ascended into heaven? I don't think so, but I believe that's exactly what happened, and if God can do that, well, I think He can work some mojo to get information out to people who need it."

"Jeez, Marcus, No need to get so sensitive. I'm just not ready to accept all this crazy stuff. Let me keep believing in accidents and happenstance, okay?"

"Fine, whatever. It just frustrates me because I've seen this stuff. I've experienced it firsthand, and even though I don't get all of it, it just bugs me that I can't convince you."

Laughing, she teased, "Well, Marcus, maybe it's not up to you to convince me. Maybe it will happen all in good time. For now, you better put the pedal to the metal so we can get there and make a difference—no matter where the information came from."

Joining in her laughter, he said, "Yeah, I guess that's pretty arrogant of me. As Fox would say, let's get it on!" He put his foot down on the gas pedal and accelerated as fast as he dared, praying that no police would pull him over.

* * *

Pastor Stone called everyone together. Looking at the clock on the Davieses' wall, he saw that it was 6:15 p.m. It was time. The group took each other's hands and formed a prayer circle. Stone began to pray, "Dear Lord, we pray Your hand of providence will guide us tonight. Help each of us to do only what You would have us do. Keep everyone at the meeting safe. We pray especially for the souls of those who are lost, specifically Michael Damious, Catherine Sunsteen, Justin Wright, Burke Smith and William Tempess." At Tempess's name, Fox flinched and squeezed Rachel's hand a little too hard. She looked at him and squeezed his gently. "Lord, You know the enemy, and You know his plans. We ask that Your will is done tonight and ask blessing upon us all. Amen." After he finished praying, he pulled out a vial of oil for anointing. As he walked to each person, he made the sign of the cross on their forehead and prayed an individual blessing. When he had finished, everyone released their hands, and Peter felt the need to yell, "Yay! God!" while raising his hands to the ceiling.

Smiling at the young man's enthusiasm, Fox said, "All right. Now everyone knows the plan. I see no reason to go over it anymore. Kids, you all leave now and go mill around the concession stands until almost everyone is inside. They nodded their heads and proceeded to skip, jump, and twirl out of the house. "I love those kids!" Fox laughed. "Okay, now, Stewart and you prayer warriors, get to giving us prayer cover. We're really going to need it. Bob, Scott, and Kevin, you guys start walking over to town hall and get your seats." Noticing the clock now read 6:35 p.m., Fox continued, "Andrew, Rachel, and myself will leave in about fifteen minutes and sneak around the back of the building to the window Rick left open for us. Okay, let's get going, and good luck!"

Isabelle walked up to Stone, flung her arms around his neck, and held him tight. "Andrew, please let me go with you!"

Drawing his lips to hers, kissing her gently, and looking into her eyes, he replied, "No. I have to be able to focus on the work at hand. There is bound to be massive spiritual warfare going on, and if Adder attacks you again, I will have to choose between the mission and you. Please don't put me in that position." Tears ran down her cheeks. As he wiped them gently away, he continued, "If you're with us, Adder will probably be able to find us. If you're here and he attacks you, Stewart will be able to cast him away. You will be safer here, and we will be safer with you staying here, okay?"

Looking dejectedly at the floor, knowing he was right, she nodded her head and walked slowly over to her father. Taking her hand, Stewart looked into her eyes. "Isabelle, we will keep you safe, and we can use you to pray with us."

"But I don't know how to pray. I'll probably just make a mess of it."

"Nonsense," Miriam replied while smiling kindly, taking her hand and pulling her over to the prayer circle that was forming. "None of us knew what we were doing when we started, but God led us. He'll lead you too."

Grateful for her friendship, Isabelle allowed herself to be drawn into the circle. Stewart joined them while Fox, Stone, and Rachel prepared for their mission.

*　　*　　*

Once the youth reached the carnival, they all bought drinks, and Kara, Peter, and Zac decided to draw attention to themselves by running up to everyone they saw and giving them hugs while yelling, "Free hugs! Free hugs!" Josh, Kat, and Eryn watched their friends and shook their heads while smiling and clapping for them. After their mirthful play, which was really reconnaissance, the six friends climbed a tree near the entrance of the building and watched the people entering.

As Bob, Scott, and Kevin walked up to the entrance, the kids started yelling hello and waving. The three men waved back and entered the building. Once inside, they walked to the council chambers and were taken aback at the sight. Bob whispered, "Are they serious? Plausible Reality? Is that anything like plausible deniability?"

Scott was fuming. "Do you notice the flag? Do you see that they put the UGSE flag higher than the American flag?"

As they were looking, Burke Smith noticed them and walked over. "Well, hello, gentlemen! How do you like the concept?"

Kevin answered first. "Global Sustainable Societal Development? Hasn't society sustained itself for all of creation? Why do we suddenly need a plausible reality? You want my honest opinion? I think it's stupid. I think it stinks of socialism or communism or some kind of negative *ism* that means people like you think you know what's best for people like…well, the rest of us." Getting right into his face, Kevin stated, "I think it and you are pathetic!" Standing back up straight, he finished, "That's what I think."

Flustered, Burke turned red with anger, but before he could open his mouth, Scott jumped in, "And what's with the flags? Why is the UGSE higher than Old Glory? Do you really think Americans are going to stand for the global government to usurp us?"

Burke's anger turned to amusement. "What America, Scott? Who's standing up for America? I mean, besides you? When are you going to open your eyes and see that the global government is here? It has already usurped ours. I mean really, do you think our president is there by popular choice? My god, man, he was raised and handpicked for this job by the UGSE. Since 2012, when the Congress gave their constitutional powers to the president and he gave them to the UN, it was over. No one in the world has actually been sovereign since then."

Turning his attention back to Kevin, he said, "And quite frankly, Kevin, those of us in power and coming to power do know far more than you, and what's more, we know what's best for this planet. Believe me, there will be ways of dealing with dissidents like you."

"Oh, you mean like brainwashing?"

"No, Mr. Davies, I mean like death." Leaving the three friends in shock, he turned and walked away to greet other people.

The three friends drew close to each other and wondered aloud if Burke really meant that and how would it be accomplished. Instead of following the plan and splitting up, the three stayed together toward the back of the room in anticipation of something worse than mind-warping. Unseen by their eyes, three angels had been surrounding them with their shields out, warning the demonic enemies poised for attack to keep away. Their light shone brightly, disturbing the demons' eyes, keeping them at bay.

At the front of the hall, Damious felt uneasy, although he didn't know why. Looking out over the crowd, he noticed the three friends huddled together near the back. Calling Burke over, he asked, "Who are those men?"

"Oh, those are Stone's followers."

"Are they a threat to us, to our plans?"

"I shouldn't think so. They came to see what would happen. I think they know about the machine, but the fact that they're staying so far away tells me they aren't going to be a problem. Actually, they look a little afraid." Letting a wicked smile play across his lips, he finished, "I think the reality of globalization is hitting them, and they realize that very soon they're going to have to decide to join or die."

Eyeing him with a little respect, Damious asked, "Did you threaten them with death?"

"Let's just say I put the fear of the UGSE in them."

"Good, Mr. Smith, just make sure you don't go overboard!"

After he finished speaking, a raucous group of teenagers rumbled into the room. Laughing and joking, one of them, a tall twenty-year-old man with short cropped blond hair and green eyes, waved at Burke and shouted, "Hi, Mr. Smith, been to Washington lately?" Everyone in the room laughed, except of course Burke, who just scowled and turned his back.

Kat, another twenty-year-old, with long shiny brown hair with blonde highlights and bright blue eyes, smacked Josh on the back of the head and said, "What do you think you're doing?"

Holding his side from laughing, he answered, "Come on, Kat, we're supposed to cause trouble. How would it look if we all just walked in like good little children, sat down, and then waited to be disruptive? Better to get the ball rolling!"

Zac and Kara and Peter and Eryn linked arms and proceeded to dance around in circles in pairs. All their parents were in the room shooting disapproving looks at them, so they slinked quietly to their seats and sat down, still being disruptive but quietly.

Bob, Kevin, and Scott were looking around concerned. They needed to get in touch with Stone, but didn't dare use their phones. Individually, they all sent up a prayer for God to protect the crowd because they knew in their hearts something was about to happen.

*　*　*

Outside of the town hall Fox, Stone, and Rachel crept silently toward the building. The streets had gone quiet, as it seemed everyone had gone inside for the big meeting. After deciding the coast was clear, the three friends hurried over to the big tree the kids had climbed, waiting for their final dash to the window on the side of the building. When Fox was about to give the signal to run, he noticed a black SUV with its headlights blinking. Turning to Stone, he whispered, "Do you see what I see?"

"Yeah. SOS...Marcus." Knowing the signal, he pulled out his cell, turned it on, and held it up so that it shone toward the vehicle. A minute later, two people exited the car and nonchalantly walked toward the tree. When they were sure no one was watching, they hurried over. "What on earth are you doing here?" Stone asked.

"Long story, brother," Marcus replied. "Amanda here has some important news."

Rachel flung her arms around Amanda. "Gosh, girl. I didn't recognize you with the wig. What are you—? How did you—? What are you doing here?"

"Long story, Rach. Too long to go into now. The important thing is that I'm working with the resistance too, and you've got to get your people out of the building. Heck, you have to get everyone out of the building." Catching her breath, she said, "Damious is planning to blow it up and blame it on the resistance."

Everyone's jaw dropped open. "What do you mean? I thought this was about mind control?" Fox asked.

"It *is*, in a way. He's going to let my father speak, and then while Catherine is giving her spiel, he's going to detonate an explosive device under the stage. When he realized that you guys had escaped, he figured you'd be coming after him, or at least be trying to cause trouble for his plans, so he came up with an alternate one. He figures that the people will already be pliable. My dad's speech will be a crowd-pleaser, so turning the people against the resistance after we get blamed for the carnage will give them even more power. We've got to do something."

"All right, let me think a minute," Stone said. "Okay, here's the plan. Jason and I will still go after the machine. After all, they still don't know we're coming. I've had some training in explosives, so perhaps I can disable the bomb. You three need to get inside and tell our guys to get ready to get people out of there. I don't know where they'll be sitting, but you should be able to find them easily enough, Rachel."

"Okay. I'm sure the kids can do something to get everyone out if we can't." Rachel said.

"Our inside guy, Ricky, can help too. He'll be helping Jason and I get close to the device." Then Stone bowed his head; everyone else followed. "Okay, Lord, we really need your help now. Guide us and please help keep everyone safe. Amen." Everyone said amen, and as they prepared to go their separate ways, Rachel looked to the sky and almost fainted. Fox rushed to her side to support her and almost fell over himself. Everyone looked up, and shock overcame them. Not only was a battle getting ready to rage inside, a battle was happening in the sky above.

*   *   *

While Damious, Catherine, Burke, Wright, and Tempess were meeting for brunch, the small church was learning about Stewart's past, and Marcus and Amanda had yet to break down on the side of the road, Angelous was calling a meeting of the demon lords. "Hail, powerful ones!" Angelous greeted. "There is a gathering storm on the horizon, and we must be prepared to meet it." Morpheus, Lucius, Jezeel, Adder, and the rest of the twenty-four lords nodded in understanding. "The One has a powerful force of prayer warriors giving cover to the enemy. They are protected by The One Himself, so we cannot locate them, but we can fight the Host protecting the others." Shouts of agreement and aggression rang throughout the cavern. "Our human ally, Michael Damious, has prepared a deliciously heinous plan to be carried out tonight. Jezeel and Lucius you will probably be losing some humans tonight. Tempess, Wright, and Smith are due to be blown up!"

Evil laughter erupted in the room, and Jezeel shouted the loudest. "Praise the dark lord! Wright is the biggest prat I've ever had to deal with! Ha! Ha! Ha! Death to Wright! Death to Wright!" The cheer rose to an earsplitting crescendo. When the moment was right, Angelous got the attention of all by drawing his sword. It glowed a wicked red with yellow and orange tendrils curling outward. Understanding the purpose, the demon lords quieted down and looked to their leader.

"Now while I quite enjoy the evil of the plan, Michael has disappointed me more than once lately, so we must fight the host of heaven and destroy them this time!" As one unit, the demon lords all pulled out their swords and held them high. A chant went up, "Hail, Lucifer! Hail the lord of chaos! Hail, Lucifer! Hail the lord of chaos!" The chant went on and on as the demons worked themselves into a malevolent frenzy. Their eyes flared, and their wings beat a cadence of fury. One by one, the demon lords ascended to their lairs to call together their minions and prepare for the battle.

* * *

In the realm of heaven, the angels of God were also preparing for battle. The archangel Michael had called forth all warrior angels in heaven. "Hail, mighty warriors of God! We have been summoned for a great battle. At this very moment, Lucifer is gathering an army of his demon lords to destroy a group of our Lord's ministers on the earth. A great explosion is set to take place, and many could die. The group of witnesses we are to keep safe is known to their guardians. As I speak, they are protecting each of their charges.

"It is our duty to not interfere with the human's plan, but only to keep the enemy focused on us to give them the time to escape." The angels all nodded. "The army of the enemy has but one purpose, and that is to stop our guardians from protecting their wards. Lucifer will bring multitudes of demonic minions to battle, and we must fight. Watch your opponents. Parry their strikes. If an opportunity opens, then slay them and send them to the waterless places. There they will suffer and find no rest until the great and glorious day that our Lord throws them all into the lake of fire for eternity to be done with their evil forever!"

Shouts of angels burst forth to the heavens. As one, the angelic host and all of heaven cried, "Holy, Holy, Holy, is the Lord God Almighty! Who was and is and is to come! Amen! Blessing and glory and wisdom, thanksgiving and honor and power and might be to our God forever. Amen!" The song went forth through the heavens, a song of joy and peace radiating to the Lamb and to the throne. At the altar of the Lord, prayers offered by the saints ascended with the smoke of the incense to the throne. All eyes were fixed on the throne, singing and praising the Lord.

When the signal was given and the trumpets blown, Michael, the archangel of God, lifted his sword high. White flame, pure and cleansing, shot from the hilt! The other angelic warriors raised their swords and proclaimed as one, "You are worthy, O Lord, to receive glory and honor and power. You created all things, and by Your will they exist!" The angels gathered and prepared themselves for the battle.

* * *

In the Davieses' home, the small group of prayer warriors, joined by others all over the world, thanks to Marcus's list of contacts, offered up scripture, prayers, and songs. Isabelle had never experienced anything like it before. While there were no magical lands or spirit guides to speak with, the power of the Spirit was all around them, filling and guiding them with unseen hands. Doris read from Psalm 108, "'O God, my heart is steadfast; I will sing and give praise...Be exalted, O God, above the heavens, and Your glory above all the earth; that Your beloved may be delivered...give us help from trouble, for the help of man is useless! Through God we will do valiantly, for it is He who shall tread down our enemies.'"

In the quiet that followed, Debbie began to sing the psalm. "Be exalted, O God, above the heavens," and everyone else joined in because it was a favorite praise song for the congregation. Isabelle had never heard the song before, so she sat, hands raised, listening to the praise of God's own words being sent forth in prayer. Her spirit began to soar, and without realizing it, she was taken up in the spirit again, just like in her room. Once again, she stood before the throne, the twenty-four beings still bowing and the strange creatures singing. Veritas stood with her, and she asked, "Why am I here again?"

Smiling, Veritas answered, "The Lord asked that you be brought up to see the battle, so that you may go back to the congregation and share the victory of their prayers."

"But why me? Why not one of the more faithful, like Miriam or Doris or—"

"It is not about who's more faithful, Isabelle. You have a gift, a gift of seeing. Not everyone has the faith to accept visions. Some will question whether what they saw was from God or the devil or if it was their mind playing tricks on them. You have a pure heart, an openness that many don't and thusly can't receive such sight. The prayers sent up for you all of your life were not in vain. The Lord has been protecting you since your baptism and allowed you to experience the other side for what He has planned for you in the future."

"What future?"

"Ah, you are not the first to ask, and I'm sure you won't be the last, but I am not allowed to reveal your destiny. It will work out in its due time."

"So are you saying that God controls everyone? Like a puppet master?"

"No, of course not. If He worked like that, do you think all the evils in the world would exist? He knows the future because He's seen it. He already has knowledge of what will happen. Sometimes He opens and closes doors to guide people, but ultimately it comes down to their choice. The Holy One allows situations to unfold to allow people to see the truth. The problems come when they refuse to see or when the enemy puts stumbling blocks in their way. He brought humanity to Himself when He became man. The suffering of the Son broke down the barrier so that all men could freely come to the Father. The invitation went out to all of mankind when the Holy Spirit was poured out into the world. Every person has a chance to come. Faith is available to all and redemption through the very blood of the man Jesus."

"Well, what about those who never heard of Jesus? Is faith available to them?"

"Faith is available to all. How God chooses to work is not our business. He spoke to you in a dream, did He not? I am called to be a messenger of His truth. You are called to share the Word with whomever God brings to you. To worry more about of how salvation works is foolhardy and useless. We need to focus on the now."

"Won't the others notice that I'm not joining in with them?"

"No. They are praying in the Spirit, and for everyone, that is different. They will assume that you are deep in prayer because you are. You are speaking to God, and He is speaking to you through me."

"All right then, show me what you want me to see."

Veritas breathed deeply, clapped his hands together, and the mist formed around them. As he slowly pulled his hands apart, the mist dissipated, and the scene before her took her breath away. She and Veritas were no longer before the throne. They were sitting on the top of the building directly across from the town hall. The sight playing out before her eyes was full of angels with white swords blazing and demons with black and red swords flashing. Smoke was flowing up to and down from the heavens, and the sound of trumpets and the screams of torment filled her ears. Wanting to look away but not daring to, she asked Veritas, "Why is smoke streaming toward heaven and then pouring out of heaven? And why does it smell so sweet?"

"The smoke you see going up to heaven are the prayers of the saints, your saints. As the prayers are mixed with the incense of the altar of heaven, it flows down to us, the angels, giving us strength. There is no greater power from the earth than the faithful prayers of the saints. Close your eyes and breathe the air. Feel the strength. Do you feel it?"

Closing her eyes and breathing deeply, she felt a filling like nothing she'd ever felt before. Her heart raced, and her breathing increased. She felt the power of the Spirit within her. Not being able to contain herself, she began singing, but in a language she did not know. She simply knew it was from the Lord, and she must let it flow from her. Her song seemed to enliven the angels, and the swords of light slashed through the demon horde, sending plumes of black smoke and red streaks to whatever hell they were bound. As her song came to an end, she felt herself fall, but Veritas caught her and held her fast.

"You are truly blessed, Isabelle. The song you sang is one reserved for the end of days."

Looking up into his face, she asked, "End of days? Are we at the end of days?"

"Only God the father knows the day."

"Veritas, I need to go back now," she whispered faintly. "I need to be with them."

As she opened her eyes, everyone in the room had their eyes glued to her. "Am I back?"

Stewart took her hand and answered, "You're here with us now. Where did you go? And what was that song about?"

Feeling the strength return to her, she lifted her arms to heaven, praising the Lord. A few moments later, she lowered her hands, announced they had won, and shared with them her vision. In awe, all of them began praising the Lord until the sound of an explosion sent them running to the door and out into the starry night.

* * *

"What in the world is that?" Rachel whispered.

Smiling, Marcus answered, "That would be our prayers being answered. It looks like God sent his angels to keep the coast clear."

Whistling quietly, Stone asked, "Is that what you saw in the parking lot, Marcus?"

"Yup! That pretty well sums it up."

Not wanting to take his eyes off the spectacle but remembering the mission, Fox interrupted, "Come on, guys. If God's keeping them busy, let's get busy getting on with this."

The wonder of the battle disappeared, and the sky was once again simply beginning to fill with stars as evening turned to night. Stone led the way to the back of the building. As planned, the window was open, and Rick was waiting for them. "Hey guys! Let's get moving. The program is about to begin."

"Thanks, Ricky!" Stone said, clapping him on the back after climbing through the window. "We've had a slight change of plans. It turns out that a bomb has been planted somewhere by Michael Damious—"

"Michael Damious? I met a Michael Damious today while Tony and I were setting up the sound system."

"What was he doing?"

"Well, he just came up to us and talked with us. Do you know that he helped in the development of it? Way cool. Anyhow, I saw his name on the business card he gave to Tony. I was a little bummed when he didn't offer me a job, but then I thought I really probably wouldn't like working with someone like him. He just had a bad vibe, you know?"

After getting everyone safely through the window, Fox interrupted, "That's great man, but what did he do? Did you see him go anywhere or do anything?"

"No, honestly. He came in, talked with us, looked over the machine, and then let us go to the carnival."

"And did he go to the carnival with you?"

"Come to think of it, no, not right away. I saw him later. He stayed behind to check out the rest of the place. We didn't think anything about it, so we just left him to it." Realizing something was wrong, he asked, "Did he do something? What's going on?"

Ignoring Rick's question and looking over at his friends, Stone said, "Okay. Rachel, take Marcus and Amanda and find everyone else. Tell them what's going on. Amanda, you should be able to blend in as long as you don't look at your dad, and, Marcus, just watch yourself. Both of you stay with Rachel and follow her lead."

"Right-o, big brother. Will do." Walking over to Fox and kissing him, Rachel warned, "Now, my crazy husband, please don't be stupid. I want to see you after this is all over."

Kissing her back, he whispered in her ear, "Don't worry. You're not going to get rid of me again."

"Blah, blah, blah!" Marcus said, rolling his eyes, "Let's get the smoochie-smoochies over and get going!"

Laughing the nervous laughter of people who don't know if they'll ever see each other again, the three friends turned and walked down the corridor toward the bathrooms and to the entrance of the meeting room.

Turning to Rick, Stone said, "I'm gonna level with you, man. If you don't want any part in this, leave now. There's more going on then we let on. The sound system is more than just a sweet mixing machine. It's actually a subliminal device set to brainwash people. We just learned that Damious is intending to blow up the town hall and blame it on the resistance."

"The resistance?" Rick asked incredulously, "I thought they were destroyed years ago."

Fox turned Rick to look in his eyes and said, "No, Rick, we *are* the resistance. All the stuff you've heard about us is false. People like Damious made up lies and created a fictional enemy. The UGSE is the real enemy. You must know that somewhere, or you wouldn't be helping us."

Going over the implications of all this information, Rick stood up tall. "I know people think I'm just some stupid surfer dude, but I'm also a patriot. I won't let them kill everyone. I'm in. What can I do?"

Patting him on the back, Fox asked, "Can you get us under the stage without anyone seeing us?"

"Naw, man. I already told Pastor Stone that I couldn't. I thought you all had a diversion planned."

Rubbing his chin thoughtfully, Stone said, "We did, but with the bomb scenario, I don't know."

"Well," Fox chimed in, "Amanda did say it wasn't supposed to happen until Sunsteen speaks. The kids could still pull something off—wait! I know you're going to hate this idea, but what if I showed my face? Tempess would go mental. If I showed up on the other side of the stage, he'd have all the guards looking to take me out, and—"

"Take you out is right. No way, man. Besides, Rachel would kill me. No, there has to be another way."

"Drew, I have so much to make up for…Wolfe." He blinked back tears. "Let me do this, man. I can take care of myself." He pulled out his 9mm.

Hugging his friend, Stone said, "I don't think I could stop you if I wanted to."

Pushing away and punching Stone in the arm, he answered, "You got that right. Pray for me, brother, and I'll see you soon, either in this life or the next." Turning, Fox ran down the hall toward the door and his destiny.

Watching his friend run down the hall, Stone turned to face Rick. "All right, Rick, man it's time. Get me to the door so we can do this thing."

"You got it, Pastor A," Rick said. "Follow me."

* * *

The meeting started on schedule. At seven o'clock, Burke, Wright, Catherine, and Damious walked up the center aisle to the stage. Tempess stood to the right of the stage near the door, watching the crowd for any sign of intruders. The police were stationed near the double doors, the entryway, hall, and outside the building. While Burke was confident of his security, Tempess would never be underestimating Fox again. As the four politicians climbed the steps to the stage, Burke stopped at the podium while Wright crossed to one table, and Catherine and Damious sat at the opposite one. "Greetings, everyone! Welcome to one of the most important meetings ever for our town! Let's begin with an invocation and the pledge of allegiance."

A voice yelled through the crowd, "Yeah! Burke! How about making the American flag higher than the UGSE!"

Knowing the voice belonged to Scott Abrams but not being able to see him, Burke chose to ignore the comment. "Bow your heads please. Dear Lord, thank you for the UGSE and the wonderful people you've placed over us. Help us to be able to accept the wonderful gifts promised by our leaders in the global government. Help us to see the glories of jobs and homes and open society they will provide our world. All praise to the UGSE. Amen." Scattered amens filled the room, followed by an uncomfortable silence.

Unseen to the leaders on stage, Rachel, Amanda, and Marcus snuck in through the double doors. Rachel assumed they must have some angels with them because the guards didn't even flinch as they entered the room.

Bob called out this time, "What are we praying to the UGSE now?"

Turning to look at the crowd with his face burning with rage, Burke said, "I'd like to ask the negative thinkers out there to keep their opinions to themselves. There will be a time of questions and answers to come. Now please join me in the pledge." Everyone said the Pledge of Allegiance together. "I pledge allegiance to the flag of the United States of America, and to the republic for which it stands, one nation, indivisible, with liberty and justice for all."

Scott, Bob, Kevin, and the kids repeated the last line, joined by a few others in the crowd, "One nation *under God*, indivisible, with liberty and justice for all."

The double doors banged open, knocking over the guards and startling everyone in the room. All eyes focused on the figure at the back of the room. "Play ball!" Jason Fox yelled. "Hey everyone, don't listen to these guys. They're maniacal dictators who want to enslave you more than you are now. Run! Run! Run! Cover your ears!"

Too stunned to react, Wright, Catherine, Damious, and Tempess stared dumfounded. Burke, not recognizing the man but realizing he was trouble, yelled, "Get that man!" The guards at the door were too stunned to react quickly. As the guards in the hall ran toward the door, Fox turned, winked at Rachel who was also gobsmacked, and bolted out the door, evading the arms grabbing at him by running as fast as he could. The few-second lead he had proved to be just enough as he dove out the window he had crawled through only ten minutes before and legged it down the road into the woods. The guards decided it wasn't useful to go after the man, instead choosing to double up on the outer doors and check all the windows around the perimeter to make sure they were secure.

The ruse worked because while everyone was staring at Fox's antics, Stone and Rick slipped into the room unnoticed and hid themselves under the stage. As they crept under the stage, Stone noticed a light blink on while Burke introduced Wright. *He must have just turned on the machine,* Stone thought as he handed Rick a pair of earplugs while he put his own in.

Whispering in admiration while placing the earplugs in, Rick said, "Wow! That guy is totally awesome! He's like some movie action hero! I sure hope we live through this all. I sure would like to hang out with him."

"Yeah, that's Fox, action hero extraordinaire." Eyeing the subliminal system, Stone stared in awe. The creation he'd envisioned was nothing like the final version. Even the one at the church wasn't this elaborate. If he'd been in any other situation, he'd be inspecting every detail of the machine. As it was, he directed Rick to show him how it worked.

"Well, honestly, I don't know. I know how the sound mixer works and everything, but I had no idea it had subliminal capabilities. I always thought that was some kind of conspiracy kookiness."

"Well, it's not. Show me the motherboard. Maybe I can find the chip."

"Sure," he replied as he pulled out a screwdriver to remove the panel. As he began to unscrew it, he noticed something out of place. Putting down the tool, he asked, "What's this?"

"What's what?"

"This seam seems to be out of alignment. Look." He moved out of the way.

Examining the seam, Stone answered, "It just looks like an imperfection to me. Why does it concern you?"

"Well, the main reason is because it wasn't like that before." Rick pushed on the seam, and to both of their surprise, it slid easily out of place. Tentatively, Andrew pulled out his flashlight and shone the light inside.

"Oh, Lord, help us." Gingerly, he reached into the opening and pulled out a very small but effective explosive device. "Ricky, I need you to get out of here and get everyone else out as well. This could take out the entire room and then some. What in God's name was he thinking?"

"I can't leave you here, man. Let me work on the subliminal thing while you do the bomb."

Giving him a cold stare, Stone demanded, "No. Now, Rick, I know you want to help, but honestly, the best you can do is get everyone out. I don't care how—pull the fire alarm, go talk to Bob, Scott, or Kevin. Just figure out a way please. We only have until Sunsteen gets going. Now get out of here and keep an eye on Damious. He won't trigger this thing until he's clear."

Never seeing Pastor Andrew so harsh before, Rick knew something bigger than the resistance was going on. "All right, I'll go, but I'm not leaving the building until you're out."

"God bless you, Ricky, and Godspeed!" He went to work on the bomb, the subliminal system forgotten.

*   *   *

"Sorry about the disruption, everyone." Burke oozed confidence. "We've had some threats from people calling themselves resistance, but as we know, they were destroyed three years ago, so let's get back on track." Everyone nervously returned to their seats, and Tempess flicked the switch to turn on the subliminal system. "It's my great pleasure to introduce the head of the United Global Society Administration, Justin Wright." The room erupted in applause for Wright, as he was very well known and respected by most people in the country.

"Thank you. Thank you," Wright began as the applause died down. "As you all know, my team has been working to help bring jobs, education, housing, and an open and accepting society that we can be proud of and, most importantly, a society where we can live in peace together. Since the environmental disaster of 2012 when the UN worked so quickly to bring the earth back into balance and 2017 when the UGSE took control of their complete inadequacy at organizing the world, we have come a long way, but there is still more to do. For years, we've been working toward sustainable development through keeping open space open and consolidating residential and business development. Since the sad days of the United Nation's extermination of the cities during the War of 2015 due to of the lies of the resistance, we at the UGSE have managed to bring together all the governments of the world into one peaceful coexistence."

Applause filled the room, but in the back, the youth yelled, "Yeah right!"

Not losing his stride, Wright continued, "As the young people in the back rightly pointed out, there are still some areas of dissent. I suppose that will always be the case, but the leaders of the world have realized that we can no longer let our differences define us. History has shown us that democracy without strong, educated leaders simply leads to mob rule and anarchy. While we here in America pride ourselves on self-sufficiency, it has been shown that without community organizations and governmental initiatives led by those with more knowledge in the ways of civilization, society descends into chaos."

Rachel cringed while listening to his words because at one point not too long ago, they were her words and her thoughts. *He's using my work,* she thought, flattered but also sickened at the reality. As she looked around the room, she noticed the rapturous expressions on the audience's faces. *The machine is working. Where's Andrew?*

Suddenly, Rick was at her side, whispering about Stone's message. "He said we've got to get everyone out!"

"But how can we do that without causing a panic?"

She didn't have to wait long for an answer. Somehow, Amanda had walked to the stage and moved behind her father. By the time Catherine, Damious, or the guards noticed her, it was too late. Holding a pistol to her father's head, she took center stage and prepared to give a speech of her own. Whispering in Wright's ear, she said, "Hello, Daddy." Knowing better than to ignore a gun to the head, no matter who was holding it, he stood still.

While Catherine sat stunned at the boldness of the young woman, Damious was trying to conceal a smile. Things couldn't be more perfect if he had planned them himself. The subliminal machine was working perfectly: He could tell by the glazed over look in the people's eyes. They were following Wright's every word. Amanda, a now-known resistance fighter, was holding a gun at the head of the UGSA in front of witnesses. All Damious needed to do was switch off the machine and let the people hear Amanda's rant without the sound system, making them believe her. Then he could blow up the building.

As Amanda began speaking, he silently motioned toward Tempess to shut down the machine by running a finger across his throat, indicating the universal sign for kill and then pointing at the speakers. Understanding, Tempess quickly flicked the switch to turn off the machine. Almost immediately, the crowd's eyes cleared, and fear replaced bliss.

In the back of the room, Bob, Scott, and Kevin moved to different locations, trying to convince people to leave the building quietly and quickly. Some acquiesced, but most were too stunned by the goings-on on stage and stayed put. To most onlookers, the three men milling through the crowd whispering looked normal, but Burke knew they were up to something. When people started leaving, he almost stood up to interrupt Amanda, but when he noticed more people than not chose to stay, he kept quiet. Rachel was standing with the group of young people, trying to get them to leave. Finally after much cajoling, the kids agreed to leave— the guys to find Fox and the girls to go tell the others what was happening.

"Hello, everyone," Amanda began as she pulled off her wig, letting her blonde locks fall around her face and shoulders. "Please don't be afraid. I am Mr. Wright's daughter, Amanda, and I'd like to tell you a little bit about his plan and the plan of the UGSE. They are not your friends. They do not want the best for you. This man you love so much beats me regularly." Gasps could be heard throughout the room. "His plan is not to bring you jobs but make you slaves. The whole stupid sustainable development plans for every aspect of life has been to control you. Check it out. It's not hard to find—" Suddenly, Amanda collapsed to the floor after a gunshot rang out. One of the guards had come to his senses and, after getting a signal from Burke, shot her.

"No!" Rachel screamed and ran to the stage to help her friend.

Wright, never one to let a good crisis go to waste, started tearing up over his daughter, pointed at Rachel, and screamed, "Guards, get her! She's part of the resistance, and she did this to my poor daughter." Cradling Amanda gingerly, he whispered, "This is what you get, you spoiled brat."

As the light faded from her eyes, she managed to say, "Burn in he…"

Two guards grabbed Rachel before she could reach the stage. Through tears, she screamed at the people onstage. "I will get you!

I will get away, and I will kill you! You're dead, you—" She didn't get to finish her words because one of the guards smacked her hard across the cheek, knocking her senseless.

The people in the room were panicking, running in every direction to get out but not being able to because the guards closed the doors to keep them in. Damious sauntered up to the microphone, winked at Tempess, who turned on the machine again, and began speaking. "Please everyone, take your seats." At first, people were still trying to figure out how to escape, but it only took moments for them to calm and sit down. Bob, Scott, and Kevin were stunned but thought it best to go along, so they took seats together near the back, trying to hide from Burke. "Now this is a crime scene, so we'll need everyone to stay calm and wait for the police to get here." Pointing at the guard who hit Rachel, he continued, "Please remove this woman to the back of the room." Looking down at Wright crying over his daughter, he touched his shoulder and comforted, "Now, Justin, please go sit with Ms. Sunsteen. We need to keep things as uncontaminated as possible." Slowly, Wright complied. As he took his seat next to Catherine, she could see that he was faking his sorrow, and if not for fear of retribution, she would have smacked him across the face.

Pleased with his control over the room, Damious instructed the guards at the double doors to open them. "Now please stay in your seats. I'm going to go out and speak to the guards at the front of the building to make sure everything is secure, and then we will be letting you leave in an orderly fashion after we get your details for the police." Burke started getting nervous. Besides Damious, he was the only one who knew the plan to blow the building up. *Surely he won't do anything with me in here.* Seeing his discomfort, Damious added, "Mr. Smith, I'm sure you'll hold the fort until I get back." Burke nodded his agreement.

Catherine and Justin whispered quietly together while Burke tried to figure out the best way to handle all this. He walked over to the two politicians and asked if either of them would like to take questions or if Catherine would like to give her speech. Catherine decided that she would take questions from anyone who wanted to speak to try and keep the peace. As soon as she stepped up to the microphone and asked for questions, the room erupted in hands going to the ceiling. She took many questions, mostly about the resistance and Amanda. Her answers were always the same. "No, the resistance had not returned. This was just a small group of instigators that had been trying to derail our plans, and Amanda was a very ill girl who this group took advantage of." Justin and Catherine had decided that they would put out background on Amanda as a manic-depressive with schizophrenic tendencies. They planned to tell people that she imagined voices speaking to her and that this group had used her to collect information on Wright. When they couldn't get anything, they drugged her and convinced her to kill her father after destroying the UGSE's reputation with the lies she spouted. By the time Catherine had finished spinning the story, the audience was ready to string Rachel up in the town square; someone even suggested burning her at the stake as a witch.

The subliminal sound system had accomplished its mission. As Rachel slowly regained her faculties and saw the rage in the people's eyes, she became very afraid. Burke had taken the liberty of directing the guards to arrest Bob, Scott, and Kevin; they were being held on the other side of the doors. With guns pointing at their chests, they dared not move. Rachel was desperately looking around for her brother or her husband, neither of which had shown their faces. At Burke's command, Tempess walked up to Rachel, pulled her to her feet, and whispered, "I'm sorry, Mrs. Fox. I have nothing against you. I'm just following orders."

Shrugging off his aid with fire and defiance in her eyes, she replied, "Yeah, I wonder how many times that was said at the UN's population-cleansing trials." Not wanting to give the leaders of this meeting the satisfaction of any hint of fear on her part, she held her head high, righted herself as she almost lost her balance from the minor concussion she had suffered and walked a few paces behind Tempess to the stage. Standing in front of Catherine, Wright, and Burke, she spit at them and received another smack to the face, this time less damaging, as it came from Catherine, who whispered, "You need an attitude adjustment, Mrs. Fox, and I think we'll let the crowd decide how to go about that." Spinning Rachel to face the crowd, Catherine asked, "Now how do you all think we should deal with this antisocial extremist?"

*   *   *

While the excitement with Amanda was happening above him, Stone came to the realization that he could not disable the bomb, so instead he decided he would have to get it out of the building. In the midst of the chaos that followed Amanda's shooting, he snuck out of the room the same way he and Rick had entered. His problem lay in the fact that the window was now shut and about twelve to twenty guards blocked his escape. Wracking his brain, he noticed that the bathrooms were only visible in this hallway but not from the entrance hall and decided to go into the bathroom and try a window. Much to his chagrin, once he entered, he realized these bathrooms were on the interior of the building and held no means of escape. Trying to figure out how to minimize the loss of human life if the bomb were to go off, he decided to remove one of the ceiling tiles and place the bomb there. Hopefully, when it detonated, the upper floor and this hallway would receive most of the damage.

Once the ceiling panel had been replaced, he opened the bathroom door and heard Damious's voice coming through the speakers. Knowing this might be his only chance, he silently crept up behind the guards who were mesmerized by the subliminal machine and used the same technique he'd implemented to put out Chef Daniel at New Life. It worked like a charm; the two guards simply slipped silently to the floor. Thankfully, the other guards had gone inside the room to arrest the rest of his gang and his sister.

When Damious came strolling out, Stone waited until he'd passed through the door, put his Walther PPK to his nemesis's head, and said, "Well, hello again, stranger. Care to step into my office?"

Completely taken by surprise, Damious stopped short, raised his hands, and replied, "My, my, my, you just never know when to give up, do you, Andrew? Just what do you think you're going to accomplish here? Maybe Fox can just shoot people in cold blood, but you aren't Fox, are you?" Turning to face him, he finished, "Are you, Andrew?"

With nothing but malice in his green eyes, Stone pressed the muzzle of his gun to Damious's forehead and replied, "Oh, I think you might be *very* surprised at what I can and can't do. I've done things that would make even you sick, and while I don't believe in torture anymore, at least by me, I have no compunction about ending evil quickly. War is hell, Mr. Damious." Looking deep into his soulless eyes, he continued, "I know you're well acquainted with the place already, and it would be my pleasure to send you there on a permanent vacation."

Motioning Damious toward the bathroom, he moved the gun back, allowing him to turn and begin walking. "What do you mean to accomplish, Mr. Stone?"

"Honestly, I don't know, Michael," he replied, allowing him to open the door and enter the bathroom. "I was thinking that I'd like to kill you, but I don't feel convicted in my spirit that that's what God wants me to do. I don't think it's my place to kill you."

"Then why all this? Why not let me go?"

Stone smiled at him, not the warm smile of friendship but the cold, knowing smile of an assassin ready to strike. "Well, Michael, I wanted to tell you that at least part of your plot failed. I want to show you where your bomb is." Stone could see that he'd struck a chord because Michael's cool facade came crumbling down. His eyes narrowed, and he bared his teeth. "Yes, that's right, we know all about it, and since I couldn't figure out how to disable it, I brought it in here and put it in the ceiling." Pointing right above Damious's head, he grinned. "Right above your noggin. How do you like that, Michael?"

Letting his shoulders fall in defeat, Damious asked, "So what now? No one will believe I did this. You have no proof." Taking a moment to think about the situation and standing a little taller, he continued, "With Amanda dead, her testimony is gone. No one is going to believe your story or Marcus's." Surprise played across Stone's face. "Ah, yes," Damious's confidence flooded back in. "You didn't know we knew about him huh? I guess he shouldn't have been so arrogant back at the hotel, waving to the cameras. Tsk, tsk, tsk."

Putting the muzzle of the gun back to Damious's forehead, Stone exuded hatred for the man. Just as fear crept back into Damious's eyes, Stone raised his hand. Instead of shooting him, he pinched the nerves in Damious's neck and shoulders and dropped him to the floor. As he prepared to drag him into a stall, a melee of gunshots and screams rang out from the meeting room. He could hear screaming people running down the main hall and officers screaming, "Stop!" to no avail. Peeking out the door, he realized this was his chance to escape. He ran into the crowd as they exited the double doors. Before joining the exodus of the crowd, he looked back into the room and stopped dead in his tracks. Up on the stage lay Rachel, motionless, next to Tempess, a puddle of blood surrounding them both. Jason Fox, head bowed, was crying in between the two bodies.

* * *

While Stone was dealing with Damious in the bathroom, up on the stage, Catherine spun Rachel to face the hostile crowd. Bob spoke up, ignoring the guns pointed at his chest, ready to die for the truth. Looking into the guards' eyes, he said, "If you're going to shoot me, shoot me. Otherwise, I'm going to speak my peace." Turning to the crowd, he yelled, "Listen, people. This whole thing is a charade. Amanda Wright was right! These people are brainwashing you into believing their words. Use your own mind. Use your common sense. Does any of this make sense to you? They're liars."

Not really wanting to shoot their neighbor, the guards looked at each other, agreeing silently about what to do and chose to hit Bob on the back of the skull, knocking him down in a stupefied haze. Scott kneeled down to help his friend and glowered at the guard who hit him. "You'll pay for that, Smitty! As God as my witness, you will pay!"

Suddenly, Jason Fox stood up in the middle of the audience, pulled out his 9mm, let off one shot into the ceiling, and said, "All right now. This is a stickup." While he was speaking, he opened his jacket, showing a vest filled with wires sticking out of various pockets. "Now I'm not saying what this vest is made of, but everyone is going to find out if Ms. Sunsteen doesn't release my wife this instant!"

Shock showed on Catherine's face, and as she let go of Rachel, Rachel turned around and punched Catherine in the nose. Wiping the blood flowing from her nose away with the back of her hand, Catherine said, "Oh, no you did not!" Not being one to back down from a fight, Catherine grabbed Rachel's hair, yanked her head back, and brought her knee up to Rachel's abdomen, knocking the air out of her. Gasping, Rachel brought her elbow up, connecting to Catherine's rib cage, and an all-out brawl erupted on stage. Tempess, Burke, and Wright backed away in shock as the two women continued to beat each other. Fox was standing in awe of his wife's tenacity, and seeing that she had things well under control onstage, he turned to the rest of the people and said, "Everyone, get out of here! I don't want to have to do anything I'll regret, but I will do what I have to do." The guards were the first to hightail it out of the room, followed by the rest of the audience.

Suddenly, Kevin shouted, "Jason! Watch out!"

As Fox spun around, he saw Wright leveling a revolver at his chest. Diving to the left seconds before Wright got off four shots, Fox pulled the trigger of his 9mm three times, hitting Justin twice in the head, killing him instantly.

The moments following Jason's takedown of Wright seemed to happen in slow motion. People were running and screaming. As Wright went down, Catherine, who had managed to escape Rachel, saw the gun fly out of his hand and grabbed for it. Lying on her back, arms extended holding the pistol, she aimed at Rachel, who had just turned to find her prey, and pulled the trigger twice.

Tempess, realizing what Catherine intended to do, pushed Rachel to the floor as the shots rang out. Time moved back to normal in Fox's mind, and as he ran toward the stage, he screamed, "No!" unloading two more shots, into Catherine this time. Jumping up onto the stage, he fell to his knees between Tempess and Rachel. He checked over his wife. Rachel was unconscious but breathing and seemed to be unharmed by the shots. Turning toward Tempess, he saw that his enemy had taken two bullets, one to the shoulder and one to the abdomen.

As Tempess lay dying, he grabbed Fox by the shirt and begged for forgiveness. "Fox." He breathed heavily, whispering, "I'm sorry. I'm sorry for Wolfe, and I'm sorry for everything. It was my choice, but I was misled." Dropping his arms, he continued, "Is your wife…is Rachel okay?"

Confused and caught between hatred and pity, Fox answered, "She'll be okay. She didn't get shot."

A smile played across Tempess's face as he coughed up blood. "Fox, I'm asking you to forgive me…please. Forgive me and pray for my soul. I'm so sorry."

Still conflicted, wanting to hate him, but feeling pulled to forgive, he looked up and saw a beam of light shining down on Tempess. A voice sounded in his head, telling him to forgive and let go of the hatred. Closing his eyes, Fox decided to place Tempess in God's hands. Taking Tempess's hands and looking into his eyes, he said, "William, I forgive you, and I leave you to God. Dear Lord, I commend the soul of my enemy, my new brother, into your hands. If his contrition is true, take him to be with you as you did the thief on the cross."

"Fox, do you see a light?"

"Yes, Tempess, I do. I think it's time for you to go."

Tempess smiled, closed his eyes, said, "Thank you," and breathed his last. Jason sat between the two crying and praying, thanking God for sparing his wife and saving his enemy.

"Jason!" Stone yelled while running toward the stage. "Jason! What happened? Is she—?" He couldn't finish as tears filled his eyes.

Looking up with tears of joy filling his eyes, he answered, "No, Drew. She's alive, just hurt."

Scanning the carnage onstage, Stone asked, "What in God's name happened?" Noticing the wires in his jacket, he continued, "And why are you wearing a bomb vest?"

Looking at his vest, Fox laughed and said, "Well, you know me, always trying to be more than I am. I figured it would be the best way to get their attention, so after deciding to come back to try and help you, I broke into the local convenience store. I stole this vest, some bars of soap, and ripped some wires of out of a couple of radios. I stuck the wires in the bars of soap to create the illusion. Was that wrong?"

Adrenaline draining from them, Andrew punched Jason in the arm and hugged him tight. "No, man, I think it was just right."

Bob, Kevin, and Scott joined them at the stage as Rachel began waking up. "What-what happened?" she stammered.

Lifting her gently, Jason kissed her and said, "You kicked some serious booty, babe!"

Smiling, she answered, "Yeah, I'm sure." She pulled him to her and kissed him back passionately.

As the small group prepared to get out of the building, a voice came from the doors. "Well, well, well. It looks like the little naughty kiddies are all together in a box."

Everyone looked toward the door and saw Damious standing and holding the detonator of the bomb, with Burke smiling next to him. "I don't know if the bomb is powerful enough to kill you in here, but I'm looking forward to finding out. Good-bye, Mr. Fox, Mrs. Fox, and Mr. Stone." The two turned and ran toward the door. As they ran out into the street, Damious pushed the button.

*　*　*

By the time the prayer warriors had reached the crowd around the town hall, three fire trucks were busy extinguishing the flames. Stewart touched the nearest person to him and asked, "What happened?"

The man turned around, eyes still glazed with shock. "The... the resistance is back. They...they...just started yelling and shooting, and one of them had a bomb vest and killed Justin Wright. I guess after everyone left, he blew up the place." Taking a breath, eyes filled with hatred, he finished, "I hope they all burn in hell. Yeah, that's just what they deserve." Numb, he turned back around to face the fire.

Isabelle whispered, "No, they're okay, I know it. We won this one. This is as it should be."

Not sure whether she was speaking emphatically or trying to convince herself, Miriam placed her arm around Isabelle and said, "Yes, I'm sure you're right, Isabelle."

Jerry was the first to notice the young people from their youth group. He walked up behind Peter and touched his shoulder. "Hey guys. Good to see you're okay." The kids turned at his voice, and all six of them hugged him at once. "Hold on there. Let me breathe. Come on, the rest of the group is back here." The seven of them walked through the crowd, back to the small group of friends standing in stunned silence.

James asked the kids, "Did you guys see what happened? What can you tell us?"

The kids motioned for the adults to follow them, and they formed a circle in a copse of small scrub oaks. Josh told the story, "Well, we got there and, you know, started being a little obnoxious, at least until our parents gave us the evil eye and the meeting started. In the middle of Mr. Wright's speech, his daughter got onstage and put a gun to his head. That's when Mrs. Fox talked us into leaving. We guys were supposed to find Mr. Fox, and the girls were going to meet you all. Well, we were all about to split up when Mr. Fox showed up and told us he was going to get back inside. That's when the gun shot went off and the guards ran inside. Mr. Fox told us to get back to you all, and then he ran in after the guards. That's all we know. We were halfway to Mr. Davies's house when *kablam!* We heard the explosion and ran back. That's all we know."

"Where did Mr. Wright's daughter come from? I thought she was with Marcus," Stewart thought aloud, looking around.

Suddenly, from out of the woods came a familiar voice, "Hey everyone." Stone walked out of the shadows. "Anyone know how a group of extremists can get out of town?"

Isabelle ran into his arms and kissed him. "How did you get out?"

Slightly stunned by her exuberance, Stone caught his balance and answered, "Darlin', I'd love to go into it, but I've got seven people hiding in the woods, one of whom is injured. Can we get them back to the house first?"

"Seven?" Stewart interjected. "What seven?"

"Well, let's see, there's Jay, Rach, Bob, Kevin, Scott, Ricky, and Marcus," Stone said quickly. "We need to get out of sight. Can you help please?"

"Well, I think Isabelle and I can help. Everyone else should probably hang around. People have seen us. If we all disappear, they might get suspicious."

"Okay," Yvonne answered, "we'll all go back to the crowd and blend in. Here, take the house key." She handed Stone the key. "Get inside and wait. We'll be there as soon as possible. They'll probably be combing the debris for your bodies, which should give you all enough time to escape. Give Kevin my love."

Stone gave her a hug, and he, Isabelle, and Stewart disappeared into the woods.

Just in time, the remnants of the group rejoined the crowd because Burke recognized them and walked over to address them. Trying to conceal his glee, he said, "Hello, Yvonne, everyone. I didn't see you at the meeting. What are you doing here?"

Boldly, Yvonne said, "Well, Burke, the explosion rocked the whole town. What did you expect? That we'd just stay home and not be curious? What happened?"

Damious sauntered up next to Burke and answered her question. "Well, can I assume these people belong to the instigators of this mess?"

Burke answered, "Yes."

"Well, Ms..." Damious stumbled.

"Mrs. Davies," Yvonne answered.

"Mrs. Davies, it seems a few people from your group disrupted our meeting with crazy conspiracy theories, ending in a gun battle that caused the deaths of both Mr. Wright and Ms. Sunsteen, not to mention one of my colleagues William Tempess and Amanda Wright, Mr. Wright's daughter." Smiling, he finished, "It seems that a Mr. Fox and his wife...oh, and your pastor, Pastor Stone—"

"Bob, Scott, and Kevin too," Burke crowed.

Damious gave him an annoyed look and continued, "They blew up the building, themselves included. I'm sorry to inform you."

The kids all got wicked smiles on their faces but quickly turned those to frowns when Jerry nudged them. The others pretended to be shocked. Yvonne broke down in tears, saying, "It's not true! Kevin is not dead!" Shocking Burke with a slap to the face, she said, "You're a liar!"

Holding his stinging cheek, Burke said, "I assure you he's dead, and good riddance to the lot of them. Bunch of pains in the backside!" Peter, Zac, and Josh started toward Burke, but they were held back by Doris, James, and Debbie. "You'd better watch yourselves. Society is changing, and those who won't conform will be taken care of."

Thomas spoke up, "What's that supposed to mean, Burke? Death or reeducation camps? I thought the UGSE promised that would never happen."

Damious answered, "Well, sir, I didn't hear anyone use those words but you. Words are a dangerous commodity these days. Be careful. I think what Mr. Burke meant was that jail will loom for those who do not conform. Society will be new, and with the death of our health administrator as well as the society administrator, the people are going to be clamoring for peace and justice." Narrowing his eyes and leaning into them, he finished, "As one of my favorite progressive leaders once said, 'Never waste a good crisis,' and believe me, we won't. Now if you weren't here when the awful events of this evening went down, you should leave. You young people are excused too. We don't need any troublemakers." He turned and walked back through the crowd to talk with the police chief.

"Good-bye!" Burke said. "I suggest you might want to leave town soon. Your kind isn't welcome here, and we will be watching you."

As one, the youth mocked him. They held up their first two fingers and pointed from their eyes to his as they said, "We'll be watching you." The group of teens broke out into hysterical laughter, and Burke, red-faced, turned and walked away.

* * *

Once the whole group was back together at the Davieses' house, Isabelle, Miriam, Thomas, and Fox tended to Rachel's wounds. "Good lord, girl, what did the other one look like?" Yvonne joked.

"Well, I think I broke her nose before she cracked my ribs, at least they feel cracked." Rachel joked back through clenched teeth. "It hurts to laugh. I think I have bruises from my front to my back."

"That's my girl," Fox said, kissing her bruised side. "Just like me, always joking even through the worst pain."

Laying back against a couch cushion, she breathed a little easier. "Yeah, it's either laugh or cry, and I just don't look that good with red puffy eyes."

At once, three of them blurted out, "Too late! Jinx, you owe me a Coke!"

The laughter coming from the couch was a welcome sound because everyone had been worried about Rachel's injuries. Thomas was an EMT, and after an initial examination, he declared that he didn't think anything was broken but that she would be in pain for a while.

Her answer had been, "Really, you think so?"

Stone came in with drinks for everyone. As they sat around relaxing, letting the adrenaline drain from their bodies, Marcus told his and Amanda's story. He was heartbroken over her death. She had become like a sister to him, and to see her shot like a rabid dog made him want to break something. He downed his drink, got up to pour another one, and finished his tale.

"In the confusion after her murder, when Rachel shouted no and Stone was nowhere to be seen, I figured I needed to come up with a plan B, so I grabbed Rick and got out of the room right before they closed the doors. I pretended that I needed to be sick after seeing Amanda shot, so the guards let us pass. We rushed down the hall, past the bathrooms, and rounded the corner that led to the window we had entered from. Being unaware that they had posted guards, I had to think quick on my feet, so I told them about the shooting and that they were needed in the hall." Looking at Andrew, he said, "They must have been the two you took out. Anyway, Rick and I got the window open and waited for the right moment. Rick took me to the backdoor of the meeting room, and we listened to everything happening inside." Staring over at the mess that was Rachel, he continued, "I would have loved to see that catfight, rawr."

Everyone laughed.

"Anyway, after the gunfire started, we realized we had to take action. We squeezed through the door just as Damious was giving his little speech on the other side of the room. Once he had turned his back, we jumped onstage. Rick grabbed Rachel, and I gathered the others. We practically dove off the stage and out the door right as the explosion happened." Eyeing Stone with a respect he held for the highest of soldiers, he said, "Good thinking, brother. If you hadn't have gotten that bomb in the ceiling, I think the blast might have gotten through the second wall. Anyway, we hightailed it to the window. I climbed out first, and Rick handed Rachel through. Everyone else followed, and Fox led us into the woods where he had hidden out. After that, you know the story."

Zac asked the question on everyone's mind, "What now? We can't go home. You all can't stay here. What happens now?"

Marcus answered, "I think if we can get to Jared's place, we can get transportation out of town. We're going to have to go tonight." Looking everyone in the eye, he stated, "Living on the lam isn't easy. It's not like in the movies where there's hotel rooms and stuff like that. I live in a warehouse. Stone and I lived in a tent in the jungle for a while. In fact, a lot of us live in tents. If you're lucky, you might go undercover, like Amanda, although she got regular beatings. There's always a trade-off. When you're undercover, you have to keep track of all the lies you tell, and sometimes you have to do things you don't want to in order to keep your cover. If you live out in the field, there's not always soap or toilet paper. People never seem to think how wonderful toilet paper is until they don't have it."

Everyone laughed uneasily at his warning. "If you want to join the resistance, you have a few options. You can stay here and be spies. You just have to pretend to fit in. You have to go along. Probably half of our operatives do that. It's not glamorous, but intel is intel, and sabotage is sabotage. You can come with us and learn a trade and infiltrate the UGSE network. Again, it's not glamorous, but it's necessary for our very survival. Finally, you can go completely underground like me and live in the shadows. It's not glamorous at all, and sometimes I have to do some pretty wacked stuff. It's not easy.

"You also have the option of getting out, although I have to be honest with you, if you tell anyone about anything you know, I guarantee you will die. Secrecy and honor is the resistance's lifeblood, which is why we don't let just anyone in. I know this is hard, so I think it would be wise to pray about it, and if you feel compelled to join, simply stay. If you feel compelled to get out, simply leave. It's"—he looked at the clock—"ten o'clock now. You have until eleven to decide." Standing up, he nodded his head toward Stewart, and the two walked out into the back yard.

Stewart started, "Okay, we need to get to the cabin and decide who will go where."

Remembering Jerry's affinity for Jenna, Marcus suggested he go stay with her and her group. Stewart agreed. "What about the kids?" Marcus asked. "Do you think they're going to want to join?"

Stewart answered, "Most of them are eighteen or older, but Kara is only seventeen. I think they'll all want to come, but leaving their parents will be a struggle. What are you thinking?"

"Well, would you say they're strong in their faith?" Marcus asked.

"I don't know, I think Andrew or Scott would be the ones to answer that."

"Because I was thinking they could go to New Life and get settled into positions in the UGSE. I know it's asking a lot, but the thing we can use the most is moles. Chef Daniel could watch over them. Plus if you think about it, those kids would fit right in with him."

"Hmmm, I don't know this Daniel, but I trust your judgment. We'll just have to see who stays and who goes."

"Hi, is this a private confab, or can anyone join in?" Stone asked with Fox and Isabelle at his side.

"No, brother, anyone is welcome," Marcus affirmed.

"So what's the plan? I think everyone is going to join, but I think the prayer group is going to want to hang around, as well as the Davieses and Bob," Stone guessed. "The kids are all hopped up on ideas of adventure, so it's fair to say they'll want in, and I think Scott and Rick will want to get in the field as well."

"I agree about the kids," Fox said.

Stewart questioned Isabelle, "So what would you think about sending them to New Life to be integrated into higher society? Do you think they are strong enough to withstand the aura of the place?"

"If we keep giving them prayer cover, I think they'll handle it well. I have lived around spirits my entire life, and I've never experienced power like that of God. He is stronger than Adder, Angelous, and even Lucifer himself." Looking each man in the eye, she finished, "And that young man Daniel will be a good guide for them. Plus, didn't you say there were others in the foundation, Marcus?"

"Yes, we do have some."

Yvonne stuck her head out the door. "Excuse me, Pastor Stone, but your sister wants to talk with you."

"All right, tell her I'll be right there." Looking at the small group, Stone said, "I've got to go see what she needs. I think you all should take Marcus's advice and pray about all of this and for guidance for these people."

When Stone left, Donald, Isabelle, and Fox joined hands and prayed for guidance for themselves, the resistance, and the small group of believers inside the Davieses' house.

*   *   *

"Hey, sis," Stone said to Rachel. "What can I do you for?"

Flinching, as she sat herself up straight, Rachel confided, "I need to talk with you about salvation."

"Go on. I'm listening."

"When I was passed out on the stage, I think I had a vision or a flashback to a vision I had before." She looked in his eyes for any hint of disbelief. When she saw none, she continued by relating her dream of the cabin while she was in the Orchid Garden.

Stone joked, "Wow! I can't believe you didn't take the crown. You were always such a princess as a kid."

Grabbing her side as she laughed, she said, "Seriously though, when I was passed out, I had the same vision. I was in the cabin, and the voice was calling me again. This time, though, I could feel all my bruises and how tired I was. When He called to me, I just wanted it all to go away. I told Him I was afraid of losing myself if I gave in. I told Him that I've worked my whole life to achieve what I have and I didn't want to lose it…but I so much wanted the pain to go away. He told me to kneel before the chair and lower my head, so this time, instead of fighting, I did it. I bowed before the little wooden chair, but when I looked up, it wasn't a chair anymore, it was a throne, and there were crowns on the ground all around me and men bowing before the throne, singing. All I saw in front of me were two hands holding a crown, the crown with my name on it. He placed it on my head. As soon as it touched me, all the pain left, and I felt a peace that I'd never felt before. It was then that I knew what you all were talking about, a peace that couldn't be explained. It was like I knew everything was going to be okay and everything was as it should be. Then I was back on the stage, and every part of my body hurt. I wondered if it had just been a dream, but I feel different now. I'm afraid of the future, but I don't fear it. Does that make any sense to you?"

"It makes perfect sense, sis, and if I'm honest, I have to say I'm jealous of you."

"Jealous of me? Why?"

"Because you and Marcus and Isabelle had these wonderful visions of heaven and God. He's never chosen to show me things that way. Not that I haven't felt what you feel. I have. It's just that I wish I could see it too. I know it's vanity to want what others have, but I can't help it."

"But your faith is so much bigger because you haven't seen and believe. Our faith must be so much less, especially mine because I didn't let Him in, even after seeing. Anyway, you were the first one to see the angel guardians. I think He shows us stuff when we need faith, and the fact is that you have faith enough for us all." Leaning forward through the pain, she hugged him hard. Leaning back and looking into his eyes, she asked, "What do I do now?"

"Well, now you just continue on. Listen and follow. Receive the sacraments and just let Him keep crowning you." He looked at his sister with deep brotherly love and realized that no one had had the sacrament of Holy Communion for a while. "Yvonne," he called, "get everyone together. We need the Eucharist."

At eleven o'clock, no one had chosen to leave, so they gathered in the living room to decide who was staying in town and who was going to the cabin. Marcus asked for a show of hands of everyone who planned to stay in town. As suspected, Doris, Debbie, Thomas, James, Bob, and the Davies raised their hands. Rick, Scott, Zac, Josh, Peter, Kara, Eryn, Kat, and Miriam all planned to leave. "Very well then," Marcus said, "the decision is made. For those of you staying, Stewart will get a missionary pastor from our group to come and lead you. He will have the names of local resistance leaders and will be our contact with you. Tonight you will go home and continue your life as usual. Keep your eyes and ears open and never do anything without the consent of the resistance unless your life or the life of another person is in danger: That will be your call. You will be trained in the use of small arms and possibly other weapons as needs be and as you are comfortable.

"You, however, already have our most powerful weapon, and that is prayer. We will need you constantly praying, and when something big goes down anywhere around the world, Stewart will call the prayer group, and you *will* need to answer. Up until a few days ago, I wouldn't have believed anything about prayer, but I have since seen the light, and I think God has spoken to us through Isabelle's vision. He is with us, and only through Him can we succeed…Andrew?"

Stewart and Stone had gotten the Eucharist prepared for one last church service together. Together, the small group called on God's mercy confessed their sins and received absolution. Then everyone knelt on the floor, and the two pastors gave the body and blood of the Lord Jesus Christ to the congregation of saints gathered together. They prayed the Lord's Prayer together and closed with the song "Here I Am Lord." After tears and hugs, the group staying in town silently walked to their homes.

Marcus had called Jared, and he had the same moving van ready to take the fugitives out of town. Jared parked the van at the entrance to the ally and left the keys tucked into the sun visor. At midnight, the small crew of renegades made their way to the van. Once safely hidden in the back of the cargo hold, Jerry climbed into the driver's seat, said a prayer, put the car in drive, and pulled away from the curb into the night toward the cabin in the woods.